THE MANY ASPECTS OF MOBILE HOME LIVING

THE MANY ASPECTS OF
MOBILE HOME LIVING

A NOVEL

MARTIN CLARK

ALFRED A. KNOPF NEW YORK 2000

THIS BOOK IS DEDICATED TO PAM CLARK:
MUSE, SCRIBE, EDITOR AND SUMMA WIFE

THANKS TO JOE REGAL, GARY FISKETJON,
CAPTAIN FRANK BEVERLY, CHARLES F. WRIGHT,
DAVID WILLIAMS AND REVEREND "BUCKY"
HUNSICKER. I AM ESPECIALLY GRATEFUL TO
MY PARENTS FOR THEIR WORDS OF ENCOURAGE-
MENT AND TO MY KINSMAN EDDIE TURNER FOR HIS
STEADFAST FRIENDSHIP. FINALLY, A DEEP BOW
TO S. EDWARD "SMILIN' ED" FLANAGAN FOR ALL
HIS HELP, SUGGESTIONS AND DROLL WISDOM.

THE MANY ASPECTS OF MOBILE HOME LIVING

ONE

IN 1969, WHEN EVERS WHEELING WAS A BOY IN WINSTON-SALEM, North Carolina, men in filling-station uniforms still checked your car's oil, pumped high-test gas out of heavy silver nozzles and cleaned your windshield with a spray bottle and a blue, quilted wipe. There was a man named Herman Stovall who worked at the West End Shell, where Evers and his family would stop for fuel and air and little Cokes with peanuts poured into the bottle. Herman was a bent, thin, wispy man, a skeletal bumpkin with a crew cut and big red ears. He could hold an inch-long ash on his cigarette, and he didn't think that astronauts had touched down on the moon and he didn't believe in gorillas, even though they'd been on exhibit in various zoos for over half a century. Herman would give Sundrop caps out of the drink machine and tin Prince Albert cans to Evers and the other kids who visited the station, and he would lean over the greasy cash-register counter to show them cat's-cradle tricks with a loop of grimy brown twine. Evers would take the soda caps home in a paper sack and scratch off the cork on their undersides, trying to win a free pop or a five-dollar bill.

Herman also did not believe in viruses, whales, the Loch Ness monster or radar that could predict the weather; he warned Evers and everyone else who came onto his one-bay, nuts-and-bolts corner lot to

3

be cautious of easy ruses, sleight of hand and men who wore vests with their suits. "I don't have no time for foolishness," Evers once heard Herman say to a woman with Texas plates while he was fitting a metal spout over a can of motor oil and telling her what he thought about rockets flying through space, traveling from planet to planet. The spout made a wet, slicing sound when it cut through the top of the can, and Herman used the noise to end his sentence.

Many years later, when Evers first got on the trail of the smiling white shrine, he had become a lot like Herman Stovall. Evers didn't believe in very much at the time, and he was socked in under a long horizon of bloodless indifference as thick as paste; he had the look and air of a cur mother suckling another gang of mongrel babies, her head and side lying flush on the ground, her fur clumped in a few spots, too weary to do much more than shift her eyes and half-ass growl if someone happened by. On the morning that Evers got his first glimpse of the albino mystery, he'd been walking into the sun, scraping down the sidewalk, burping up squalls of alcohol and two-in-the-morning microwave lasagna. He had just passed by a can of garbage spilled in an alley when he thought he heard someone say his name. Evers was dizzy, the sun was sharp and combative, and he was trying hard to get to his office, so he didn't stop moving right away.

"Judge Wheeling? Sir?"

Evers looked around for the voice, put up his hand to shade his eyes. "Huh?"

"Good morning."

Evers stopped and looked to his left. His balance wasn't all that good when he stood still.

"Would you come in here, please?" The woman speaking to Evers was a stranger—beautiful, handsome, well dressed and tan—and he had a muddled thought that perhaps she was talking to someone else, even though she had called him by name and was looking right at him, smiling. She was standing in front of a coffee shop not far from the courthouse where Evers worked.

"Me?" Evers looked over his shoulder, then down at his feet on the sidewalk. The woman was so pretty that he did not want to see her face for very long. He dropped and bobbed his head in choppy, pell-mell pecks, up and down and from side to side, like an old bird eating seed, and he put his hands in his pockets, took them out and put them back in again. A fat man with leather sandals and short pants walked past Evers and bumped him, brushed his back. "Are you talking to me?" Evers looked up for a moment and blinked and took his hands out of his pockets.

"Yes."

"Who in the world are you?" he asked.

"Would you come in here? I need to speak with you. Please?"

"What do you want? I don't think I know you. Is it about court, about a case?"

"No. But you are Judge Wheeling, aren't you? Judge Evers Wheeling?" The lady had taken a step and was standing right in front of Evers. "I'm Ruth Esther English. I go by Ruth Esther."

"Yes . . . nice to meet you." Evers turned and watched a tall man with a package walk past. He heard a car horn blow. "You really startled me or something—not startled, I guess, just made me uneasy." Evers kicked the sidewalk with the toe of his shoe.

"I didn't mean to upset you. Sorry."

"That's all right. I don't know why I feel so odd. People stop me all the time and want to talk." Evers stepped back and looked at the woman. She had blond hair and her hands were clasped in front of her, her two index fingers pressed up into a point. She didn't move, didn't offer to shake hands, just pulled her hands closer to her chest.

"I would like to discuss somethin' important with you for a little while. I know that you're busy, but I'd be grateful. It won't take long."

Evers shuffled his feet on the sidewalk; he felt his soles catch on the cement. His head hurt. He looked out at the traffic driving by.

"Judge Wheeling?"

Evers didn't say anything. He noticed that Ruth Esther's pants were loose around her ankles, and that she wasn't wearing hose or socks.

"Sir?" Ruth Esther touched her lips with the tips of her fingers. "Would you let me talk to you?" She kept her fingers in front of her mouth and spoke through the spire.

It was May in Winston-Salem, already warm, and Evers was wearing a suit coat, tie, long sleeves and a T-shirt. "What do you want to talk about? I have to be in court in just a few minutes." Evers began to think he was still drunk from the night before. He saw the corner of a building start to wash out; the hard brick edge turned into a lazy, aimless blur.

"I would like to speak to you in private about a personal matter."

Ruth Esther was younger than he, probably twenty-four or twenty-five, Evers decided. He felt his heart beating in his head, and his back and chest were starting to sweat. When he tried to look at Ruth Esther, he could see only her face and a jumble of swirls and streaks. He squinted and strained, struggled to get things to quit fading. The people behind her were blots and noise, and the sidewalk next to the restaurant was full of currents and eddies and erratic hues, breaking around him like a dappled creek. Evers' hands started to shake, and he rubbed them together. He rolled his head, squeezed his eyes shut, then opened them and focused on the lady in front of him: she looked more like a painting than a person, boxed in by the doorway, full of grace and goodness, like a perfect Renaissance child, all eyes and face and cheeks. "I guess I could. For a moment. I need to clear my head. I don't feel right. It's like watercolors or . . ."

Ruth Esther held out her hand, but Evers didn't move, so she touched his arm and they walked into the restaurant. The White Spot Grill and Coffee Shop was about three minutes away from the Forsyth County Courthouse. Evers rarely ate at the "Spot"—it was small and too crowded. He stepped inside the door, just ahead of Ruth Esther, into the smell of bacon and cigarette smoke and Ruth Esther's perfume, a sweet, quiet scent he'd never run across before.

"I'd like to talk somewhere private," Ruth Esther said.

"How about right here, ma'am?" Evers felt some of his balance returning. It was cooler in the restaurant than on the street, and the colors were darker and didn't seem as skittish.

"Do you think that it would be possible for us to step into one of the restrooms? I know that sounds strange, but I don't want other people listenin' to our conversation."

"Are you serious? Here? The toilet?" Evers' tongue was so dry that it didn't come off the roof of his mouth when he said the last word.

"Yes."

"Did I understand you . . . hear you right?"

"I think so."

"Are you a hooker or something? Is this some state police scam to test my integrity? You think that I'm going to walk into the toilet with a woman I don't know seven blocks away from the courthouse where I punish people for minuscule moral lapses and running red lights at three in the morning when nobody else is there? Are you—"

"If you run a red light at three in the morning and no one sees it, does it make a sound?"

"You mean like an alarm or some sort of device. . . ." Evers stopped.

Ruth Esther unfolded her hands and laughed. It occurred to Evers that she had kept her fingers in front of her, still and steepled, almost the whole time they were talking. "And someone would have to see it for it to end up in court."

"Thank you, Descartes." Evers' mouth was a thin, ill line.

"I wasn't trying to be smart. You seem pretty uncomfortable, and I was just trying to make you laugh, break the ice, that sort of thing."

"It's a pretty somber morning for me, ma'am."

"Well, why don't you go in to the men's room first? I'll follow you in. That way, if things go wrong, it would be easier for you to explain. And I'll leave my purse here on the counter, in case that's somethin' you're worried about . . . you know, that I might shoot you or stab you or try to hurt you."

"Miss, I appreciate the intrigue and your good looks, I like your sense of drama, I like the way your suit fits and how you try to look me in the eye when we talk even though we're strangers. But I'm going to go to work, get a couple of Cokes from the vending machine, put on my polyester robe and spin the wheels of justice." Evers' legs felt heavy, and the crowd and smoke in the cramped grill were making him queasy.

Evers and Ruth Esther stood beside each other in the restaurant entrance and didn't say anything else. Evers wanted to leave, to get out, to finish this encounter as best he could, but three men and a woman in a sundress had pressed in behind him, all of them smoking and craning their necks to look for a booth. A waitress with a stack of dirty plates and glasses told Evers and Ruth Esther to sit wherever they wanted to; a fork fell off one of the plates when she turned her back and pushed open the door to the kitchen.

Evers was sick from drinking, and he had walked into this woman who wanted to talk to him in a bathroom, and she was probably crazy or working for the police or full of spit and ire because of some quirk or hiccup or imagined slight. "I'm sorry that I'm no more helpful. I'm not trying to be rude, but I need to get to work." He shrugged and turned his palms up.

"What I need to speak with you about is very important. I've approached you, and I'm asking you to go with me, not the other way around. I understand that you need to be careful about things. I understand. I'm not crazy or mean or trying to make any kind of sexual offer or—what's the word—entrap you, set you up. I just need a private moment."

"You can't talk to me on the phone or come by my office?"

"I'd rather not wait."

"Why?"

"There's a lot at stake. For me and for you. For both of us."

"For me?" Evers was still avoiding Ruth Esther's face. He saw that the fork had not been picked up.

"Please."

"This involves me?"

"Yes."

"And it's not connected to my work?"

7

"No," Ruth Esther answered.

"You're certain?" He took a brief look at Ruth Esther's eyes.

"Yes."

"Why not, then? Let's have a peek at the prize behind the curtain," Evers said, and he turned and started toward the rear of the grill. "I guess if you're a lunatic, at least the story will be fun to hear. If you're worried about people reading our thoughts through satellites or TV screens, you can stop them by wearing a tinfoil hat. If that's the problem, we don't have to go into the bathroom. Any kind of thought snatching, a tinfoil hat will stop it. I run into the problem two or three times a year, so I know the solution. Just Reynolds Wrap your head—they can't get past the foil."

"I'll remember that. I'm sure the spies and aliens are hard at work on new tricks, though, ideas to get around the hats."

Evers opened the door to the restroom, and Ruth Esther walked in behind him. The room was clean and the walls mostly white, and drops of water had turned the sink bowl green around the drain opening. There was no stopper in the sink, and a bar of orange soap with brown, dry webs and bubbles was on top of the basin. The floor was dark, made from eight-sided tiles.

"I would be grateful to you if you would let Artis English go free when his case comes up in your court," Ruth Esther said as soon as she closed the door to the restroom.

Evers walked to the sink and saw his reflection in a small mirror with a cardboard frame. The mirror was hung on a short, black nail. He turned on the cold water. "Ma'am, if he's innocent, I will let him go. If he's guilty, I will find him guilty. That's the way it works." Evers was washing his hands and didn't look at Ruth Esther when he spoke. "And sometimes, guilty people are not punished because of constitutional problems or technical concerns."

"I don't know much about the facts in his case." Ruth Esther was leaning against the door.

Evers had finished his last drink about five hours earlier, and he felt the red wine in his stomach surge toward his throat. He imagined a cartoon thermometer, red mercury rising up the scale and exploding out the top. He stepped back from the sink and bent down, so his head was over the bowl. "It would seem that you lied to me. I thought that you didn't want to talk about a case or my work."

"You look sick, Judge Wheeling."

"Stomach flu."

"I'm sorry."

8

Ruth Esther sounded so earnest that Evers turned and looked at her over his shoulder. "Have we ever met before?"

"No."

"Do you know my wife? Are you a friend of hers?" He ran some water into his hands and splashed his face.

"No. I mean, your wife and I are not friends. We've never met or spoken. I just wanted to speak with you about Artis' case. It's important to me. Artis English. He's charged with cocaine possession."

"Are you a relative or something?"

"Sister. I'm his sister, although we don't look alike." Ruth Esther walked to the sink, and Evers straightened up.

"Well, it's good of you to be so supportive. I'll be fair to your brother."

"I know you will. You have that reputation. He may need more than that, though."

Evers turned toward Ruth Esther. She was solidly in front of him now; the spinning and whirling had stopped. Everything stayed inside its outline. Ruth Esther's top and pants were white, and she wasn't wearing any jewelry. He heard the water dripping in the sink, and silverware dragging across a plate out in the restaurant. "Then he is going to be shit out of luck, Miss English."

"Oh . . . "

"What else can I say?" Evers closed his eyes a little longer than he usually would, like heavy blinds lowered and lifted, and then he raised his eyebrows.

Ruth Esther's expression changed; her face crumbled, filled up with creases and puckers, and her features came undone, fell apart. She put the point of her chapel fingers under her chin, bowed her head, and then she turned and hurried into the commode stall, almost ran. The heels on her shoes beat and slid on the floor, made spastic taps that came and quit and rolled along like frantic jig steps. She banged the stall door shut, but the lock's clasp bounced against the frame, and the door swung open about a foot or so. From where he was standing, though, Evers couldn't see very far into the stall. He saw Ruth Esther's hand and some of her sleeve flash forward, heard her shove and rattle the small deadbolt into the metal loop that kept the door in place. He looked up at the ceiling, thought about cameras and peepholes, and reached toward the door to the restaurant even though he was still near the sink, too far away to get to the knob. "What are you doing?" he asked. "What's going on?"

Ruth Esther didn't answer. Evers heard the last part of a sob, sniffling and some muffled, blunt gulps. It sounded like she was trying not to cry.

There was a gap between the bottom of the stall door and the floor—the opening private eyes and psychopaths always check to see if someone's hiding in the john—and Evers could see that Ruth Esther's pants were bunched around her ankles, and that her underwear was pulled across above the pants, stretched tight, connecting leg to leg. The front partitions of the stall were bolted to the floor with silver brackets; the brackets and screws were nicked and pitted and spotted with rust, and a thick piece of cotton mop string was caught underneath the edge of one of the brackets. "What are you doing?" Evers asked again. "Are you okay? Are you crying?"

"I'm sorry. I'm okay. I'm comin' right out. Don't leave. I'll be right there. I'm embarrassed . . . I'm just upset some. Nervous."

"I can't be late for work. What else do you want, anyway?" Evers frowned. "This is a crazy confrontation. So far, I know you want me to let your brother go. I've told you that I'll follow the law and be fair. If two fat-ass police officers are out there eating McMuffins and thinking about bowling uniforms while they're recording this, I'm telling them the same thing. I'm sorry. If you're offering me sex, then I am declining. I don't want money, either. There's nothing that you can do or say that's going to change my sentiments. I didn't mean to upset you, but I can't help."

"Please don't leave yet."

Evers waited another minute or so, didn't say anything more to Ruth Esther. He heard someone shout for a waitress out in the restaurant, and a man's voice ask for more coffee. "Ma'am, I really am going to go," Evers said. "I have to. You're okay, aren't you?"

Ruth Esther opened the stall door and bumped it toward Evers with her shoulder. She was disheveled when Evers saw her, not all the way dressed, stuffing the tail of her blouse into the top of her pants, and after a couple of jabs and tucks, she gave up and left several uneven folds hanging out of her waistband. She put her hand inside her pocket, and Evers' mouth opened and he took in his breath—a hard suck that the tiles trapped and echoed, the sound circling the room two or three times. He stepped away from Ruth Esther until he felt the edge of the sink hit him in the back. "This is my business card," she said before she took her hand out of her pocket. "I'm going to leave it on the windowsill for you. Please give some thought to freeing my brother. He has information I need to help me locate property that belongs to me. I can't get my property unless he's out of jail."

"That's all very interesting, but I cannot and will not help you. I'll decide your brother's case on its merits."

Ruth Esther nodded. "I'll leave my card. Please just keep an open mind." She worked on her shirt a little more, pushed it into her pants, and she touched the corner of her eye where some makeup had dried into a tiny, blue-black ball. "Just think about it."

After Ruth Esther left, Evers leaned against the restroom wall and patted his pockets, looking for his cigarettes. Ruth Esther had walked right past him on her way out, and was face to face with him when she opened the door to go back into the restaurant. Evers locked the door. He lit a cigarette and smoked part of it while he was resting on the wall; after a few minutes, he slid and slumped down until he felt the floor underneath him, and he sat there looking at his knees and at his hand holding the cigarette. He finished the cigarette, put it out in the sink and walked across the room to pick up Ruth Esther's card.

When Evers walked by the stall, he glanced inside, and he saw—he stuck right where he was, didn't go any farther, reeled and spun and herky-jerked to get a better look—there was a perfect white curve lying on the floor in front of the toilet, five flat alabaster drops, this albino arc that looked like a row of marble dimes laid down into a big grin, small bright circles, a vivid Morse code smile: dot dot dot dot dot. The circles were all the same size, and Evers stepped closer and crouched down. Light from outside was coming into the bathroom through a window, and occasionally a moment's worth of brightness would reflect off the water in the commode and settle on his jacket or the crease in his pants. Evers stood above the smiling drops until he heard someone out in the restaurant knocking on the door. He rubbed the white circles with the toe of his shoe until they disappeared, picked up the card from the sill and put it into his pocket without reading it.

A s soon as he got to the courthouse, Evers went into his office and dialed the district attorney's number. He was able to find the chief deputy, a woman named Joan Anderson, who was about to leave for court. Evers told her that he had been approached by a lady claiming to be the sister of a man named English, and that the sister wanted Evers to help Mr. English. "Does the name ring a bell?" Evers asked. "Is this guy noteworthy?"

"Not that I'm aware of," Joan said. She sounded distracted. "I'll check and let you know."

"I just wanted to give you a call. I always try to when something like this comes up. Just to be safe."

"It's not a big case, as far as I know. I've never heard of the guy. Do you recall his first name?"

"Artis. Or Artist. Something close to that."

"I'll have someone run it down and get back to you if we find anything important. How long are you going to be in Winston?"

"What's today?"

Joan laughed. "You sound like me. Today's Friday, Judge."

"I'll be here for another two weeks."

"How are things in Norton?"

"Okay." Evers looked at his watch. "I can't complain."

"Thanks for calling. I appreciate your letting me know about this."

"Sure. I'm glad to do it. It's generally a good idea to try to cover everyone's butt."

"No doubt about that. Maybe I'll have a chance to work with you while you're here. I hope so. Do you have many criminal cases?"

"A bunch." Evers heard someone in the background talking to Joan. "I'll let you go, and thanks for the help. Give me a call if you find out anything."

Evers took Ruth Esther's card out of his pocket. He had looked at it as soon as he got to his office, before he called Joan Anderson. Ruth Esther was a "sales associate" at a car dealership in Winston-Salem. He turned the card over; there was nothing written on the back. Evers phoned the clerk's office and had them bring him Artis English's file; when he read it, there was nothing exceptional about the case or the paperwork. He asked his secretary to put a memo in the file regarding his contact with Ruth Esther, and had a copy sent to the chief judge and the district attorney's office, addressed to Joan Anderson. Evers put the card back in his pocket. He drank a Coke out of the can, smoked another cigarette, put on his robe and started work.

During a break in the morning docket, Evers had one of the deputies check Ruth Esther's background. The officer handed Evers two sheets of computer paper with Ruth Esther's name printed in large type across the top of each sheet. She was licensed to drive in North Carolina, Evers discovered, and she had no criminal record or traffic convictions. He put the two pages on the bench beside his pens, gavel and rubber bands, laid the card on top of the report and kept glancing at the pile throughout the day. During a long, tedious case after lunch, Evers started doodling on the sides of Ruth Esther's driving record. He drew a house and a man with a beard, and eventually blackened in all of the "o's" and "a's" on the page. While he was listening to his last case, he circled the address on the card and tried to recall if he'd ever seen Ruth Esther anywhere else. Evers remembered the white drops on the floor, how bright they were, five thin pearls he could still see if he kept his eyes closed. He figured that if traffic wasn't heavy, he could get from his office to Ruth Esther's car lot in about fifteen minutes.

The Ford-Lincoln-Mercury-Jeep-Eagle-Isuzu dealership was about as nice as possible, given that the heart of the trade was selling superfluous extended warranties, defrauding buyers with shell games and counterfeit invoices, hiding used oil from the EPA and rebuilding whole transmissions that probably needed little more than a bolt tightened or a dollar gasket. The salesmen were wearing tasseled loafers and suits with pleated pants, and two had mousse in their hair. The cars were new and clean, rows of them in color gradations like a sheet-metal spectrum, lined up by size and model, Escorts to Lincolns. Evers looked at them from small to large and thought about a xylophone. The showroom was full of heavy-paper brochures that showed cars and trucks parked on wet black driveways and in front of streams and mansions. The floor inside the building was made from large, slick tiles, and the ceiling had several rows of recessed lights and one bright brass chandelier. Ruth Esther walked up just after Evers stepped inside the door to the showroom. She was wearing the same suit she'd had on when Evers talked to her in the bathroom of the restaurant.

"Good evening," she said. "I'm glad you came by." Ruth held out her hand, and Evers shook it. She had a soft grip. Evers couldn't feel any bones or joints while their hands were together.

"I would never have thought that you sold cars. You seem a little . . . elegant for this."

"Thank you for the compliment, but it's a good business. I make a lot of money. Old men think that they can take advantage of me, young men think that they have a chance to have sex with me and women trust me. I moved a hundred eighty-six units last month. One hundred eighty-six automobiles. That's one of the best figures in the nation, and we're in a small market. I was by far the leader in North Carolina."

"Are you honest?"

Ruth Esther nodded several times, but she didn't smile or speak. "I am," she finally said. She took a step back and leaned against the trunk of a car on the showroom floor. "Do you want to go to my office

I 3

or walk through the lot? Would you like a snack or a drink? We have bottled water, soft drinks, pretzels."

"How do you get paid for something like this, if you don't mind my asking?"

"I get paid a commission on the above-cost profit that we make on each vehicle. Depending on the model and promotion, that margin is anywhere from two hundred dollars to two or three thousand. In addition to that, I get bonuses and incentives for meeting certain sales targets."

Evers thought for a few seconds. "You're making thirty or forty thousand dollars a month selling cars? Is that possible?"

"I make more than that when you take my target bonuses into account."

"Damn."

"So where would you like to talk?"

"I don't think I want to go to your office." Evers rubbed his neck with the heel of his hand. Ruth Esther was paged over the intercom system. "Do you need to answer that?"

"They'll take a message."

"Let's take a test drive. I suppose that if we're being monitored, there's about a six-hundred-to-one chance that they've bugged the right vehicle in advance."

"I'll go get a plate. Which vehicle do you want?"

Evers looked into the lot and saw a black pickup about forty yards from the door. "The black truck." He pointed.

"I'll go get everything."

Evers watched the truck while she left to get a tag and the keys. No one went near it. Ruth Esther walked and moved so quietly that Evers didn't realize she was back until she tapped him on the wrist. "Here are the keys."

"Let me see them. And the plate."

Ruth Esther handed Evers the keys. The key ring was attached to a rectangular, yellow piece of plastic with black Magic Marker writing on one side of the plastic. The keys were flat and metal. The plate had two springs running from corner to corner and a clip in the center. Evers turned it over and stretched the springs. The coils were stiff and close together, two silver tunnels that didn't give much when Evers tried to pull them apart.

"I can't see inside the springs. Can you unhook the ends?"

"No. But the plate will be on the outside of the car, so that shouldn't bother you."

"You'll need to get a temporary tag. One of those flat, cardboard, thirty-day deals."

"I can't do that unless I transfer title. There has to be a sale." Ruth Esther's hands were back in front of her, her two index fingers pointed up.

"Then I don't guess we can do business," Evers said.

Ruth Esther took the plate from Evers and looked at the fasteners. She pulled the springs, then pressed the license tag under her arm and worked and twisted the ends of the coils, trying to separate them from the corners of the plate. "I'll take the spring off and get some screws from the shop."

"I'm paranoid now; try to get a paper tag. And let me tell you again that I'm not going to do anything venal or corrupt or misuse my office." A beer would taste good, Evers thought, a cold beer in a clear bottle that would sweat in his hand when he picked it up. He rubbed his neck some more. "I've notified several people about our first contact and your entreaty."

"So why are you here?"

"To find out what it is that you want."

"If your intentions are good, why are you so concerned about bein' overheard?"

"People take things out of context from time to time." Evers half smiled, very quickly, and then reached into his pocket for a cigarette.

"I'm not trying to cause problems. Really, I'm not."

"That's good to know."

Ruth Esther stopped trying to bend the ends of the springs. Evers had found a cigarette and had it in his hand, but he hadn't lit it. He leaned very close to Ruth Esther and whispered, "Get a cardboard tag." She left and walked through a door and out of sight.

A salesman with chain-saw cologne and his hands on his hips had walked up and was half-sitting on the hood of one of the showroom cars behind Evers. "I wouldn't think that you'd care for a truck," he said. "You look like a sport-utility man to me. Grand Cherokee or Explorer. In fact, we're just about giving away an interior package on some of the Explorers. Of course, everyone can use a good truck." The citrus and musk fumes settled on Evers.

Evers turned his head, twisted his neck as far as he could and looked at the salesman. He didn't move his feet or bother to get any closer. "Was it Lionel Hampton who played the xylophone? I can't recall. It's a great instrument, though, isn't it? I like the name. I like the name 'harpsichord,' too." He looked away from the salesman, back outside at the truck. "So what do you think? Was it Lionel Hampton?"

"I'm not sure. I've started getting into some New Age stuff myself. Yanni, you heard of him? Or John Tesh? He's the guy from *Entertainment Tonight*, but he's also a great music composer. Women—let me tell you—they love the stuff, too. You ought to try some." The salesman winked. "I've got a disc in my car—you're welcome to borrow it if you want to."

"No thanks." Evers didn't look back.

"Let me know if you change your mind."

Ruth Esther returned with a cardboard tag and two screws, and she and Evers walked to the truck. She fastened the tag to the front bumper and handed Evers the keys. Evers had never driven a truck before, and he was surprised by how high he was off the ground and how awkward he felt inside the cab. The length and size of the interior made his hands and legs look small. He shifted the truck into drive and pulled out onto the interstate.

"You are going to have to take off your coat and shirt and let me see them."

"I'm not carrying any sort of listening device," Ruth Esther offered.

"Then I won't find one."

She took off her suit coat and laid it on the seat. Evers looked in it and felt along the lapels and seams and pushed his hands into the pockets. Ruth Esther handed him her blouse, and he held it up and patted it and turned it inside out. She was wearing a white cotton bra with a plastic snap in the front.

"You'll need to take off the bra, too."

"I'm beginning to think that you want to be entertained rather than safe. This is sort of low and ugly." Ruth Esther was looking out at the road, not at Evers.

"This must be important to you."

"It is, obviously. And it upsets me to have to undress in front of you like this." Ruth Esther glanced at him. "You know, if I were trying to get you into trouble, my being almost naked in a truck with you would be pretty hard to explain, don't you think? You're being so guarded and careful and now you're tellin' me to take my clothes off."

"You really don't have to do anything. You approached me and asked me to misuse my office. I think I have the right to be wary and ask for some concessions. And I'll probably enjoy seeing you naked— you're right about that. You're attractive, and I'm a fan of form and pulchritude." Evers looked in the rearview mirror. "For what it's worth, I've already seen you with your pants down at the restaurant anyway. Saw your shins, the bottoms of your knees."

"It's a combination of things, I guess."

"I'm not trying to be a cad. I hope you can see why I might be concerned."

Ruth Esther snapped open her bra and handed it to Evers. "Would you turn so that I can see your back, please?" he asked.

"I suppose that I'm going to have to finish undressing, my pants and all?"

Evers remembered that he did not have his seat belt on, and he reached up and pulled the belt and harness across his lap; the metal ends made a clicking noise when they caught. "Sorry."

Ruth Esther put her bra and shirt back on and gave Evers her slacks to search. She pulled down the front, rear and sides of her underwear, but did not take it all the way off.

"Thanks," Evers said. He had begun to feel embarrassed and shabby. "I feel better."

Ruth Esther didn't acknowledge his contrition. She closed two air vents in front of her and put her head and back against the seat. "About four years ago, my brother Artis, my father and I took one hundred thousand dollars from a man named Lester Jackson. He owns an antique store on Cherry Street here in Winston-Salem. At one time, as hard as it is for me to believe, he held some position in the North Carolina Antique Dealers' Association. To be more precise, we went into his business—broke into it, really—and took the money. I drove the car, and my father and Artis went inside. The police came before my brother got out of the building. My brother is very simple, and you can't count on him for much. He'd stopped in the store to look at an old phonograph and several records and was trying to pull the record player off a shelf. My father and I got away, but the police found Artis in the store. It was impossible for us to do anything for him. He had climbed up a three-hundred-pound bookshelf and tipped it over, and the police found him trapped underneath the thing with Ink Spots and Mills Brothers records lyin' all around him. We simply didn't have time to go in and lift the furniture off him. My father was . . . well, he just couldn't believe it. Then, for a while, he was bitter. He used to say that Artis was so stupid that he had a record even before he went to court."

Evers chuckled. "Pigs get fat, hogs get slaughtered. Ever heard that? He should've been satisfied with the money."

"No, but it seems pretty appropriate in this situation. But that's just

Artis. Anyway, my father had the money when he came out of the store, and after a while he hid it. There are three clues that tell where it is, three directions that my father wrote down. We agreed we wouldn't get it until Artis got out of jail. My father gave me his clue. He's dead now. Artis has the other one. He was free for all of six hours before he got picked up again. If he's found guilty and goes back to jail, I've been told he will have to serve his punishment for this new crime as well as some additional time that was over his head because of the burglary."

"He probably had some suspended time for the theft and was out on parole. That will be revoked if he gets another conviction, especially for something drug related."

"All the while my money stays hidden somewhere. Artis won't give me his clue until he's free."

"Why would your father give him a clue if he's so stupid and caused all the trouble and delay?"

"My father believed in the importance of a bargain. And, I guess he figured that Artis would need the money. He's just about helpless."

Evers turned on the radio and rolled the window down. He drove for another mile or so, until there were fewer cars on the road, and then pulled into a convenience-store parking lot without giving a turn signal, very abruptly. A pregnant woman was pumping gas into a Volvo station wagon, resting against the car while the gas ran in. Her skirt was higher on one side than the other because of the way she was leaning; her calves were heavy, and there were black and blue veins showing on the backs of her knees.

"Why are we stoppin'?" Ruth Esther asked.

"I wanted to get out of the truck."

Evers and Ruth Esther walked inside the store and sat down at a table with a Formica top. There were some salt grains spread around on the table, some orange crumbs, a mustard smear and a cold, burned french fry. Several napkins were falling out of a silver container, the bottoms tucked behind a tin lip, the tops bowing out of the holder one after the other.

"That's a fairly bald-faced story, isn't it?" Evers said. He was sitting with his chin in his hand. "You're a burglar, and you want me to make it possible for you to profit from your theft. Your brother is a dolt and a thief and a drug user, and you want me to let him go so he can gain from your wrongdoing. There are nothing but villains in this piece— pencil-thin mustaches, Iron Crosses, sidecars and pith helmets. And there's no reason for me to risk anything to help you, is there?" Evers picked up a salt shaker and set it in front of him.

"I'll offer you half of my share. That's twenty-five thousand dollars. Of course I'm sure you don't need the money. And I'll let you come with us to retrieve the cash—that's where all the tangles and turns are, the maze, the trip, you know, trackin' it down. I think that's what you'd like the most."

"Where is it?"

"I truly don't know."

"You want me to go to jail over twenty-five thousand dollars and a treasure hunt? Lose my job? That's really all there is to this? I figured that after all the hype and tease and jugglers and clowns and dancing bears and barkers and buildup, there'd be a little more." Evers looked around the store. He decided to buy a six-pack of Miller beer and a quart of tomato juice and let Ruth Esther drive him back.

"I seriously doubt that anyone's going to end up in jail. If it makes you feel any better, Lester Jackson isn't entitled to the money anyway. Why do you think that an antique dealer would have a hundred thousand dollars in cash lying around his office? He came by it illegally." Ruth Esther leaned forward and put her elbows on the table. "He—"

"Don't put your sleeve in that mustard," Evers warned her.

"He doesn't deserve it."

"Doesn't that just make it even worse? Exponential thievery? I'd be knee-deep in thugs and losers."

"That's a strange thing to say. I'm not sure I know what you mean."

"So how did Lester Jackson get the money?"

"Drugs, mostly."

"Why are you so concerned about it?" Evers asked. "You don't seem to need fifty thousand dollars that badly. Certainly there are some risks involved for you."

"Artis needs his share. And even if I split my portion with you, twenty-five thousand is right much money for me."

He handed Ruth Esther the truck keys. "Would you like a beer?"

"What time is it?"

Evers looked at a clock behind the store counter. "Almost seven."

"I usually leave work about eight-thirty. What did you have in mind?"

Evers smiled. "My plans are a little more immediate. I meant on the ride back."

"Sure. Why not?" Ruth Esther slid out of the booth. "So what are you going to do?"

"I don't think I care for the truck."

"That's sort of avoiding the question, isn't it? What about Artis and my offer?"

"If I change my mind, I'll let you know." Evers was still sitting down.

"His trial is not too far off. Please let me know soon."

"Why would your father hide this money? Why didn't you simply take your share, Dad take his and put Artis' in safekeeping? Or put it all in an account that required all three signatures?"

Ruth Esther smoothed the front of her shirt with her hands. "Are you going to get your beer?"

"Yes." Evers stood up. He was exactly six feet tall, and he noticed for the first time that Ruth Esther was a tall woman.

"It was sort of a sense of family for my father, and fairness. We had to get it at the same time. Artis had pneumonia one Christmas and was in the hospital, and we didn't open presents until he came home and felt good enough to get out of bed and sit around the tree. My father felt that fairness was being treated the same way at the same time."

"There's a sound rule. I suppose he didn't pay for you to go to college until your brother was ready as well. No car for you at sixteen; it was only fair to wait for Artis. What an inane idea."

"I'm younger than Artis, so I wasn't on the short end of things too much."

"Isn't this scheme a little unfair to you and your brother? Forgetting for a moment that it was a dumb idea to hide the money until Artis was free, aren't you and your brother completely vulnerable? Perhaps there isn't any money. Your father may have taken it or spent it. That's not a really good checks-and-balances system you had, is it? Am I overlooking something? Couldn't Dad take the whole thing and leave you and your brother penniless? Or he and Artis fuck you over? Obviously, he didn't trust you completely."

"I have faith that the money is safe and unspent. I have faith in my father." Ruth Esther and Evers were walking toward the beer cooler.

"Faith is pretty much a sightless, hopped-up, fervent guess, isn't it?"

"For some people, I suppose."

Evers laughed. He slid open a glass door and took out a carton of beer. He handed the beer to Ruth Esther and closed the door. "Your father is a thief. You trust a hundred thousand dollars with a thief?"

"My father is my father, that's the most important thing. He is what he is. And of course you're a lawyer and I'm not, but taking money from someone who hasn't earned it, who doesn't really own it or deserve it, that's not larceny, is it?"

"Only if you plan on giving it to the poor and needy or the rightful owners." Evers got a quart of tomato juice from another cooler. "Do you want tomato juice in your beer or just beer?"

"It doesn't matter."

"I'll get two. I can drink some for breakfast if we don't use it all."

"Lester Jackson has no more claim to the money than we do. In fact, he has less claim—we didn't victimize people and prey on their addictions. Do you think we should give it back to him, or that he should get to keep it? Do you think he needs to be rewarded for sellin' dope?" Ruth Esther's voice was very calm. She had returned the beer to Evers and was talking over the points of her fingers again.

"Why did you steal it in the first place? Unless you were going to do something noble with it, or use it as seed capital to buy capes and masks to fight crime, you are simply a thief. Jackson probably didn't deserve it, but neither did you and your family. The moral cloak doesn't exactly fit you, does it?"

"I'm not tryin' to say that we were completely in the right. I just wanted you to know that we didn't rob a bank or dip into widows' pensions. You're not making a wrong worse by helping us get this money—that's what I'm tryin' to say. I certainly don't like stealin', even from a spotted tick like Lester Jackson."

"So why did you steal his hundred thousand?" Evers asked again.

"I suppose part of it was for personal gain. That's true enough."

"That's what I would have guessed." Evers paid for the beer and tomato juice, walked outside and stepped up into the passenger side of the truck. He had forgotten to buy cups, so he drank the beer by itself on the ride back to the car lot. Ruth Esther finished her bottle very quickly, and she handed it to Evers when she was through and asked him to put it in the carton and not let it drip on the floor or the seat.

When Ruth Esther and Evers got back to the dealership, he walked to his car and she walked with him. "I hope that you'll go with us," Ruth Esther said.

"Who knows." He was standing by his car with his hand on the door handle. "I don't see much on the bill of fare but risk and mischief, though. Not much in this for me that I can discover."

"Do you truly think that?" Ruth Esther looked confused. "I know you don't need the money. I know you don't have to work and that you're wealthy. But this is like a trip, a vacation. It has a beginnin' and an end. Drops and curves. Maybe we'll ride over a steel bridge or walk through a thicket. And your life now isn't that hot, and I'm not trying to sound rude, not at all, not in any way, but it's not that great. You

have a wizened marriage, no hobbies, no interests or children, nothing important that goes on. You were hungover this morning, weren't
you? You're hungover a lot. Your work is dull and numbin', refereeing
squabbles between criminals in tanktops and listening to the same
dumb old lies over and over and over. Why wouldn't you want to do
this?" Ruth Esther paused; her voice was direct and soft. "I'm not trying to be mean about it, okay? I just don't understand why you're so
hesitant. Why would you even come out here if I'm not right? That's
why you came, came today, because your life is just boredom and beer
and bourbon . . . and, like I said, I'm not trying to be critical, but you
came out here—that's why. Has to be."

"Is this the big close, where I get another hundred bucks knocked
off and a free oil change just as I get ready to walk away?"

"Well, think about it. If I'm wrong, I'm wrong."

"I'm not a very bold person, Miss English."

"We'll see."

"And I'm not going to bother asking you how you think you know
so much about me."

"How hard could it be, Judge Wheeling?"

"By the way, what was going on in the bathroom at the restaurant
this morning?"

"What do you mean?"

"When you ran into the stall," Evers explained.

"Nothing. Nothing, really. You know . . . I just needed to go in
there," Ruth Esther stammered.

"How did you do that trick with the white, uh, the white . . . smile
in the toilet?"

"It's not a trick."

"So what was that on the floor? The white stuff."

"That's a pretty strange thing to be askin' about. Why were you
pokin' around in there? Looking in? I'm not trying to offend you—for
sure, I don't want to do that—but that's sort of out of the ordinary."

"The door was open when I went by to get your card."

"I was very uncomfortable talking to you, and I was upset. I got real
upset for a moment. You know, because things weren't workin' out;
you weren't goin' to help me, and I felt pretty stupid. I just sort of lost
my composure for a while."

"So?" Evers had been holding on to his car door. He let go of the
handle.

"So I was cryin' some." Evers noticed that Ruth Esther occasionally
dropped a "g" or puffed up an "r," but she really didn't have much of
an accent.

"With your pants down?"

"I . . . I didn't want you to think I was just sitting in there."

"So you're telling me—let me get this straight—that you went in there and cried and your tears look like five Elmer's glue splatters? White?"

"Yes."

"All the time? You always weep white tears?"

"Yes," Ruth Esther answered.

Evers swatted at a gnat buzzing around his ear. "So you can do it now?"

"I guess. Probably."

"That's hard to believe. I'd like to see you do it again."

"Really?" Ruth Esther asked. "Are you serious?"

"I am," Evers said.

"I don't understand."

"I think that something's up, something you're not telling me. I don't know what you were doing in there this morning, but I really don't think that you were in the stall crafting fey white tears, or that you were flustered and shy and all unhinged."

"What do you think, then?"

"How about that you were wearing a wire that came loose and you had to take your clothes off and put some kind of adhesive on the microphone?"

"Will it help me? Help me get you to think about doin' something for Artis?"

"It will certainly hold my interest a little longer, that's for sure." Evers watched a salesman on the other side of the lot open a car door for an elderly man.

"Why?" Ruth Esther asked. "How come?"

"I like oddities and aberrations, I guess. But basically because I don't believe you, or your story."

"I'm not sure." Ruth Esther's voice was a murmur.

"It's up to you."

"I guess I'll try, then . . . as long as you don't ask me to start cryin' out here. That would really look crazy, standing out here bawling. I can go in the restroom as long as you don't follow me in. That might cause me to get in trouble and lose my job. You're welcome to check before I go in. And you certainly know there's nothing hidden on me."

"Why can't I watch you do it?" Evers demanded. "You know, see for myself?"

"I'm not like a movie star or somethin', so that I can just get upset and start crying on cue with you standing here breathing down my neck."

They walked back inside the building, and Evers went into the men's restroom and looked around. While he was checking the bathroom, Ruth Esther had gone into the employees' lounge and taken the small, clear top off a squeeze bottle of ketchup, and she had stuck two strips of cellophane tape onto the ends of her fingers. She went in the restroom after Evers came out, and he heard the door shut and the lock button pop into the center of the knob. Ruth Esther was in the toilet for about five minutes, and while she was gone Evers picked up some matches and a refrigerator magnet from a table near the front of the showroom. When Ruth Esther reappeared from the bathroom, she handed Evers a wad of toilet paper.

"Jesus Christ." He pulled his hand away, and the paper fell onto the floor. "What's in there?"

"Tears. In the little plastic top with tape over it." Ruth Esther folded her arms across her chest. She was standing close enough to Evers that he could smell the beer on her breath.

"I don't think I really want to carry around who knows what wrapped up in half a roll of toilet paper. How do I know what's in there? It could be poison or toxic or infected or—hell, I don't know, it could be anything."

"So what did you have in mind? You're the one who asked me to give them to you."

"I don't know. Why are they buried in toilet paper?" The toilet paper was still on the floor, between Evers and Ruth Esther. One of the loose ends was touching the top of Evers' shoe.

"Open it up and look. You're actin' just about silly. It's won't bite you. I just wrapped the top up in case it came open or started leaking."

"This is too bizarre." Evers kicked at the tissue with his foot, moved the lump around on the floor. He could feel the plastic top inside the ball of paper.

"I'll have one of the mechanics give me a sandwich bag. You can feel safe carryin' it that way and look at it whenever you want to. In your kitchen or something, with gloves on. And one of those surgical masks. You're sure acting like you think I'm tryin' to do something to you." Ruth Esther sounded bewildered, resigned, but not angry.

Ruth Esther went into the garage area, came back with a clear plastic bag, picked up the wad of tissue and sealed it in the bag. "Here."

"Why is it that you have white tears?"

"It's just the way I am."

"Are you sick, or taking some kind of medicine?"

"Nope. Not at all."

"I've never heard of anything like this before. It would make a hell of a sideshow attraction."

Ruth Esther handed Evers the bag. "What are you going to do with them?"

"I don't know. I think I'll take them to my friend Dr. Rudy, let him make a slide, and we'll all have a few drinks and look at it under the microscope."

"No kidding?"

"You never know," Evers said.

"I really don't like you asking me to do this. I just hope you know I sort of felt that I had to, so you wouldn't think something was going on or that I was tryin' to trick you."

"I still think something is up, only I'm not sure what it is." Evers loosened his tie, pulled the knot away from his throat. "For all I know, you got a bottle of correction fluid while I was in the restroom."

"Well, thank you for coming, regardless of what happens. And thank you for the beer. Do you want me to walk you to your car?"

"No, that's okay."

"Okay. Well, God bless you."

Evers grimaced. "What exactly do you mean by that?"

"I mean that I hope things go well for you."

"Oh." Evers turned and took a step toward the door. "Take care," he said, and he heard Ruth Esther's name called over the intercom again.

Evers walked out of the showroom into the warm air, and he heard the sounds of cars passing on the highway and a few people talking in the lot. He was wearing a Brooks Brothers suit and carrying a taped-up ketchup top wrapped like a mummy in a clear sandwich bag. He thought about a beer, and about driving home, and then he stopped walking and thought about his mother and the smell of her food in the kitchen at three-thirty, after school, and the dishwasher when she opened it and bent over, the bottom rack, plates and bowls. Evers noticed that he'd stopped moving. He looked down at the asphalt and over at his car. He turned back toward the showroom, where Ruth Esther was standing in the door watching him, and waves from the pavement lifted her up in little shimmers and rises, like she was rocking on water. Evers knelt down and put his hand on the parking lot; it was warm, but not hot.

When he got into his car, Evers' head and stomach felt good enough to take on some more alcohol. He poured part of a beer onto the ground—emptied the bottle down to the top of the label—mixed in tomato juice, and started drinking with an eye toward finishing at least three of the beers before he got to his apartment in Norton.

When Evers got home from the car dealership, he took a cooler out of a closet in his apartment, twisted two plastic ice trays into the cooler and dropped the bag with the albino tears into the ice. He sat down on the arm of an oversize chair, leaned forward, balled up some of his hair in his fist and looked around his apartment. There were two water glasses on the floor beside the chair, one empty, the other with flat soda and cigarette butts in it. Evers slipped down into the chair, picked up the phone and dialed his wife's number. She answered almost immediately. It was already past nine, and Evers told her he wasn't going to drive to Durham for the weekend. Jo Miller was quiet for a moment. "Okay," she finally said, and then she and Evers talked about where she had eaten lunch and a few other things.

"You're not mad at me, are you?"

"You know, Evers, you haven't been down here in over a week, and you left early the last time you came. And you've called just once. One time in a week. At three in the morning, remember? You and Pascal had been outside watching a toad, and you kept going on about how it looked prehistoric when it jumped and about the gold ring in its eye. You weren't sounding all that normal."

"Sorry. I'll try to make it up to you." Evers glanced at the cooler. It was sitting on the kitchen floor, next to the refrigerator. "You could come up here to see me if you wanted to. I'm just worn out; I had to work all day."

"We've had that discussion before." Jo Miller coughed and cleared her throat.

Evers could tell she had turned her head away from the receiver. She coughed some more, and Evers waited for the noise to stop before he said anything else. "Well, it wouldn't kill you to drive up here just once," he suggested.

"Probably not, but I'm not going to."

"Right." Evers didn't push the issue. "Maybe I could come down, you know, late tomorrow or early Sunday."

"Just call first to let me know."

"Do you want me to come?" he asked.

"That's up to you."

"If you don't want me to, if you don't care one way or the other, then I might just ride down and visit Pascal."

"Look, Evers, if you want to see your brother, then go see him. If you want to come down here, then come on. Please just don't do this chump dance and try to get me to bless your choice even if I don't like it." Jo Miller's voice hung and scratched in her throat.

"You sure are sputtering and hacking a lot," Evers said.

"I always get a cold around this time of the year, when the seasons are changing."

"Well, I'll let you know. I'm not trying to be hard to get along with."

"Fine. Call me in the morning. If you're not coming, I'm sure I can find something else to do."

"I'm sure you can," he answered sourly.

"We need to talk about some things, Evers. In person. Face to face. I need to . . . to get this cleared up. And, I guess, I need to tell you some things."

"Tell me what? What do you mean?"

"I need . . . we need . . . I don't want to talk about it on the phone. I just want to get some things out on the table."

"Why not tell me now?" Evers asked. "I'll be miserable and worried until you tell me. You're going to drop this ominous, curdled hint and leave it hanging until I see you, right? That's not very thoughtful."

"You deserve a little discomfort, Evers. And you have a good idea what I'm going to say." Jo Miller blurted out the last sentence. "I'll talk to you later. There's no need to belabor this now." She hung up the phone. Evers heard a click and then an empty, disconnected line. He felt his stomach stir up, like the first boils in soup or porridge— big, slow, plopping bubbles started turning over in his middle. " 'A good idea what I'm going to say,' " he muttered.

Evers still had the receiver in his hand and he started to call Jo Miller again, tapped in the area code and two more numbers, then stopped. He let the receiver drop, didn't hang it up, just opened his hand, and the receiver hit the floor beside his chair and pulled the rest of the phone along behind it—train cars crashing over a cliff, one pulling the others along, banging and clanging and piling up when they hit bottom.

Evers picked up the cooler, took an opened bottle of cabernet out of the refrigerator, walked down the stairs to his car and headed toward his brother's.

When Evers got to Pascal's trailer, it had been dark for several hours; a couple of lamps were turned on inside the mobile home, and a purple bug zapper was mixing up the light and turning everything near it—the shadows, the ground and Pascal's face, hands and clothes—an unnatural, bright gray. Evers shut his car door, and his brother waved at him. The bug zapper electrocuted an insect with a violent, hissing snap.

"I'm glad you're here, Evers," Pascal said while Evers was still walking down the driveway to the mobile home. "We are, in this season of frolic, cotillions and lawn parties, recumbent here at my house trailer, smoking dope and drinking and talking about things. And, of course, we always look forward to hearing your thoughts, given that the state of North Carolina pays you for your opinions." Pascal grinned. He was barefoot and had not shaved in two or three days.

Evers sat down next to Pascal on a long cloth sofa in the yard in front of the trailer. One cushion in the sofa was damp because Pascal had forgotten to put a brick on the corner of the large plastic sheet he used as a cover, and rain had made the seat soggy. Pascal's friends Rudy and Henry were sitting in lawn chairs, facing the two brothers.

"So, if you had testicular cancer, okay, and you could live for sure but had to have your balls cut off, or you could leave them intact but have a seventy-five percent chance of dying, what would you do? That's the question." Pascal had picked a piece of foam out of a rip in the sofa and was rolling it around in his hands.

"You're using a lot of poor medical assumptions, Pascal. This is fairly bizarre. Hard to imagine such an odd set of circumstances," said Rudy. Rudy was a physician. He was drinking expensive merlot out of the bottle. He had brought the wine with him to Pascal's trailer since Pascal drank only beer and the cheaper varieties of hard liquor.

"It's a philosophical question, Dr. Strangelove, not an empirical one." Pascal gave Rudy an impatient look. "Don't be so literal."

"I'd want to die with my balls on," said Evers.

"No doubt," remarked Pascal. "How about you, Dr. Rudy?"

"I don't have sex as much as you guys. I'd be happy to be alive and work on cars and drink quality wine."

"The doctor to the cars," Evers quipped. His pants were soaking up dampness from the wet cushion. Pascal handed him a blue plastic picnic cup half full of warm scotch. "What about you, Henry?"

"I'm married, don't use them anymore. I'd let Rudy do the work, too." Rudy was the kind of physician who probably would do well in a critical situation—blood geysering from a cut artery or a toddler with a Tinkertoy lodged in her throat—but he drank too much and couldn't be trusted around all the whiz-bang hospital gadgetry, hemostats, pharmaceuticals and other doctor's prerogatives, all the means and tricks and palliatives that are best just left alone or used on others. The doctor to the cars spent most of his time working on automobiles, boozing and filling in at the local emergency room during summers and on holidays.

"You know, there aren't a lot of people with balls anyway," Rudy said. He was almost supine in his chair, his bottle on the ground beside him. "The world's full of eunuchs and jesters and egg-laying roaches."

Henry nodded several times. "I saw my buddy Bono the other day, in this old video with Frank Sinatra. Bono has on these dumbass sunglasses and is disgorging his world-weary Irish wraparound minstrel spleen onto one of Frank's songs. 'Under My Skin,' I think it was. It was perverse. Terrible. Bono has no balls at all. He's the worst kind. Puts on this cinders-and-fury show, and, probably, the high-water mark of his virility is smashing a hotel lamp or cursing a hair stylist."

"Sinatra had balls," Evers said. "Always did."

"I agree," Pascal added. "Even though he was wearing a wig for a few years before he died."

"Good call." Henry looked at Rudy. "I wonder what Frank made of Bono?"

"Let me tell you something, brother." Evers sat up from the back of the sofa. He lit a cigarette. "Something of interest. I have a chance to spend a couple of weeks trying to track down some money. About a hundred grand. It's a pretty unusual situation. This lady—and I don't know that much about her—has two of these clues that will lead to the money, which is hidden somewhere. She has a partner, her brother, who has the other clue."

Rudy waved his hands. "Slower, Evers. And don't put more than one idea in each sentence. We're stoned, okay?"

"I'll go slowly."

"We would get more out of it if you did."

"There are three clues. We have two. You need all three clues to find the money—one hundred thousand dollars. My potential partner is a lady, very attractive, as a matter of fact. She's blond and dresses well. If I help her and we find the money, I get twenty-five thousand dollars. If you guys go with me, I'll split that with you, so that—"

"We would each get sixty-two hundred and fifty bucks." Pascal finished his brother's thought.

"Around sixty-two hundred. Yeah." Evers drank some scotch.

"Who's the lady?"

"She sells cars. Her brother's in jail. I'm not sure about this yet. I just thought you guys might enjoy the trip. I mean, I realize it will be hard to leave the lawn sirens and tar-baby embrace of the doublewide, but I wanted to mention it. It might be fun, sort of a glorified road trip." Evers paused and looked sideways at Pascal. "Like the mazes on the back of cereal boxes. A trip with some curves."

Pascal was making another marijuana cigarette. He sprinkled the dope into a paper, rolled the paper, licked the edge and twisted the ends. "I'm fairly smoked up, Evers, but it's fair to assume, I guess, that this is not a radio promotion or buried Civil War treasure. Dick Clark's not on the envelope?"

"It is my understanding that the money's stolen, probably from someone who gained it illegally."

"Where is it?" asked Rudy.

"What a stupid question." Henry frowned at the car doctor.

"That's not what I'm asking. Is it, you know, in this state, at the bottom of the sea, where? Six thousand is okay if all we have to do is pick up a duffel bag at the Asheboro bus depot, but a little short if we have to battle jackals and walk over skulls and rats and pools of acid in Nepal."

"I think Evers' point is, Rudy, that it might be an odyssey." Henry took the joint from Pascal. "Thank you for including us, Evers. I'll go if it promises to be a good drive and a fun trip. I hope that we will have plenty to drink and some reefer, and . . . a bus would be nice, too. Let me know when you make up your mind."

"Does this involve your job, Evers?" Pascal asked. "It certainly doesn't seem wise to risk your career over money you don't need. And very little money at that."

"Well, I haven't decided yet; I'm not sure about the whole thing. I didn't mean for you to think that I was definite about it. And there's something not right about the story . . . the setup doesn't make much sense. The story about these clues and how everything got to this point is hard to take at face value. But still . . . I don't know . . . it still might be okay. This has sort of a little hook in me."

"Is it the woman?" asked Henry.

"I just met her. I guess it's a lot of things." Evers took the joint from Henry and sat back on the sofa. He inhaled the smoke, and the end of the cigarette turned bright orange. "The weirdest thing about this lady—she's very pretty, very attractive, long, blond hair, very composed, and she has a voice that, if you're in a crowd, sounds like it comes out of her all over, like a speaker, not just out of her mouth. At least it sounded that way to me. I was hungover this morning, but that's the way it sounded. Plus, it was like everything around her kept—I don't know—sort of melting and jumping at the same time, like I was looking at things over the top of a charcoal grill. Or like the tar and gravel roads in the summer, the way the heat waves come up and distort everything for about three feet. And the strangest thing is . . . is—and I saw this—she has white tears. Snow-white tears. That lined up on the ground in a smile. That's what got me to begin with, stayed in my head all day."

Pascal and Rudy and Henry started laughing—bursts and giggles and snorts. Henry sat his drink on the ground beside his lawn chair, put his hands over his face and leaned back in his seat.

"How the fuck would you know this, Evers?" Rudy asked.

"I saw her cry. Today. She did it twice."

"So you watched this woman cry? What are you talking about?"

"As queer as it sounds, yes. More or less. Twice."

"And then a host of cherubs and fairies appeared and sprinkled rosewater from their soft fingers and buttercups danced with peacocks." Henry waved his fingers in the air.

"I brought some with me. They're in the car. I wanted Rudy to test them."

"Brought what? We're fucked up. Am I hearing things right?" Henry asked. "You're fucking with us, right?" Henry looked at Evers, then at Pascal. He and Rudy began laughing again.

"They're albino tears," Evers said.

"No way, Evers."

"This is like a college prank, frat initiation or something. It's a bunch of miniature marshmallows or something, and you're going to eat them or do some fake-ass Halloween riff to fuck with us." Henry picked up his drink. "I'm too stoned for this."

"Is there a punchline, Evers?" Rudy moved his feet and almost knocked over Pascal's cup.

Evers ignored him and went on in the same tone of voice. "The other thing is, after I talked to her, when I was leaving, walking to my car and—wait . . . okay . . . let me back up. Before I left she said something like 'bless you' and when I walked outside I had this strange feeling, like I was seeing my thoughts, things were in vignettes in front of me—if that makes any sense—and I was thinking about our mother, Pascal. I felt really good for an instant, despite how many things have been bothering me lately."

"Have you ever seen the *Jungle Book* when you're stoned?" asked Rudy. "King Louie, the Ape King, is like a beatnik or something."

"Shut the fuck up, Rudy," Henry said.

"Whatever you decide is fine with me, Evers." Pascal had tilted his head back and was staring up at the sky.

Evers drank some more scotch and finished the last of the marijuana. No one said anything, and the men sat in the glow of the bug zapper and watched insects and moths fly into the electric trap. Evers started doing stoner regressions, thinking about his feet, the grass, the dirt, the bugs in the dirt, the center of the earth, China, Chairman Mao, then forgetting the first thought in the sequence and quizzing himself on why Chairman Mao was in his mind. He went through this paradigm about every thirty seconds.

After Pascal finished his drink, he leaned over and put his hand on Evers' shoulder. The bug zapper was quiet, and Evers heard a whip-poorwill start up. "So where is the white lamentation?" Pascal asked.

"They're in my car, in a cooler. In the trunk. I'll just leave them here for Rudy to look at when he's not fucked up."

"Leave them on the porch."

"Okay."

"I'll get my lab coat and beakers and get right on it. First thing tomorrow." Rudy started laughing again.

"It may be some sort of hoax, Rudy. Who knows. They may turn out to be glue or skim milk or white paint. That's why I brought them for you to check out."

"Check out?"

"Yeah." Evers scooted forward, put his elbows on his knees. "Check out. See what's going on."

"We can start right now, do some science and heavy-duty research, test the luck in those things," Henry offered. "That's one way to determine if they're authentic."

"What luck? What do you mean?"

"Our good fortune in being blessed by this lady and her pallid teardrops. White things are lucky. Remember the albino crocodiles they found in—I think it was Louisiana. They're legendarily lucky. White horses, white deer, all lucky. If they're genuine, we'll know soon enough."

"What should we do?"

"Torch another doobie, for starters," Rudy said.

"Let's go play the lottery. Drive into Virginia and buy a bunch of lottery tickets. Maybe that will give us a sign," Henry said.

"Nothing better than scientific analysis that involves travel and gambling. Let's go."

Evers, Pascal, Henry and Rudy covered the sofa and climbed into Rudy's Buick, an Electra 225 with velour seats, cruise control and a Radio Shack cassette system. It was over an hour to the Virginia border, and Evers and Rudy slept in the back of the car until they stopped driving and Pascal shook them awake. Evers was weary and sluggish when he woke up. His stomach felt heavy, and occasionally the scotch would bubble up into his throat.

"Which game are we going to play?" asked Pascal. "The instant one or the long one, the one with the TV drawing?"

"Instant one," said Rudy.

"Think we can figure it out?" wondered Henry. "I'd hate to be so fucked up that I threw the winning ticket away." Henry looked at Evers. "We continued to do the correct thing while you were napping."

"I can probably figure it out, Henry," Evers offered.

The clerk at the convenience store was a skinny redneck girl in a smock. It was after two in the morning, and she seemed glad to have company.

"What's the best lottery game?" Evers asked. There were rolls of different colored tickets in clear dispensers, strange color combinations and designs—horses and purple and yellow. The lights inside were clear and electric; the store was lit everywhere, the brightness falling from every part of the ceiling.

"I like 'twenty-one,' " the girl said. "It's like blackjack."

"Great. Give me one of those." Evers gave the clerk a dollar and scratched the face of his ticket with a penny. The covering scratched off into little black balls. Evers tossed the ticket at Henry. "Great idea. I have nineteen."

"Sorry." The clerk smiled.

Pascal took the next ticket. He tried a new game that had worms, hooks, boats, boots and fish. "You need fish to win," he said after reading the front of his ticket. Pascal did not win. He bought ten more tickets and none were winners. "Fuck this."

"Do any of the tickets have the numbers twelve-twelve-seventeen?" Henry asked. He looked at Pascal. "The date Sinatra was born. Bound to be good numbers."

"No. That's the lotto. They draw the numbers out on TV. Have you guys never played before?" The thin clerk looked at the men.

"No," said Evers.

"That's a cute boy," she said. A small child had walked through the door and asked for a grape drink. He seemed awake and had picked up a rubber dinosaur from a box near the entrance. A lady with cut-off shorts and a plaid shirt had come in after the boy. "What's his name?"

"Eddie," the lady said. She looked at Evers, then took the child by the hand and walked down an aisle, past canned meat, pork and beans and cellophane packs of saltines.

"I've got two kids. Garth—we named him after Garth Brooks—and Richard—after Richard Petty," the clerk told the brothers, Henry and Rudy.

"Do you sell fireworks here?" Henry asked. He looked around the store. "I'm not talking about the spectacular kind, the ones that explode and shower sparkles and comets in the sky. We want some of the little runty ones that will blow holes in the dirt and bend drink cans."

"I know what you're talking about, but we don't carry none of them. You can get those at Myrtle Beach and places like that." The clerk brushed some cigarette ashes off the counter.

"We would like a Chow, too. Pascal needs a Chow for the trailer. A black one, on a chain." Henry slurred several of the words. "The ultimate trailer pet."

"Good call," Rudy said, and he and Henry laughed and cackled and slapped high-fives. Rudy stumbled into a potato chip display after following through on the high-five.

"Shit," said the clerk. "I know you guys are making fun of Chow dogs, but I think they're pretty." She was grinning.

"They're probably serious about the dog, ma'am," Evers said.

"So we can't get twelve-twelve-seventeen on an instant ticket?" Henry asked again.

"Not really. These tickets really aren't like that. You can get one of the lotto tickets and use those numbers."

"But then I won't win right now?"

Pascal laughed because Henry was so earnest. "Just get a ticket, Henry. This isn't atom splitting or anything."

"Okay. I want the numbers twelve-twelve-seventeen. The lotto thing."

"You have to pick six different ones. You can't have two twelves. Pick four more."

"Four, because there are four of us. Seven, because it's lucky. Ten for my birthday. Twenty-four—it's the two twelves added together." Henry handed the clerk a dollar.

"Are you going to tell your wife about the clues?" Pascal asked Evers as they left the store. It seemed like an odd question, and Evers noticed that Pascal and Henry both looked right at him to see what he was going to say.

"Why?"

"Just wondered."

"I hadn't thought about it, really," said Evers.

"So far we're the only ones who know, right?" Henry kept looking at Evers.

"Yeah." Evers looked at the ground. He was standing next to the car door. The interior light was on.

"I hope you don't," Pascal said. "I don't want to tell you what to do, but I hope you don't. It's our trip. That's the way I see it."

"You're probably right. I won't mention it," Evers promised.

Pascal looked up. "Rudy, where the fuck are you going?" The car doctor had started walking away from the other men and the Buick, toward the end of the convenience store's parking lot and the highway. "Rudy. Hey, Rudy! Code blue for Dr. Rudy." Pascal chuckled and nudged Henry with his elbow. "Check him out."

Rudy didn't answer Pascal; he just kept going. Evers turned around, and Pascal raised his voice and called out again. "Rudy. Rudy? The car's over here, Cortez." Pascal looked at Evers and Henry. "He's fucked up."

Henry laughed. "It's got to be pretty severe if we notice it."

"Rudy, don't wander out into the highway." Evers started to walk after his friend while he was speaking; Rudy was at the end of the parking lot, in the last shadows of the outdoor lights, standing beside the road. "Damn."

Pascal and Henry also started walking. A car's headlights appeared over a crest, dropped out of view, and appeared again. Rudy started a slow, serpentine shuffle in the gravel alongside the road, walking into the dark. The car caught Rudy in its headlights, blew its horn, swerved across the center line and passed him by.

Pascal, Henry and Evers caught up to Rudy, and Pascal touched the car doctor's arm. Rudy jerked away and walked faster for a few steps, twisting stabs and stumbles that kicked into the stones and dirt beside the asphalt. The men were a good hundred feet from the parking lot, near the beginning of a curve that dropped out of sight.

Evers looked back, and two cars were coming up behind them. "Shit, Rudy, get in the fucking car or you can walk all the way back home. I don't have time for this nonsense."

Pascal put his hand on Rudy's arm again, and Rudy spun around very abruptly, stopped moving. Henry jumped a little, and Pascal's mouth opened. "Damn," they said at about the same time.

"Jesus, Rudy," Pascal said. "Are you okay? Are you sick? What happened?"

Rudy shook his head. "I'm not sure. It's not . . ." He quit talking but kept shaking his head.

"It's not what?" Henry asked. "What are you talking about? What's wrong with you?"

Rudy shuffled his feet, swayed and pushed his hair back with both hands. "I feel bad."

"What are you talking about?" Evers asked. "Rudy?" Evers hesitated. "You look . . . look . . . ill or strange or something."

No one moved for a few moments, then Rudy started mumbling and sniffing. He rubbed his nose with the sleeve of his shirt. "Something bad's going to happen. I have a bad feeling about this money."

"You're just drunk and stoned and sick. Come on, Rudy." Evers looked Rudy in the face. "Let's go home. You don't know enough to have any feelings, one way or the other."

A car slowed down and turned into the convenience store. Another passed the men on the opposite side of the highway, and the sound boomed all around them for a few seconds.

"If anyone touches me anymore . . . lays another hand on me . . . I'll beat the shit out of all of you," Rudy declared and started off again.

Pascal went back for the car, and the three of them paced Rudy for nearly a mile, following his comatose gait, creeping along in the Buick with the emergency flashers going, until he collapsed onto his knees into the gravel alongside the edge of the road and tipped over onto his hip and arm. Pascal stopped the car, and Henry and Evers got out to pick Rudy up. His knees were cut, bleeding through his pants, and he'd fallen beside some roadkill, a decaying cat or possum or rabbit, bones and a few bunches of gray hair, the remains flat and dry, lying in the dirt beside a pop-top and a paper napkin.

TWO

J O MILLER COVINGTON HAD MARRIED EVERS WHEN HIS THROAT
and lungs weren't singed by devilish streams of cigarette smoke
and when he could still bench-press two hundred and five pounds
twelve times. When Jo Miller met Evers, she was a sublime, boyish
girl with short brown hair and skin that tanned evenly in the summer
months. She was gifted and calm, immune to the moods, panics and
tumults that ran over Evers like hard blue tides; Jo Miller was smart
but not smug, different, clever and playful. The first time Evers saw
her, she was standing in line at a vending machine, searching the
change in her palm, turning the money over, checking for old, rare
coins. Evers and Jo Miller fell in love with each other at the same
time. They married before he began law school.

Before that, Evers had lived a fairly good life. In 1961, when his
brother Pascal was three years old, Evers was born at North Carolina
Baptist Hospital in Winston-Salem. When Evers was growing up,
Winston-Salem was a city that had all of the hallmarks of New South-
ern elegance very early on: museums, a college, a private school for
girls, a revitalized downtown with an arts center and, most important,
a family-run, ham-at-Christmas industry (R. J. Reynolds Tobacco) that
provided the region with both jobs and an aristocracy. For two summers, Evers worked at the tobacco company loading pouches of chew-

ing tobacco into cardboard boxes, and when he was old enough to develop an interest in such things, he and his friends would park their bikes in the forest below the athletic fields at Salem Academy and lie on their stomachs at the edge of the woods and watch the girls' field hockey team practicing in shorts and kilts.

Purvis Wheeling, Evers' father, had been a tall man, very frail, with large ears and dark eyes set like two unlit caverns in his skull. Evers' mother was a beautiful, fair-haired lady, the daughter of a Chicago minister. She was a believer in the New Deal and Dr. Peale, a beneficent, likable woman who hand-sewed name tags into Purvis' shirts, made cakes and brownies from Duncan Hines mixes and organized trick-or-treat outings for the children in her neighborhood. She and Purvis met and wed in 1949, while Purvis was a student in Charlottesville at the University of Virginia, and they moved to Winston-Salem soon after he completed college because Purvis thought that the area would provide him with the opportunity to earn a good living. Purvis Wheeling had been a paving contractor, a lanky man in baggy pants who bribed state legislators—not something that made him a bad or unfit father in his sons' eyes—into granting him contracts to build roads and blacken parking lots.

While the boys were growing up, both of their parents cared a great deal about Evers and Pascal, although, in a certain sense, neither had any emotional pitch where their sons were concerned—their ages and interests put them, Evers believed, somewhere between middle C and E flat, no more, no less, no variance. They were good at handling the big things, the highs and lows which occurred in their sons' lives, but they never had a clear view of the shades between the absolutes. For all the years that Evers could recall, the Wheeling family had been more concerned with equilibrium than depth; not such a bad way to live, really. Evers loved his parents, and he felt good about the way they treated him and his brother.

Not surprisingly, Evers was brokenhearted for several weeks when Purvis Wheeling drove into a tree several hundred yards off Silas Creek Parkway, killing himself and causing a fracture in his wife's ankle so severe and painful that it never truly healed. Evers and Pascal did all they could to help their mother after she took off her cast, but she never would put any weight on her foot and leaned on a cane when she walked. She died in her sleep two years later, a thin gold bracelet and a pair of emerald rings on the nightstand beside her bed, her robe folded across the back of a chair. For one of the same reasons he had loved her, Evers particularly missed his mother after her death: she resembled him a good deal, in her countenance and in

her habits, and he worshiped the frank assurances that came from seeing his parts and image in someone so much like him.

At the time of his father's accident, Evers was twenty years old, old
enough to appreciate the substantial inheritance and trust benefits
he would receive. He and his brother each inherited one-third of
a good deal of money. Pascal had already graduated from William
and Mary College and used his portion of the money to embark on a
route of revelry and spectacle matched only by, say, Liberace or a Thai
king. Evers was satisfied with two new stereo speakers and a small
sailboat.

Although Pascal quickly spent his father's money—pissed it away,
their mother frequently said—Evers considered this Pascal's prerog-
ative and enjoyed his brother's tales of long-legged women and
wrecked automobiles with a smile, questions and no censure. Evers
had cried in the car before his father's funeral, but whether or not his
brother spent the money their father chose to leave them had no bear-
ing on anything, as far as Evers could tell, other than Pascal's judg-
ment. Evers explained to their mother that he might well have pissed
his money away also, but as a college student, didn't have the time or
desire or decadent vision to do so.

When their mother died, she left only one dollar to Pascal, and this
struck Evers as so unfair that he gave half of his mother's estate to his
brother, who, true to form, managed to turn it, after several months
of sloppy endeavor, into a mobile home, a Lincoln with a broken
windshield, a car phone, three Arabian horses and some tin mines in
Chile. The remainder of the money, somewhere over nine hundred
thousand dollars, evidently was invested in high times and hijinks.
Pascal once called his brother from Jamaica—an expensive toll, no
doubt—to list his favorite three movies while stoned: *Casablanca*,
Easy Rider and anything with dubbing and Godzilla. "Write that
down now, okay? My short-term memory's fucked-up these days."
Evers laughed, and acknowledged that his brother's choices were
probably impeccable.

Evers was sixteen years old when he left Winston-Salem to enroll
at the Woodberry Forest School, a wonderful place near the base of
the Blue Ridge Mountains in central Virginia. It was a venerable insti-
tution; it had roots, a history, an unavoidable solidness. Woodberry
was started hundreds of years ago and appeared perpetual to Evers
when he was there; like Elastic Man, the school had one leg back in
the nineteenth century, its crotch above the First World War and the
other leg planted in the 1970s, still stretching. All male, coat and tie at
dinner. Not teachers, but masters. Every boy on campus participated

in athletics, everyone showed up for the Friday-night cultural perfor-
mances, and everyone made his bed before nine-thirty or he received
demerits. Everything the boys needed was there at the school: a store
that sold WFS ties and cuff links as well as Pepperidge Farm cookies,
a pool, a golf course, fifty milk cows and seven negroes, who tended
the cattle and bought beer for the students.

On weekends Woodberry had mixers. Evers would stand on the
front porch of the Walker building, peering out from behind a smooth,
white column to watch the girls from Madeira and Saint Anne's–
Belfield step off their buses and giggle out into the late afternoon.
These were girls, not ladies or women or womyn or females or broads
or dikes or wenches, not jaded or nagging or coy or active or naive
or impressionable or anything else—just girls. There were so many
things these girls did not know. And so many things they did know.
They could sail, cook, speak French, ski, drive a straight shift and
shoot skeet. They liked Virginia Gentleman, pinot chardonnay and
marihuana, which they spelled, in their perfect-script missives, with
an "h," even though the radicals at the public defender's office and
High Times preferred the hipper "j" alternative. They knew who
Petrarch was, who wrote *Instant Replay* and how to do logarithms.
They didn't care much about Jimmy Carter, Joan Baez or Watergate,
didn't like any illegal drug that came in pill or capsule form and
didn't have time for rallies, protests, marches or fasts. In short, they
were not women's women.

The girls arrived on Saturdays for the mixers. Evers would wear a
blue blazer, a black and orange tie (the school colors), khaki pants
with cuffs and penny loafers without socks. The girls and Woodberry
boys listened to bands and danced. Real bands. Not dopers and hip-
pie trash like the philistines who show up at motel bars too drunk to
play, not dirty fools in flannel shirts shouting and twitching and cat-
erwauling, not bands with five-necked guitars and a double bass. This
was 1978, and at the Woodberry mixers they listened to real bands,
bands that played songs by Tommy Dorsey, Benny Goodman and
Harry James.

The sex was perfect, since anything beyond a kiss was a good and
great gift. Sweet, warm, tentative, one button at a time, often alcoholic, eyes closed and blind. The young, melting, perfumy smells; the
girls *smelled* warm. They smelled soft. And it was all new and com-
plicated. De Soto, Ponce de León, Neil Armstrong, Alexander the
Great and Evers Wheeling. There was no need to feign interest in
Chinese cooking, the politics of de Gaulle, the greedy denuding of
rain forests, Joyce Carol Oates, or a ban on nuclear weapons. Evers

was barely able to drive a car, and was years and events away from evenings with harridans who would, where their favors were concerned, bicker and haggle like hucksters in a tent carnival to ensure that none of their kindnesses went unacknowledged. He enjoyed women more when he was sixteen than when he was thirty-nine, and according to his wife this was his biggest problem in life. "Arrested mentality," she called it. "No, it's not a bad thing. It's yearning," Evers often said in his own defense. "These were very black-and-white times."

College was more of the same. Evers graduated from Woodberry and went to Princeton. He was content there. His favorite days were Friday afternoons in November and December, when he didn't have to worry about classes and everyone was showering and shaving and steaming up the hall bathroom, getting ready to leave for parties and movies and dates. Evers would work out in the gym on Fridays and then come back to his dorm and shower. As soon as he was dressed, he would put on a heavy coat and wool scarf and step outside into the evening, tired and relaxed from five sets in the weight room, warm as could be in his winter clothes. Sometimes he left a trace of soap on his face so that it would pull especially taut for a few moments, and he never wore a hat or covered his head. Evers would step outside even if he had nowhere to go, just to feel the winter air on his skin and hear the noise coming out of the residence halls.

But then it all began to run out. Evers could sense it when he looked around. The days of typing term papers, drinking beer at the student union and weeklong road trips were being eaten up locust-quick, and at the close of the good years he began to worry. *A posse ad esse.* By the time Evers arrived at law school—he went to Duke—he had begun to feel like all the continuity and joy in his life were vanishing. Evers began to sit in the law school library, in the basement behind the regional reporters, and think about slippage, about Howard Hughes or Henry VI mewing in the Tower of London or Greta Garbo or poor William O. Douglas limping around the Supreme Court. The last semester at Duke was odd, funny, melancholy, often anxious. The fraternities were different, and Evers was, uh, married. He had been since arriving in Durham. No more dorms, no more softball games . . . just like that, he was buying dress shirts, selling rugs and chairs instead of moving them and talking to a college friend about life insurance.

When Evers walked across campus on his last day of law-school classes, he turned around in the crowd and realized that he was only weeks away from becoming another doctor or lawyer or banker with a wife from St. Catherine's, a "WFS 78" license plate, an Irish setter, an Ortho lawn, Louis Vuitton luggage and a timeshare town house at Sugar Mountain. About a month before, in April, he and his spouse (as the white cardboard invitation from his fraternity described her) had driven to Cambridge for a Princeton-Harvard baseball game, and he was worried because none of the kids were wearing coats and ties, even though they had been the year before and the year before that. And he got pissed off because some cretin wearing a papier-mâché tiger's head spilled a rum and Coke on his car. After the trip, he was spent, weary for days, in spite of the fact that he'd slept during the entire ride back to Durham.

Pascal, during this period, had very little to say that Evers found helpful, although Evers felt sure his brother was doing all he could and wasn't just being flippant. "Be feckless and come live with me. Fuck it. Enjoy the many aspects of mobile home living and cable TV. When we get tired of that, we'll tour the country on a Greyhound and meet Roy Clark. The Catskills, Atlantic City, Nashville, whatever. Big-time shit, my brother." All this from an honors graduate of one of Virginia's oldest and finest colleges who now smoked dope, lived in a trailer and shot trees and stumps with a twenty-two-caliber pistol. It was about this time that Pascal had lost his job as a loan officer at Wachovia Bank and Trust, this because he'd loaned a fifteen-year-old and her boyfriend six hundred fifty dollars for an abortion. "Fuck it. I'll become a fireman or a veterinarian," Pascal said when Evers asked how he planned to support himself.

"How about police work?" Evers offered.

"Whatever."

While Pascal understood his brother's feelings and had no solutions, Jo Miller simply could not understand her husband's discontent. They quarreled from time to time in the months before Evers was due to finish law school. "I don't think you make a whole lot of sense, Evers. I just don't. What's the matter with you? Look at your future. What else do you want? You'll have a good job. You'll have me, and I love you. We can do just about anything."

"But everybody else has already done all of the things I'm going to do. Thousands of people make law review. Thousands of people become judges or senior partners or whatever. So what? As for falling in love and the rest of what follows from all that, it's pretty straightforward. I love you; you know that. Don't take what I'm saying poorly, okay? You know what I mean?"

"Do you want to be famous or something, is that it? Or better than everyone else—or just keep going to school and never get a job? Maybe you should have been born around 1810, when so many people hadn't already done so many things. You would've had a lot more possibilities then. You could've invented the steam engine or the cotton gin or something like that."

"What it is, I guess, is that I'm not happy to have to stop going to school. But I don't really have any problem with getting old *per se;* I really don't care about that at all. And I really don't mind accepting responsibility, despite your hints to the contrary. The biggest thing is that after I stop going to school, I'll lose a lot of order and standing. You see what I'm getting at?"

"What? Jesus, Evers, no. I really don't, I'm afraid. You can be excellent in what you do. You can make your own order. The world won't end because you don't have a class schedule. Don't get pissed off, but I really don't see the problem."

"Really, you don't? You're not just trying to badger me? You don't have any idea what I'm saying?"

"Nope. You just need to grow up and get on with things."

"There's more to it than that. I just don't want to be alike, to be another sad sack standing in a long line and then, on top of that, lose all the structure in my life. It's a kind of ontological engineering, you see. It's depressing to know that there's a shitload of people out there just like me, all of us just sort of being carried along, bumping into things."

"What's the last thing you did that you really enjoyed, Evers?"

"I don't know, okay?"

"Come on, if you think back far enough, you'll be able to come up with something. Don't be so puerile."

"Do you really want to know?"

"Yes."

"I should be candid with my wife and psychologist, huh?"

"Yes."

"A couple of days ago, I felt good about telling you to go fuck yourself." Evers was serious.

"How nice. What about something before that cathartic undertaking? Can we go back a little further?"

"Well, during Evidence class today I started to get drowsy, and I was right there on the cusp of sleep and I thought for a moment I was a wizard and that I had cast a spell on your friend—what's her name? Ellen, Ellen Wyatt—and shrunk her to the size of a cashew nut and then dropped her into a cup of espresso, a double of course. She wasn't able to swim and died a hot, brown drowning death with her pulse racing. I shrunk her clove cigarettes, too; they were in her pocket when she perished."

"I think that sometimes you must hate me," Jo Miller said.

Despite wanting to stay longer, Evers completed law school, graduating with honors. He did so well, in fact, that at age twenty-six, almost immediately after finishing school, he became a judge. A district court judge in Norton, North Carolina. During his final year of law school at Duke, Evers sent out résumés to law firms all over the East Coast. He received job offers from two firms in Washington, D.C., from firms in Miami, New York (White and Case), Richmond, Raleigh, Tampa Bay, Atlanta and from Boyd T. "Baby" Hicks, Esquire, a sole practitioner in Norton, North Carolina. Boyd's letterhead carried precisely that heading; all of his correspondence had both the infantile nickname and the title of "esquire," a juxtaposition that struck Evers as stupid and silly when he read it for the first time.

Boyd was a kingmaker, a sweet-talking fellow who had his hand in everything and a file cabinet full of uncollected favors. When Evers visited Norton, Boyd promised him that two judicial spots would be opening up in the next two years. Boyd had the votes to get Evers a job on the bench, and Boyd wanted someone in the courthouse who would be indebted to him and would listen to what he had to say when he stopped by at five o'clock with a bottle of bourbon in his briefcase. Boyd liked Evers immediately and recalled that Evers' father had paved a lot of roads in Surry County. He also had a good sales pitch: "Shit, Evers, all them bright boys at the top of your class will be working eighty-hour weeks and kissing your ass, begging for a continuance or a little docket time. And me and you will be teeing off no later than three every afternoon that you want to head on over to Pinehurst to play."

Jo Miller was frenetically happy around this time. Even though she and Evers had been married for nearly three years, she viewed their time in Durham as no more than an uncomfortable stopover on a long trek that was supposed to get better as it went. After three years of academia, spaghetti dinners and her husband with greasy hair in sweatpants, she was eager to start her life. She was living for it. And when you live for it, it beats you. Evers had told Jo Miller this on more than one occasion. When you really want something, when you lust, seek, desire, await, anticipate or expect, when you sit in front of the TV after the late news twirling a plastic spoon in a bowl of lukewarm skim milk and saturated puffs of Special K, praying for nine or so hours to pass so that you can check the morning mail to see if the college accepted, the one-night stand wrote, the tax refund arrived or Publisher's Clearing House made you the winner of a dream house in Wisconsin, when you're really looking forward to something, that's when Fortuna dispatches a couple of her handmaidens to drop a load of shit on you. Jo Miller wanted more than anything in the world to leave North Carolina and move to Atlanta.

Evers did not want to go to Atlanta. He wanted to go to Norton, and he did everything he could to change his wife's mind. "You've never been there, honey. You've never seen the place. You don't know the people, what the economy's like, where we could live—anything. You just don't know anything about the place or the man I'll be working for. And it's only twenty-five minutes from Winston-Salem. All you know is what you've read in the two brochures the chamber of commerce sent to you—one was about the local fairy stones and the other was about some Civil War battle. What kind of decision can you make from that?"

"Doesn't that give you a tiny hint, Evers? They send me a flyer on rocks and an obscure battle when I asked them for 'any relevant literature regarding cultural, social and economic opportunities in the area.' That pretty much says it all."

"You're not giving the place a chance. You won't know about it until you go there."

"I know, Evers. I know exactly what kind of place it is. Norton, North Carolina. I drive into the local filling station, and a pack of newts in coveralls is hunched over a checkerboard. And what do I do? Join the D.A.R. chapter and thaw out fish sticks and scheme about having an affair with a pudgy insurance salesman who was an all-district basketball player for the Norton whatevers? Shit on that, Evers. We need to go to a city that has something for both of us. We need to go to a city that will give me a chance to find an interesting job and make interesting friends."

"Don't paint with such a broad brush. Small communities attract a number of good people. Really. And picture this. A farm—a real farm out in the country, with horses and hardwood floors. We're lying in our bed, a brass job from Neiman Marcus. Toasty under a quilt. Across the room is our fireplace, and the coals are still warm and orange from the fire the night before. We get up, put on clean clothes, clothes with a lot of starch, go for a horseback ride through the forest, come back, play with our basset hounds, drink brandy, take our shoes off, maybe then have a meal and some light sex—a languid sixty-nine on the sofa downstairs under the skylight. And then—"

"Could we wash our hands after rubbing the dogs? I think that would improve the food and sex a little."

"Let me finish. After we —"

Jo Miller interrupted again. "Picture this. You're sitting here in our apartment in lovely Durham, North Carolina, at our cable-spool kitchen table with the stolen Pizza Hut plastic tablecloth, and a process server brings you the papers for a divorce. I'm serious, Evers. I love you and will make sacrifices for you, but I won't make myself into your shadow. You have to give some as well. I'm more interested in doing something substantial with my life than I am in living in a Harris Tweed commercial with dogs and horses."

"The reason we have such a shitty apartment is because you're so compulsive about making our own money. Anytime you want something, you can have it. You know that. I'm rich. And you know you don't have to get a job. Why do you want to work, anyway?"

"It's not that I necessarily have to have a job. I just don't want to waste away, Evers. Why do you have to have a job?"

"I will enjoy practicing law. I like it."

"I will enjoy what I do, too."

On the day in March that Evers let the deadline pass for accepting the job in Atlanta, he skipped class, smoked dope and drank vodka before lunch, walked home from a bar, knocked over a glass half full of orange juice beside the kitchen sink and vomited in the bed. By the time Jo Miller got home, Evers had rolled around in the puke, and it had dried on the sheets and on his hair, hands and arms. His pants and underwear were pulled down, twisted and wrapped around his thighs, his shoes and socks still on his feet. Jo Miller woke Evers up, and he told her he was going to go to Norton. They began arguing, and Jo Miller put her hands over her face and started to cry.

"But what are you going to do, Jo Miller? That's my point. I mean, just what kind of career choices do you have? You're so damn vague. What do you want to do?" Evers asked. He felt dizzy, and there was a lot of throbbing in his head.

"Something that interests me and I'm good at. And don't make some obnoxious remark about that, either. I just need an area where there are a number of options so I can try things and find out what I want to do. I'll be the first to admit that I don't know exactly what I want, but I'm willing to look at a lot of things. Is there anything so wrong with that? I'm still young, Evers." Jo Miller wiped her cheek.

"I see. So the bottom line is that even though you don't know what you want to do, we can't go to Norton because you're sure there's nothing there for you. Even though I want to go and already have a good job there. And you're only a few minutes away from Greensboro and Winston-Salem." Evers pulled his pants up. He felt sick.

"It's a hole, Evers. A boring, small hole. I don't want to organize the Christmas parade and spend my afternoons with bluehairs named Mary Ruth and Miss Lilly."

"It has the kind of law I like. Very low-key. And, like I've told you, there's a strong possibility I'll become a judge if I go there. It's a great opportunity."

"How do you know that for sure?" Jo Miller had stopped crying.

"I just do. Boyd Hicks is very political. It seems pretty certain."

"So you become Judge Evers Wheeling. That doesn't really help me any. I'm still in the same boat. I just don't want to go; it isn't fair."

"Well, let's be analytical. What do you want to do? Let's just list things. Now, there's a big demand for psychology majors from Hollins, so our biggest problem will be paring down the list. Maybe you could—"

"Fuck you, Evers. I had better undergraduate grades than you did. I had better S.A.T. scores, and I took the law boards and could've gotten into any law school I wanted. But what you do is boring, Evers. You've said so yourself. Law school is a tedious trade school filled with pimps and robot pimps. All you've done for the last six months is mope and carp about how you hate what you're doing. I went to school and did something that I enjoyed and that's far more interesting than the study of real property. Lawyers have no imagination. Lawyers are douche bags for the rest of the world." Jo Miller's tone was steady now; she had folded her arms across her chest.

"You don't think that dealing with life, whether people live or die, whether they're incarcerated or free, whether they're married or divorced, you don't think any of that's relevant and exciting? I guess it's not up there with smoking dope and going to the lab and watching rats run through a maze, but it's still not boring. And I've never really complained about law school itself; I've told you why I've been a little bit uncomfortable recently, and it has nothing to do with my like or dislike of the law. And one more thing. All your whining about making our own money, all your petty perspectives about being self-fulfilled, all that shit you pick up at the women's center from the assorted hirsute lesbians down there, all your talk—and you've never had a real job. You've never made one cent. But Mr. Massengill here had job offers all over the country. I can get a job. I can make money. Can you?"

"You can make money at a boring job. I could do the same. That's my only point, Evers. And I'm sure, of course, that you'll be getting a lot of life-and-death cases in Norton. Like cow theft and farmers sodomizing sheep. Really big stuff."

"It's still a living."

"You're a sexist, too. Sometimes you are from the depths. A blind fish. A squid."

"So how come sumo wrestlers shave their legs?" Evers asked.

"What?"

"Why do sumo wrestlers shave their legs?" he said again.

"Why?"

"So they won't be confused with feminists."

"Nice sixth-grade mentality, Evers."

"Get a sense of humor, dear." He sat up in the bed. "You know, something else that you haven't mentioned or thought about . . . I don't want to move too far away from my brother. Pascal's pretty close to Norton."

"The prince of white trash?"

"Jo Miller—"

"I'm sorry. I like your brother. I do. He's bright and handsome and carefree. I shouldn't have said that about him just because you're being a prick."

"I'm not being a prick."

"Well, you do what you want to do. You're making a huge, monstrous, terrible decision. You're going to suck the marrow and patience and affection out of us. I do not want to go to this place. I do not want to go."

Jo Miller got her wish, at least partially. She never lived in Norton, North Carolina. Evers did, though, lived there by himself in an apartment above the Coin-O-Matic laundry, and drove more than eighty miles on the weekends to be with his wife. She came to Norton only twice, the first time to help Evers move books and boxes and clothes into his five rooms above the Laundromat, and the second to witness her husband's swearing-in ceremony at the Hite Mountain County Courthouse. Jo Miller stayed in Durham on a small farm, where she acquired a cat, a supply of Kahlúa, a bottle of bubble bath, a *Norton Anthology of Short Fiction* and a pair of black riding boots. She worked as an assistant for Professor (Dr.) Hirsch Brockman in the psychology department at Duke. Brockman had hired her on a part-time basis during Evers' final year of law school and gave her a full-time position just after Evers left Durham. Evers worried that she was having an affair with this "fascinating man," or, at any rate, that a tryst was imminent. Evers was jealous. He considered Brockman an unemployable, pipe-smoking fraud.

In the months following their separation, Jo Miller would talk about her job and Brockman and the projects she was working on, and Evers would talk about radar guns, drunks in public and knife fights. There was soon an eroding of their common interests and, in inverse proportion, an increase in their sex. Because they really did try to care about each other, Evers and Jo Miller's sex became more frequent, sustained and important. Evers wanted to keep them together; their union, the idea of their being and remaining joined, was important to him, and sex is a very good adhesive when there isn't enough time or will to sit in the kitchen after work and sort through all of the small, stubborn marital knots and problems. Orgasm obviates.

"Sex conquers everything," Evers would say before he and Jo Miller fell asleep on clean sheets at the Durham farm. "Sex conquers everything. Wouldn't that be an interesting addition to the children's game, the one where you have scissors and rocks and dynamite and paper and you make signs with your hand to represent each one and certain signs prevail over others? You ever play that game?"

"Yes, I did. Scissors cut off the dynamite fuse, but a rock crushed the scissors."

"And paper covered the rock."

"But it wouldn't work if you had sex and nothing conquers sex."

"That's true, I guess." Evers actually thought about the implications for a moment. "And what would the sex sign be anyway?"

"I'm not happy about all of this, Evers, you not living with me, and me not living with you. We're like two-sevenths married or something."

"It could be better, I guess. But don't dare do anything that you don't want to do."

"I don't even know the things I don't want to do. And don't be sarcastic. It comes out more as a whine than a bite with you. You're so rigid, so distant sometimes."

"So why do sumo wrestlers shave their legs?" This had become Evers' favorite interjection over the years.

Jo Miller smiled, just a little. "We need to do something about this."

"It's so weird how things happen. You get married and it's all just fun and new and sex, drinking and just hanging out, and now we've got all these problems. Complications really complicate things."

Evers came to hate Norton.

This is not to say that he disliked the town when he first got there; in fact, for several years he enjoyed himself and his new job a great deal, despite occasional fits of self-doubt and ceiling-staring. Evers continued to worry about his "alikeness," but more and more, like scores of other small-town men, he began to smile and end conversations with the four-syllable defense that "it's not so bad." He enjoyed the one meat, three vegetable meals at the Owl Diner, he enjoyed his metal mailbox with the red flag, and he enjoyed selling brooms door to door for the Rotary Club. He enjoyed Norton for some time. And then—snap—months of sentiment were transformed in seconds. Jo Miller had been right.

Harry Truman Moran was a deputy sheriff in Norton. H. T. was pure stereotype: he had carved out, with no more than a straight razor, steady hand and shaving bar, a continuous facial hair network of two triangular sideburns which were connected to a turn-of-the-century mustache by a narrow, hairy isthmus on each cheek. H. T. drove a red El Camino equipped with white-letter tires, wore zip-up, pointed, synthetic white boots—even while on duty—and owned a tiepin shaped like a miniature pair of handcuffs. He would take the tiepin off and tap it on the witness stand when he was testifying in court. Harry Truman Moran thought that Judge Evers Wheeling was a minor deity. H. T. was absolutely loyal to Evers.

This fidelity was no small asset. Because of the lie-detector tests, H. T. was a valuable ally for Evers, a regular Lafayette. The lie-detector scenario went something like this: H. T. would arrest some local for disorderly conduct at a fiddlers' convention or for a drunk in public violation at the county fair or, as was more often the case, for a bogus breaking-and-entering charge just as the suspect was preparing to eat dinner. The person in custody would invariably deny any wrongdoing and usually was telling Officer Moran the truth when he professed his innocence. Nevertheless, H. T. would take the suspect to the Norton jail and hold him in the interrogation room, all the while demanding a confession. Evers once asked H. T. if he'd ever heard of *Miranda v. Arizona*. H. T. suggested that since that case was decided in 1966, and 1966 had come and gone, the case didn't apply any longer.

Upon failing to obtain a confession, H. T. would ask the suspect to take a lie-detector test. In his experience, crooks and hoodlums always thought they could beat these tests, and innocent people were anxious to take the test so as to escape his bullying and braying and bad teeth. Consequently, just about everyone whom H. T. decided to apprehend—guilty, innocent or in between—was subjected to his examination. He would escort his prey from the interrogation room into another, darker cubicle, tape a collection of wires to the poor fool and fit some kind of hat over his head, then ask a question. "You was the one that helped shoot President Kennedy, weren't you?" The suspect would answer, and Harry Truman would push a button on the machine's controls and out would come a large sheet with the word LIE printed on it.

The object of all this forensic magic, usually some plant worker or farmer who was afraid of the cordless microphone on *The Old-Time Gospel Hour,* would, as H. T. put it, "lose his shit." Evers had actually watched H. T. putting someone through these paces; the poor man really did become unnerved. H. T. would then say something along the lines of, "Well, if you ain't lyin' about the question I just asked you, then there must be something what's not true inside you. Says right here that you're a lyin'."

The witless questionee had no idea he was connected to an office copy machine with a metal colander resting on his head. H. T. kept the room lights low and stood behind a sound board which had been illegally seized from a high-school band at a keg party. When the sound board came on, it was full of red and green lights, and H. T. would turn dials and slide levers and push buttons. An eight-and-a-half-by-eleven piece of paper with the word LIE written on it was waiting in the copy machine, and H. T. would ask a question and then punch a button on the sound board. The button was wired to start the copier, and the copier always gave H. T. the same response. This proved to be a useful tool: rather than risk involvement in a presidential assassination or the burglary of Fort Knox, people would volunteer information about affairs, gambling debts, old grudges, stolen livestock, illegally manufactured liquor, or the locations of growing marijuana plants.

It was Harry Truman Moran's revelation that caused Evers to become unhappy in Norton, and the bruit came on cat's feet, early in the morning when Evers was reading the newspaper at his desk and thinking about where he was going to eat breakfast. He'd returned from his brother's the night before and gone to bed early, around nine-fifteen. He had left the albino tears on Pascal's porch for most of the weekend, until the ice in the cooler began to melt and Pascal put the sandwich bag and plastic top in his freezer. Evers had tried to call Jo Miller from his brother's, and again when he got back to Norton, but she didn't answer the phone. He knew he had a mess on his hands with his wife.

Harry Truman walked into Evers' office and asked if he recalled a local farmer, a man named Hobart Falstaf. Evers knew Falstaf; he remembered him because Falstaf had been before Evers in court, once for a charge of careless and reckless driving, and once as a character witness for a neighbor accused of larceny. Evers remembered Falstaf because of the man's hair. It was thick, rich, black hair, combed straight back. It had just a little wave, near the front, and Evers wondered why God had wasted such a fine head of hair on Hobart Falstaf, who probably would never think about what a blessing he possessed.

Evers remembered dismissing the driving charge against Falstaf because he liked the man's hair and because he liked Falstaf's looks—handsome but not pretty, very rural and straightforward. He was particularly fascinated by the fact Falstaf's hair glistened—it glistened at nine-thirty when court opened, and it glistened at noon when he stood up from the defendant's table to leave. But it wasn't wet or dirty or oily; it glistened, like a snake's skin, dry and shiny wet. Hobart Falstaf had snake hair and wore Red Camel work pants, and Evers incensed the state trooper who'd made the arrest because he didn't convict Falstaf. This is what Evers remembered when H. T. Moran asked if the name was familiar.

"Why, H. T.?" It was a Monday morning, and Evers knew, of course, exactly why H. T. was asking. H. T. ran the copy machine on Friday and Saturday nights, then reported any results of interest to Evers and the sheriff on Monday mornings. Evers enjoyed these visits and looked forward to them.

"You know him, Judge?"

"Careless and reckless driving. Black hair, pulled back." Evers laid his paper down. "Seemed kind of quiet, fairly well spoken. Was a character witness once, too. What about him?"

H. T. took off the tiepin and began tapping it on the front of Evers' desk. The desk was wooden. "I hate to be the one telling you this, Judge. Shit. God. I'm doin' it 'cause, well, 'cause you and me is friends and because I've got a duty to you as judge."

Evers could see he was agitated. "So tell me, H. T. I know you're my friend, and that you're trying to do what's right. Don't worry about it."

H. T. wasn't listening to Evers. He continued tapping the wood and looked down at the floor. "I didn't sleep a lick wonderin' if I should tell you this. I found out nearly four weeks ago. Didn't want to do nothin' or say nothin' till I done checked it out real good. Seen things for myself."

"Seen what?"

"Falstaf's datin' your wife."

"What?"

"He's been datin' your wife."

"Dating?" Evers looked at H. T.

"In a motel."

Evers laughed. "Her boss, maybe. Or some sensitive sort with a beard and good lines about wines and Barcelona and Vermeer. But not a farmer with greasy fingernails. She's never been here but twice, Harry. I trust you, my friend, but I think you're off base here. And I see her on the weekends, and talk to her on the phone during the week." He laughed again. He laughed because H. T. seemed both worried and earnest, like a puppy who had pissed on the floor while its master was fumbling with the door. "Don't worry. Really."

"But it's true, Judge. I know it's plumb hard to swallow, but it's true. I reckon it's hard to believe what with you bein' a judge and so smart and all, but I got it out of him on the lie-detector test. They date at the Iron Duke Motor Inn—it's right outside Hillsboro, about halfway between here and Durham."

"And you've checked this all out?"

"Usual procedure. Had the suspect in custody on breakin' an' enterin'. I asked him a question, told him he was lyin' and that there must be some powerful untruth in his system. So then he up and told me that he'd been seein' your wife. Kinda smiled when he said it. I put my gun to that fucker's head and I said to him, 'You've done slandered upon a fine woman and man, and I'm goin' to get you a phone and let you call the judge's wife and prove to me you ain't lyin', or I'm gonna shoot you right in the side of the head.' I was figurin' he might just be smartin' off, so I wanted to test him."

"And?"

"I got him a phone and he called a number in Durham—he knowed it by heart—and he talked to this lady, Jo Miller, your wife. Here's the number what he dialed. It's her number. Anyhow, when he called, she knowed him and all but said she couldn't talk and to call her back. I reckoned that you was right there when he called. So I watched him after that, and on the next Monday she met him at this motel. I got some pictures of 'em. I mean, you know, pictures of 'em goin' in and then leavin'. Ain't got none from the inside. Damn if I ain't sorry about this."

Evers believed H. T. now. He remembered the telephone call, and he remembered Jo Miller's tone on the phone. "Just one of Brockman's students." Evers felt drained . . . practically instantaneously, he began to despair. . . . "Let's see the pictures. How did they meet?"

"I made a report for you to read."

"You read it to me." Evers' secretary buzzed him on the phone. He ignored her, and she poked her head into his office. "Mr. Blake in the clerk's office—"

"Fuck it, and do not bother me until I tell you to, understand? Go away and do not come back in here."

"But it's—" She saw Evers' glare and didn't finish her sentence. She pulled her head back and shut the door.

H. T. was reaching into his pseudosuede briefcase. "Read it to me, Harry. Read it." Evers stopped talking and thought for a moment. "There's no order after a certain time in your life, is there, H. T.? Everything gets to be random. Canadian air masses are random. Drawings are random. The Virginia lottery is random. My wife is random. Justice is random. I let him go—random. Goddamn it. Goddamn it, Jo Miller."

Evers bit his lip and pressed his temples with the bottoms of his palms. It occurred to him that the largest, most hideous things, unexpected and wicked things, take only seconds and a few words and breaths to get completely into you and sour your blood; gargoyles, cancers and betrayals pour into you in no time at all, like water filling a bottle. Evers felt angry and ruined. He slid down in his chair, closed his eyes . . . and he saw a hand, strong and larger than life, pull a piece of dripping, bloody bone from out of his back, and he just stopped moving, paralyzed, seized and broken.

"I agree, sir. Things get all mixed up." Harry Truman Moran always agreed with Evers. "You okay, Judge?"

"I guess I just took a lot for granted," Evers said, ignoring H. T.'s concern. "It's been a bunch of years, her down there, I'm here. You just get used to things. . . ." Evers' voice trailed off. It was hard for him to talk. "And, I mean, you know, I knew this was coming, just . . . just . . . not like this."

"You know, Judge, the way ol' Falstaf acted, he knowed the machine was a trick. He ain't dumb. I guess he told just to be spiteful."

Two days later, Evers was sitting outside the Iron Duke Motor Inn in H. T.'s El Camino (the "El Demeano," Evers called it), both of them smoking cigarettes and listening to a John Boy and Billy Big Show cassette entitled *Rocket Science*. H. T. collected comedy recordings—Jerry Clower, Redd Fox, George Carlin—and he had been listening to one after another since they left Norton, repeating the punch lines, rewinding his favorite bits and chortling and slapping the steering wheel whenever someone worked in a little profanity at the end of a joke. They waited at the rear of the motel for about an hour, smoking and listening to comedians, watching cars drive into the parking lot and staring at the people inside them. Evers felt his stomach squeeze and turn when he saw his wife's profile through the window of Falstaf's car, a blue Cadillac. Falstaf drove the car into a space in front of one of the rooms and turned out the lights before the car completely stopped. Coasting into darkness. Evers saw his wife touch her eyelashes with her thumb and finger. She was always doing that, fooling with her lashes.

Room 118, a brown door, a yellow light. Falstaf opened the door to the room and then went in with Jo Miller. He walked in before she did, Evers noticed. A light came on, and the curtains were drawn until only a slim, tall crack of white space showed in the middle of the room's window. Falstaf came back outside and got something out of the car, something in a brown grocery bag.

"I'll go get the key, Judge."

"You mean a room key?"

"Yeah." H. T. cleared his throat.

"How?"

"I just will."

"That's a bit irregular, isn't it, H. T.?"

"What? What do you mean?"

"Wouldn't that be sort of unlawful?"

"So's what they doing, huh? Plus, I am the law, right? I got me a badge and a hat and all that other good shit, all of which says I am the law."

"That's a pretty good analysis, H. T., given the state of things."

Harry Truman Moran was gone for a few moments, then returned with a key that had a square metal head and a hole cut through its top. "You wanna 'comp'ny me inside, Judge?"

"Sure, let's go." Evers opened the door of the El Camino and noticed the cigarette smoke when the interior light came on. "Unbelievable," he said.

Evers' wife, his fiancée, his girlfriend, a bright, engaging, porcelain-fine, boyish girl was in the room. Evers' wife. He and H. T. walked to the door, stood in the air, both of them looking down. Evers could hear noises through the door, but he couldn't understand what was being said. A few times he heard laughter.

After five minutes or so, a car pulled into one of the spots near where Evers and H. T. were standing and left its lights on. The room had turned quiet, no sounds, no voices.

"Let's us go in, Judge. Pretty soon now."

"Let's." Neither man was eager to open the door.

Evers could hear noises again, coming out of the room, as he and H. T. stood outside, not looking at anything, but he couldn't tell who was speaking or make sense of any of the words.

When H. T. opened the door, Jo Miller and Falstaf were so engrossed in their flailing that they continued on for several moments after H. T. and Evers entered the room. Evers recalled that his wife's mouth was rounded open, her legs lifted, both of them perpendicular to the bed and going up as high as she could push them, and—this he especially saw—Falstaf's hands were cupped over Jo Miller's rear, one on each side of her, dark hands with veins all the way up to the knuckles.

They were pounding each other when Evers first saw them. Slamming. A pair of white, tiny panties with a cotton band was lying beside a man's boot that had a thick black sole and laces crisscrossing their way well up past the ankles. Jo Miller looked at her husband, saw him over Falstaf's shoulder and arm, and pulled away from the man on the bed. "Jesus." Her eyes were wide, and Evers could hear her breathing. She put her hand against Falstaf's chest, rolled off the bed and stood up.

"Good to see you, Jo Miller."

"Evers—"

"Officer Moran, would you draw your side arm and point it at the man in the bed?"

"Yessir. Ten-four." H. T. was the law. The law drew his gun.

Falstaf licked his lips and held his hands in front of his chest, palms out, fingers spread.

"Okay now. Would you, Mr. Falstaf, get up and leave?" Evers was surprised how little animosity he felt toward the man who was just violently screwing his wife. Perhaps he was simply numb. His stomach felt knotted, heavy, as if it were full of rotten earth and slick, red nightcrawlers.

"How 'bout my clothes?"

"Just hit the road, okay?"

"No problem. Right. I'm not lookin' for trouble." Falstaf walked to the door. He was naked and large and still wet from being inside Evers' wife. He looked at H. T. and Evers and then opened the door and walked out. Evers heard the Cadillac start and saw the car's lights through the curtains.

His wife, his girlfriend, his fiancée. He had made her hot soup from a can when she was infirm, and allowed a cat into the house when they lived together before getting married. And now Jo Miller was standing on matted shag carpet in front of a motel sink with yellow-brown cigarette burns all around it, transformed into a bare, naked woman with angry red splotches on her neck and cheeks, a different, foreign, shadowy thing, staring at Evers and H. T. Moran, her arms folded across her breasts.

"Let me get my clothes, Evers," Jo Miller said.

"No."

"I want to leave." Her voice was low.

"Then go."

"Don't be an asshole, Evers." She looked at H. T., who looked away. "How big of a surprise can this be?"

"I can see where you must feel aggrieved," Evers said.

"You could be decent."

"Even though you haven't been."

"Even though I haven't. At least not right now."

"Nice understatement."

"You've probaby cheated on me, Evers. I'll bet you have. What's the difference?"

"You know better than that. What a pathetic thing to say, Jo Miller."

"Well, you've certainly been a sorry husband in a lot of other ways, Evers. Selfish and cold and headstrong."

"Officer, would you gather up the adulteress' clothes, please." Evers nodded at Jo Miller's pants.

"That's so childish and silly, Evers. I mean, in terms of all this it's just small, what you're doing. It's like letting the air out of my tires or signing me up for a record club or something. Really impotent. Better to do nothing if you can't be effective." She didn't raise her voice.

H. T. picked up the clothes in the room, getting to Jo Miller's underwear last and balling it up inside her shirt and pants. Evers collected Falstaf's clothes and then the towels from the bathroom, the sheets from the bed. Jo Miller watched him, stepping back when he passed, her arms still folded.

"Great, Evers. Just great. What is it exactly that you're trying to accomplish here?"

"Are you taunting me, Jo Miller?" Evers looked at his wife. "Are you? Do you remember what you just said? Or are you coming unglued, standing there naked and guilty?"

"Do you think that it matters that you're taking my clothes?"

"Who knows?"

"You've caught me, I'm committing adultery, our marriage is in trouble, and you and Sergeant Pinhead are acting like two sixteen-year-olds. I'm waiting for you to demand your preengagement ring

THE MANY ASPECTS OF

and AC/DC tape back. Why don't we just cut our losses and go? Or you beat and bloody me. But don't be sophomoric about this, okay?"

"I'm going to leave you. You know that, don't you, Jo Miller? And, I'm going to make sure that you have to get off your ass and get a job and that your sport shopping and nouvelle cuisine lunches from noon to three end. Perhaps that will be substantive enough for you."

"The fuck you will."

"We'll see."

"We will," said Jo Miller.

"Nice Cadillac your boyfriend's got."

"Why don't you just give me my clothes and let's leave."

Evers was quiet for a moment. He leaned against the back of a chair and put his hands in his pockets. "Officer?"

"Yessir?"

"Would you please handcuff the adulteress?"

"Ten-four, sir."

Jo Miller's mouth opened. "What the hell are you suggesting, Evers? Are you mad? You can't do something like that." She moved her feet. There was a trace of fright in the last few words. Fright and uncertainty.

"Sure we can."

"I haven't done anything. He can't do something like that. You know better, Evers. It's against the law. God."

"Officer Moran *is* the law. Behold the badge and gun and hat. Am I correct, Officer?"

"Affirmative," H. T. replied, hands on hips, legs spread.

"Affirmative, my ass. You and your friend will regret anything you do. I promise you that."

Evers thought, listening to his wife, how odd it was that she was undressed and splotched and that the three of them—Evers, Jo Miller and Moran, a stranger really—were standing in a motel room debating points of honor and justice. "How bellicose," Evers said.

"You'd better not do anything to me, Evers."

H. T. had very little difficulty subduing Jo Miller, and Evers was surprised at the policeman's strength and proficiency. Jo Miller, at first, shook away, swung at H. T. and tried to bite his arm. He moved behind her, caught one wrist and trapped her leg between his calves, and the scuffle was over. He put handcuffs on Jo Miller. "What now, Judge?" H. T. asked.

"There's a town not too far from Greensboro called Climax. Climax, North Carolina. It's next to another town called Julian. I've seen the road signs. Let's drive out there."

"Ten-four. Yessir. How do you want to transport, uh, the lady here? Is she gonna be a ridin' with us or what?"

"I think we should wrap her in these sheets, toss her in the back of the El Camino and roll."

"Have you lost your mind, Evers? Have you? Are you mad? Fuck you, Evers. Fuck you."

Evers looked at his wife. "I just want my retribution to meet your lofty standards."

"You're crazy," Jo Miller shouted.

They set out in the El Camino with Jo Miller, naked and trussed, lying in the back of the half-car, half-truck underneath a sheet and bedspread. H. T. and Evers smoked cigarettes and listened to a Jeff Foxworthy cassette, but didn't talk much. A large truck passed them about twenty miles outside of Greensboro, and the driver blew his horn and pointed at the bed of the El Camino as if he thought Evers and H. T. somehow might be unaware that a nude woman was riding behind them. Jo Miller was screaming at the truck driver and flopping around like a fish on a stream bank. "I hope no one calls the state police or something," Evers said.

"I am the law, remember?"

"Good point, H. T. I appreciate the reassurance."

Evers had H. T. stop the El Camino at the Climax exit sign. The two men left Jo Miller, without clothes, at two-fifteen a.m., tied to the metal support pole of the road sign, along with a note:

> I am an Alpha Sigma Sigma pledge.
> I must stay here until sunrise. No matter
> what I tell you, you must leave me here.
> If you release me I will not become an
> Alpha Sigma Sigma sister.
> > Thank you,
> > Jo Miller Wheeling
> > Class of 2003

Jo Miller was enraged, kicking, cursing, twisting, crying, threatening. "You're a judge, Evers. Think about it. I'll get you for doing this. I promise you that I will fuck up your life."

"I'm just a really pissed-off husband. Women have a way of defeating our titles and pretenses. Strip us right down to the nub."

"There's not much I can do now, but you'll regret this. You will." Jo Miller pulled against the pole and strained toward Evers. "And, Evers, you know, no matter what you do to me, I'll always have the upper hand—I'm the one who left you and chose to be with someone else. That's a rejection you'll carry around forever, and you'll have self-doubt that eats you alive. I'm just bulletproof where you're concerned, and what you're doing now is feeble and weak and pitiful."

"Perhaps you're right. We'll see, I guess." Evers looked at H. T., who looked down at the highway.

A car passed while H. T. and Evers were starting back to the El Camino. It seemed loud and fast, and Evers heard the wind and the engine's sound as it went by; he shielded his wife with his body so she wouldn't be seen and the car kept going, red lights getting smaller and smaller. Evers felt strange standing in the gravel and dirt beside the road. Everything outside was large, empty and dark. He got into the El Camino and shut the door. Jo Miller was tugging at her bonds, screaming and crying, a jerking white form with dark hair.

H. T. and Evers drove home in the El Camino. Evers managed to smile as they were driving, in spite of all that had happened, in spite of the fact that the certainties in his life, all his routines and braces, were now little more than vapors; everything now would be different, even the past, the things that already had happened. H. T. glanced at Evers and saw the smile. "You done showed her ass, Judge. Yessir."

"I don't guess that we're quite even though, huh?"

"I don't guess so, nope," said H. T. in a flat, literal voice.

"Oh well."

H. T. paused. "So how come we done drove all the way down here, Judge? I reckon there was closer signs, weren't there?"

"Metaphor, H. T."

"Gotcha." He nodded sharply.

Right, thought Evers.

"How come you think she kept seein' Falstaf after I done jumped him?" H. T. asked a few miles later.

"I don't know. Either he didn't tell her or she just didn't give a shit."

"I guess."

"You know," Evers told Harry after they had ridden for about thirty miles and not said a word, "I just figured something out. This is the second part of the equation. Not only do you leave Princeton and become paler and paler and paler still, but you also discover that acts swirl and dance and fall without your ever touching them, just above your head or out of your reach. It's bad that the trestles crumble, and worse that you have no idea where the debris will fall."

Harry Truman Moran didn't understand what Evers was saying, just as Evers hadn't understood it himself until the deputy had told him about Jo Miller, his wife, and they found her in a motel with Hobart Falstaf.

Evers didn't go to work the next day. He stayed at his apartment by himself and cooked hamburgers and hot dogs on the grill on his balcony and drank red wine. He drove to Winston-Salem to Vaughn Ford-Lincoln-Mercury-Jeep-Eagle-Isuzu, but he did not turn in. He rode past several times, back and forth on the highway. He finally saw Ruth Esther at about seven-fifteen, talking to a man and a woman in front of a green Crown Victoria. She shook hands with the couple, and they walked off. Evers drove his car into the turn lane, slowed down and blew the horn. He'd just opened a beer and set it between his legs. Ruth Esther turned toward him and looked at his car for a moment. When she recognized him, she smiled and motioned for him to pull into the lot. Evers didn't turn in and stayed in the road, stopped and blocking traffic. A car jerked up behind him and flashed its lights. Ruth Esther started walking toward the highway, and Evers rolled his window down and waved at the driver on his bumper. The car didn't move. Another car appeared and passed both Evers and the vehicle waiting on him. Ruth Esther opened the door, got in Evers' car, and he steered back into traffic. The car behind him turned into the dealership.

"Goodness. It smells like alcohol and cigarettes." Ruth Esther reached down to the floorboard and picked up a fast-food bag and an empty soft-drink can. She put the can in the bag and dropped the trash into the back.

"I've been drinking beer and smoking."

"I'm glad you're here. Did you decide to help Artis?"

Evers drove and didn't say anything. "Do you want me to strip again? If that's what it takes, I will."

Evers turned to Ruth Esther and then looked back at the interstate. He rolled his window down several inches and lit a cigarette. He put his hand in his shirt pocket and took out a napkin. He held the napkin between his thumb and index finger and nodded at Ruth Esther. The napkin had OK written on it, and Ruth Esther moved closer to Evers so that she could see it.

"So you'll help?" she asked.

"I've told you I can't," Evers said. He nodded his head and shook the napkin at Ruth Esther. "I just came to see you about the truck."

"You don't have to be so paranoid."

"About the truck?" Evers asked.

Ruth Esther sighed. "Yeah. About the truck."

"Good."

"I have a lawyer. You'll need to talk to her."

"A lawyer? About what? A lawyer. Shit. You're kidding, right?"

"Her name is Pauletta. I'll give you the address. She lives in Charleston, West Virginia."

"Why would I want to talk with your lawyer?"

Ruth Esther reached across the seat and lifted the can of beer from between Evers' legs. "Do you have another one? May I finish this one?"

"Sure." Evers licked his lips. "I can't imagine why I'd need to see your lawyer about anything. You must be out of your mind."

"To draw up the truck papers, of course." Ruth Esther giggled. She put her feet on the seat, her knees in her chest and set the beer in her lap.

THREE

THE LIGHT SHINING IN FROM OUTSIDE THE DOOR CAUSED
Evers to see his shadow on the wall, and he and his shaded
image looked like Pan straining to avoid a cattle prod. Evers was
standing about fifteen tiles away from his target with his feet spread
past shoulder width, his knees locked, and his eyes slit and sotted.
That much wasn't particularly distinctive. What caught his attention
when he saw his outline going up the wall, what he noticed more
than anything, was the exaggerated bloat in his middle, the way his
back was arched and his abdomen was convexed well past its usual
position. Evers was not heavy or fat or overweight, nor was he as
unbalanced as his posture would suggest. To grow so misshapen, he
had contorted his form intentionally, stretching and swelling himself
so that he could transform his midsection from a thin, bland drop-off
into one of the brazen, brown-'n'-serve guts which you generally find
brooding atop a warehouse shipping crate or squirming free from the
flesh-packed shirtfront of a third-world policeman. Evers rubbed his
eyes, peered down at the sway, blinked once and closed his lids.

Even though this position grew uncomfortable after several
moments—the weakest portions of his lower back were aching—Evers
enjoyed the stance, liked it because it was, well, symbolic, indicative,

if you will, of his life just now: leading with his groin, a pair of testicles as his trump suit and, in their wake, on his other side, his rear tucked and drawn, secure against rogue Olympian bolts and braced for any mischief that might be worked by the gods' swift feet. The quintessential Evers. Mary's essence is captured in the *Pieta*, L.B.J. regaled the country with the shot of the scar from his gallbladder operation, and Evers Wheeling's most recent history, if it had to be summed up by a single pose, was best described by his standing on a tile bathroom floor pushing his pelvis forward and balling up his butt with every sinew and muscle he could muster.

Evers smiled, even though he was alone in the room. His single, helmeted trooper, the Il Duce of organs, was poised in front of him, exhorting the rest of his body. For just a moment, Evers thought of his brother and how once, in Key West, in a hot room without air conditioning or screens in the windows, the two of them had fucked sisters at the same time, each pair in a single bed, flashes of gray-white skin in the dark, Marvin Gaye singing, quiet voices and sheets moving. Evers looked down; Il Duce, defiant, stared back. "Dictator." Evers said the word aloud.

The loins on the run and the task before him caused the rest of his body to appear warped and out of whack. Behind the abominable curve, Evers' shoulders were pulled back toward the tub, his chin was near his chest and one of his hands was resting on his hip. He was about to pee, hard as it is to urinate through an erection. It is even more troublesome when the person involved is drunk, and Evers was drunk. He was wearing a crewneck T-shirt and nothing else.

"Evers, you okay?" Outside the bathroom, on a motel bed with rough sheets, a dental hygienist named Naomi was waiting to have sex with Evers. Naomi's parents had given her two other names as well, but he couldn't remember either one.

"Yes, Naomi, I'm fine. I'll be out in a second."

After two futile spurts that splattered the toilet and wet the floor, Evers grew tired of bending Il Duce like a Krazy Straw in an effort to correct the proud ruler's errant aim. There was a solution, of course. Evers turned and—what the hell—emptied himself into the tub, a larger and more approachable goal. Judge Wheeling finished the enterprise with a sigh—a long, exaggerated ahhhhh exhalation—and a glance down at his feet on the tile; he returned his middle to its normal dimensions.

"How did this happen?" Evers wondered. Two weeks ago, on his way to work, he had seen Ruth Esther English for the first time, a hazy, dim, hungover day of entropy that started in another bathroom and ended when he put a taped-up top full of white tears into a cooler and drove to his brother's trailer. Two days after that, he had talked to Harry Truman Moran, and now Evers was in a Charleston, West Virginia, Ramada Inn, drunk and rash and mad-brained, pissing yellow parabolas all over the bathroom.

"How did what happen? Are you talking to me? Are you okay and all?" Naomi called from the bedroom. "Evers?" Evers had not shut the door completely when he went into the bathroom.

"I'm fine. I'm coming right out."

Evers stood with one hand gripping the towel rack and watched the yellow circle around the silver drain shrinking away. A slender, yellow ring remained in the indentation surrounding the plug, and Evers washed it into the drain with cold water. After he turned off the tap, Evers started to think about what Naomi was going to say after he fucked her. That was the correct word—"fucked." Evers despised "make love." The term was silly, banana-daiquiri-*cum*-umbrella silly; it was slick, cheap and evasive. "Intercourse" was all right, and "screw" was acceptable. Perhaps even "do it" would pass scrutiny. Evers had no use for all of the euphemisms coined in stark moments, all of the nervous glosses designed to add a sheen of intimacy to unions which were, during their brief life spans, little more than hedonistic and carnal couplings. Evers liked Naomi, and there was no malice at all in his choice of words, just an instinct to be direct and fair. Lust without the luster. " 'To thine own self be true.' Shakespeare," Evers said out loud. He left the light outside the bathroom burning and closed the bathroom door when he returned to the bedroom. No other lights were on.

"A little light makes fucking better, don't you think?"

"You're the judge." Naomi paused. "Who were you talking to?"

"What?"

"Who were you talking to in there?"

"I'll tell you after we fuck."

"I wish you wouldn't always say the f-word. You're a very nice man, and very interesting, but that word really isn't very attractive." Naomi tried to smile a little.

"It bothers you?"

"Yeah, sort of, I guess. It's so harsh and everything."

After he fucked Naomi, Evers did not go to sleep. He lay on his side and studied a chair not far from the bed. A light from across the street came into the room through an opening in the middle of the curtains and caused two irregular shapes to appear on the back of the chair. The shapes looked like a pair of fairy silhouettes. One was turned to the side, a profile with a single wing shaped like an inverted "L" attached to its shoulder. The other was facing Evers, with both wings thrust upward like a small, smooth phoenix. The pair held their position on the rear of the chair, flickering more or less incandescent depending, Evers supposed, on who walked past the storefront or porch light or street lamp that created them. Evers felt uneasy; he had not slept with anyone other than his wife since college. He heard traffic passing nearby; the roads sounded wet, so it must have rained since he checked into the hotel. Evers closed his eyes and fell asleep after a lot of effort.

He woke up. He looked at his watch; it was the first time he'd needed to use the glow-in-the-dark digits since he had lit them seven times during a two-dollar matinee showing of *A Passage to India*. According to the green figures, he had slept for only half an hour. He went into the bathroom, placed a clean towel on the floor in front of the tub, knelt down on the towel, turned on the cold water and wet his face and hair. He combed his hair straight back, using a complimentary Ramada Inn black plastic comb, and he noticed in the mirror that his hair was thinning at the crown. Christ. Evers was more sober now. He drank several glasses of water—too much fluoride—turned off the bathroom light and went back to bed, back to sleep.

And he woke up again; it was very dark in the room. His hair was still damp. He went into the bathroom and urinated again, this time into the commode, through a more helpful organ. When he came out of the toilet, he sat down on the double bed across from the one where he and Naomi had been sleeping. Evers watched her. Earlier, he'd been surprised to discover that she was so fit—trim thighs, a flat stomach and a smooth tightness in her back and arms. She had admitted to Evers that she was forty-two, and that she had a child, who was staying—since it was an odd-numbered weekend—with her nefarious ex-husband, a man named Cleo. Cleo had beaten her once, she said.

Evers held up his hands, palms toward his face, and looked at the skin and outlines of his fingers, trying to get a fix on himself, trying to make sure he was held together; he felt displaced and listless. He thought about what he was doing, and about the woman beside him in a bed in West Virginia. He had met her for the first time several hours ago in the bar at the Ramada Inn, had just walked up and sat down beside her and her friend. "Hi, I'm Evers, and I'd very much like to know your favorite lizard." Beyond his introduction, Evers hadn't felt the need to be too assertive or overly clever.

He had talked to Naomi, very intelligently, about things in magazines. In Evers' apartment above the Coin-O-Matic Laundry in Nor-

ton, in neat stacks beside his dresser, he kept a year's worth of all
the major women's magazines—*Vogue, Cosmopolitan, Redbook* and
Self, to name just a few of his holdings. Evers read all of these, pored
over them at his apartment and hid them between the oversized covers of *Black's Law Dictionary* so he could peek at them during especially dull moments in court. He wandered through hundreds of
pages on fall fashions, career choices and diet tips because it was
important to know what women were thinking. He felt like a pirate
buying up maps and charts at a super savings subscription price of
twenty-two dollars per annum. Evers the plunderer.

A carpet salesman from Bluefield had solved the problem of
Naomi's girlfriend, and Naomi herself was pleased after Evers offered
that he was "a lawyer . . . well, actually, a judge," who was thinking
about coming to Charleston more often because he had business to
attend to. "Could we date some then," Naomi asked, "when you are
up here and everything?"

"I'd like that." Evers had enjoyed talking to Naomi.

"Me, too. Will you be working as a judge when you come up here?"

"No. I'll be doing some things on my own time."

"Are you married or anything?" she asked.

"Yeah. Yes. I guess I am. You either are or you aren't, and I am."
That was about all Evers could bring himself to say, although he could
have said plenty more.

Where is my life going? Evers wondered. He put his hands down
and noticed that the silhouettes had disappeared from the back of
the chair. He thought of the hot room in Key West, thought of all the
bass in Marvin Gaye's songs. And he thought of his wife, whom he
despised. For some reason, Evers began thinking about pinball. PIN-
BALL. Bright silver balls banging off little poles with rubber bumpers,
steel circles flying through gates and ringing bells, rolling across the
painted face of the game into flippers and holes and chutes, making
lights flash and blink. Pinball. "Pinball," Evers mumbled.

"Huh?" Naomi opened her eyes and looked at him.

"Nothing. I'm sorry. I didn't mean to wake you up. Go back to
sleep."

"Did you want to talk or something?" Naomi was struggling to stay
awake.

Evers smiled wanly. "Thanks. It's been . . . a while since I did something like this. I'm trying to take it all in, get used to it, see what I
think about everything. I appreciate the offer."

"You're welcome."

"Good night."

"Good night, Evers."

Evers stretched out on the bed, on top of the covers, and closed his eyes. He lay there by himself until he fell asleep.

Evers and Naomi left the motel room early in the morning, just as the night was ending and light had started rising up over the hills into the city. Naomi woke up first, and Evers heard her in the bathroom. They rode together in Evers' car across the city, across two bridges, talking about hangovers and the songs on the radio. They kissed at the door to Naomi's apartment, but he did not go inside.

"I hope things work out for you and that we can get together again," Naomi said.

"I hope so. Thanks."

"And thanks for driving me home."

"You're welcome." Evers paused. "Thanks for having sex with me."

Naomi looked at Evers' face. She swallowed, and Evers saw her neck move. He heard the keys in her hand rubbing and bumping against one another. "Okay," she answered. "I hope you don't think, you know, I'm a slut or anything. You being married and us not knowing each other too long. I just liked you."

Early in the morning after sex qua sex, very little is on your mind and the world is at once primal and linear. Evers wanted to have breakfast—tomato juice, eggs, biscuits and meat—alone in a Naugahyde booth, check the prices of silver futures in the newspaper, then return to his room and sleep in his wrinkled pants and shirt underneath a hint of a headache, his worth affirmed, his face unshaven, his hair twisted and tired.

Evers stopped at a pancake house about three minutes from Naomi's apartment. His waitress had a name tag and was very kind. She brought Evers a newspaper and smiled each time she ended a sentence. "Let me know if I can get you anything else," she said when Evers was almost through with his meal.

"How about the power of incantation so I can kill my wife from afar?"

"Would you like anything else with that, sir?" Question-mark smile.

"That's all right, thanks," Evers said, but her answer had come without a breath of hesitation, so quickly and naturally that Evers immediately wondered what had actually come out of his mouth. "What did I just say to you?" he asked her.

The waitress had already walked away and did not turn back to answer; she was pouring coffee for two men in suits.

There was a single flower, white and nondescript, in a white glass vase on the table. Obtrusive thoughts of his wife and her misdeeds began to worm through Evers' mind and interrupt his early-morning reptilian nirvana, so he focused on the flower, on its center and petals, and recalled—the image appeared clearer and clearer in his mind, like a Polaroid photograph filling itself—his parents' house and lawn in Winston-Salem. Along the west border of the Wheeling lawn was a flower garden belonging to Evers' neighbors, Mrs. Lizzy Blankenship and her husband, H. Robert, the architect. In the summer, all sorts of flowers appeared in the Blankenships' garden, the blooms at different heights, here and there in fits and starts of color—yellow, orange and red—surrounded by green leaves and green stems and cut grass. Evers shut his eyes and saw zinnias, roses, hollyhocks, snapdragons, gladioli, delphinia, meadow rue and petunias with soft, downturned petals and beads of yellow in their middles. There were other flowers there as well, some that he couldn't identify.

Evers left a five-dollar bill beneath his plate and took the flower from the white glass vase. He put the flower in his pants pocket, in the front. He left the pancake house and stood outside on a cement step, looking into a glass window, his eyes just above the red R and E in RESTAURANT, the two letters outlined in black. On the step, near his feet, were three flat tan cigarette butts with singed tobacco pushed out of their ends, one with the filter open and split into webs and threads of dirty, tight cotton. The mind of the cigarette, Evers thought.

The waitress was clearing his table, and Evers watched her. She picked up the paper money tip without looking at it for very long and put it in a large pocket in her apron. The money wasn't the first thing she reached for, or the last. She wiped the table with a cloth, and Evers could see the water swirls on the tabletop, until they evaporated. He wondered . . . why . . . he was watching this woman and her work. He hadn't thought about it until now, had ended up on the step without really meaning to.

When Evers returned to his motel room, he lay down on the bed and called Pascal. After four rings, a tape from an answering machine came on, and Evers heard Mr. Spock describing a rare telekinetic phenomenon through which certain humanoids can communicate without talking. Pascal the rascal, Pascal the wit. "Will that be all, Captain?" Evers had begun to leave a message when his brother interrupted him. "Evers?" Pascal sounded groggy and distant.

"Hello, brother."

"Time, please." Pascal coughed.

"Star date 20:00.6, Captain's log, supplemental."

"I recall sleeping for a while. What day is it?" Pascal asked.

"I didn't know you were a *Star Trek* fan," Evers said, ignoring his brother's confusion.

"I'm not, really. Rudy gave me the answering machine tape a week or so ago for a late birthday present. And the TV show's pretty good if you're stoned." Pascal paused. "Some . . . some huge acting and hopeless props." He hesitated again. "I've got to wake up. It seems so early."

"Listen. My wife has fucked me over, and I've decided that I want you and Henry and Rudy to go on the trip with me."

"Call the navy if you want to go on a trip. And I like your wife."

"I used to. No more." Evers took off his socks. A black piece of lint was wedged between his nail and the skin of his big toe.

"Where are you?"

"Charleston."

"Is that my wife?" Evers heard Henry's voice in the background.

"Shut up, Henry. It's Evers. You'd do well in espionage, dumbass." Pascal cleared his throat. "Charleston, South Carolina?"

"West Virginia," replied Evers.

"Oh god. How's the chromosome nondisjunction up there? Lots of people of indeterminate phylum and kingdom?"

"You'll go, then?" Evers asked.

"Sure. If you'll pay for everything. I've squandered most of our father's bequest and have no job. But you already know that."

"Sure."

"Why are you in Charleston, West Virginia, Evers?"

"I looked at a map and liked the colors of the roads leading here."

"Yeah?"

"I'm here to see someone."

"Are you really pissed at Jo Miller?" asked Pascal.

"Yes."

"You haven't said anything about it." Pascal stopped talking for a moment. Evers heard him light a cigarette.

"I know."

"So where are we going? Where're the gold cups and doubloons? Do you know yet? We'll need to know how much to pack." Pascal sounded more alert.

"I'll let you know when I find out. I hope it's somewhere hot and decadent, where we can be clearly American and sit in bars with ceiling fans. I want a lot of angst and boozy exchanges with my brother."

"Sounds good to me." Pascal yawned. "So what are you doing now? What's the deal? Who's in West Virginia?"

"Jo Miller is a mean, petty, dishonest bitch who cheated on me. She's screwing some guy like there's no tomorrow."

"You were just down here. How come you didn't say anything?" Pascal sounded upset.

"I found out right after I got back, after I saw you guys and charmed you with the albino sorrow. I go to work on Monday morning, and my life turns to shit. Maybe there's some symbolism there, huh? And, well . . . I don't know. I just haven't felt like talking about it, I guess."

"You didn't mention the trip and everything to Jo Miller, did you?"

"No. Why? That's a strange thing to ask."

"Just wondered." Pascal almost mumbled.

"Oh, I almost forgot. How's Rudy doing? What was wrong with him?"

"He's fine. He was just drunk and stoned and melodramatic. He doesn't remember much and he was sick for a couple days, but everything's back to gaiety here at the doublewide. It was just a bad night for him—that happens occasionally when you get fried as much as we do."

"Maybe he was right, Pascal. Maybe this trip could be a little dark."

"Whatever. I guess he's right in a sense. Everything has a downside, even good dope and fine scotch. Planes fly vaccines to save the sad kids in the Sally Struthers pitch and the *Enola Gay* pops a whole city. In the end, it's just how you work things that matters." Pascal sucked on his cigarette and quit talking.

"I just fucked a woman I don't know," Evers said.

"Good. That'll bring Jo Miller to her knees. Call her and tell her." Pascal laughed a little.

"That's not good. Not a good idea, Pascal."

"Then I'll do it for you. I'll call Jo Miller."

"Don't do that," Evers said, but he knew his brother probably would. Pascal was reckless, and the idea would seem sound after a couple of joints and some scotch, late at night, around two in the morning.

"I'm going to tell her that the woman moaned a lot, too. In French— French moaning. Beaucoup French moaning."

"You do that."

"Whatever." "Whatever" was Pascal's favorite response, his type-O, white-bread answer, he called it: always in context, always suitable, always unassailable. Pascal would never be at a loss for words. "I don't really care" was also popular with Pascal.

"So you'll go?" Evers asked.

"Are you serious about this, Evers?" Pascal's voice changed, became heavier, slower. "This is all pretty abrupt and drastic."

"Jo Miller cheated on me. What else do you need to know?"

"She probably was drunk and it was her prom night and all."

"Fuck you."

"Good answer. Let's see what our studio audience said."

"Come on, Pascal. This isn't funny. Don't fuck with me. It's different with men. It is. For us, it's instinct, but women take it seriously. It means that she's going to leave me. That's what it means. And I don't give a shit what you or anybody else says. Everyone knows what I'm saying is right, even if nobody will admit it. Fucking someone else would be an end for me, but it's a start for Jo Miller."

"You've never cheated on her, have you?"

"No." Evers raised his voice. "I haven't."

"I'll bet that it was pretty wild, having sex with someone else after such a long time with the same person. That would have to chart pretty high."

"I'm glad you're tuned in to the critical parts of all this, Pascal."

"So you're leaving, huh?"

"She obviously doesn't love me now."

"Love's just lust spread over time, Evers."

"There's more to it than that."

"Whatever."

"Yeah, whatever," Evers answered.

"Who's the guy?" asked Pascal.

"I'll tell you later."

"Do you know when we're supposed to leave?"

"I'm not sure. I'll call you when I find out."

"Just let me know." Pascal yawned again. "I'm going back to bed."

Evers tried to sleep in the room where he and Naomi had just been together. The covers on the bed felt stiff and smooth. Velveteen— Evers wondered how it was manufactured. He had never slept under it before, and he had been surprised when he opened the door to his room for the first time and saw the counterpane. "People paint on this stuff," he said, lying on his back, his hands rubbing the tough fuzz above his stomach.

Evers needed to sleep. He stopped rubbing the bedspread. His meeting with Pauletta Lightwren Qwai in a few hours was important, and he needed to be sharp.

•   •   •

Charleston is dim and sluggish in the morning, and Evers was frazzled and shaky, even though he'd slept for over an hour after driving Naomi home and eating breakfast at the pancake restaurant. And the hills were foreign and queer for Evers as well. They seemed to ring the whole city, a simple congruity, a rugged, uneven band of transition from earth to sky—the rough hills—as if god had built the ground first, the sky second, and then, dissatisfied with the lacuna between top and bottom, joined the two together by wedging in the Appalachian Range. The wall of hill and colorless sky made it appear to Evers that airplanes might have to fly straight up quite a distance before they could get out.

While he was getting dressed, Evers couldn't stop yawning and had trouble getting his hair to stay in place. Despite his fugue state and the early hour, he felt compelled to order a drink with breakfast before driving to Sparkman, Roberts, Plunk and Small to meet Pauletta Lightwren Qwai. After all, he had just fucked a stranger and become baffled at the pancake house. Evers didn't want to drink so early in the day—he needed to be tightly wrapped when he spoke with Ruth Esther's lawyer—but, he thought to himself, a drink was appropriate, necessary, very much in character. "Gin, straight, ma'am." Evers the gangster. The waitress in the hotel coffee shop had to go into the lounge and bring the alcohol out in an orange juice glass.

Evers was early for his appointment with Pauletta, and while he was sitting in the reception area of her law firm, six floors high in the Kanawha Bank and Trust building, he reached into his suit pocket and found a page he'd torn from a newsweekly in the public library about a month before. He recalled that he had picked up an old magazine, from March, and while he was trying to locate the Newsmakers section, he had found an odd story about Westland, Michigan. Evers' cousin lived in Westland, sold pets and pet supplies there, so Evers had stopped and begun to read. He had read the article over and over and over and over. He read it again, then folded it in quarters and put it back into his suit pocket.

THE BOWLING-BALL MURDER

Will and Helen Wood of Westland, Mich., were driving home one night last December when a 14-pound bowling ball smashed through the windshield of their car. Will Wood, 40, died of massive cerebral injuries, the victim of a seemingly random act of mayhem that led to the arrest of 19-year-old Charles Anglin. Anglin had been in similar trouble before—he had recently completed a year's probation for running a carload of teenagers off the road and then trying to run one of them down—and Wayne County prosecutors charged him with manslaughter, which in Michigan carries a maximum sentence of 15 years in prison.

Anglin pleaded no contest. But when Wayne County Circuit Court Judge Richard Owens announced he might not sentence Anglin to time behind bars, the community erupted. Last week Owens—son of the judge who recently freed with a fine and probation two autoworkers who had clubbed a Chinese-American to death—bowed to pressure and sentenced Anglin to 12 months in jail and three years of community-service work.

Evers started to taste the alcohol in his mouth, a bitter, acrid broth that settled into his throat and fought off his coughs and hard swallows. He left the reception area and walked down a bright corridor into a bathroom. It struck him that you appear differently in every mirror, depending on the light and the cut of the glass and the colors of the tile and how far away you have to stand. Evers looked different in the Sparkman, Roberts mirror, better than he had in the mirror at the hotel the night before, but not as good as he did in the $4.98 Kmart full-length he had tacked onto the back of his bedroom door in Norton. Evers wondered what he actually looked like. He couldn't see the thinning spot on his crown in the Kmart mirror; that's how he wanted to look. Evers hoped the thinning would stop. He needed all his hair, since he was going to be single again.

He flushed his mouth several times with cold water, scrubbed his teeth with his index finger. He combed his hair again, tightened the knot in his tie and put two sticks of gum in his mouth at the same time. The gum was old, dry and brittle, and it broke into stoney little pieces that were hard to chew. Evers decided, after breathing into his hands, that the water and gum were not going to eliminate the taste of the gin, or the smell. He left the bathroom and found a coffee machine and mugs beside a secretary's desk. He poured coffee into one of the mugs and took several sips. Each time, before swallowing, he sucked the liquid through his teeth, like a stream through tiny enamel turbines. "Not much different from eating Jell-O," he mumbled. A secretary was talking on the phone near the coffeemaker, and the lights overhead made her seem white, almost luminous. There was a picture of two dachshunds on her desk, and a picture of a child standing beside a fat horse.

"Pardon?"

"What?"

"Did you say something to me, sir?" The secretary was looking at Evers.

"Uh, no. Not really. I was just thinking about how sometimes you get a chunk of Jell-O in the front part of your mouth, between your teeth and gums, and inhale it back through your teeth. Kind of suck it back, strain it between your teeth. It's a good feeling, in a weird sort of way."

She seemed perplexed, looking at Evers with her head cocked like a parrot's and her lips packed together. Thinking. Trying to decipher an end without having the start. And then her face relaxed. "I do know. I know what you mean. We used to do it at supper all the time. My sister said it was like French-kissing the Jell-O."

"I never thought of it in quite those terms. But I'm glad you know what I'm talking about. I wouldn't want you to think I'm just babbling on. Mind you, I do that on occasion, too, but I was on fairly solid ground here. Thank goodness for your sister, huh? If she didn't French-kiss Jell-O you might have thought I was a full-blown idiot."

"I like to give people the benefit of the doubt. Although you were talking to yourself."

"I do that a lot."

The secretary leaned over her typewriter. "Who are you here to visit?"

Evers hesitated. He was anxious, a little paranoid. "One of the attorneys."

"Oh."

Evers looked at the mug in his hand. "You must be Evelyn, and you're an Aries, right?"

"Evelyn doesn't work here anymore. She quit. I'm Sherri. I'm a Capricorn. Evelyn had to leave her mug. She wanted to take it, but Mr. Jarvis wouldn't let her. Said the firm bought it, and the firm would keep it."

"Never know when you'll have another Evelyn Aries."

Sherri laughed. "Never know."

"Do you believe in astrology and signs?" Evers asked.

"I guess some folks are lucky and some aren't."

"That sounds more Calvinist than astrological." Evers wondered if Sherri understood what he was talking about.

"I guess."

"Well, thanks for the coffee. Maybe we'll see each other around."

Evers noticed Sherri's hands. There were rings on almost every finger, mostly silver bands with designs and inlays, but her fourth finger was empty.

"Okay. It was nice talking to you."

Evers took a step, then stopped. "I was thinking . . . if you're not married or doing anything, I thought you might want to go out for a drink this afternoon. Maybe after work. Or later, later in the evening. Whatever would suit you." Even though he was talking, Evers could barely hear what he was saying; the words popped out and were gone before he could get a hold on them.

"That's a pretty sudden invitation." Sherri smiled. She sat back in her chair, and Evers heard the chair squeak when she moved. "I'd like to, I guess, but I have a boyfriend."

"Oh."

"But I'm glad you asked. I'm flattered. Maybe some other time."

E vers began to sweat immediately after he entered the door to Pauletta's office. Wet comets fell from beneath his arms and burned down across the skin covering his ribs. Evers thought of his family, sitting on the screened-in porch in Winston-Salem, in the summer, with all the night noises—traffic and insects and radios—starting again, and he remembered that his mother would serve ice tea, and that the glasses on the table would soon become covered with tiny drops of moisture, water balls hanging . . . hanging . . . hanging . . . until they cut clear paths down the sides of the tea glasses. That was what Evers was thinking about when he realized he was seconds away from losing his mind. Cerebral meltdown. Evers' mind began to think things over which he had no control. This was different from his ruminations before the Ramada Inn toilet; this time there was no stopping and starting the images and pieces and bits that came into his consciousness.

He was confused, considerably. He had opened the door and discovered a forest, a rain forest. He was in this foliage, these trees, and the temperature was so extreme that he could feel his pores expanding into craters, as if small subcutaneous faults were causing his skin to cave in, leaving rows of sinkholes all over his body. And the pores might keep expanding until they overlapped and—damn—his skin would expand away. Gone.

Evers didn't want to think about losing his skin. His mind made him. It also made him think about a Frank Sinatra line in three-quarter time. "Only a Barnum & Bailey world, as phony as can be."

And bowling balls. Bowling balls were in his head, falling like rain from an overpass. His mind made him think about a kitchen sink and a scrambled-egg pan filled with yellow islands floating in greasy water. Evers' mind was slipping and grinding. He thought about Bob Lilly and Black & Decker power tools.

The forest's trees moved, and in front of him, pushing toward him through the bush, there was a savage. Stalking him, Evers felt sure. He shielded himself with his briefcase, but his mind was locked onto power tools.

"Skill saw. Skill saw."

"Mr. Wheelings?"

"Skill saw," Evers repeated.

"Mr. Wheelings?"

"Skill saw," he said again.

"You're not all right, are you?" Pauletta later told Evers that at first she thought his falling to one knee on her carpet was an elaborate slight, a mocking, tongue-in-cheek pose of supplication. "May I help you? Should I get help?"

"The skill saw."

"You need a skill saw?"

"What?"

"I'm going to call someone," Pauletta said a second time.

"What?"

"You're—what is wrong? You want a saw?"

It wasn't a rain forest. The dark woman in the trees wasn't a savage. Evers was regaining his senses. "No. No, I don't. I mean, well, no. I was just thinking about a skill saw. Jeez. I'm sorry."

"What is the matter?"

"Nothing. Don't worry." Evers tried to smile.

"Nothing?"

"I'm really sorry. I guess I've upset you, huh?" Evers stood up and held out his hand. He left his briefcase lying on the floor. "I'm Evers Wheeling."

"I know. I know who you are. What happened to you? Are you sick?"

"My . . . damn. I . . . I know that seemed like a pretty bizarre entrance. I'm sorry." Evers paused. He was disoriented but recovering, except for his breathing, which was too quick and ineffective. "Goodness." Another pause. "You see, I've been ill. Ill. Some physical problems. And affairs with my wife. Nothing long-term or disabling— if you don't call spells of rambling disabling—but my medicine gives me equilibrium problems. I'll soon be through with the whole mess, though. I'm okay. Don't worry. Why don't we sit down? I'll be fine."

"What sort of medication are you taking?"

"I don't remember the names. Just the reactions. There are several of them. Medicines, I mean. One's a liquid, like cough syrup." This was all a grand lie. Evers was startled by his mind's mutinous bent. All of this stumbling and straining was unpleasant and unexpected.

"I see. You should be more careful. And if I were you, I'd see my physician, Mr. Wheelings. You act like you're on dope."

"Wheeling. No 's.' "

"You're sure there's nothing I can do? You looked pretty bad. And you're still pale."

"Don't worry. I'm just sorry I've upset you. I'm afraid I haven't made a very good first impression."

"Quite the opposite, I promise," Pauletta said as she sat down behind her desk.

"Why do you have all of these plants in here? Friend on vacation or something?" Pauletta's office was crowded with tall green plants; they occupied every inch of floor space, except for a clearing around two chairs and a narrow path which led from the office door to her desk. Evers had settled onto the edge of one of the chairs.

"Keeps up my image as the wild nigger, you know?"

"Maybe I could come here and work with you—the hallucinating judge and jungle lawyer."

Pauletta Lightwren Qwai didn't smile. She was laying papers and files and a *Southeastern Reporter* into a briefcase open on her desk. "We have a problem. I don't mean, Mr. Wheeling, to seem inconsiderate, but I'm afraid that right before you arrived, I was called down to court. One of my mother's sisters' sons has a case, and they just contacted me about representing him. I'll have to get right to the point of our business." Her enunciation was perfect, every syllable given its due, every vowel sounded.

"That's fine with me." Evers' armpits and the weak, fleshy pockets behind his knees were becoming sticky from the drying sweat. "I certainly don't want to inconvenience you, though. If you want to go, I can wait for you to get back. Or perhaps I could walk out with you. Whatever I can do to accommodate you." His breathing was still too rapid.

"Let's not jerk each other around, Mr. Wheeling."

"Pardon me?"

"Let's not act as if things are as we know they aren't." All traces of concern had left Pauletta's voice. Her tone was flat and formal.

"How are things not?" Evers repeated.

"You could fall into my office like a drunken sailor, spewing non sequiturs, and it wouldn't matter to you one way or the other, I suspect. I have a feeling you probably have a certain measure of disdain for women like me." "Non," when Pauletta said it, rhymed with "bone;" it had a long, hard "o."

"I'm sorry you feel that way."

"I'm sorry that's the way things are."

"Why are you being so confrontational?" Evers asked. "Are you this senselessly militant with everyone?"

"I think it's important that you and I know how we stand. I'm just very plainspoken. Things work better that way. It's a trait that I also admire in others, even when I'm on the receiving end of unvarnished thoughts. It's not any sort of hostility, Mr. Wheeling; it's simply that you don't have to fight through a lot of hulls and rinds to get to the center with me."

"Oh. Okay." Evers looked at Pauletta. There was a window behind her desk, and he suddenly wanted very much to be outside, to be walking between the buildings and shops in the morning air. He picked up a pencil from Pauletta's desk and leaned back in his chair. Evers rolled the pencil in his hands. "I'm glad you're so candid. I'll be candid as well. I've seen your résumé, read it in *Martindale-Hubble* along with everyone else's in the firm before I came up. In my opinion, and I hope you won't take this personally, part of the reason you're sitting in a comfortable office in the top law firm in this state is because you are, number one, black and, number two, a woman. So I suppose part of what you said makes sense. But that doesn't mean, of course, that you're not a good lawyer, not at all. I've discovered that people who have been given things without earning them—black women in government jobs, doctors' sons in Ivy League schools, dairy farmers sucking up subsidies—are always on the defensive. I don't know why you want to take it out on me, though, to think poorly about the kind of person I might be. You should be happy that you've gotten a break—at least I would be. And I don't think any more or less of you than I do anyone else. I don't begrudge you your good fortune."

"You're exactly right, Mr. Wheeling. I was given a history of slavery and illiteracy, and I was given a white-oriented society, and prejudices, beatings and laws and courts which discriminated against me. Quite a cornucopia, and it was all mine for the taking." Both of Pauletta's hands were still, lying on top of her briefcase. Evers thought it strange that she didn't gesture while she spoke.

"Maybe them, but not you. You weren't around when that happened." Evers wanted the last comment. "Anyway, I don't hold any of it against you personally."

"Nor do I hold the injustices you've done my people against you, Mr. Wheeling."

"You pretty much take the shackles-and-chains hard line, don't you?" Evers tried to relax in his chair and rein in his breathing. "No gray areas in your world."

"No, things are pretty much black and white for me."

"Clever but untrue, I'm afraid. Erasmus said that—"

"I'm not impressed by quotes from writers who died in Europe before Jamestown was settled. For that matter, you could make up any quote you wanted. The effect is lost on me."

"That's a shame. Perhaps LeRoi Jones is more to your liking. He's still alive, isn't he? The angry black poet? Though he's changed his name, I understand."

"I'm sorry I don't have more time to discuss this with you, but I've got to be in court and I'm sure you need to leave here in time to get back to North Carolina for the John Birch smoker. Here is Ruth Esther English's offer." Pauletta cleared her throat and folded her hands together. "You will be entitled to one-fourth of any recovery she makes relative to the hundred thousand dollars in currency which was removed from Lester Jackson's antique business. You will be responsible for your own expenses, and you will be allowed to accompany Miss English as she and her brother search for the money. In return, you must see to it that her brother, Artis English, is not convicted in the case pending in your court in Winston-Salem, North Carolina. That is her offer. Do you accept?"

"I'm not exactly sure what it is that you're talking about."

"Then why, Mr. Wheeling, are you here in my office, hundreds of miles away from home?"

"Miss Qwai, your client approached me one morning on my way to work. She attempted to bribe me and wanted me to make sure her brother would not go to jail. I told her that I would not help her. I reported the contact to the district attorney's office and to my chief judge. I followed up—"

Pauletta shook her hand at Evers and interrupted him. "You don't need to detail the steps you've taken to cover your ass if this endeavor proves to be a sting or if it falls apart. I would do the same things."

Evers continued. "I followed up the first meeting with another contact to find out if perhaps I'd misconstrued Miss English's proposal. I'm distressed to have to say that your client offered me the same bribe that you're offering me now. I'm convinced that this is a serious bribery attempt and, of course, will have to respond accordingly. And I certainly plan to notify the SBI, unless, of course, you are the police and this is some sort of scam. If that's the case, you can close your file. The bottom line is that I'm not going to do anything illegal to help Mr. English. I'm not."

Pauletta leaned back in her chair and looked at the ceiling. "I see," she said, without looking back down.

"And what is it that you want from me? Why did I drive up here to have the same offer repeated to me by another person? Do you want me to sign a contract or some sort of agreement? Is that it? Do you think that I'm a lunatic? It doesn't make any sense to me that Ruth Esther wanted me to drive to West Virginia to see you. This whole thing seems pretty crackpot, all leprechauns and snipe hunts."

Pauletta was still focused on the ceiling. "Not a written contract, just your promise. I guess in that regard I'm both the messenger and the witness. It shouldn't surprise you that Ruth Esther would like a little leverage in this deal. Certainly you can understand that she doesn't want to pay you, get nothing in return and have little to show for her investment beyond a swearing contest."

Evers squinted at Pauletta; she kept her head tilted and ignored him. "Well, of course, I'm not going to take a bribe . . . but if I were going to—help me with this now—Ruth Esther wouldn't be paying me until *after* her brother is freed and then only if she finds her money. I'm the one with complete exposure, right? Am I missing something here? I would be the vulnerable party, not your client."

Pauletta finally looked at Evers. "Ah, you're right. Most important in all of this, Ruth Esther thought that you might be . . . concerned. She wants you to know that she has faith in you and wants to protect your interests. It goes without saying that you could let Artis go and never get either your payment or the trip. You would have a pretty difficult time enforcing the agreement if Miss English decided to renege." Pauletta moved closer to her desk, closer to Evers. "It would be hard to recover your twenty-five thousand, given the consideration for your payment."

"And you're going to eliminate that problem?" Evers was careful with his words.

"Yes."

"How?"

"I am going to give you collateral, around twenty-five thousand worth of gemstones. That's your security." Pauletta opened a drawer in her desk and took out a bag with a drawstring across the top. The bag was red and smooth; Pauletta set it on top of a file, closer to Evers than to her. She had to reach forward when she placed the sack on her desk. "Mostly emeralds, from the Bahamas. The stones are—obviously—not set and not distinctive. Nor are they stolen. If Ruth Esther fails in any way to honor her end of the agreement, you will be made whole by keeping these gems. If you complete the agreement, you may keep them or exchange them for your share of the currency."

"Oh."

"And of course it's to our advantage to have you on board before the trial, committed now—not worrying about whether or not the money exists, or if you'll ever see your share."

Evers stared at the bag. He was having more trouble breathing, getting enough air in, and his chest and belly were moving and struggling so much that he folded his arms to keep Pauletta from seeing the fit going on underneath his shirt and tie. He was trying to breathe without panting, and he opened his mouth, gapped his teeth and lips and pressed the point of his tongue down hard against the bottom of his gum. He noticed that some of the plants almost touched the office ceiling. Evers reached out, and he watched his hand and fingers catch the bag and wrap it up, and then everything stalled, quit for a moment, and the tableau was there for everyone to see: still life with hand and red velvet bag. He pushed down harder with his tongue . . . and he thought about the bursting deadness that hangs in important hitches, in the pause while the clerk of court unfolds a jury verdict or a physician—Dr. Rudy at the Tri-County Hospital—turns to the second page of a pathology report, quiet providence suspended on a spider's string. Evers shook the stones out of the bag onto Pauletta's desk; there were ten or twelve gems, mostly green, with a few that appeared to be diamonds.

"Payment in advance," Pauletta said. "We trust you."

"So why is it so important to Miss English to recover twenty-five thousand dollars, given all the risks involved and given the fact that she seems fairly wealthy? For all you know, I could just keep these emeralds and you're out a lot of money. It doesn't make a whole lot of sense to risk twenty-five thousand on a fifty-thousand-dollar long shot."

"With Miss English, it's principle."

Evers heard quick footsteps, and suddenly the door to Pauletta's office opened. He spun around in his chair, and a man in a suit was coming up fast behind him. The man had come through the door without closing it. He was walking down the path through the plants, taking long, agile strides, so that after about three steps he was beside

Evers, and Evers' breath just stopped in his stomach and he closed his eyes. "Shit." The man took another step, halted right in front of Pauletta's desk.

"I'm sorry. I didn't know you had someone with you." The man turned to Evers. "I apologize for barging in."

"Where's my secretary?" Pauletta asked.

"I'm not sure. There was no one at her desk. You said we had to get these requests for admissions in the mail today. When you get a chance, look at them and sign them if everything's okay." The man handed Pauletta a folder. Evers exhaled and felt his senses start to return.

"Thanks. Ray, this is Evers Wheeling. Judge Wheeling, this is Ray Watson, one of our newest and most gifted associates."

Ray and Evers shook hands and talked about law school and baseball for a few minutes before Ray left.

"You look a little pale again." Pauletta was trying not to smile.

"Ray startled me, coming in like that, without knocking."

"I bet he did."

"So what were you telling me, what were we talking about?" Evers asked. "Damn."

"Principle. The reason Miss English feels so strongly about recovering her money."

"Right. Exactly." Evers took his handkerchief out of his coat pocket and held it in his hand. "You know, Miss Qwai, there are three red flags for a lawyer. The first comes when your client begins your initial meeting by saying, 'My other lawyers told me. . . .' The second comes when there's a Camaro or a Rainbow vacuum cleaner involved in a divorce. And the brightest and biggest red flag appears when someone says, 'It's not the money, it's the principle.' Especially in this instance, where the morally aggrieved party is a thief."

"I'm not here to talk you into anything, Mr. Wheeling," Pauletta replied. "And I have to leave for court."

"What sort of case is it?" Evers asked.

"Assault and battery." She stood up.

"Is that the sort of work you do most of the time?"

"You mean helping poor black people not to get screwed by old white men with shriveled scrotums?"

"I suppose poor white people have no problems with the judicial process? The miners and hillbillies never get screwed?"

"Not by white judges they don't. I'll bet Judge Rieckert hasn't convicted a white woman under thirty in the last year."

"How about by black judges? No racists among their ranks?"

"Black judges? In West Virginia?"

"All I meant when I asked you the question was, do you do primarily criminal litigation? That's all. Everything isn't cocked and armed. I feel like I'm talking to Angela Davis."

"Yes. I do mostly criminal work. As a matter of fact, Mr. Wheeling, I do more than I can handle. I'm overworked. And you can go ahead and wipe your hot, shiny forehead with your handkerchief if you'd like."

"I hear a lot of criminal cases, too. Maybe we have one common denominator," Evers said. "The handkerchief, I just took it out to wave at you—white flag, truce, that sort of thing."

Pauletta laughed. It surprised Evers that she had such a pleasant face and striking smile. "You're pretty oblivious to a lot of things, aren't you? Either that or you just don't care."

"Probably a little of both," Evers answered.

"I have just the case for you."

"Oh?"

"Black man accused of murder."

"Great. Is he guilty?"

"It's nice to meet you, Judge Wheeling. You're a different sort of fool, I'll give you that." Pauletta's voice was still emotionless and her diction perfect. "His name is Marvin Ross; he killed his wife. Perhaps we can discuss it when we continue our dealings. I've heard that you're a better-than-average judge. I'd be interested to hear what you have to say, although I guess that I'll have to catch you on a day when you're a little healthier."

"Continue?"

"Yes."

"What else do we have to do?" Evers wondered.

"I'll be going with you, Mr. Wheeling. With you and Ruth Esther to recover the money."

"No shit? Really?"

"Really."

"Damn. Huh. You know, I'm still not sure why I'm dealing with you. Ruth Esther could've handed me these stones, and I doubt that you'd be in any position to support her story if I backed out of the plan. Not that I'd do anything wrong, of course. But you'd end up in jail and disbarred."

"I'd end up in jail if I had tried to bribe you. I wouldn't end up in jail for merely giving you gems that I bought with my own credit cards to settle a dispute you had with Ruth Esther. Let's see, you were going to sue her for an injury you claimed you received on a test drive. She was afraid of losing her job. You demanded cash. That's what the file memo would say. I think we'll be able to show that you got the stones from me, and that you came here to get them. You're all over the security cameras by now. I didn't know anything about a bribe, but I know you got the gems. Like I said, Ruth Esther wants me to be in a position to reassure both sides."

"I see." Evers dropped the bag of stones into his inside pocket. He felt the *Newsweek* article he had put back into his coat; the magazine page was slick when it touched the back of his hand. "Then I'll have to include that in my report to the detectives. And I'll need these gems as evidence."

When Evers returned to the hotel, he discovered that there was a motorcycle convention lodged there. Large, bold men and women with jean vests and chains on their wallets were everywhere. They were in town, according to the desk clerk, to kick off "Wheels for Seals," a charity event for abused animals. Evers extended his stay by a day—he did not feel like traveling back to Norton—and was informed by the clerk that because of the bikers, she'd decided to buy some "maize" for herself. "To protect me personally," she said.

"It's mace, isn't it? Maize is the stuff the Indian lady in hip-huggers on TV used to talk about."

"Well, I've never seen none of it advertised on TV."

"Whatever," Evers replied, using his brother's omni-response.

He rode the elevator to his room and lay down on the bed to take a nap. Before falling asleep, he decided to call Naomi. N. Hankinson was the listing in the phone book. Evers made a note to mention to her that only women listed their last name and first initial. "Not many trolls and panty sniffers are put off by that trick, Naomi." Evers talked to her even though she wasn't there. He picked up the phone and held it between his ear and the pillow. When he dialed the number, the phone rang several times, then an answering machine came on. Evers hung up, didn't leave a message.

"Damn." He really did not want to spend the entire evening alone in West Virginia, cooling his heels, watching TV, brushing his teeth over and over again, trying to find something to do. He wanted to call the twenty-year-old waitress who'd served him lunch after he left Pauletta's office, but, of course, he couldn't do that. He was sure that he didn't want to try the Ramada Inn Lounge again, and he was sure he didn't want to watch in-room movies and eat room service food. "So." So Evers called Pauletta, first at her home on Harnette Circle and then at Sparkman, Roberts, Plunk and Small, where he found her working. She could go for a drink with him, but, because of her workload, not until nine-thirty. Evers thought to himself when he hung up the phone that it had been odd for him to call Pauletta. He wondered why she was going to go somewhere with him.

Evers left the hotel and drove out MacCorkle Avenue to a shopping mall. He parked his car well away from the mall's entrance, in a space fifty yards or more away from the nearest vehicle. Evers thought that walking in the mountain air would be good for him. He got out of his car and walked, very slowly, to the doors opening into the building. The evening was cool, cooler than normal for June, and the mountains and hills had become smudges, almost disappeared into the dark. When he reached the entrance, Evers turned and traipsed back to his car, paused and touched it with his hand, then returned to the mall. This time he went inside. At a drugstore, he bought a pound bag of M&M's and a gallon of sweet milk, which he took back to the Ramada Inn room to eat and drink while he was waiting for Pauletta to pick him up. A biker and his girlfriend—all leather and inked-up arms—got out of the elevator on Evers' floor; he offered the couple some M&M's, and the woman reached in the bag and grabbed a handful of candy.

The phone rang and Evers picked up his jacket, then the receiver. The cap to the milk was on the nightstand, the jug on the floor. "Thurgood Marshall Scholarship Fund. May I help you?"

"Evers?"

"Yes?" Evers hesitated. "Yes?"

"Evers Wheeling?"

"Yes." The voice sounded familiar, but it wasn't Pauletta.

"This is Judge Wheeling, right?"

"Henry? Is this Henry?" Evers was surprised.

"Yeah."

"I thought it was someone else. I was waiting on someone to pick me up. Sorry."

"That's okay," Henry said. "You don't sound like yourself."

"What's up?" Evers wondered. "Why are you calling me? Is something wrong? How did—"

"Believe this. I won the fucking lottery. I fuckin' won. Close to two million."

"Bullshit." Evers sat down on the edge of his bed.

"Well, it's really not two million. They say that it's two million, but you get yearly installments. In my case about eighty-five grand a year for fifteen years. That's after taxes."

"Unbelievable."

"I'm pretty happy. You guys want to go with me to Richmond to pick up the money? Suites and limousines, wine, rich food, decadence? Maybe try to spend it all in one day?"

"You're kidding me."

"All true. It was the smiling albino tear numbers, too. I played them a couple more times. We're going to declare the pallid drops a relic."

"Sounds like a good idea. A smiling white talisman. . . ." Evers still couldn't believe it.

"It is a good idea. We're going to Kmart tomorrow and get a decanter to keep them in, some nice faux crystal. Pascal said that we can house them in his freezer; they're at the hospital lab now—the charmed tears, that is, not Pascal and the freezer—where Dr. Rudy left them. I hope nobody's thrown them away; we may ride over and get them tonight, just to be on the safe side."

"When you pick them up, see if you can pull some more strings and make my wife's life miserable."

"I'll see what we can do." Henry laughed. "Look, I've gotta go. I'm using Pascal's phone. He and Rudy went to get some chicken and beer. Took me five hotels to find you. I'm serious about sharing the money. Let's all go together to cash in the ticket."

"Okay." Evers started to hang up. "Oh, Henry. Henry?"

"I'm still here."

"So Dr. Rudy actually analyzed them, to see what they are?"

"You bet."

"So what is it?" Evers asked.

" 'Human lachrymal secretions,' to use Rudy's words. How about that?"

"Really?"

"That's what he said."

"How's that possible? Is it a disease or something?" Evers wondered.

"I'm not certain. He . . . he . . . I think I hear them outside. Do you want to hold on? Want me to get him?"

"Yeah. Yes, would you? Let me talk to him." Evers heard Henry shouting Rudy's name and then all three men—Henry, Rudy and Pascal—talking about how Pascal had forgotten the coleslaw and had left his hat on the take-out counter at Hardee's. When Rudy came on the phone, Pascal and Henry were in the background debating whether to call the restaurant about the hat or just drive back and pick it up after they finished eating.

"Dr. Rudy?"

"Evers. What's up? Greetings from your favorite motor doctor."

"Sorry to hear about the slaw."

Rudy laughed. "I think that next time we'll call our order in from here and then go get it. It's getting harder and harder to remember things."

"Tell me about the tears. Henry says you checked them out."

"I did. And that's just what they are."

"How does that happen? I mean, is it a trick or something?" Evers could still hear Pascal and Henry arguing.

"I don't think so. You could probably control the color to some extent by failing to treat an illness or infection or by introducing some kind of drop into your eye. For instance, radiologists use something called a barium swallow to diagnose certain problems, and you drink a barium milkshake and you shit white for a couple days. Same principle here. But there's really no evidence of any sort of dye or coloring agent. Of course I didn't send it to the FBI lab or anything; I just did some tests myself and sent it to the local folks at the hospital."

"So why are they white?"

"Well, the simple answer is that they have an unusually high amount of dead white blood cells and cellular debris mixed with the normal tear secretions. That would be pus, for those of you who didn't go to medical school. But the thing that's way out of the ordinary is that there seems to be an exceptional amount of aqueous humor fluid in the secretions you gave me. That's hard to figure, and that's what really sets the tears off and colors them up."

"What else can you tell me? Is that it? What is 'aqueous humor'?"

"Damn, Evers. You asked me to tell you what it is, and I just did. I spent an entire drug-and-alcohol-free day working on this at the hospital. I'm waiting for kudos and a Nobel Prize and your gratitude."

"Sorry. This whole thing has gotten me tangled up, and I'm not sure I'm following what you're telling me."

"I'm not an ophthalmologist, but generally here's the way your eye works. The space in front of your lens is filled with a fluid—usually clear—called aqueous humor. The aqueous humor fluid is provided by filtration from capillaries, and usually drains off into the blood vessels that supply the eye. Somehow, this woman has a leak or drainage problem, some defect or blockage or routing abnormality that allows this fluid into her tears. In her case, the fluid is white, there's also a little pus present, and there you have it—white tears."

"Is it common? Have you ever heard of anything like this?"

"Not really, no. The best I can figure is that she has some sort of chronic, low-grade infection coupled with a strange congenital duct and capillary connection. You can't have constant, significant releases of aqueous humor fluid; your eye has to be kept under pressure, and this is the stuff that does it. On top of that, if the aqueous humor was milky, it would be hard to see . . . sort of like looking through fog or mist. The fluid should be a lot more transparent. This would certainly take the brittle edges off the world for you, though; you'd be peeking into gauze or a cloud all the time." Rudy put his hand over the phone and said something to Pascal and Henry. "At any rate, you now have the benefit of my medical expertise. And let me add that I agree with Henry—I think the white tears are charmed. He wanted me to tell you that."

"Maybe he's right. Although they're sure not doing much for me. Thanks for looking at them, Rudy. That was good of you, and I appreciate the sacrifice."

"Sure." Rudy chuckled. "Of course, the magic could be in the ketchup top or the clear tape, huh? I'll keep everything intact."

"Good idea. I'll see you guys soon." Evers hung up the phone, put his coat on the side of the bed and leaned back against a pillow and the headboard.

This seems like a nice enough place," said Evers. Pauletta had met him in the lobby of his hotel, and they'd driven for about fifteen minutes—past a string of strip malls, a Wal-Mart, an electronics store (red neon wrapped around a Bauhaus box), a factory and three or four ramshackle stores and gas stations—to a bar on a narrow street in a crowded part of the city. The bar was called the Galaxy 2000, and the waitresses wore shiny silver skirts and hard, metallic lipstick.

Pauletta and Evers sat down at a table and ordered drinks. Evers asked for a scotch and soda, Pauletta a gin and tonic. They talked— Evers enjoyed hearing her voice—and while he listened, Evers watched the condensation on his glass, the water balls falling down the side making clear paths that came to an end on a cocktail napkin. The napkin stuck to the bottom of the glass when he lifted it off the table. After two drinks each—and in the middle of a third—Pauletta asked about Evers' wife. "Ruth Esther suggested in one of our conversations that you have a strained marriage."

"My wife is a radioactive shrew."

"So why are you with her?"

"I'm not. We're not together at all, not at all," Evers said.

"Then 'strained' seems like a very charitable way to put things."

"Why does Ruth Esther think she has so much insight where I'm concerned, anyway? I don't even know her."

"You're a well-known person in a small community, I guess." Pauletta rattled the ice in her glass. "Who knows. I suppose you'll just have to ask her."

"I will."

"If I could ask, what happened? I don't want to pressure you if you don't care to discuss it."

"Does it matter? I mean, well, does it make any difference? She's not around, so basically that's all there is to it."

"Do you miss her?" Pauletta leaned forward in her chair.

"Of course."

"Then that's not all there is to it."

"It's not something I like to dwell on," Evers said. "I'd rather just not talk about it."

"That's fine."

Evers paused. He looked to his left at the man and woman sitting next to them, then at Pauletta. "I didn't mean to cut you off or anything. It's just that I think it's good to draw a line and forget about some things. It's easier if—"

"I understand. Perhaps I shouldn't have asked. We don't actually know each other, anyway. Some people like to talk about it, some don't. It's always hard to talk about someone you love, or someone who was close to you whom you miss. No matter what the circumstances."

"You say that fairly well."

"What do you mean?"

"You ever in love, Miss Qwai? Do you miss anyone?"

"Sort of, I guess." Pauletta's enunciation was still immaculate, but her speech had slowed; she almost paused between words.

"Sort of?"

"It's difficult to explain. To verbalize."

"Give it a try. You're a lawyer."

Pauletta tapped her fingers on the table. "Well, for me, romance and love and everything else are much like reading a book. The intriguing parts are finding out about a person, his likes and dislikes, his background—his uniqueness. Especially with African American men. But that's why it's like reading a book. There's only so much to know with one person, to *do* with one person, before you duplicate and begin to level off. We're all sort of finite like that. Like a book, you see, only so many pages and you reach the end. Of course, some books are worth reading twice. But eventually you know everything and there's nothing left to excite you, and the story's over."

"So you just read them and shelve them, huh?"

"Come on, Mr. Wheeling."

"Well?"

"What's better than the feeling-out part—the unwrapping, the discovery?" Pauletta asked.

"Stability? Love? Certainty?" Evers was sincere.

"Sure."

"And for you love's a ream of pages?"

"That's why I think people with poor intellects are more prone to think they're in love; they're slow readers with weak memories. They keep finding new chapters or forget old ones, even when they're dealing with folks who're about six or seven pages long. Or sometimes they just stop in the middle of the story and start over. Look closely and you'll discover that children and handicaps and madmen are the most devoted to love. Ever go to a lunacy hearing? Hear all the crazies talk about how they love everyone from their doctor to the trashy relative they just tried to stab with a kitchen knife? Love does better with simpletons."

"Jesus. That's a pretty sorry attitude." Evers shook his head.

"No it isn't. Not at all."

"Lots of bright people fall in love. I've been in love."

"For how long, though? I'm not saying that you don't fall in love, just that it comes to a close. It decelerates, Judge Wheeling—fades and wanes and flickers and goes away."

"You really believe that?"

"Oh, maybe not. Maybe not. Too many drinks make me overly cynical. Maybe that's all it is."

"Are you saying all this because of my wife?" Evers asked.

"How could I? I don't know you or your wife." Pauletta smiled. "Don't act paranoid."

"I see. So are we in our unwrapping stage now?"

"No. No, we're not. No rooms at the inn, Jose." She smiled again.

"No?"

"Never fuck your clients, Mr. Wheeling."

"And if you do, then don't stop, right?"

"Exactly," she said, still smiling. "Have you ever made love to a sister?"

"That would be incest."

"You know what I mean. At least I hope you do."

"Why do you talk like it's 1968? Why do all glib African Americans talk like it's 1968? I like Benjamin Hooks and all the old-timers who still call people 'colored.' "

"I'm sure you do. So have you?"

"What do you think?"

"No."

"Good guess. Of course I haven't. I've never even thought about it." Evers laughed. He bent over his glass and blew air through the small straw, caused his drink to bubble. "Bubble, bubble, toil and trouble."

"Blowing off steam?"

"Have you ever done it with a white man?"

" 'Done it,' Judge Wheeling?"

"I don't like the term 'make love.' It's stupid."

"Yes, I've fucked white men."

Evers and Pauletta talked some more, then Pauletta asked him to dance. During the first two songs, fast songs, Evers just shuffled his feet and shook his arms by his side; he was uncomfortable about dancing—even though he was almost drunk—and unsure about dancing with Pauletta, who was black. Pauletta was very active, springing and circling around Evers and twisting toward the floor until her knee and thigh came out of the split in her skirt—a blue cotton skirt, with several buttons undone along the split side. The third song was slow and old, the Commodores' "Three Times a Lady," and Evers and Pauletta danced together, touching each other.

"Ever slow dance with a colored girl at Woodhill Forest?"

"Woodberry Forest." Evers and Pauletta had talked about schools and vacations and places while they were driving to the club.

"Woodberry Forest?"

"No. It was an all-boys school. We didn't admit colored girls, you see."

"Didn't even think about it, I'll bet."

Evers and Pauletta sat down after the song ended. Evers stood behind her chair and pulled it out for her to sit. "We learned good, courtly manners at Woodhill Forest."

"Are you feeling all right, Mr. Wheeling?"

"Sure. Why?"

"Your illness." She looked at him.

"Oh. I'm almost over it, like I said. I really am embarrassed about what happened this morning."

"What was going on with that, Mr. Wheeling?"

"Maybe you should call me Evers. I'll call you Pauletta."

"Maybe not. So what was the story with you this morning?"

"Just a balance problem." Evers smiled.

"I'll say."

"I appreciate your concern."

"It's not concern," said Pauletta.

Evers ducked his eyes and rubbed his brow with his thumb and middle finger. "Just a lot of weird shit going on in my life. Stress and so forth. I'm really not taking medicine."

"Are you enjoying yourself, Mr. Wheeling?" Pauletta didn't show any reaction to Evers' admission.

"Yes. Yes I am."

"Good."

"So tell me about Ruth Esther English." Evers tried to sound casual.

"She's a client and a friend. And I safeguard my clients' confidences."

"How does a white car salesman from Winston-Salem end up with a black firebrand attorney from West Virginia?"

Pauletta didn't answer for a moment. Evers thought she hadn't heard him.

"I have no idea. She just called me one day. Out of the blue," Pauletta finally said. "I have no idea," she repeated. "I've known her for two years now."

"And you're acting as middleman in a bribery scheme?"

Pauletta ignored Evers. "She's a very compelling woman. Very compelling." Pauletta took a drink and kept the glass in her hand. "I take it that you don't know anything about her either."

"No. I'd never—"

"You know, she rarely eats. Did you know that? I've been with her for two or three days at a time, and she rarely eats. She drinks bottled water. Picks at a salad."

Evers looked around the bar. "Miss Qwai, is this some sort of sting or scam?"

"It is not. That's all I can tell you."

"So a highly principled black female attorney, who deplores injustice and unfairness in the system, is offering me a bribe to fix a case?"

"The system, Mr. Wheeling, is a venal, nasty quagmire. You know that. You've let a defendant go because you hunt with his lawyer, or you don't like the cop in the case because he gave your cousin a speeding ticket. You've convicted a twenty-year-old black kid because his pants hung too far down on his butt even though his mother swears he was home in bed when the crime happened. You're right. I do believe in the system—I believe that it's frail and full of foibles, that it's rigged and crooked, and that most of the time poor people and minorities are shot out of a cannon for sport and to make sure that people who read the paper know that you guys aren't asleep at the switch."

"Actually, the butt-crack plus fours don't irritate me as much as gold chains and gold teeth."

Pauletta smiled. "So are you going to let Artis go?"

"Sure. If he's innocent." Evers snapped his head up. "Oh, so . . . shit." He slid his scotch away from the edge of the table. "So . . . that's why you decided to come out and have a drink with me, isn't it? You're not really sure about all of this, either. Despite all the blast-furnace, mau-mauing, Nubian-dominatrix pushing and shoving at your office, you're still a little in the dark about all this and about Ruth Esther English, aren't you? Aren't you? You're trying to get a read on what I know."

"I came because of your charm and power-tool poise, Judge Wheeling. Don't sell yourself short. And, naturally, I came to help my client by encouraging you to take her up on her offer. I consider these billable hours."

Evers took hold of his drink. "Right." He finished the whiskey left in his glass and looked around for his futuristic waitress. "Let's change the subject. Your family from around here?"

"I grew up here with my aunt. In a trailer. In a trailer park. The two of us."

"In a trailer?"

"That's what I said." Pauletta's voice had an edge to it. The last word was tense and sharp.

"With flamingoes and a yard car and a satellite dish?"

"I'm not ashamed of it. Do you see something wrong with that? Perhaps we should have made other arrangements—taken a home by the river, lolled with our spritzers under the big oaks."

"I'm not being critical, not at all," Evers said. "I think that it's great. My brother lives in a trailer. He's not all self-righteous about it, though."

Pauletta didn't smile, didn't frown. She looked at Evers and didn't speak.

"I just hope that you bought the aged black aunt with silver hair a new Lincoln when you won that first big trial." Evers grinned at her.

"You'll say just about anything, won't you? You're a loose cannon."

Evers and Pauletta drank some more and danced again. Evers

thought that he looked more at ease dancing now. He watched himself in a mirror when he and Pauletta were on the dance floor. This time, they both were drunk. "Entering the supernova stage," Evers stated. When they returned to their table, they decided, after Evers suggested it, to start ordering hybrid drinks. A black Russian–greyhound for Evers, and a grasshopper-sunrise for Pauletta—"Looks like a bad Impressionist painting, I'll bet," she offered. The space waitress pointed out that the drinks would cost double the standard price, since the bartender would have to make each drink separately and then mix them together.

When their drinks came, Pauletta and Evers stopped talking to each other, just sat in their chairs sipping half-breed cocktails and listening to the music. Evers watched other couples dancing. Two men were trying to pick up the women at the next table over. He noticed that the men said "Aw, come on" a lot.

"These drinks really suck, don't they?" Evers finally said.

"Whose idea was it to mix them up?"

"Mine, I guess. Sorry. Of course they'd be even worse if we were sober."

"Are you a happy man, Mr. Wheeling?" Pauletta asked the question abruptly.

"What?"

"Are you happy?"

"Now, or in general?"

"In general."

"Sure. Why? Why shouldn't I be? My wife's banging a stranger, and I'm in West Virginia. Are you concerned about my happiness as well as my balance?"

"Pardon?"

"Forget it," said Evers.

"You seem a little—I don't know—glum. Worn down. What's wrong with you?"

"What page are you on?" Evers slurred the "g" in page. "Damn—do I sound drunk? I'm starting to feel pretty buzzed."

"What page?"

"Your book theory," he said.

"Oh. Just looking at the illustrations so far."

"Don't move your lips when you read, okay?" Evers had his hand on his glass, his palm touching it, his fingers arced. "What's wrong with me is . . . is that I turned pale after Princeton and right after that discovered that, that, well . . . in a word, things happen. Houses burn, cars collide, your wife sleeps with a man who sells cows for a living. That's it, really. The world happens and there's no rhyme or reason. It just does."

"You used two words, not one."

"Part of it has to do with my wife. I really loved my wife. That was my first clue. Do I sound drunk?"

"Yes. And I would've guessed that you thrived on being pale. The whiter the better."

"You don't follow me, do you?"

"Not completely."

"Just as well." Evers paused, lifted his glass. The drink was bitter and strong.

"Maybe some of this is your fault. You seem passive and stubborn at the same time. And I'd bet you were that way with your wife, too."

"Who knows." He sighed and shrugged.

"See what I mean?"

"Do people like Al Sharpton and Marion Barry embarrass you?" Evers was looking past Pauletta, watching the bartender. He thought about ordering a different drink.

"Yeah. Sure." Pauletta answered. "You guys got all the saints and stars—Jimmy Swaggert and Jesse Helms."

"Let's drink a tequila shot before we go. That should about put us over the top."

"I've had enough; it would only make me sick."

Neither Evers nor Pauletta was able to drive, so they left her car at the Galaxy 2000 and took a cab to her house. After they went inside, Evers sat down next to Pauletta on her living-room sofa. Pauletta brought a cup of coffee from the kitchen and set it on a table in front of Evers. He drank only a little. Evers smoked some of a cigarette and put it out by dropping it into the coffee left in his cup. The butt sizzled and then floated on the surface.

"May I spend the night with you, Miss Qwai?" Evers asked.

"You mean you want to stay here in my house?"

"That's part of it."

"What's the rest?" she asked.

"I want to stay with you."

"I'll be here, too."

"In your bed," Evers said. "I want to sleep with you."

"You want to fuck me, Mr. Wheeling?"

"Yes."

"Yes what?" Pauletta's face was close to Evers'.

"Yes, I want to."

"To what?"

"To fuck you."

"I see." She turned her head, leaned through the little bit of space left between them and kissed Evers, lightly at first, then with her tongue. "A new realm for you, huh?"

"The dark ages."

"Well, Mr. Wheeling, it's not going to happen for you. Not now, not tonight. Sorry."

"What's not going to happen?" Evers wondered if his speech was slurred.

"No fuck. No dark ages. Maybe a night in my guest bedroom."

"Oh?"

"That's all."

"Sounds lovely."

"You're being facetious," Pauletta said.

"Oh no. I consider it real progress. I've never slept in the same house with a colored girl before."

"It's better than sleeping in the street outside the colored girl's house."

"Why no fuck?"

"I don't like one-night stands, plus we're drunk and it would put us in an uncomfortable position later."

"But comfortable enough now." Evers looked at Pauletta.

"Maybe. Maybe not."

"Well, if you change your mind in the middle of the night, creep in and get me, okay?"

"Don't hold your breath waiting."

"I will, though. And I might die from doing it. What would you do then?"

Evers slept poorly and woke up with a headache and plaintive stomach. When he looked around Pauletta's house, she was gone. No note, no explanation, no car. It occurred to him that he had tried to have sex with almost every woman he had met since leaving his wife. He decided that this was healthy, correct, moral, just and sane.

Evers left West Virginia about four o'clock and began to drive to Norton, alone and weary. A few weeks ago his wife had treated him poorly and changed some of the things he had thought were immutable. And now she was causing him to lose his mind. God keeps his hands in his pockets sometimes, divine laissez-faire. Things just tumble on. Evers pulled his car—a Datsun 280Z, old but in good shape—to the side of the road after an hour or so of driving. He got out of the Datsun and then got back into the passenger's seat. He wanted to rest on the shoulder of the road, listen to traffic, watch the sky, think about his wife. Go over things in his mind. . . .

While it was still night, a policeman rapped on the window and told Evers that he couldn't park beside the highway, so he finished driving home before the sun rose and lay down on the sofa without taking off his shoes. He could not recall ever having been so tired, so torpid. He bit the corner of one of his fingernails and began thinking about college: the friends he'd never see again, who probably looked different now anyway; the quiet, unencumbered walk in the dark from the library across campus; getting drunk and playing bridge on a snowy afternoon, four nineteen-year-olds bidding and turning up beers in a cracker-box dormitory room; throwing a baseball around the quad after an exam; knocking on a girl's door at three a.m.; passing by Nassau Hall early in the morning on his way to get a bagel and New York paper; songs he had heard at a certain time and a certain place, both now lost. Evers looked up at the ceiling in his apartment. "There's nothing I can do about Jo Miller, about any of this," he said.

FOUR

OH, SHIT." THAT WAS ALL EVERS COULD SAY WHEN HE first saw Artis English; it just came out of his mouth—even though his lips didn't move—not too loud, one part voice, three parts thought, not directed at anyone, more sough than words. After Artis' case was called, the jailer had to go fetch him and bring him from his cell into the courtroom. When Artis walked through the metal door from lockup, he was wearing an orange jumpsuit, and he was no more than five feet tall, fat, unkempt and dark-skinned. He had kinky black hair that was matted on one side and spiraled and twisted like black corkscrews near the crown of his head. Artis had thick lips and heavy eyebrows—a dark, moping, unraveled spot of a person. Evers was confounded; he gave Artis a slack-jawed, slapstick mug, his head down, eyes popped, neck stretched like a rubber chicken's. Evers leaned toward his bailiff. "You sure this is the right guy? Artis English?"

"Yep."

"Are you Mr. English?" Evers asked the man in the jumpsuit.

"Yeah." Artis didn't look up at Evers.

"Artis English?"

"Uh-huh."

"Okay, good. Have a . . . seat at counsel table with your attorney."

Evers watched him walk across the room. His legs were in chains and his feet skidded over the floor; his shoes never came off the ground. Artis sat down beside his lawyer. James Turner was one of the better public defenders in Winston-Salem; he was usually prepared and smarter than most of the other attorneys. Tall and bald-headed, around fifty years old, Turner was polite when Evers met him from time to time, but not gregarious.

After his initial shock at seeing Artis, Evers began to feel better about the deal with Ruth Esther. Certainly the state police would be more discriminating with their plants and operatives—they would not cast a short, black troll in the role of an ethereal white woman's brother. Evers was still convinced that something was queer, but now he felt fairly sure the police weren't involved; they were hardly this creative. Evers tried to calm down. He opened Artis' file and picked up a pencil. He thought about Toulouse-Lautrec, then imagined Artis in a beret, drinking warm wine in front of a bordello. "Would the lawyers approach, please?"

Turner walked to the bench, along with the district attorney, Paul Otis. Otis was one of ten deputy district attorneys in Winston-Salem. He had been hired about a year ago, and he had come to Winston-Salem after graduating from the University of North Carolina Law School. Evers had worked with Otis only a couple of times and didn't know that much about him.

"Good morning, Judge." Turner nodded at Evers. Otis spoke as well.

"Good morning." Evers put his pencil down, then picked it up again. "Mr. Otis, I've already informed your boss that the family of Mr. English contacted me about his case. Since then, I've had some conversations with the Englishes' family attorney as well. As you know, these things happen from time to time. Mr. Turner, I wanted to disclose everything to you as well. If either side wants me to disqualify myself, I will." Evers spoke in a quick monotone. He squeezed the pencil in his hand.

"No need for that," Turner said. "I appreciate your letting us know, though. They didn't do anything rude or threatening, anything like that?"

"No. I can hear the case with an open mind. Nothing unpleasant happened. I always like to let everyone know when something like this transpires. As I said, I've already talked to the D.A."

Turner folded his arms. "It's not a problem for us; we appreciate your telling us about it." He shifted his weight, took a step closer to Evers. "Judge, while we're here, maybe we can streamline things a bit. We've filed a suppression motion to exclude the cocaine from my client's trial. If you grant our motion, the case will be pretty much over in terms of guilt or innocence. Without the cocaine, I think we can all agree that the state has nowhere to go. If you deny our motion, then we will enter a guilty plea and ask for a presentence report." Turner looked at Paul Otis. "That's pretty much what we talked about, isn't it, Paul?"

"That's correct, Judge. James and I discussed it this morning."

"What's the basis of the motion? I saw it in the file." Evers turned to the last paper in Artis' folder.

"The police officer found three grams of cocaine in Mr. English's car. We don't think he had a right to search my client's vehicle."

Evers glanced at Artis, then at the lawyers. He tapped the court file with his fingers. "Good enough. I appreciate your narrowing the case down for me. It's your motion, Mr. Turner. Call your witnesses and let's hear it."

"I'm only going to call the police officer. And, perhaps, my client."

"Who's the officer?" Evers asked.

"Warren Dillon," said Turner. Both he and the district attorney watched for Evers' reaction. Otis put his hands behind his back and briefly rocked forward on his feet.

"I thought that he was suspended," Evers said. "Or at least . . . doing more administrative kinds of work."

Otis spoke up. "The sheriff said that they had two complaints about him, one about some missing evidence, one about him losing the file on a really bad malicious wounding case. Evidently, the SBI cleared him on the problem with the evidence, and he just flat told the sheriff he'd made an error on the wounding case. Just misplaced his file, and the sheriff appreciated him telling the truth and admitting his mistake."

"Everybody makes mistakes." Turner grinned. "At any rate, he's been back about three or four months. No new problems that I'm aware of."

"Where is he?" Evers asked. "I don't see him in the courtroom."

"He's at the sheriff's office. I told him we'd let him know when he was needed. Mr. Turner subpoenaed him about two weeks ago." Otis was up on the front of his feet again, tipping forward.

"Go ahead and get him here then," Evers instructed the lawyers. "I'm ready when you gentlemen are."

While waiting for Warren Dillon to arrive, Evers adjourned court and went into his office. He shut the door and stood in front of his desk. The office belonged to another judge, and Evers used it when he worked in Winston-Salem. He thought about looking in the drawers for a bottle and taking a drink, and thought that it would be seedy and loutish, ripe, perfect for what he was contemplating doing. He looked at the books and diplomas in the room, the computer on a stand next to the window. He cracked the door and peered out into the courtroom, watched the deputies, lawyers and people talking. A lawyer he didn't know, a young woman, had her hand on her client's shoulder and was telling him something. The client wiped his eyes several times while his lawyer was talking to him.

"Officer Dillon's here," Evers heard one of the clerks announce out in the courtroom. "Go let Judge Wheeling know that we're ready as soon as he is."

Warren Dillon was a pale, white gibbon in a suit and vest. He had a small head, flat mouth, wide nose, pasty skin and a full black beard the same color and texture as his hair. The beard and hair were almost identical and circled his head, an unbroken, woolly ring that caused him to look like he had pushed his face through a tricycle tire. Dillon's legs were long and spindly, his hands elongated and his wrists on hinges. When he sat down in the witness stand, he moved his head and eyes in tiny starts and jumps so his head seemed to constantly chase after his eyes, a staccato pursuit going on all over his face.

Turner stood up behind his table, beside Artis. "Good morning, Officer."

"Good morning." Dillon's voice was squeaky and nasal, like his throat and teeth and tongue were in the middle of his head.

Turner moved a sheet of yellow paper on the desk. "You're Officer Warren Dillon, is that correct?"

"Yes."

"And you're employed by the Forsyth County Police Department?"

"Yes." Dillon looked at Evers when he answered.

"And you were so employed on the third of last month?"

"Yes."

"Did you have occasion, on that date, to come in contact with Artis English, the defendant seated on my left?" Turner pointed at Artis, and the small man seemed startled. Artis dipped his head, ducked and snarled like a stubby orange vampire sprinkled with holy water. Turner stared at Artis for a moment; Artis stayed crouched and wound, but his face became blank again. Turner's expression didn't change—he had seen a lot of things, seen his clients piss on the canvas cushion in the defendant's chair and smother in the coils of Laocoönian lies, and he had learned to turn his back and walk right past the mess without hesitating or flinching.

"Yes, I made contact with the defendant on that day. Yes."

"Were you on duty and in uniform?"

"I was."

"And what were your duties on that day?"

"What are you getting at?" Dillon's voice squeaked out of his nostrils. Evers noticed that his mouth didn't move much when he spoke.

"Well, what were your job responsibilities that day?"

"I guess I know what you're gettin' around to. I'd been placed on paid leave for about a month back in February because of some complaints about my work. I was cleared by the state police regarding some evidence that turned up missing, and to be truthful about it, I lost a file and a piece of evidence involving two cousins in a knife fight. It was my error, and I owned up to it. When this happened with your client, with Mr. English, I was fully reinstated, working as a road deputy."

Turner shook his head. "I didn't mean to get into all of that, but thanks for the candor and background. I just wanted to note that you were working as a police officer for the county of Forsyth on the day that you encountered my client."

"Yes. I was. I was working as a road deputy here in Forsyth County."

"Why did you stop my client's vehicle?"

"The defendant was driving a 2000 Ford Taurus, blue in color, which failed to stop at a traffic signal. The car was a four-door sedan." "Sedan," when Dillon said it, came out as "see dan."

"I see. What sort of signal?"

"A stop sign."

"And my client didn't fully stop, is that what you're saying?" Turner asked.

"Correct."

"Where is this sign located?"

"At the intersection of East Third Street and Cleveland."

"I see. How did you bring Mr. English to a stop?"

"I turned on my blue lights, and he pulled into a parking lot at a convenience store." Dillon turned through some pages in his file. "Uni-Mart parking lot. The subject was initially detained at sixteen-thirty hours."

"Was there anything else irregular or uncommon about his driving?"

"No. He just ran right through the sign."

Turner stepped to the side of his chair. Artis looked up at his lawyer, then buried himself so far back into his seat that his head was almost even with the top of the table. "Officer Dillon, after you stopped Mr. English, did you ask to see his driver's license and registration?"

"I did."

The courtroom seemed quiet to Evers. It was full of people, but it seemed still. No one was moving or talking or folding newspapers or popping gum. The metal detector was mute, the attorneys waiting for their cases looked lethargic, doodling and napping and staring at the floor.

"Were they in order?"

Dillon looked at his file. "He had a valid driver's license. The car was registered to a dealership here in town. I was concerned that, you know, it might've been stolen. It had dealer tags. I checked while we were on the scene, and dispatch called and everything was okay."

Evers heard a door open, and the metal detector sound, and when he looked out over Dillon's head, Ruth Esther had started into the courtroom. She walked about halfway into the gallery and sat down on the end of a bench, beside an obese woman wearing a black Lynyrd Skynyrd T-shirt. The two women smiled at each other. Evers looked around the room, and stopped when his gaze returned to Dillon.

"How was it that you came to find the cocaine?" Turner asked.

"It was in the trunk."

"I'm not sure that you understand my question." Turner smiled and looked at the paper on the table in front of him. "Let me put it like this. Obviously, you didn't have a warrant, correct?"

"I didn't have a warrant."

"Right." Turner smiled again. Evers looked at Ruth Esther. She was wearing a silk shirt under an off-white suit. As far as Evers could tell, it was the same outfit she'd been wearing at the restaurant and at the car dealership. She opened her purse and offered the fat lady in the T-shirt a Life Saver; the lady shook her head no.

"And you didn't have my client's permission to go into his trunk?" Turner had taken a step back so that he was standing behind Artis.

"Right. I guess you could say that. I asked him, and he didn't make me a reply." Dillon turned and faced the district attorney after he answered.

"So he didn't consent."

"Well, you know, he didn't refuse, either." Dillon's eyes and face continued to twitch away. Evers recalled placing round magnets on the utility-room floor when he was a child, lining them up so the poles pushed apart, and chasing one with the other across the linoleum.

"Officer Dillon, you and I both know this wasn't a consent search. You would agree that he would have to give you clear and unequivocal permission to—"

Otis stood up and spoke at the same time. "Judge Wheeling, I hate to object, but I'm not sure that the officer can be called upon to decide a purely legal question. He can address factual matters, but he's not in a position to decide the law."

Turner started to say something, and Evers interrupted him. "There's no need to quibble. We all know that the defendant's consent has to be clear, and that silence is not consent. Let's go on. Is this supposed to be a consent search? Is that where this is going?"

"No, sir," said Otis.

"No, not at all," said Dillon.

"Then why are we arguing about it?"

Otis shrugged. "Because we're lawyers, I guess."

A few spectators laughed, and Evers smiled for a moment. "Next question, Mr. Turner."

"So it's not a consent search, and there's no warrant. How did you discover the drugs?"

"Well, I found them in the trunk." Dillon's mouth barely moved and very little sound came out of the slit in his lips. His eyes kept up the kinetic chase with the rest of his head.

"Officer, why did you think you had a right to open the trunk? Why did you look in there? That's my question."

Otis objected to the question, and Evers overruled him. "You'll need to answer the question, Officer Dillon."

"Well, you see . . . " Dillon looked at his notes. His voice was in the insect range, beyond human octaves, coming straight out of the middle of his face. "You see, a number of things went into the decision to search. First, it was a high-crime area. Very bad for drugs. And second, the defendant was extremely nervous. Very nervous. In fact, he never looked me in the eye but one time. And that's the third thing. His eyes was red. Very red. And there was the car, this new car, and the fact that he wasn't willing to let me search when I first asked made me think he was suspicious. Based on my experience as a police officer and the totality of the circumstances, I felt I had probable cause to search the car."

"That's it? Those are all of the factors? I want to make sure you're telling me everything."

Dillon stared fixedly at his notes before answering. "Well, yeah. I mean, you know . . . I was right. He had the dope in the car."

"Oh, by the way. If you didn't have my client's consent, how did you physically get into the trunk? How did you get it open?"

"I . . . well, since I had what I thought was a legal right to search, I stuck my hand inside the car and just, uh, removed the keys out of the switch."

"So Mr. English didn't hand you the keys or open the trunk himself."

"That's right."

Turner sat down in his seat beside Artis. "Okay. Let's take the car first. You checked that out and there was nothing wrong, correct? Isn't that what you said?"

"That's right."

"So that could not serve as the basis of any wrongdoing or some suspicion of a crime, could it?"

Dillon rubbed his chin. Evers noticed that his fingers all looked very similar, all about the same length and thickness. "I guess that's true enough."

"And you thought that his presence in a certain part of town, in a certain location, just driving through, gave you a reason to search his car for drugs?"

"It's a high drug-traffic area," Dillon answered. He turned to look at Paul Otis again.

"But you never saw this defendant stop, slow down, signal another party or have any contact with any other person or vehicle? In fact— quite the opposite—he ran a stop sign, correct?"

"I guess."

"Well, don't guess. I'm correct, aren't I?"

"Yes."

"So if, for example, Judge Wheeling were driving through this area in a new 2000 Taurus, you'd assume he was carrying drugs?"

"No. I wouldn't think that. No sir."

"So what's the difference?"

Dillon moved some papers around in his file. Artis looked up and saw his sister in the crowd. Ruth Esther waved at him, held her hand in front of her chest and moved it back and forth.

"Officer Dillon?"

"Well, just his look. He—"

Turner put his elbows on the table. He interrupted the gibbon's answer. "So you're telling us you search people based on their physical appearance?"

"No."

"Really? Isn't the bottom line that you thought you had probable cause to search the defendant because he was in a bad neighborhood, in a new car he lawfully and legally possessed, but he looked a little less normal than, say, Greg Brady?"

Otis half stood. "I object to that question. It's rhetorical."

"I don't know a Mr. Brady, anyway," Dillon said.

"Which part is objectionable?" Evers asked.

"The Greg Brady reference."

"I sustain the objection, although I understand where your questions are going." Evers looked down at Dillon. "Greg Brady is a very homogenous, wholesome character on a TV show called *The Brady Bunch*. There was also a movie recently, I believe."

"Oh yeah. Thank you, sir."

Evers began to think that Dillon was a prop, an early Nipponese failure, constructed by the same people who'd built Mothra and his brother's dope-favorite Godzilla; his lips missed his voice, and his eyes and face were always a beat separate from each other.

"While we are on the subject," Turner said, "what do you mean by a 'high-crime area,' Officer?"

"I mean there's a lot of crime going on." Dillon attempted a mechanical smirk. "As compared to other places."

"I see. And you have these comparisons, correct? You can tell me, statistically, that more people have been arrested and convicted in this area, than, for example, in the Skyland Park area or around Reynolda Road?"

"No real, uh, statistics. Just what I know from experience and information."

Evers looked at Otis, and Otis sheepishly looked back. The district attorney rubbed his brow and stared down at the table in front of him. Evers tapped Artis' file with the eraser end of a yellow pencil.

"Tell me, then, the number of arrests you have made in this area in the last year as compared to other areas."

"I'd say more here, around King and Cleveland, than in other parts of the city. Sure. More."

"Who was the last person you arrested there?"

"That would be a . . . a Lowery guy, for stealing." Dillon sniffed.

"You wouldn't be suggesting that this area is a 'high-crime area' because a large portion of the population is black, would you?" Turner raised his voice when he asked the question.

"No sir. Not at all. Just a lot goes on there. A lot goes on in other places, too. Places with mostly whites, like Mountainview Trailer Court out off Interstate Forty—there's always trouble with that bunch. And there's a lot more places with real bad trouble."

The public defender nodded his head up and down. "So really, this area, in terms of its incidence of crime, is no different than a lot of other places."

"That's not what I mean." The long-fingered gibbon's voice almost gave out midway through the sentence. He looked at the floor and slouched.

"Thank you, Officer. Those are all my questions."

Otis made a halfhearted attempt to save Dillon. "You've been a police officer for over twenty years, correct?"

"Yes."

"Almost all in the Winston-Salem, Forsyth County area?"

"Yes." The gibbon raised up in his seat.

"And based on that experience, and the location of this car in a high-crime area, you felt that you had probable cause to search the defendant's trunk?"

"Exactly. And I was right. He was carryin' almost three grams of cocaine."

Turner stood quickly and very straight, his hands by his side. "Judge, I object to the last part of the answer. It is fairly fundamental that the officer needs probable cause before he searches, not after the fact. The search and seizure is not validated because the officer violates the Constitution but happens to be correct in his guess. Bad conduct isn't salvaged because of good results." He sat down.

"I'll sustain your objection, Mr. Turner."

Otis asked Dillon about Artis' eyes.

"They were red. Very red."

"Thank you, Officer."

Dillon stood up to leave, and Turner stopped him. "I'm sorry, Officer. I apologize. Just to follow up on that, you didn't smell or see anything that would lead you to believe that drugs were in the car, did you?"

Dillon was standing in front of the witness stand. "That's right."

Otis pulled his chair closer to the table in front of him and took another file from the stack on the table.

"May I be excused, Judge?" Dillon asked Evers.

"Yes. Thank you for your time, sir."

While Dillon was still walking through the gallery, Turner stood and asked Evers to suppress the cocaine, and he pointed out that the police officer did not have legal justification to look into Artis English's trunk. "In fact, this is not even a close call. Basically, he searched the defendant's vehicle because of the way god created Mr. English and where Mr. English chose to be. That's about it."

Evers glanced at Ruth Esther, saw her surrounded by punks and petty thieves, her expression composed, her hands folded in her lap. She was staring toward the front of the courtroom, but her eyes weren't letting anything in; she was focused somewhere else, rarely blinking, looking past Evers and over his head.

Otis stood up, and he left a little bend in his back, leaned onto the table in front of him with both hands. "Judge, the state will concede that this is not the strongest case we have ever had in this court involving a warrantless search. Still, we would argue that the officer had probable cause given all of the circumstances and the officer's training and experience." He sat down and returned to reading the file for his next case.

"This is not a difficult decision," Evers said. "There is no probable cause to search. The cocaine is suppressed." Evers saw Ruth Esther get up and leave, watched her back and blond hair walk out of the courtroom. He was relieved that the case was so clear.

"Judge, on behalf of the defendant, I would ask that the charges lodged against him be dismissed."

"There's not much we can do without the evidence," Otis replied.

"The charges against Mr. English are dismissed." Evers motioned to the lawyers on either side of him. "Would you gentlemen please approach the bench?"

Otis and Turner walked up. "That was terrible, Mr. Otis," Evers said. "What's Mr. Dillon's problem? It's like he's trying to screw up."

Otis' neck and cheeks turned red. "I'm sorry. I didn't talk to him that much. I'll mention it to the sheriff."

Turner cleared his throat. "I really do think he doesn't know any better. He's not a bad guy. In fact, it would've been easy for him to concoct something that would win the case for him."

"If he knew what to say," Evers remarked.

"I guess you'd expect that after twenty years, he could do a little better job." Turner sounded as if he felt sorry for the gibbon.

"He's definitely not our best officer," Paul Otis remarked.

Two days after he let Artis English go, Evers stopped at Honey's Qwik Stop just outside of Norton to buy beer and snacks to take to his brother's trailer. Evers was world-weary, tired of so many things. And, he hated Norton. He wondered whether or not he would have cheated on her someday if his wife hadn't been unfaithful. He bought a case of Michelob and opened one for the ride, almost an hour and a half of traveling in the dark. The beer was warm.

While he was driving, Evers decided that every great rock-and-roll song—or at least every song he really enjoyed—had either an organ or a saxophone in it: "Wooly Bully," "Light My Fire," "Louie, Louie," "Born to Run." Pascal would be interested in this observation; it was the kind of thing he liked talking about.

It was black and quiet when Evers got out at Pascal's. Evers opened the door to the trailer, shouted his brother's name and got no answer. The spring on the screen door was stretched and loose, so the door did not return to the frame, but just hung open and still. The light in the kitchen was on. Evers went into the den and switched on the television. He had left his bags and the beer in the car; there was too much to carry in one trip, and he could sleep in his underwear and use his brother's toothbrush. *Love Connection* came on the screen, but the volume was turned down. Pascal had left a bag of marijuana and a pipe on a plastic tray in the floor, this despite Evers' warnings to be more careful.

Pascal, Rudy and Henry were sitting in Pascal's bedroom, passing a water bong back and forth and watching *Fantasia*. "Didn't hear you, brother," Pascal said when Evers walked into the room. "We're celebrating our American president and Henry's good luck."

"You mean Bill Clinton?" Evers asked. "You guys just discover that Reagan's out?"

"Bill Clinton smoked dope. Can't be all that bad," Henry said.

"He probably just said that so cool people would vote for him. That's my only concern." Rudy's eyes were red, and his shirttail was hanging out.

"So what's cool these days?" asked Evers.

"Don't know. I watch MTV, read *Rolling Stone,* let them decide for me." Pascal grinned. "You seem out of sorts, Evers."

"Gee. Hard to imagine, huh?"

"Come live with us. No ambition, no disappointment. And no worries—not with Henry's good fortune. No money problems, at least. Have a bong hit." Pascal stretched out on his bed and handed Evers the water pipe.

"I'm tired of people, places and things. I'm tired of queers, mayhem, politicians, Betty Friedan, network TV, Hobert fucking Falstaf, affirmative action, the welfare system and my job."

Rudy and Henry held up their hands. "Easy on TV, now. We saw some great TV not long ago. 'A Special Celebration: Phil Donahue's Years in TV,' and a miniseries on the Jackson Five—'The Jacksons: An American Family,' or something like that. That's entertainment." Rudy nodded after he spoke to emphasize the point.

"That's unreal." Evers shook his head. "That's like doing a special on Jimmy Olson, cub reporter, and the Archies. You know what I mean?"

"Don't be so humorless and grim, Evers," Rudy said.

"I'm about to go crazy. I want some normalcy and insight."

Rudy giggled. "Gee, Wally, that Eddie Haskell sure is a pest."

"Fuck you, Rudy."

"If you're not going to use that bong, Evers, pass it back." Rudy snapped his fingers.

Evers looked at Pascal. His brother rolled onto his side and propped up his head. "Whatever."

Evers lit the bowl of the water pipe and sucked the smoke into his lungs.

"That should cheer you up," Henry said.

"Speaking of cheer, I was listening to Handel the other day, and it dawned on me that there's no mirth in classical music. Not even in *Fantasia*." Rudy was locked onto the TV screen; he didn't look at anyone when he spoke.

"Damning and profound critique from someone watching a children's movie," said Pascal.

"There's precision and synchronization, but no mirth."

"Do you really think this lady's going to come?" Pascal said. "We're anxious to meet her."

"The mother of the albino shrine." Henry stood up and stretched. "You said she was nice looking, too."

"Why would she come, though?" Pascal wondered. "I mean, her brother's out of jail. You don't know anything about her. She may not come."

"I'll tell you guys one thing." Rudy tried to tuck some of his shirt into his pants. "I'm paranoid as shit. When she comes in here with a pistol and about forty chubby guys with yellow FBI letters on their nylon windbreakers, I'm going to swear that I don't have anything to do with any of this."

"You're paranoid because you've been smoking dope for the last five years with very few interruptions," Evers said.

"This is a Byzantine tale, brother." Pascal had the bong between his knees and was tamping dope into the bowl with the top of a pen. "And it's not like you to get into something like this. You don't need the money. Are you sure she's not working with the police?"

"I'm not sure, but I don't think so. If she were a cop, they would've arrested me by now. In fact, they would probably have done it at the courthouse—a lot of metaphor and populist justice in that image." Pascal handed the bong to Evers, who passed it to Rudy without smoking any more of the marijuana. "And the other thing is, I didn't do anything. I made the right call. It wasn't even close. It was a minor drug possession case, and the police officer completely fucked up. The D.A. pretty much tossed in the towel."

"But you lusted in your heart, Evers. You were conspiring to let him go."

"I don't think you should get arrested for using drugs anyway," Henry said.

Evers laughed, and so did Pascal. "Really, Henry? I figured that you'd come down hard on the drug scene. Especially pot. It makes you impotent and leads to heroin addiction. In another month or two, you'll be full of infected needle marks and wearing some guy's old tuxedo jacket for a winter coat."

"So her brother was innocent?" Henry sat down in a recliner beside the bed. "If you didn't do anything to help, maybe she won't come."

"I let him go. That was the deal." Evers looked at the TV. Mickey Mouse was dancing with a broom. "And she called *me* after the trial, not the other way around. I guess we'll see. Of course, she has sort of paid me. That's the only thing that's troubling me about whether or not she'll be here."

"Paid you? Already?"

"Yeah. Well, she gave me . . . a deposit, I guess you could call it. I really don't want to get into it."

"I'm sure you don't." Henry wiggled his eyebrows.

"It was a payment I can divide with all of you, Henry. Sorry to disappoint your prurient side."

"She's supposed to be here around ten, right?" Pascal asked.

"What if she's crazy or something? Or, you know, starts transforming in front of us, turns into a big-ass scaley lizard or some shit like that." Rudy pointed his finger at Evers. "I'm serious."

"I'll watch her hands, Rudy," Evers said. "The first hint of a claw or a skin change and the deal's off." Evers and Pascal started laughing. Henry smiled and shook his head.

"I'm just cautious, that's all." Rudy reached into a bag of Doritos on the floor beside the bed and started eating. "I'm looking forward to meeting her, too, I guess."

"Well, Rudy, there is something peculiar about the whole thing. You're right—"

"Shit, that's her. I heard something." Rudy twisted his head so his ear was turned toward the driveway. He was chewing the Doritos and still had a few of the chips in his hand. His speech was dry, and his tongue and lips were orange.

The men went to the window and then to the kitchen door, but no one was outside or in the driveway.

"I know I heard a car," Rudy insisted. "And saw lights."

"Whatever," said Pascal. Everyone was standing in the kitchen. "We may as well move the reception outside anyway. It's a nice night.

I'll turn on the bug killer and uncover the sofa. It'll be good to keep an eye on things. I'm getting a little anxious myself."

Henry picked up the bong, and everyone followed Pascal outside. They left the TV in the bedroom on. When they got to the couch, an old pickup truck passed by on the road in front of the trailer and kept going. The bedroom window was open, and the classical music from *Fantasia* was loud enough that the men could hear it in the yard. The scenes in the movie changed and made the light coming out of the bedroom dim and stutter, brighten and fade. A big green moth flew into the bug zapper, and it took several seconds before the electrical buzzing stopped and the moth died.

"There is absolutely no one out here, Rudy."

"I know I heard a car. I know I did. And I saw lights. Headlights. Through the window."

"Shit."

"I'm going in for some scotch," Evers said. "Anybody want anything?"

"Bring me a coat or shirt or something." Henry was wearing a short-sleeve shirt.

"Hang on." Pascal put his hand on Evers' leg. "I hear a car."

Evers heard something as well, and he saw lights start around the turn in the gravel road that passed Pascal's mobile home. The vehicle was moving slowly and almost stopped when it came into view of the trailer. Then the lights picked up pace and the driver signaled to turn into Pascal's driveway, even though Pascal lived next to an unpaved rural road and there was no other car in sight. Evers watched the rectangular yellow signal blinking; the vehicle cut into Pascal's drive.

Ruth Esther shut the car door and waved at Evers and the others. She was driving a new white Explorer with a dealer's tag. When she stepped in front of the Explorer, it appeared to Evers that she was wearing the same white suit and silk shirt, though the glow from the bug zapper made her appear purple from head to toe. The classical music was still coming out of the bedroom, Mussorgsky's "Night on Bald Mountain," rapid violins and deep bass. Evers introduced Ruth Esther to everyone, and they decided to go inside, into Pascal's trailer.

"Artis is in the car. Do you care if he comes in?" Ruth Esther asked when Rudy walked through the trailer door. Rudy was behind everyone else, carrying two glasses and the bong.

"It's fine with me," Pascal said. No one else said anything.

"Well, it's fairly important that he come as well. He has the third clue."

"And you haven't opened yours yet? That's what you're telling me?" Evers asked.

"Artis opened his the day he got it. I haven't opened my father's or mine. I guess I should put it this way. Artis wants to come in to make sure that the clues are all looked at together, and that he isn't left out."

Evers went to the refrigerator and opened the door. He took out a beer and unscrewed the top. "So how is he your brother? He's black. Or Samoan or something. He's hardly your brother."

Ruth Esther smiled. "May I have a beer, too?"

"I'll get one for you," Pascal said. "Evers can be an ogre sometimes."

"Artis is my brother, Judge Wheeling. We just don't look anything alike. My mother is white, and her grandfather was an albino. There must be some dark genes somewhere else. I don't think that the colors managed to mix much in either case. I don't have any reason to mislead you about it. In fact—"

"How do you . . . how do you cry and have it look white?" Rudy interrupted. "How do you do that?"

"Damn, Rudy." Pascal rolled his eyes.

"What?" Rudy's eyes were almost closed, his hair flat and straight. He'd been wearing a hat, and taken it off when Ruth Esther came into the trailer. "What?" he said again. "Like you guys are Linus Pauling and Wernher von Braun and you already know?"

"What about Artis? Are you going to get him?"

"We have, like, a shrine for the charmed white drops. We keep them in a decanter in the freezer." Rudy grinned and swayed a little bit. "I'm a doctor."

"I'm flattered." Ruth seemed calm and steady.

"They're like enchanted."

"Rudy, let's get the clues for the trip, then worry about the shrine."

"There's no way that Artis is your blood, biological brother." Evers returned to the subject.

"Does he have magic tears too?" Rudy stepped back and bumped against the refrigerator. He started laughing and rubbed his hands across his face. Pascal and Henry started to giggle.

"I'll go get him. You can ask him yourself."

Ruth Esther was gone for a few minutes. The men heard a car door slam, then voices outside. Artis came in first, Ruth Esther right after him.

"This is your brother?" Pascal asked. He squinted at Artis.

"I told you so. Didn't I tell you?" Evers ignored the fact that Artis was in the room.

"No way." Rudy had collapsed down the side of the refrigerator and was sitting on the floor with his legs crossed. "Shit."

"This is my brother, Artis." Ruth Esther put her hand on Artis' back. He looked shorter and darker than Evers recalled from court. He had combed his hair, and it was dry and puffy, parted down the middle into two frizzy hemispheres. Artis was wearing sandals; his toes were dirty, and his toenails were cracked and yellow, banded with runs of grime underneath them. "Artis, this is Evers—Judge Wheeling, you remember him from the other day—and his brother Pascal. Rudy's sitting on the floor, and this is another friend of theirs named Henry."

"Hello. Nice to . . . meet you," Artis said.

"This is very strange," said Henry. "Flying-buttress-and-trapdoor strange."

Ruth Esther sat down at the kitchen table between Evers and Pascal. She laid two envelopes on the table and then opened each one. "Artis, give me your clue, please."

Artis bit his lip.

"Show us your clue, Artis," Pascal said.

"No. I don't know."

"You don't trust your sister?"

"I don't trust nobody." Artis narrowed his eyes.

Pascal pushed his chair away from the table. "Let's go look outside, Evers. Henry, you and the car doctor stay in here with Miss English and her brother and the clues."

"Where are you going?" Rudy wondered.

"Outside. To see if anyone's there, okay? Now I've gotten jittery."

"No one's there. Why would there be?" Ruth Esther sounded weary. "Why would we drive here to open my two envelopes if we weren't sincere about this? Or why would we drive here and then have someone steal the clues? Who do you think is out there?"

"We'll just enjoy the evening more if we satisfy our paranoia."

Evers and Pascal walked outside, and after he started down the steps from the trailer, Evers had to turn around and push the screen door shut. The air was pleasant, with some breeze in the trees and leaves. The movie and music had ended, and the bug zapper was quiet. Evers and Pascal walked to Ruth Esther's vehicle and looked inside. The driver's side door was not locked, and Pascal opened it. A light and a buzzer came on. The keys were in the ignition. The Explorer smelled new, and the backseat still had plastic stretched across it. The interior was completely empty except for a map, a pair of sunglasses and a car phone.

After they finished with the Explorer, Pascal and Evers walked around the trailer and the perimeter of the yard. They went to a path at the edge of the woods and looked in. Evers felt something very primitive and unusual, rushes in his belly and chest and hands.

"There is no way that guy's her brother, Pascal."

"Maybe he is. Whatever."

"What do you think they're up to?"

"Who knows. Perhaps they are simply honoring their agreement."

"We'll see." Evers lit a cigarette. He could see the smoke from the match even though it was dark outside. "Should we check to see if they're wearing a wire?"

"You decide—I don't really care. I'm sorry I got all freaked out."

"I don't blame you." Evers looked out at the gravel road. "Stay here with me for a minute while I finish my smoke. I'm not ready to go back in yet. Just keep your eyes open—that's about all we can do."

Evers finished his cigarette, and he and Pascal walked back inside the trailer. When they opened the door, Ruth Esther and Artis were sitting at the kitchen table with Henry. Rudy was standing beside Ruth Esther, holding the decanter with the albino tears, plastic top and two strips of tape. The shrine had become cloudy, fogged in under condensation. There were three pieces of paper on the table, and Henry was writing on the back of a napkin with a dull pencil.

"Evers, check it out. We have the clues. This is a treat. It's like *Wheel of Fortune.*"

Evers walked to the table and looked over Artis' head. Two of the sheets were clean, the folds still sharp and clear. One sheet—Artis', Evers surmised—was dirty, flat and limp, and had begun to separate at the creases in two or three places. A thin metal key was lying at the end of the three clues. The first sheet had Na written on it, the second ke, U and the third Cl La. Under Na was the number 100. Under the Cl La was a single 0. Under the ke, U was an arrow which pointed down.

"It's in Canada," Artis said. He was agitated, rocking back and forth in his chair. "Canada. That's it. Canada."

"You mean like he omitted the 'd'?" Rudy asked. "And threw in a couple of 'l's' that we don't need?"

"That's a pretty big leap, isn't it? Hell, it could be Colorado or California if you use that theory." Henry continued to study the clues.

"It's Canada, the country that's right above us," Artis insisted.

"Then it would need a 'd,' Artis," Ruth Esther pointed out. "I think you're close, but let's look at it a little longer."

"Then let's see you all think up somethin' better," Artis snapped.

Rudy sat the shrine decanter on the edge of the table. The glass was clearing, and the frosted white top was visible; crystals and intricate patterns were frozen on the top, and it was stuck to the bottom of the container, fastened by several icy webs.

"We need some more dope for this," Henry suggested.

"Whatever. I'll go get the bong," Pascal said, walking out of the kitchen.

"Bring enough for everybody," Rudy said.

"Sure." Pascal hesitated, then motioned to his brother. Evers walked up to him, several steps down the hall. "Are you all right with this, partying in front of these people, your job and this guy just being in your court and everything?" Pascal whispered. "It's probably a little late now, but it just occurred to me—I just thought about it. I suppose it might have been better to consider possible problems before we met them in the front yard with a bong."

"I guess that's the least of my worries, huh? But thanks for asking. It is sort of strange when you think about it."

Evers went back into the kitchen and looked down at the letters on the table. Artis had his head in his hands, winding and tugging strands of his hair. Evers heard a cigarette lighter click in the den, and his brother walked back into the kitchen with his hand over the opening in the top of the dope pipe and his breath held in.

"Nake La . . . can lake . . . a clan . . . shit, this is tough," Henry said.

"Maybe it's Louisiana," Rudy suggested.

"Or Los Angeles."

"Or Canada," Evers remarked. "You guys have more frigging letter problems than your buddy Artis."

"We're just trying things out, Evers," Henry said. "La could be an abbreviation you know, for Los Angeles."

"Or La Crosse. It's in Wisconsin, not far from Canada." Evers winked at Henry.

For about fifteen minutes, the men and Ruth Esther gathered around in a circle and pushed the sheets of paper over the tabletop, guessing at words and states and countries, putting together syllables and scribbling possibilities on paper napkins and the back of an envelope.

"Why in the world would your father make it so difficult?" Evers asked Ruth Esther.

"Probably to protect me, in case someone got all three clues when he wasn't supposed to." She shifted her eyes toward Artis; he was rubbing his hands together and staring at the table, oblivious to the reference.

"Oh."

"I got it," Rudy shouted. "It's Salt Lake City."

"How do you figure that? There's no—"

"Start with the 'Na,' then the 'Cl,' " Rudy said.

Ruth Esther lined up the papers. "Na Cl La ke U." She read the clues out loud. "I don't get it."

"Shit." Henry snapped his fingers.

" 'NaCl' is salt. It's the chemical symbol for salt. So you get 'Salt Lake U,' " Rudy said. "Salt Lake City, Utah."

"It could be," Evers agreed. He read the second row of clues. "One hundred, zero, arrow. One Thousand Arrow Street, maybe? Is there an Arrow Street in Salt Lake? The key looks like a bank key. The second part has to be a street or place."

"How about One Thousand South Street?" Henry offered. "The arrow points that way."

"All we need to do is check those addresses for a bank or storage building. I think we're hooked up."

"Salt Lake City," Pascal said. "Huh."

"That fits. It makes sense. It all works." Ruth Esther turned toward Evers and smiled. She reached out and squeezed his hand. "That's bound to be it. I'm happy. Pack your bags. I'm going to call Pauletta, have her meet us in Greensboro at the airport."

"Meet us for what?" Evers put his hands on his hips. "Was she serious about going with us? To Salt Lake City?"

"Yes," Ruth Esther told him. "Her goin' doesn't affect your deal at all."

"Why is she going?"

"Because she wants to, and because I invited her."

Evers caught Pascal's eye and bent over to put his cigarette out in an ashtray on the table.

"Whatever, Evers. The more the merrier. Does your lawyer enjoy dissolute living and sleeping until noon?"

"Fine with me, too," Henry assured Evers.

"Who keeps the key?" Evers demanded.

"Yeah, who keeps the key?" Artis asked. He was staring at the clues and the key. His hands were gripping the edge of the table.

"You can, if you like," Ruth Esther said to Evers.

"Are you going to stay awhile?" Rudy asked Ruth Esther. "There's plenty to drink and another quarter of pot."

"I will," Artis volunteered.

"Sure. For a while." Ruth Esther got up from the table and poured her beer into a glass. " I wonder what time it is in Utah? Is it two hours difference or three? Maybe we could find out tonight about this address, if that's what it is. I'll bet it's a bank address. It would make sense to talk to them and make sure we're in the right place before we fly out there."

"It occurs to me that we've done an awful lot for one evening," Pascal said. "Let's just concentrate on celebrating our success tonight. We don't want to take on too much at one time, get rushed and shoddy, that kind of thing. Calling *and* doing time-zone math might cause a little meltdown."

Ruth Esther drank some of her beer and looked at Pascal over the top of her glass. "I'm sorry. You're right; we should all enjoy ourselves. I'll look into the address tomorrow."

"Thanks. Given that our lives are—by choice—fairly uneventful, we like to stretch out our triumphs as long as possible." Pascal smiled and toasted Ruth Esther's glass with a coffee cup full of cheap scotch.

"I wonder why your father would travel so far—almost across the country—to hide the money?" Evers asked Ruth Esther. "Why not Hilton Head or Pensacola, or for that matter, somewhere nearby like Chapel Hill or High Point?"

"I think he probably felt that Salt Lake City was a good, safe place where our money would be properly watched over. And it's the kind of place you and Pascal had in mind, isn't it? Hot and entertainin' and far away, different from everything around here. I told you it would be a pretty big trip."

"Entertaining? Are you serious? Salt Lake City's the damn desert, and Mormons, and no coffee or tea, and the Osmonds. What a terrible spot," Evers said. "I wanted something a little swank and edgy. So much for a wobbly table outside a crumbling tropical hotel—or a few days in South America, dealing with venal sugar planters who're sweating circles in their suit jackets and mangling English through a couple of gold teeth. Shit. Maybe we can go to Las Vegas while we're there or—"

"Hold on, Evers." Henry leaned forward. "Salt Lake's a very solid area. I've been there . . . seen it . . . red dirt bluffs and sandstone and rock castles, stone arches, bands of pale colors—it looks like another planet out in the desert. And the Mormon Temple—this big Edgar Allan Poe deal right in the middle of the city. It's not like Old Master tripping, but with a bag of hooch and some mescal, the place can treat you right. Trust me, it's a good call."

"Sounds great to me," Pascal offered. "A perfect destination."

"We'll see," Evers grumbled.

"I'm so relieved to get this figured out. Thank you all. Thanks." Ruth Esther walked around the table and hugged all the men. "The only problem we still have is Lester Jackson. I know he's keeping an eye on Artis, followin' him. He's called me a couple of times, too. And I'm pretty sure he had someone watchin' Artis before we left to come down here. We went out the back of the lot, left out of the garage, so no one could track us. But the sooner we go, the better."

"Fuck Lester Jackson . . . whoever he is," Rudy exclaimed, drunk and high and sloppy.

Ruth Esther, Henry, Rudy, Pascal and Evers sat in the kitchen drinking and smoking pot out of the bong for several hours, until the morning sky started to arrive; spills and pushes of daylight began to come up over the trees and behind power lines and poles, and turned everything outside into silhouettes and cutouts. Artis had gulped down several beers and some of Pascal's liquor and had fallen asleep on the sofa after about an hour of hard, unbroken drinking. Pascal still owned a turntable, and just before the sun came into view, he took a Pink Floyd album out of a red Sealtest milk crate. He held the edges of the record between his middle fingers, fitted it onto the silver bump in the center of the turntable, lifted and lowered the needle with a little lever, and, when the music came on, closed the cracked plastic dust cover. Evers heard scratches and jumps in the music, and the needle skipped once.

"I love the idea of records, that you still have them. It's very nostalgic to hear songs played like this." Ruth Esther closed her eyes. She'd drunk several beers and tried the marijuana pipe one time. She coughed and her eyes watered after she inhaled the marijuana smoke.

"I have a great idea," Rudy said. "Let's use the shrine and all make a wish. Use the good mojo." He looked at the decanter; someone had set it on the counter beside the kitchen sink. The glass was clear, and most of the frost and ice had melted so it was possible to look right in on the white tears. "Henry won the lottery. It's lucky." Rudy waved his hand. "Turn the lights out in here."

"Let me start the record again," Pascal said. "This is a superior plan, Rudy. Excellent."

"This should be an especially good time since Ruth Esther's with us."

The four men put the tear shrine in the center of the kitchen table and sat down around it. Ruth Esther stood behind them, in front of a window; her two index fingers were pointed at the ceiling, as they had been when she talked to Evers for the first time.

"Should we hold hands or anything?" Henry asked.

"I don't think so. Just make a wish."

"Who's going to go first?"

"I will," Rudy volunteered.

"So what will it be?" Pascal lowered his voice.

"I would like a perfect, immaculate, Packard limousine."

"Good wish, Rudy. Good choice," Pascal said.

"How about you?" Rudy looked at Pascal.

Pascal put his hands behind his head and shut his eyes. "I want to be beatific."

"Henry?"

"I'll pass since I've already had my turn. I don't want to risk drawing too much juice off of the relic before everybody's been taken care of."

"Evers?"

"I'm not sure." Evers paused. "Are you going to make a wish, Ruth Esther?"

"I've been very blessed. I think it would be greedy of me to ask for anything else." She was still standing in front of the kitchen window. More and more light was coming in from behind her, around her head and shoulders; it was hard to see her features in the brightness. "I'm sort of like Henry, I guess."

"Are we embarrassing you?" Pascal asked. "I apologize if we are."

"I'm not embarrassed, no."

"So what is it, really?" Evers asked. "Why won't you tell us?"

"What it is—really—Judge Wheeling, is a plastic top and a little water in a cheap whiskey container. I thought Rudy was goin' to confirm that for you."

"I did, ma'am. I told him exactly what he had." Rudy laughed. "I told you right after you gave it to me, Evers."

"I'm sorry if we're embarrassing you," Pascal said again. "I didn't really think of all of the connections when we started making wishes."

"It's not like I reached down through her mouth into her duodenum and pulled out a fistful of dinner, Pascal. Ruth Esther invited me into the bathroom on my way to work and ended up handing me the sacred contents of the shrine at her car dealership."

"That doesn't mean—"

Ruth Esther interrupted Pascal. "So are you going to make a wish, Evers?"

"Yes."

"What is it?" Henry asked.

Evers stood up. "I wish my wife were dead. How's that? I wish that Jo Miller would drop dead."

"Good call, Evers. She deserves it." Pascal stood up beside his brother. "She does." He held his scotch in front of him, above his head. "Let's have a toast. To our wishes. To Salt Lake City. And a good trip."

FIVE

PASCAL AND EVERS WERE SITTING IN THE LOUNGE OF THE SALT Lake City Hilton, watching the World's Strongest Man competition on ESPN2, drinking some kind of pale ale with a picture of a bear and a mountain on the label, and enjoying a sterling combination of cold alcohol; gothic, arid culture; and local pot, a bacchanalian trifecta. It was almost ten-thirty at night, and they'd landed in Salt Lake City about four hours ago. Their suitcases and travel bags were all scattered on a bed in their room, still packed except for two shaving kits and two clean shirts.

A picture of James Brown appeared on the television, and then some footage of him prancing and chugging onstage, tucked into a sparkling blue suit that was too snug around his middle, his hair raised into a prom bouffant, spun and stacked the way he wore it a long time ago. Song titles started up the screen, and a voice-over explained how to order all of the Godfather of Soul's best music on two tapes or compact discs. James was sweating, and all the songs were fast and sounded alike, although the words were different. In a close-up right before the commercial ended, it occurred to Evers that the Godfather looked a lot like a cast member in *Planet of the Apes*, one of the later films. *Beneath the Planet of the Apes* or something like that. Evers took a drink from his ale. When he turned up the bottle, the bear flipped over on its back.

"You know," Pascal said, "James could get work as a sort of chubby swinger in one of those *Planet of the Apes* movies. *Planet of the Apes Dating Game,* maybe. *Beneath Club Med.* Look at him." Pascal pointed at the TV screen.

"That's unnatural."

"What is?" Pascal asked.

"What you just said." Evers looked at his brother.

"You've become an apologist for the Godfather of Soul?"

"No. But that's just what I was thinking," Evers said. "The same thing."

"What were you thinking?"

"That our man James Brown looks like a man in an ape outfit. *Planet of the Apes.* No shit, Pascal. That's just what I was thinking."

"It's the hair."

"It's probably the dope, too," Evers said, and Pascal laughed and nodded.

"You weren't really thinking that, were you?"

"Yeah, I was." Evers rocked back in his chair.

Pascal hit the table with his open hand. "Fuckin' A. Yeah."

"How about that."

"It's good to have James out of jail. And good to be here with my brother." Pascal looked around the bar for a moment. "You know, Henry was dead on target about this place. Did you see that temple and the metal seagulls? Metal birds. And then you get all the peaks and canyons and shadows out in this flat, parched plain that goes on forever. With some nice low-grade colors. This is some fine reefer backdrop, Evers. Just superb. And it seems so safe here; you can enjoy your buzz without looking over your shoulder all the time. Just a nice clean city."

"I miss Rudy and Henry—I think they'd enjoy this," Evers said.

The car doctor and Prince Hal had both decided to stay at Pascal's trailer while the brothers headed west. "All four of us can't be on the same plane—like the president and vice president, same kind of concerns," Henry had suggested. "And if something goes wrong, Dr. Rudy and I can help out from the East Coast. We'll be like the command center." So they'd rented several *Star Trek* movies and *Willy Wonka,* purchased a half gallon of gin and vowed to the brothers to always be by the phone, day and night.

"I miss them, too, Evers. They're good people."

Evers was tired, tired from the flight and the beer and the dope. He went to the bar and ordered a Miller and some tomato juice. While Evers was waiting for his drink, Pascal got up from his seat and started talking to two women who were about to walk out of the lounge. Pascal turned and looked back at Evers, then took a step closer to the women. One of the women was tall, almost as tall as Pascal, and she was smoking a skinny cigar. Her hair was all over the place, pulled up on top of her head and falling out in long curls on her forehead and on the back of her neck. Her friend was smaller, with short blond hair, small eyes and flawless teeth. Pascal waved Evers over. "Come and meet Marie Curie and Betty Ford, brother." The women smiled and flirted and the tall one held her cigar between her teeth and pushed back some of the hair in her face.

"Not tonight, Pascal. I have that sunrise meeting with the church elders, but you go ahead."

"My last name isn't Ford; your brother just made that up," the blonde said. "But you probably already knew that."

"You're sure?" Pascal asked.

"Come on—we're going to go to a party out in the desert." The blonde held up a wineglass.

"I can't." Evers watched the glass; the woman had it up in the air, over her head.

"You're positive?"

"I'd love to, but we've got to get cracking on Jedidiah's barn raising first thing in the morning. You folks go ahead and enjoy yourselves."

Pascal laughed, saluted his brother, put his arms around the two women and walked out of the bar, leaving his bear ale bottle on a table beside the entrance. Evers heard Pascal and the two women laughing and whooping after they were out of sight; the blonde had missed a step as they were leaving, and she had stumbled out with her glass still raised, the wine rocking and sloshing as she went.

Evers rode the elevator to his room, but he was restless and fidgety and he couldn't fall asleep. He lay on his bed weary and awake, listening to a quarrel through the wall and ice cubes bouncing into someone's plastic bucket out in the hall. He went back to the bar and drank two quick scotches and ordered some french fries. He started a third scotch and began to feel drunk, warm and weak and off balance.

Alcohol incites small passions, makes tiny ideas flourish, transforms tatters of sentiment into grand, full emotions, and sometimes causes stale reminiscences to spring to life with an almost supernatural vitality. Evers wanted to keep drinking, to get drunk, to poke around in the liquor and his memory. He thought of landing a trout, a lake at night, a bicycle trip through the mountains, a college sweetheart he should call who in his mind's eye seemed pretty and solid; and he thought about Jo Miller, the way she stood in the shower when she shaved her legs, and then he decided—a little idea that was becoming unruly—to call her on the phone, to talk to her, without really knowing why he was calling or, on a more practical level, whether she would want to be awakened late at night to talk to him.

Evers asked the bartender to let him use the phone beside the cash register. He was a good barkeep, slow and easy and generous with his pours and ice, and he took Evers' phone card and punched in the credit card information and then Jo Miller's number. He handed Evers the phone, and Evers took the receiver with both hands. He heard a ring, barely, and then, very distantly, another voice.

"Hello. Jo Miller?"

"Hello."

Evers strained to hear. "Where are you?" A drunken non sequitur. "I mean—"

"Evers? Is that you? Do you know what time it is?"

Evers said nothing, just listened. He imagined his wife standing in her panties at the wooden kitchen table, and he just gave the black receiver back to the bartender and walked out of the bar into the city, drunk and a stranger, his big ideas subdued.

When Evers returned to the hotel room, Pascal was lying on one of the beds, his front and face down, his shoulders, back, rear and legs uncovered and bare. He was a beautiful, handsome man, larger than Evers, and since the age of shared baths and cotton pajamas the brothers had developed a rapturous affection for each other. Never a fight, a sulk, a lie or hard word, never a hint of envy, anger or resentment— good companions, Evers and Pascal. They would go days without talking, and Evers didn't know his brother's birthday—it was in the fall sometime, during cool weather—but the two men had their own sequences, their own rituals, their own way of getting along.

The room smelled like pot and cigars, and the tall woman with loose hair was asleep in the bed with Pascal. Evers was worn out and drunk. He walked down the hall to Ruth Esther and Pauletta's room; no one came to the door when he knocked. He went back to his room, lay down on his bed on top of a clean shirt and beside their two suitcases. He left his pants on and finally was able to fall asleep, spinning for just a few moments after he closed his eyes.

Several hours later, Evers woke up and left his brother and the woman in bed and went outside. The sun was hot and strong; it seemed so close that it was reachable. Evers hadn't bathed, his clothes were wrinkled and he felt a little dark from drink and lack of sleep. He hadn't checked the time, did not know if it was morning or afternoon, only that it was daytime. He saw people eating eggs and ham and toast at outdoor tables and assumed it must be sometime before midday. He breathed in the desert air, baked and dry, felt it going down and pushing his lungs, traced it from his nose to his throat and into his chest. A horse-drawn carriage loaded with a family of tourists passed by on the street. The kids in the buggy—a boy and a girl—waved at Evers, and the horses' metal shoes clopped and danced on the asphalt.

Evers started walking toward the capitol, and he stopped at a kiosk to get some bottled water or a can of fruit juice. Just as he leaned down on a wooden counter under a canopy of newspapers, magazines and calendars, Evers heard a sound above all the business and shuffling of the city, a voice right outside his ear, sharp and trilled, like a bug scratching its legs and feelers together, and he choked with panic, felt his throat plug and his cheeks and feet tingle. "What in the world . . ." He spun around and looked up and down the sidewalk, across the street and at the windows above his head. The man in the kiosk took a step back, and Evers kept spinning and searching, jerking his head back and forth. "I thought I heard someone I knew, someone from home," Evers explained when he stopped turning in circles and looking at the sky. "Guess I was just hearing things." The vendor smiled, but didn't seem inclined to venture any farther out of his shell. Evers looked around some more and left without buying anything to drink.

He was sober now, awake, filled with adrenaline, and he decided to call Jo Miller again. He used a phone booth, a closet with a folding door, in the hotel's lobby. Strange how things bite and worry you and become immediate; Evers was committed to calling his wife from another time zone, thousands of miles away.

"Hello?" Jo Miller sounded disoriented and startled, although it couldn't have been too early in the morning in Durham.

"Jo Miller?"

"Yes."

"This is Evers."

"What the fuck do you want? Did you call here last night?"

"Good morning."

"Where are you?" Jo Miller wondered.

"I wanted to talk to you."

"About what?" she asked.

"About settling our problems."

"I don't have a problem, Evers."

"I mean money, divorce, property—you know, settling things."

"Did you call here earlier?"

"No," he lied. "I wanted to talk about all our marital affairs."

"Affairs, Evers? What's that—some heavy-handed humor?"

"Things. Not a great word choice. Sorry." Evers was trying to be civil. "It would just be better if we could get this behind us. We'd both have less discord and worry."

"What do you want?" Jo Miller seemed agitated.

"Let's do a separation agreement and get on with our lives."

"That presupposes we can agree."

"What do *you* want?" Evers noticed two fat, pale men in shorts passing through the hotel lobby. They were pink on the tops of their arms and legs, white everywhere else.

"Half of what you have."

"Half? Jesus. That's fair. You contributed nothing to my getting it, ridiculed me for being rich, live like some regal exile on a farm that I bought you and drive a fucking Lexus that I hate but bought because you whined incessantly. That's not enough, huh? You want my fucking money, too?"

"You should've thought about that when you bound me to a sign." Jo Miller's tone was restrained, the remark pointed enough without inflection.

"If you're so bitter and angry about the sign thing that you want to drag this on for a long time and refuse to throw me a crumb, then so be it." Evers almost yelled. He was mad.

"You don't want to push me on this, Evers."

"Why?" He shifted his weight.

"Your career and reputation won't stand it." Jo Miller raised her voice. "I'm sure that you'd look none too good in a divorce court. Your personal habits won't stand the scrutiny, Evers. And I'll do whatever's neccessary to make sure I'm treated fairly."

"Meaning?"

"Meaning, Evers, that I'll testify about how much dope you smoke, how you abhor minorities and how you treat women like concubines—good qualities for a judge, huh? And anything else I need to swear to, I will."

"Whether it's true or not?"

"Exactly." Jo Miller hesitated. "Whether it's true or not. Whatever it takes. And if I do have to compromise the truth, we both know that's not altogether unfair."

"I don't plan on leaving you destitute." An Asian woman with an oversize purse tapped on the glass door and gestured at Evers.

"Anything else, Evers? I don't think this is very productive, and Ellen and I are going to Siler City today. I'm buying a horse."

"A horse?"

"Horses, actually. Two."

"Where'd you get the money?"

"I took it out of your savings at the bank. They bent the rules a little since I'm your wife."

"Bitch." Evers leaned against the back of the booth.

"I took a little extra for living expenses, and since you and your white-trash brother are into travel and leisure, I thought maybe I'd take a trip as well. Mr. Falstaf and I."

"You had better put my money back. That's theft and forgery and everything else," Evers shouted.

"Just to keep you stewing in your juices, I thought you'd like to know that I called your office today and let it slip that I knew you were on vacation, not at home sick. Good-bye."

"You are a brutal cunt, Jo Miller." He had to squeeze past the woman waiting to use the phone. She had posted herself right outside the door to the phone booth and wouldn't budge. "Fuck you," Evers said as he pressed by her. Not knowing what language she spoke, he gave her the finger to emphasize his message.

Evers left the lobby and, after walking several blocks, found his brother outside an old hotel eating at a table with an umbrella. Pascal was wearing shorts and deck shoes, his hair wet and slicked back. He smelled like shampoo and had not shaved.

"Evers. Come and buy me my food and let me tell you about my night." Pascal smiled. "Did you come in last night?"

"For a while."

"Sit down."

Evers sat down in a metal chair with a hard back. "What a morning."

"Whatever. Mine's been pretty tolerable. The little while I've been up."

"Did you fuck that woman?" Evers asked.

"I can't remember, to be honest."

A waitress stopped at the table and filled Pascal's water glass. She asked Evers if he wanted to order, and he told her that he wasn't hungry.

"Good waitresses are heroes, Evers. Not heroines, heroes."

"Especially those who have to wear dresses without backs or work more than four tables at a time. You're right." Evers took a piece of toast from the edge of his brother's plate.

"What were we—oh, so—I got major-league drunk, and we sat around in the desert and looked at the lights in the distance and rolled in the sand. I don't think that I fucked her, though. What did you do?"

"Drank and sulked. Slept for a while."

"I'm sure it was very forceful sulking, huh?"

"Yeah. I tried to talk to Jo Miller."

"And?"

"It didn't work. I called her just a few minutes ago."

"Whatever." Pascal assumed that Evers had told him all he had wanted to tell, and didn't explore all of the possibilities.

"What am I going to do about Jo Miller?"

"Whatever, my brother."

"What the fuck, you know. Now I really want to sear her ass and see her suffer." He looked at Pascal. "I've always been a good provider and a decent person, don't you think?"

"Always have been to me."

Evers was hot, sweating. He bit the middle out of the toast. He chewed for a while, but the bread was dry and hard to swallow. "This is poison, Pascal. Arsenic. Jesus. I want to cry. Five years ago everything was so perfect. Now my marriage is gone, my wife is gone, my job's probably going to end up tied to this money and I'm in Utah with zero future plans and a stunted Moor with a drug habit. And I'm completely jumpy and about to lose my mind—just a minute ago, I thought I heard the cop who arrested Artis. When I was in West Virginia, I almost passed out in Pauletta's office, started thinking about power tools and imagined I was in a jungle."

"Don't give up, Evers."

"Let's start drinking and get some more dope—maybe we can find the same guy who sold us the bag yesterday. I'd like to be thick-tongued and happy, at least for a few hours."

Pascal smiled. "I may have to go visit my new friend. She said come by."

"I'm going to take a shower. Come up and talk to me while I'm getting ready." Evers finally swallowed the last of the food.

"Great. Then why don't you come with me, maybe hook up with her friend, the blond girl? And while we're on the way, maybe we could pick up some souvenirs for Henry and Rudy."

"You go ahead. I'm going to drink and smoke dope and see the city and sit in the hot sun and wallow in self-pity. And I don't want to tag along and weigh you down with the smoking Medusa."

"Whatever."

"I want to do some stultifying things. I want to walk around in the Delta Center. I want to ride a bus somewhere. I want to see some of those stone arches. I'm just going to get ripped and wander around in a stupor doing asinine things. You can be the coital carpetbagger— just spend a few hours drinking with me before you leave to cast your nets. Okay?"

"Okay." Pascal wiped his mouth with a cloth napkin.

"What time are we going to go to the bank?"

"Noon tomorrow. I don't know why we're waiting until tomorrow, though," Pascal said.

"What time is it now?"

"About nine-thirty."

"I wonder if that's all there is to this, just stopping by to collect a hundred thousand dollars. There has to be something else." Evers was beginning to feel light-headed.

"Whatever." Pascal picked up the check from the table and handed it to Evers. "I don't have any money. I'd be grateful if you'd cover breakfast for me; I was going to have to use a credit card."

Evers looked at the bill and reached into his pocket for his wallet. He noticed a man in an expensive shirt standing a few feet away from him and his brother. The man was looking at them with his head slanted at an odd angle. Pascal stood up from the table, and Evers took a five and several singles out of his billfold. The man took a step closer, so he was standing between Evers and Pascal.

"May we help you, sir?" Pascal smiled at the man. "Are you with the restaurant or something? Do you work here?"

"No."

"Do you know us?"

"Yes." The man offered Pascal his hand. "You are no doubt Pascal Wheeling, Judge Wheeling's older brother."

Evers was putting a water glass on top of the paper money and he hesitated, stopping the glass in the air for an instant before setting it on top of the cash.

Pascal shook the man's hand. "I'm going to guess that you didn't see us get off the shuttle at the airport with our name tags on. So how do you know us?" Pascal held the stranger's hand while he talked to him.

"May I sit down?"

Pascal looked at Evers. "Sure. Whatever."

The man sat down in a chair between the two brothers. He sat very straight; his back and arms were rigid, and his neck was stiff. "I've not had the pleasure of meeting either of you. But we have something in common."

"What's that?" Evers asked.

"I'm Lester Jackson." The man put his hands on the table.

"Damn." Pascal raised his eyebrows.

"Should I know you? I don't think your name sounds familiar," Evers said. His mouth twitched, and his eyes shifted toward Pascal.

"Evidently, it struck a chord with your brother."

Evers picked up his glass off the pile of money. "Pascal, do you know Mr. Jackson? Ever heard the name?"

Pascal's face was blank for a moment, then animated. "Of course. Everybody's heard of Reverend Jackson. He ran for president and does those great speeches with all the rhyme and rhythm and urban cadences. He's the Rainbow founder. Or was that Sammy Davis, Jr.? No. He was the Candyman. Right? You know, though, I've got to tell you this, and don't think I'm being a racist, but on TV you look like a black man. Even with a tan, it's apparent to me that you're white."

Evers looked down at the table. "I think the gentleman said his name was Lester Jackson, not Jesse Jackson."

"Oh." Pascal raised his eyebrows again. "I thought he said Jesse. Jesse Jackson. I misunderstood. I've never heard of a Lester Jackson."

Lester Jackson seemed amused. He smiled, and the corners of his eyes and the ends of his mouth wrinkled. He was not as tall as Pascal and Evers, and he was quite trim. He was wearing a green linen shirt, long pants and leather sandals; his hair was short and parted on the side. Evers guessed that Jackson was probably older than he, but not by much. Lester Jackson was a nice-looking man, neat, and very measured when he moved or spoke.

"I'm not here to cause either of you any problem," he pointed out.

"That's good news."

"I'd be grateful if you would sit down, Mr. Wheeling." Jackson was talking to Pascal. "I'd like a word with you and the judge, and your sort of looming above me makes me uncomfortable."

Pascal waited for a few seconds before sitting down on the edge of his chair.

"What is it that you want from us, Mr. Jackson?" Evers asked.

Jackson sighed. "My property. No more, no less. That's not an unreasonable request, is it?"

"My brother and I don't have anything that's yours, as far as I know. Maybe you've made a mistake."

Pascal raised his hand and waved it back and forth. "Perhaps this is my fault, Evers. It's the soap and shampoo, isn't it? From the room? I've already packed it, along with the shoe-shine mitt. You're with the hotel, aren't you, Reverend Jackson? Hotel security?"

"You're welcome to all the soap you can carry. I would like to recover my property from the Englishes, however."

"What property is that?"

"Ruth Esther and Artis have not told you the true depth of this endeavor, have they?" Jackson was still very formal, full of hard angles.

"What would that be, Mr. Jackson?"

"Do you know what you are looking for here?"

"That's an excellent question." Evers was beginning to feel the sun on his arms and the back of his neck.

"It is hard for me to believe that a judge would be involved in this type of . . . of scheme."

"Perhaps you could just tell us what you want," Pascal said. "All this bluffing and feinting and Boris-and-Natasha shit has already lost its appeal. What the fuck are you up to?"

"Fair enough. Mr. English and his sister have a significant amount of money which belongs to me. They stole it from me. I assume you are here to help them find or retrieve the money. I simply want what is mine returned to me."

"How did you get this money?" Evers asked Jackson.

"To be honest, some of it I gained in transactions that traditional commerce would frown upon. So be it. But I'm not really here for the money. I simply feel that I've been victimized by thieves, and I am upset by that."

"So what do you want?"

"Do you think that these two are here to pick up fifty thousand dollars each? Do you? Think about that. What are you getting out of this? Twenty thousand? Ten?"

"We're not getting anything." Evers shifted his weight in his chair. He picked up his glass, tapped the bottom with his fingers and knocked some ice free and into his mouth. "Pascal, check Mr. Jackson and see if he's recording this. Pat his clothes." Evers looked around at the people at other tables and on the sidewalk and street. Jackson seemed startled but held his hands up while Pascal felt up and down his arms and stomach. He got out of his seat, and Pascal checked his waist, legs and ankles. Several people stopped eating and watched what was going on.

Jackson sat down and put his hands back onto the table. "What possible reason would I have to record any of this? I will gladly give the two of you fifty thousand dollars. That certainly must be better than the division you're getting now."

"If you're not after the money," Evers said, "what is it you're here for?"

Jackson wiped a small line of sweat off his forehead with his finger. "Redemption. Principle. That's all."

"Somehow, I don't think that you came all the way to Utah to prove a point, Mr. Jackson."

"What offer would convince you to share your information with me?"

"I think we like things just as they are," Pascal said.

"I agree," Evers added.

"Certainly there must be something I can offer you."

"We just came for the trip, Mr. Jackson. Jack Kerouac, Ken Kesey, Hunter S. Thompson, Pascal and Evers Wheeling. We came for the flight and hotel and souvenirs and to see the big organ in the tabernacle. We came to get out of North Carolina. We came to travel. That means, of course, that you really can't give us anything. We're getting all we want."

"Well said, Evers." Pascal nodded his approval. "You could pay for our breakfast if you wanted to, Reverend Jackson. You could do that."

Several birds landed on a table next to Evers'. They began to jump and cry and pull at a piece of bacon.

"Judge Wheeling, I do not intend to be taken advantage of, and in that regard I am prepared to do whatever it takes to protect my interests. You and your brother are being sold short. If you are going to continue in this pursuit, might I suggest that you inquire of Ruth Esther the true nature of her search? I might further suggest that despite your fairly clumsy efforts to camouflage your trip here by using your friends' names, the North Carolina Bar Association could be easily convinced that you're involved in an unseemly mess; in fact, your attempt to conceal your identity only makes matters worse."

"Might I suggest that you get the fuck out of our faces," Pascal said, mimicking Jackson's careful speech.

"Mr. Jackson, you can tell anyone anything you want. You can tell the bar that we are here. It's a big city. Our travel agent screwed up our tickets; originally four of us were going and two canceled. The agent voided the wrong two tickets, and we didn't discover this until the day we left, a Sunday. It was easier simply to pick up our friends' driver's licenses, since I don't think we could've changed the tickets at the last moment. Who knows? And I'm sure you'll have an excellent explanation as to why you're here and what you're trying to find. In short, Mr. Jackson, no one wins a nuclear war." Evers glared at him.

"Gentleman, I'm not a bad person. I'm simply trying to recover my property. I certainly do not wish to alienate either of you."

"So what's everyone after besides the money?" Evers asked. "Perhaps we could be more helpful if we were enlightened."

"As I said, this entire trip is simply a matter of principle for me. The money is secondary."

"That's not what I asked you."

"Then I'm sorry that I am unable to provide you a satisfactory response." Jackson reached under the stack of money and took out Evers and Pascal's bill. "I would be honored, Pascal, to buy breakfast for the both of you. I'm staying at the Red Lion. Give me a call. Let me know if you change your mind or would like to propose some terms." He folded the check in half and stood up. "Enjoy the day. Salt Lake is an exciting city, isn't it?"

"What a fucking creep," Pascal said after Lester Jackson walked away.

"I wonder what's going on?"

"Whatever."

"Perhaps we should press Ruth Esther a bit."

"Good idea," Pascal agreed. "Should we tell her about Jackson?"

"Yeah, I think so."

When Evers and Pascal got back to the hotel, Pauletta and Artis were sitting on a sofa in the lobby, facing the entrance to the building. Evers saw Ruth Esther standing at the counter, talking to a clerk. Evers sat down next to Pauletta, very close to her, and put his arm on the cushion behind her.

"Good morning, Miss Qwai."

"Good morning," she answered. "Why are you putting your arm around me? Have you and your brother been drinking? Lost track of time and place? It's ten in the morning. This is a hotel lobby, a public place. I'm not your girlfriend."

"It's a conspiratorial gesture, not an amorous one." Evers lowered his voice. He looked past Pauletta at Artis, sitting on her other side. "I didn't plan on including Tiny Don Ho there in our conversation."

"I see."

"What conversation?" Artis asked.

"Here's our question." Evers ignored Artis and looked right at Pauletta. Pascal was standing in front of the sofa, his hands in his pockets. "What is it that we're here to find?" Evers almost whispered.

"Money. A hundred thousand dollars."

"I think there's more to it than that."

"Well, then, I guess you'll find out when we go to the bank, huh?"

"We have some bad news, Miss Qwai. Lester Jackson stopped by to break bread with us this morning. It's an extremely safe bet that his being here is not just coincidence. He bought our meals and sat there like Himmler on holiday, dropping hints about how we're being duped and fooled and misled. We have always figured we were, too, but we had hoped to find out what's behind door number two at least a few moments before the curtain's pulled back."

Pauletta tapped Artis on his leg. "Go tell your sister to come over here, please."

"How come? I ain't afraid of no Lester Jackson."

"Please, Artis. Go get her."

"Why?"

"Artis?"

"Okay."

Pauletta pivoted on the sofa so she was facing Evers. "We are here to get one hundred thousand dollars in cash. That was your deal. Assuming for the sake of argument that we're here to get a million dollars or a lost da Vinci manuscript, it shouldn't matter to you. We have an agreement. You get twenty-five thousand. Period. That's what was offered and what you accepted. If you don't like those terms anymore, leave. Or go cast your lot with Lester Jackson and spend the day wearing sunglasses, ducking behind newspapers and trailing us in a midsize rental." Pauletta had raised her voice and narrowed her eyes.

Pascal had been standing in front of his brother and Pauletta, listening. He crouched down next to Pauletta and rested his elbow on the arm of the sofa. "Listen, Pauletta, we're not trying to hold you guys up or get more money or anything. We just want to know what's going on. We didn't come here for the money; you know that. At least I didn't."

"Exactly." Pauletta's tone was more pleasant when she spoke to Pascal.

"So what is going on?"

"We're going to go to a bank and pick up the money if all goes well. That's about it."

Ruth Esther walked up behind Pascal. Artis was beside her. "So where did you see Lester, Judge Wheeling?" She looked down at Pascal. "Good morning, Pascal."

"Good morning." Pascal stood up. "He was about two or three blocks down, at a restaurant on the sidewalk."

"I see."

"We were just asking Pauletta why he would fly across the country for money he knows he won't get. Perhaps you could let us know why. There's got to be more to this than the money."

Ruth Esther put her index fingers together and pointed them toward the sky. Her hands were near her chest, her other fingers wrapped around one another. "For you . . . I thought you understood. There is more to it, there is the satisfaction of traveling here and finding the money. We talked about that. We did." Ruth Esther's voice was faint, almost too muted to hear.

"Pascal just told Pauletta—right before you and Artis came over here, in fact—that we're not trying to change the bargain or make new demands or renege or back out or screw anyone over. We just wanted to know why we're here and what's going on. You guys can keep the Holy Grail, okay?"

"You'll know a bunch more in a few minutes. I got directions from the hotel clerk. I called the bank and they said that we could come any time. We don't have to wait until tomorrow. We might as well go now. The man I talked to before we left North Carolina isn't working today, but he left word with another man. It's definitely the right bank—Wells Fargo—and right address. I'm gettin' excited."

"What about Lester? There's a pretty good chance that he'll be watching us, don't you think?"

"I thought about that," Ruth Esther said.

"So did I," Pauletta agreed. "Let me make this suggestion. We should all leave separately. One at a time, about five minutes apart. Those of us left behind can see if Lester's following or if there's anything unusual. We all meet at the same spot. I would suggest the temple in Temple Square, in front of the entrance. If Lester is following us, or if someone else is, we'll know it when we all get there, and it should be easy to lose him in the crowd. And if we can't lose him, at least we won't have led him to the money."

"What about the key?" Artis wanted to know. "Who keeps the key?"

"Judge Wheeling keeps the key, Artis. That's not open to debate. We can trust him." Pauletta turned to Ruth Esther and rolled her eyes.

"Which one is the temple?" Pascal asked. "The one with the dome or the one that looks like Notre Dame?"

"It's the big building, the tallest one," Ruth Esther answered.

"Oh, okay. Right. That's good. I wanted to see it up close before we left anyway."

"So we leave separately, all meet there and keep our eyes open along the way?" Evers repeated.

"Right."

"You know, that temple really has a lot going on all at once—arches and points and spires. And it's huge." Pascal took a piece of gum out of its wrapper, folded the stick in half and popped it into his mouth.

"It is very impressive," Ruth Esther agreed.

"Well, I understand there's always a crowd there," Pauletta said. "Everyone be careful and pay attention to what's happening."

"So we're going now?" Pascal asked.

"Yes."

Pascal touched Evers on the arm. "Could you give me some money for the cab? If it's okay with everyone, and not too far out of the way, I might stop and let my new friend know that our plans have changed. I've got her address."

Evers handed his brother two twenties and a ten. "Make sure you get to the meeting point, Pascal. Don't screw around."

"Who goes first?" Artis asked.

"Ruth Esther," Pauletta said. "She's the one most likely to be followed."

"See you at the entrance to the Mormon castle," Pascal said to Ruth Esther.

"Okay."

Evers was the last to leave the hotel. When he got out of his cab at Temple Square, he stopped on the curb and let an older man and woman pass in front of him. The man had a long gray beard and was dressed in a plain white shirt. He held on to the woman's arm right behind her elbow, and they shuffled along the sidewalk. The woman was wearing a simple silver cross around her neck, and she was stooped enough that the cross hung down and dangled in front of her without touching anything. Evers walked into the square and found everyone else standing in a group near the entrance to the temple. Pascal was reading a guidebook he'd bought from a vendor, and Ruth Esther had her back turned and was looking up at the tall, solemn building.

"No sign of Lester," Pauletta said when Evers walked up. "Everything looks clear. Did you see anything?"

"No. Nothing."

"Let's wait a few minutes and head to the bank."

"Okay."

Pascal looked up from his book. "We ought to come back, Evers. I like it here. It's cool and still, and I like all the trees that somebody took the trouble to plant. To put this thing up took a shitload of effort and commitment, huh? If we'd been the first settlers, there'd be some tents and pop-ups and a couple doublewides with the nice tin skirts around them."

Evers had expected that it would take several meetings, managers and garbled inquiries to get into the safe-deposit box. He was prepared to spend most of the day waiting in a stale lobby, looking over his shoulder, blowing into his palms, smoking cigarettes and staring at stories in *Reader's Digest*. Right before he opened the door to the bank, it occurred to him that he and Pascal and the three others must look like a carnival troupe, conspicuous and mismatched, and all of them, except Ruth Esther, as nervous and fidgety as a pack of teenagers in bulky army jackets trying to steal beer from a 7-Eleven. And then there was Artis, the crown jewel of the clan, a runty, sloppy ball of a person who drew stares and turned heads everywhere he went.

As it happened, the receptionist took the group to an older, gray-headed man in a small office. He looked at the key Evers handed him and took a ledger from his desk. He asked to see Ruth Esther's driver's license and had her sign two forms. The banker was wearing a tie but not a jacket, and he didn't seem very interested in Ruth Esther or her request. When she signed the last paper, he turned the book toward her so that she could read it. The entry for Box 303 listed three names: Ruth Esther English, Artis English and John English.

The banker led everyone into a drab room behind a door made out of bars. There were no tables or chairs in the room. A fluorescent light was hanging from the middle of the ceiling, and it had started to hum and flicker, so much so that it almost turned completely off several times. Evers followed the banker to Box 303, and the two men inserted their keys at the same time and opened the door to the deposit box. The container was black and about two feet long when Evers slid it out of the space in the wall. Evers could feel his palms sweating; he looked up at the light above his head and then at his brother. The box was made of metal, and it felt heavy when Evers got it completely removed from the cavity in the wall.

"Thank you," Ruth Esther said to the banker, who smiled and bowed and walked out of the room. He pushed the door shut when he left, and everyone was locked in, behind bars, looking at the box in Evers' hands.

Artis took several rushed, clumsy steps toward Evers and tried to open the box. He got both hands on it and pushed himself up on his toes, tugging and pulling and twisting as soon as he touched the lid. Pauletta and Pascal grabbed him, and Pascal jerked him away from Evers by the arm.

"Well, open it," Artis yelled. "Why are we waiting?" Pascal did not let go of Artis' arm. Artis looked like a recalcitrant child being dragged through a store aisle by his father. Pascal had his hand wrapped around Artis' wrist and was holding the tiny man so his feet just barely touched the floor.

Evers put one hand under the bottom of the box, opened the lid with the other hand and looked inside. Pauletta was standing next to him, peering over his shoulder. Lying in the box was an envelope, and the first thing Evers noticed was that it wasn't sealed; the flap was not stuck to the front. Underneath the envelope there were stacks of one hundred dollar bills wrapped in red rubber bands. Evers knelt down and set the box on the floor. He took out the envelope; it was yellow-ish, made of thick paper and addressed to Ruth Wright at a street in New York. The script on the envelope was elaborate; the letters had tails and curls, and every word was written with a flourish. There was no zip code and no return address.

Artis was trying to get his arm free, and Pascal had lifted him com-pletely off the ground. Artis' legs were kicking in the air, and he was screaming. Spit came out of his mouth. "Let me see. Let me go, Pascal. I want my fucking money. I want to see."

Ruth Esther turned to her brother, and for the first time since Evers had met her, she sounded angry. "Artis, be quiet." She took several steps toward him. "Quit kickin' your legs. Do you hear me?" She pointed at him with her index finger. "Do you?"

"I want to see in the box."

"The money's in the box, Artis. You'll get your money."

"Is it in there?" He stopped kicking, and Pascal lowered him back onto the floor. "Is it?"

"It is," Evers said. "The money's in the box, Artis. Calm down."

"Is there a letter for me, Judge Wheeling? An envelope with 'Ruth' written on it?" Ruth Esther was calm again.

Evers picked up the envelope and handed it to her. She reached for the letter and when she touched it, it occurred to Evers that some-thing important might be in it and he held on, clamped down on the envelope with his thumb.

"What is it, Judge Wheeling?" Ruth Esther asked.

"What's in here?" he asked.

"It's not any of your concern, and the letter is mine." Ruth Esther was polite.

"Perhaps—"

"I want to get my fucking money, Ruth Esther," Artis shouted. "Why are we talking about your stupid letter?"

"Artis, shut your mouth," Evers snapped. "If you don't shut the fuck up, I'm going to have Pascal drag you outside, kick your ass and go give all the money in this box to the Mormon kids over in Temple Square." He and Ruth Esther still had the envelope between them, each holding an end.

"Why don't you let me have the box," Pauletta suggested, "and your brother, Artis and I will divide the money and stack it into our bags. I'm sure Pascal will let you know if something is hidden in the box or if anything's out of the ordinary, Judge Wheeling. There would be the added advantage of gratifying Artis."

"Sure. Go ahead. That's a good idea."

Pauletta slid the box across the floor and opened her briefcase, and Pascal let go of Artis. Pascal had brought a gym bag with him, a nylon giveaway from *Sports Illustrated*, and Evers heard him pull open the zipper.

Ruth Esther took her hand off the letter. "You're welcome to look in the envelope and read anything in there. Go ahead. I just, you know, would like to have it back when you get through. It has . . . a lot of meaning to me." Ruth Esther put her head down. "Go ahead."

"It could have more clues. Or it could have—I don't know—it could be something valuable."

"In which case you're not entitled to it." Pauletta stopped counting and looked up from the stacks of money. "It's none of your business at all. Your money is right here. That's all you should be concerned with. Why are you being such a lout? Such an asshole? Why?"

The banker came to the door. He had put on a blue blazer. He looked through the bars at the people in the room and the money on the floor. "Is everything well?" he asked.

"Yes," Ruth Esther answered.

"Good. Very good. I thought I heard some noise."

"Noise?"

"Some loud talking," the banker replied.

"No, everything's fine."

"We have a private room, if you would like to go in there. A lot of people take the box from here to the private room. You wouldn't have to be on the floor that way. You're welcome to use the other area."

"We're almost through," Ruth Esther said. "Thank you, though."

"Certainly. Push this buzzer when you're ready to go, and I'll be back here to get you." He nodded and walked off.

Evers looked at the letter. "What do you think, Pascal?"

"Whatever. I'd give it to her. It's none of our business. Pauletta's right. Our money's here, and the box is empty. Even if it's a check for a million bucks, we're just being nosy."

Evers held the envelope close to his face and moved it back and forth in front of the fluorescent light. The envelope was heavy and there was a row of stamps stuck across most of the top border, so Evers couldn't tell what was inside. He took the envelope down from beneath the light and held it in both his hands. "Sorry," he said, then took out four sheets of paper that were as yellow and stiff as the envelope. The letter was written in the same elaborate script that was on the envelope; the writing was so full of tails and slants and words on top of each other that it was difficult to read. The letter began "Dear Ruth" and, on the first page, mentioned that the writer hoped she was doing well and that he'd just gotten back from a trip. Artis began screaming to leave and shaking the bars in the door, and Evers quickly looked up and down the rest of the pages. Everyone except Artis was staring at him. Ruth Esther's fingers were underneath her chin, church and steeple.

"Oh well," Evers said. "I'm sorry. Here." He handed the letter and envelope back to Ruth Esther. She opened her purse and dropped them in without putting them back together.

"No treasure map, Judge Wheeling?" Pauletta had finished placing three-quarters of the money into her briefcase. "No bearer bonds or gold coins?"

"I'm sorry. I apologize. I just wondered if there was more to this than the cash."

"That's not the point." Pauletta shook her head. "That's not the point at all. What were you going to do if you had found something valuable in the envelope?"

"I wasn't going to keep it. I told you that before I looked. I was just curious. I was going to . . . I would have given it to Ruth Esther. I would have."

"You had no right to look," Paulettta scolded Evers. "It was a classless and offensive thing to do. Base. Just common."

Artis had his hands on the bars of the door and his face stuck into a narrow gap, looking out. "When are we going to get out of here?" he demanded. His back was turned to everyone when he spoke.

"I'm sorry," Evers said again. "But I'm not going to keep apologiz-
ing over and over. And I might point out that I'm not the thief in the
room, okay? I'm not trying to be a prick—"

"I accept your apology, Judge Wheeling." Ruth Esther snapped her
purse shut. "It was nice of you to say that you're sorry." She paused.
"Are we ready to go?"

"I certainly am," Pascal said. He looked at Evers. "I've got our
money." He held up the gym bag. "Or at least we're pretty close. It's
hard to be completely precise in here with so little time. Pauletta and
I can finish when we get back."

"You'll have to use the buzzer, Artis. Shaking the bars and looking out won't open the door. Remember what the man told us?"
Ruth Esther pointed at the button beside the door, and he crabbed
over to it and pushed it in, held it for several seconds without letting go.

The banker returned with another document for Ruth Esther to
sign, then let everyone out of the room. When Evers walked out of
the bank onto the street, it had gotten hotter, and a car and pickup
had wrecked at an intersection a block away. Traffic was stopped, and
two men were talking to the police. One of the men was holding
his stomach, standing near an old Volkswagen Beetle with a broken
windshield.

"Let's walk a couple streets over and catch a cab," Pascal said.
Everyone glanced at the police and the accident and kept moving,
Pauletta in front, Artis behind her. The two women and Artis got into
a cab together, and Pascal and Evers flagged another, jumped in before
the car completely pulled to the curb. When he got inside, Evers
rolled both of the back windows all the way down and undid his shirt
until only the last button was still fastened. There was a song on the
radio, and Pascal started humming and rocking his head even though
he didn't know the lyrics. "So far, so good," he said.

"Yeah."

"This was pretty entertaining, the way it worked out."

"So far," Evers agreed.

The cab pulled off and rushed in behind a small Chevrolet—drove
right up to the rear of the car—before veering left to accelerate and
speed by. Evers crossed his ankles in front of him and turned his face
toward the wind blowing in through the window. He smelled
exhaust, dry air and the city's roasted exhalations, felt every dip and
shake in the road. Pascal was bobbing and swaying, listening to a song
he'd never heard before. The driver was a dark-skinned man who
tried to talk to the brothers in broken English, questions about where

they were from and did they like the Dallas Cowboys, but Pascal and Evers didn't have much to say.

As soon as Evers got out of the cab at the hotel, he saw Lester Jackson standing on the sidewalk, near the entrance to the lobby. He and Pascal walked past, and Jackson barely acknowledged them, just shifted his eyes in their direction when they got close. They stopped at the threshold of the lobby, held the doors open and looked out at Lester Jackson. Evers felt the cool hotel air and the heat from outside at the same time, cold and hot curling around each other, bumping and butting.

"I trust that you recovered my property," Jackson said to Ruth Esther when she started heading into the building, several yards behind Evers and Pascal. Artis was in front of her and Pauletta beside her, carrying their share of the money in her briefcase.

Pascal pushed the door open a little farther, and caught it on his hip and shoulder so his hands were free.

"Mr. Jackson, I have *my* property. Do you understand that? I cannot imagine why you decided to come here. You are an evil, greedy man."

"I would gladly settle for my currency, the letter and some other modest payment. That's the very short end of the bargain; you may keep the rest."

"You're a horrible man. You sell drugs. You gave Artis drugs and made him steal and turn on his family. You'll never get anything from me. Never. Maybe this will teach you a lesson."

"I will get my money, Miss English." Jackson took a step closer to Ruth Esther, and Evers noticed another man separate himself from a group across the street and begin walking toward them. The man had bright white skin and curly black hair, but he was behind Artis and the women, and Evers couldn't really see his features. A boy a few yards down the street—skinny, without a shirt, wearing sunglasses— started up a motor scooter.

Evers jammed his hand against his brother's back and pressed, but Pascal had already started outside again, toward Ruth Esther, so Evers' hand never touched much, just the tail of Pascal's shirt and, for an instant, the small of his back. The shirt was wet with sweat. Lester Jackson had kept walking until he was in front of Ruth Esther and Pauletta, just a few feet away from them. The milky-white man crossed the street; Evers saw him wipe his forehead in the crook of his arm. He searched the street behind the man to see if anyone was along with him, and when he looked back, Jackson had crowded in as far as he could, was directly in front of Ruth Esther and Pauletta, blocking their way. "Certainly, we can reach some agreement."

"Mr. Jackson, fuck off." Pauletta pointed at Lester Jackson. Artis glanced up at Jackson and moved closer to his sister. Artis' head did not reach Ruth Esther's shoulder.

The man from across the street was right behind Pauletta now, and the skinny boy was up on his toes, striding the scooter, revving the engine, twisting the throttle, angling forward. Lester pointed back at Pauletta, and the white man took his last step and reached for her briefcase. She sensed him behind her, turned toward him just a little and moved her feet and twisted her shoulders. Pascal got his hand on the case at about the same time as the pale thief, and for an instant all three of them were holding on to Pauletta's briefcase. Pascal put his other hand on the handle and pulled, and the case came out of Pauletta's grip. Pascal had been crouched, bending down, stretching for the briefcase, and when it flew free, he tumbled backward, fell onto his rear.

As soon as the men and Pauletta began wrestling with the brief-case, Artis had run away, bolting halfway down the block, where he stopped and looked back, his mouth opening and closing and his arms hanging down straight and flaccid. Evers stepped between Ruth Esther and Lester Jackson, put his hand on her shoulder and shoved her toward the door of the hotel. The bleached man turned right and disappeared into a gang of people who had come out of a store and restaurant; they all looked alike—black hair, colorless skin and white shirts. The group of men hurried off down the sidewalk, and the boy on the scooter rode by, watching everybody, his bike popping and sputtering when he took his hand off the throttle and stopped the gas. Pascal stood up and joined Evers in front of Lester Jackson.

"Thieves and pickpockets are rarely a problem in this city. It's certainly fortunate that you gentlemen were here to help these ladies," Jackson said. He was standing so close that Evers really couldn't see him, just some of his face and nose and eyebrows smeared together.

"Right," Evers said.

The three men stood in a tense knot for a little while longer, then Pascal and Evers turned and walked off.

"Be careful, gentlemen," Jackson yelled when the brothers went into the lobby. He hadn't moved, was still thin-lipped and stiff in the middle of the sidewalk, simmering under the hot sun, people walking around him on either side.

"Thank you both. Thanks," Ruth Esther said once everyone was inside the hotel, standing in the lobby. She was holding on to her purse with both hands.

"You're welcome," Evers said. He was breathing hard.

"You're welcome," Pascal echoed. He handed Pauletta her briefcase.

"Yes, thank you." Pauletta put her hand on Evers' shoulder. "That was good of you. I had no idea what was happening."

"Maybe my positive deed will offset some of my earlier bad conduct and put me back in good standing with you."

"I had already forgiven you," Ruth Esther said. "Remember?"

"I guess Lester just waited for us to come back. Saved himself some cab fare." One of Pascal's shirtsleeves had rolled down during the scuffle, and he was pushing it back up while he spoke.

"I guess so." Ruth Esther was the only one who didn't seem unsettled.

Pauletta wiped something out of the corner of her eye. "I figured that he'd try to follow us. But he couldn't have known for sure that we were bringing the money back here. I'm sorry; I should've thought this through a little more. He's either lucky or shrewd—I'm not sure which."

"Don't worry about it," Pascal said. "Nothing bad came out of it. We still have the cash."

"So what's so important about the letter?" Evers asked.

"I told you it means a lot to me. It's a big part of my family. Lester is just so spiteful and angry that he wants it. He'd probably tear it up or throw it away or somethin'. Lester just wants money; he doesn't care about anything else. He's just runnin' his mouth."

"I believe that, don't you, Pascal? For a while things weren't making sense, but now I understand." Evers frowned. "I really don't see why you won't tell us what's going on. Especially now."

"You are a nosy man, Judge Wheeling, like an old apartment crone, all binoculars and police scanners, got your face stuck in the window all day. Damn." Pauletta pushed her briefcase underneath her arm.

"It would seem that you just emptied out the goodwill reservoir, Evers," Pascal said.

"So it seems, so it seems."

When evening came, Pascal wanted to celebrate. He'd smoked a joint, had a few drinks and called Rudy and Henry back in North Carolina. "The wombat is on the nest," he told them, and they all cheered and laughed and hooted on the phone when Pascal mentioned the coded signal that things had worked out.

Evers and Pauletta were concerned about leaving the money in their rooms, and finally they agreed that Pascal and Artis would stay behind with the cash while the others went to eat, and that Pascal could go out and drink and defile himself when everyone else had finished dinner and come back to the hotel.

Evers ate some chicken and a salad in a small restaurant, but he was still jittery six hours after his standoff with Lester Jackson, and his food did not sit well in his stomach. It took about an hour to eat, and when Evers and Pauletta walked back into the hotel, they spotted Pascal sitting at a table in the hotel bar, drinking a beer.

He saw them coming and stood up. "Evers, come here." Pascal took several strides toward his brother and Pauletta, almost ran. "Hurry up."

"What? What's up?" Evers walked into the bar in front of Pauletta.

"I have bad news."

"Shit."

"What?" asked Pauletta. Pascal had her by the arm and was leading her back to his table, where he'd left an empty bottle, a napkin and a glass with a little beer in the bottom.

"Shit," Evers said again. "What is it?" He was following along, pacing his brother and Pauletta.

"Our money's gone, Evers."

"Gone? Where?"

"Yours is, too, Pauletta. I don't know that for sure, but it's a pretty good bet."

"Where is it?" Evers repeated. "Gone? What happened?" He reached for a chair and sat down without thinking about what he was doing.

Pascal knelt down next to him and looked up at Pauletta; she sat down across from Evers. "What are you talking about?" she asked.

Pascal's knee was touching the floor. "Artis fucking took it. He—"

"Artis? How could Artis take anything?" Pauletta demanded.

Pascal put his hand on her leg. "Wait a minute. Let me finish. Let me tell you. He was with someone, another man."

"Who?"

"I don't know. I've never seen him before." Pascal's voice was steady. He reached up and took his glass of beer off the table.

"So it wasn't Jackson, it wasn't him? It wasn't Lester Jackson?" Evers asked.

"No. Absolutely not."

"Maybe he was working for Lester," Pauletta offered.

"Whatever. I couldn't tell you."

Evers winced. "Was it one of the guys from today? The guys on the street?"

"No. This guy didn't look like that." Pascal had his glass in his hand but wasn't drinking.

"How did they get the money, Pascal? How?"

"Artis came to the door and knocked and said he wanted to watch TV and that the one in his room wouldn't work. To tell you the truth, the first thing that went through my mind was that he was too stupid to figure out how to turn it on. He's completely worthless. So I looked through the peephole, I see Artis standing there in a pair of shorts, no shirt, no shoes, and I figured I'd let him in for a moment, but I sure as shit do not want to spend an hour with him in our room. Basically, I was just going to tell him how to use the remote and send him on his way."

"So Artis took our money, Pascal?" Evers' mouth stayed open when he finished the sentence. "Unbelievable."

"Jesus, Evers. Let me finish."

A waiter came by the table. Pauletta ordered a beer, and Pascal stood up and sat down in a chair between her and his brother.

"Go on," Evers said before the waiter had finished writing on Pascal's tab and was still standing at their table.

"I opened the door to let him in and when I did, when I opened the door, another guy in a suit comes in right behind him. You know, you can see pretty well out into the hall through the peephole, and this guy wasn't in the hall to begin with. He opened the door to the room across from ours and came running in behind Artis." Pascal swished the beer in his glass. "I should've ordered another beer. When he comes back, tell him I want another beer."

"Fuck, Pascal, you were probably messed up when this happened," Evers said. "That's half the problem."

"There's no need to get prissy about it, Evers. Or mad at me. What happened, happened. I can't change it, get in the way-back machine or something. And I had smoked some dope, but so what? This would've happened regardless of what I was doing, and it was my money, too."

"He has a point," Pauletta noted. "And if you hadn't interrupted every five seconds, we would probably know what happened by now."

"I'm not sure it matters a lot how long it takes to get to the end of this story, Pauletta."

"Listen. Calm down, Evers. Okay? I'm sorry."

Evers shrugged. "What did the man with Artis look like? You're sure it wasn't Jackson? If you were stoned, you might not have recognized him. Remember the time Henry and I came to see you and you sat there for an hour thinking that Henry was our cousin? It could've been Lester, especially if it happened quickly."

"I had smoked a little, but, shit, Evers, it takes more than a few joints to bother me, you know that." The waiter came back with a Budweiser for Pauletta, and Pascal asked for another beer and a clean glass. "This man was . . . weird-looking, really strange. Like a monkey. He looked like a monkey. A monkey with a beard. An Amish monkey. That's it."

Evers' mouth hung open again. "A monkey?"

"Yeah."

"The beard was just like his hair—same color, same length, a circle around his head?"

"Right. Exactly." The waiter brought Pascal his beer and set it on the table. Pascal twisted off the top and forgot about the glass he'd asked for, left it sitting on the table and never used it.

"Someone you know, Judge Wheeling?" Pauletta asked.

"Probably. I think." Evers picked up his brother's beer and took a drink out of the bottle. "Did he have a funny voice, really high, locust, cicada, cricket range?"

"That's him," Pascal said.

"Shit."

"Who is it?" Pauletta pulled her chair closer to the table.

"Un-fucking-believable." Evers drank some more of Pascal's beer.

"Who is this guy, Evers?" Pascal asked.

"It sounds a lot like Warren Dillon. He's a police officer, in Winston-Salem. Shit. Remember this morning, when I told you I was so whacked out that I thought I was hearing things? I stopped to buy something to drink at one of those sidewalk booths, and I thought I heard his voice. I think he was trying to hail a cab."

"Why would he be here?"

"You'll love this. He's the cop who arrested Artis on the cocaine charge. He's also the cop who stepped all over his dick at trial and made it ridiculously easy for Artis to walk."

"Damn." Pascal laughed. "We've been hoodwinked by Artis and Sasquatch." He laughed some more. "By two fucking monkeys. Sub-humans. Marginal primates."

"You don't think he's after us, do you?" Pauletta asked Evers.

"Hardly. I doubt he'd be robbing people if he were here on legitimate police business."

"True." Pauletta was quiet for a moment, thinking. She scratched off part of the label on her beer. "That makes sense; you're probably right. I guess that's the good news, huh?"

"So why did you give those two idiots our money, Pascal?"

"Because the tall, bearded one had a gun. That's easy."

"A gun?" Pauletta seemed surprised.

"Yeah. Evers' policeman friend walked right through the door and pointed it at me."

"No shit?"

"And when he pointed it at me, I told him where the money was. They would've found it anyway."

"Did they say anything?"

"Not really."

"I'm sorry about this, Evers. But you know, when I looked, it was just Artis, and I did look before I let him in. And he couldn't have done anything to me by himself. The other guy just came out of the room across the hall so quickly, and I wasn't going to test his resolve, you know? When I saw the gun, I gave him the money. Sorry."

"I don't blame you for that, not at all," Evers said.

"I don't either," Pauletta agreed.

"I wonder . . . " Evers stopped. "Where's Ruth Esther? You didn't see her, did you, Pascal?"

"Nope. She left with you guys, remember?"

"She wasn't hungry, though. Pauletta and I ate by ourselves. She said she was going to walk around the city some."

Pauletta's expression changed, her face tightened. "I would hope you don't think she participated in this." She was looking at Evers, hard.

"I don't know what to think."

"You still have your bag of stones, don't you, Evers?" Pascal asked.

"Yes. I do."

"So why would she take your money? Our money? We're protected either way." Pascal slid forward in his chair.

"And the rest of the money belongs to Artis and to Ruth Esther," Pauletta pointed out. "It's hard to steal from yourself."

"What about you, Pauletta?" Pascal wondered.

"None of the money belonged to me."

"So Artis basically took his fifty thousand, stole his sister's twenty-five and our twenty-five. I wonder if he knew that Ruth Esther gave Evers the gems to hold?"

"I doubt it," Pauletta said. "But I'm sure he wouldn't have cared."

"What if the gems aren't real?"

"Didn't you have them appraised?" Pauletta asked Evers. "I gave them to you well in advance so you could. And I know they're genuine, that much I can promise you—I helped buy them, remember? I am—"

"I'm sure they're real and worth what you say," Pascal interrupted Pauletta. "I don't doubt that."

Evers' head started to ache. "If the stones are fake, then we're out twenty-five grand."

Pauletta folded her arms across her chest. "If the stones were fake, why the fuck would Ruth Esther even bother to bring you out here? Why would she come to your brother's home, open the clues, meet you at the airport and fly to *Utah,* and then have her brother take your pitiful little twenty-five thousand? Once she got Artis out of jail, she didn't need to see you again. She didn't have to do a damn thing for you the instant Artis walked out of court. You're the most paranoid, pessimistic, faithless man I have ever met. And I resent your questioning my word."

"I'm prudent and healthily skeptical. It's my personality type that got us off the flat-world theory and discredited the medicinal use of leeches. As for your word, I believe what you're telling me; it's just that you're not a jeweler."

"You are a blindly cynical man. You should be ashamed of yourself." Pauletta picked up her beer. "You really should," she said after she had drunk some of the beer and set her glass down.

Pauletta, Evers and Pascal stayed at the table drinking and smoking and talking for another hour or so, until Ruth Esther came into the lobby. She waved at them and walked into the bar. Before she could sit down, Evers explained that Artis had stolen their money and that he was most likely gone.

"Did he really? Did he?" Ruth Esther was still standing. She put her hand over her mouth.

"He did," Pascal said. "He and another man."

"He took your money and our money, too?" Ruth Esther asked.

"Yes."

"Who helped him? You know he had to have help." Ruth Esther caught the top of a chair and slumped forward, held herself up with her palms and straight arms.

"Judge Wheeling thinks it was the police officer—Dillon? Is that his name?—who arrested Artis." Pauletta cut her eyes at Evers. "And, of course, the judge has been curious as to your whereabouts."

"Oh my."

"Yeah."

Ruth Esther sat down. "I am so sorry. No one was hurt, though, right?"

"Right," said Pascal.

"Well, certainly you've done your part, Judge Wheeling. You should just hold on to your payment from Pauletta." Ruth Esther put her hands over her face and dragged them down until just the tips of her fingers were touching her chin. "I am so disappointed in Artis. And this policeman, what's he doing here taking our money?"

"Imagine that," Pauletta sneered. "A cop on the take."

The four of them sat there, quiet and thinking, sipping beer, looking around, smoking cigarettes, watching the waiters, the door and people at other tables, until Pascal started to grin and then laughed. Evers smiled some, too.

"Who the fuck knows?" Pascal said, and started laughing harder. "What a funhouse trip. You were right, Ruth Esther—we travel across the country with strangers to a dandy city with the biggest lake I've ever seen, find a treasure, get stung by two half-wits, end up without our money and still aren't sure what happened." Pascal picked up his cigarette from an ashtray.

"You have a good attitude, Pascal. Thank you." Ruth Esther touched the top of his hand.

"And we still have another day here, correct? We were supposed to go to the bank tomorrow, then leave the next day, right?"

"Yes." Pauletta nodded.

"Great. Then I guess we just need to enjoy the rest of our road trip, chew what's left of the party feast right down to the bone."

"I agree," said Pauletta. She held up her glass. "To the trip."

"I'm glad everyone is so damned ebullient," Evers said. He sat back in his chair.

"I think things will work out for you," Ruth Esther said.

"I do, too," Pauletta volunteered. "And I couldn't help but notice that you were smiling a little bit a moment ago. That's good. Everything will be fine."

"I hope so. It's nice of you both to say that." Evers held up his glass, and everyone toasted and drank. Pascal left soon afterward, headed back to the desert, looking for the woman with wild hair. Evers went to the front desk and asked about a bus tour and the This Is The Place Monument; he brought some flyers and brochures back to the table.

About twenty minutes after Pascal left, Pauletta noticed something peculiar about one of the waiters, noticed that he had come out of the kitchen empty-handed, turned left toward the guest elevators and never returned to the bar or restaurant. She whispered several sentences to Ruth Esther, and both women put their purses in their laps and covered them with their hands. She told Evers what she'd seen, and about ten minutes later the man reappeared. All of them, at just about the same time, recognized Lester Jackson goose-stepping back to the kitchen in a tuxedo shirt and black pants; his hair was dyed black, and he had a mustache glued to his lip.

Evers shouted at him just as he went through the door. "Lester. Hey, Lester! Couple more Buds and some bar nuts, please."

Lester looked over his shoulder before the doors swung shut, but he didn't stop or come back out.

"What a fucking dunce," Evers said. "Does he think we'd just leave the money in our rooms unattended?"

Pauletta and Ruth Esther started laughing. "Oh, goodness," Ruth Esther said. She and Pauletta laughed harder, until they both were gasping and sputtering and wiping their eyes. "He looked like Charlie Chaplin!" Ruth Esther barely got the words out.

"Actually, I thought he looked sort of like Johnny Depp in that stupid Don Juan movie," Evers said. "And you know—you just know—that he has trashed our rooms, gone through everything we own and thrown our clothes all over the place. One more pain in the ass, huh? But I'm glad you guys think this is all such a riot."

Evers could not decide what to do with Pascal's clothes and luggage, whether he should take them with him or leave them at the hotel. Since leaving everyone to go to the desert two days before, Pascal had not returned to the hotel, nor had he called. Evers finally decided to take Pascal's belongings with him. Evers himself had barely unpacked; he had worn the same shorts every day, most of the time with the same shirt, wandering around impaired and ratty.

Pascal was not at the airport thirty minutes before time to leave, and Evers began to worry. He called the hotel, but there was no word from Pascal. Evers finally saw his brother after about half the passengers had been loaded onto the plane; Ruth Esther and Pauletta had waited with him until their seats were called to board, leaving every few minutes to check the bar and other gates. Pascal was wearing shorts and cheap plastic flip-flops he'd bought in Salt Lake, and his eyes were red.

He walked up to Evers but didn't sit down. "I forgot what time we were going to leave. Shit."

Evers grinned. "Today. Now."

"I tried calling all morning, and they said the fucking room phone was out of order. How about that?"

"Yeah?"

"Well, I figured it was time to go when they said you'd checked out." Pascal rubbed his hand through his hair.

"I'm glad you're back."

"I had a good time," Pascal said. "I hope you didn't get worried about me."

"I knew you were fine."

Pascal spent a good portion of the flight back to the East asleep under a fuzzy yellow blanket; Ruth Esther and Pauletta put on headphones and watched the movie. When dinner came, Evers didn't wake Pascal to let him know that it was being served. Cheese, butter, hard rolls and grapes. Evers drove his plastic fork into the top of the roll and said, "Now the bread is sporting a turret." The man to his right looked at him, then at the bread and fork. Evers realized that the statement was strange, and that the passenger beside him probably thought that he was crazy or drunk.

The plane landed in Atlanta, and while Pascal and Evers were walking toward their connecting flight to Greensboro, Evers told his brother that he didn't like the airport, started rambling and hawing, shaking his head as they went along.

"What the fuck is wrong with you, Evers?" Pascal was looking at a blond woman in front of them. "You're just going on about nothing."

"I don't know. Sorry. I have a weird feeling."

"Whatever."

"Shit. What do we do now that we're back?" Evers asked.

"I don't know. What I've always done. Pretend I'm a pro bowler, a blithe vagabond, a swallowtail on a dandelion breeze."

"Things are not good. I've fucked up. I've been fucked up, and going to Utah didn't change a whole lot. Jo Miller is still screwing a stranger, and my life is in total upheaval. Pascal, I don't know if I can get away from this. I can't really live like you, be like you, just let things go. And I tried, I did—I tried for the last couple of days."

"But you didn't fuck anybody while we were gone. Good for you. That'll help you with the gods."

"Did you sleep with the cigar woman?"

"You know I did. Of course." Pascal kept walking, looking ahead. "I'd fuck just about anybody."

"How about Jo Miller?" Evers asked.

"Sure. I think she's attractive."

Evers looked at his brother. "Have you fucked my wife?"

"Does it matter?"

"Of course." Evers suddenly had a dark, numb feeling. "Of course it does."

"Well, I haven't."

Evers slowed down but didn't stop walking. "You're lying. I can tell. You are." He felt sick and thought about sitting down.

"What does it matter?" Pascal asked.

"It *does* matter. You're lying, aren't you?"

"No, I'm not."

"Swear it. Swear you haven't."

"I swear," Pascal said.

"You're fucking lying. You've never lied to me before, and now you're lying."

"Whatever."

"Jesus."

"Tell me about the sinister airport again." Pascal tried to change the subject.

"I can tell you're not being honest." Evers shook his head. He felt wasted, tired. "I guess it doesn't make much difference anyway. Not now." He looked at his brother. "I wonder if she did it just to irritate me?"

"You're my brother, Evers, okay? She's your wife."

"I can't believe you fucked my wife. I can't believe you would lie to me. Jo Miller has managed to poison and fuck up about everything in my life, and this is the coup de grâce."

"Evers, I don't know why you think I slept with Jo Miller. You're a good brother; I wouldn't do anything to cross us up."

Evers didn't say anything.

Pauletta and Ruth Esther caught up with the brothers at the Greensboro gate, and Ruth Esther offered Evers a Tums tablet. "You look a little peaked," she pointed out.

He took one of the tablets and crunched it up in his back teeth. "I may have to go to the toilet before we get on the plane. I'm just about ready to puke."

"Let's get aboard, Evers," Pascal said. "Come on. You can just use the john there. Let's go home."

SIX

ONCE HE GOT BACK FROM UTAH, ON A THURSDAY, EVERS WENT to see his wife. While he was driving to Durham down Interstate 40, Evers thought about Jo Miller, and how the two of them had been separated—a sad, sorry and unexpected division he was still unaccustomed to. About ten miles away from her farm, in the middle of familiar turns and looking out at signs, barns, stores and ponds he knew by heart, Evers thought about reconciliation, about putting this behind them, and then he got angry and boiled and seethed again, hurt bleeding into pride around the edges.

When Evers walked into the house, Jo Miller was sitting in the kitchen reading a hardback book. She was in a small, straight wooden chair, and one of her cats—Steinem, the oldest—was sleeping on a rug in front of her. Jo Miller looked up at Evers and smiled some. "Hello, Evers." He'd called her before he left Norton, told her that he wanted to ride down for a visit, asked about her family and if she'd finished painting the guest bedroom.

"Hi."

"You look good." She sounded sincere.

"Thanks."

"You're welcome."

"Think we could talk again for a minute or so?" Evers was nervous. He felt dizzy and flushed, and could taste the spit in his mouth.

"Sure." Jo Miller put her book down.

"I'm sorry things have deteriorated so much," Evers said.

"So am I. I don't want us to get to the point we got to when you called from Utah. I'm sorry; some of that was my fault." She didn't look at Evers.

"I'm sorry as well. I shouldn't have blown up like I did."

Jo Miller paused. "Certainly you don't think I've been a bad wife, or that I shouldn't be treated fairly."

"What I wish is that our marriage had worked out and . . . do you think if I tried . . . that maybe we could get back together?"

She didn't say anything.

"Jo?"

"Evers, I'm not trying to be cold or hard or a bitch, but I don't think so. I don't want us to be as bad as we were when this all started. I want us to be decent to each other, but I'm happier now than I've been in two years. Too much time and space wore us down."

"So, I mean . . . " Evers closed his eyes for a few seconds, and everything went black.

"I'm not sure what else to say."

"So you're choosing that fucking farmer over me?" Evers' voice was low; he bit his lip when he finished talking.

"It's not a question of choosing you or him."

Evers noticed that Jo Miller looked thin. She coughed when she finished speaking, put her head down and her hands over her mouth. "Are you okay?" he asked.

"Yeah. It's just my seasonal cold; they hang around for a while."

"Are you sure about us, Jo Miller? This is what you want to do?"

"I'm sure."

Evers hesitated, looked at a bowl of apples on the counter and fingered the plastic lighter in his pocket. "Well, why can't we put this behind us, at least? Work something out?"

"I want to," she said.

"Do you still want half of what I own?"

"I do, Evers. I do. And I think that I'm entitled to it and to alimony, also."

"Entitled?"

"For over sixteen years—with one exception—I've been a faithful wife, and, for five out of every seven days, lived here like a war bride while you do as you please and come here on the weekends and screw me and watch TV and have me wash your clothes. Life is short,

Evers, and a real good piece of mine's gone, completely wasted. And think of how much money you've given your brother to piss away."

"That's not fair. And what is it with all the numbers? You're John Maynard Keynes now?"

"You've handled this poorly, Evers. You and that simpleton policeman. I haven't forgotten that. Even though I haven't done anything about it yet." Jo Miller was still calm.

"How should you react when your wife is balling a stranger?"

"Rationally, Evers. And, you know, you do have a bad attitude about women. A prep-school boy's attitude. Treat us nice, get us drunk, screw us, see us next month at the mixer. Did it ever occur to you that you left me, refused to stay with me? Did you know you've never said you'd miss me when you leave here on Sundays? That we haven't been on a vacation in over a year? I'm not trying to be harsh, but it's true."

"I had a good opportunity, and you refused to come with me. You're doing nothing, have no ties, no plans, and you won't live with me. I didn't ask you to give up anything. I begged you to come with me, and when you didn't I bought you a farm and drove down here every weekend. If you missed me, you could've driven to Norton. You didn't want to see me badly enough to drive a couple hours."

"And when you come here, you ignore me if there's anything you want to watch on TV, piss all over the bathroom and leave the soap lying in the tub so it turns to paste before I get around to picking it up."

"Those are pretty small failings to use as a justification for adultery, Jo Miller." Evers was watching a crow through the kitchen window.

"You just see the world strangely, Evers. Women, people, school, everything."

"I think it's strange that you are treating me so badly, that's true."

"It's just one of those tensions, Evers. I don't feel bad about my choices, and you don't feel bad about yours."

"I guess," Evers said. "Did Falstaf tell you that I might know what was going on?"

"He mentioned it, yes."

Evers didn't want to argue. "I'll try to think about things; we'll see. Maybe we can work something out. I don't have the stomach for a pitched battle over IRAs and pots and pans." Steinem was arching and rubbing against Evers' leg. He bent down and picked up the cat, and then headed toward the back door to put her out into the yard. The instant he stepped into the hall, she started screeching and hissing and battling with her legs and claws. Evers held her away from him, and he looked right at a large, flannel shirt hanging in the laundry room. He turned around and faced Jo Miller, dropped the cat from chest height. "Are you kidding me?"

"What?" She stood up.

"That's Falstaf's shirt in the laundry room, isn't it?"

"Yes. That's no surprise, is it, Evers?"

"Has he been here?"

"Why do you care?"

"Has he?" Evers' voice caught.

"Yes."

"In the house that I paid for?" He glared at her.

"It's my house, Evers."

"Is he living here, Jo Miller?"

"That's none of your business. Our marriage is basically over, and I shouldn't have to answer to you."

Evers watched the cat flounce back toward the kitchen, and everything seemed to evaporate, to burn off into the walls and ceiling, until only the stupid cat was registering, and Evers began counting how many steps she was taking. "Three, four, five . . . ," he mouthed. His mind was reeling, and he thought about slugs—not snails, but slugs, the kind with gleaming brown antennae and slick, dotted bodies, the plump globs that appear on porches in the summer, and if you pour salt on them the slugs dissolve, just bubble away into moisture. Carbonated mollusks, Evers thought. Effervescent pain. He felt tears welling in his eyes, and the room and Jo Miller started to come back to him. He walked out of the kitchen and the house, angry and bewildered and cut all at the same time. "You're just a shitty person, Jo Miller. You are."

She came outside, followed him out the door. "I'm not trying to be mean to you, Evers. I'm not saying you're a bad person, or spending time with someone else so I can upset you."

"That's great to know."

"Evers—"

He threw up his hands. "Just do whatever you want to, Jo. It doesn't matter to me."

Soon afterward, Jo Miller hired a lawyer and filed for divorce and alimony. Evers suspected he knew why. When he left Durham on Thursday afternoon, he drove to his brother's house and drank beer and smoked dope with Henry and Rudy and Pascal. They went to a bar and played darts and video games and listened to Dwight Yoakam and ZZ Top on the jukebox. After the bar closed and during the trip back to Pascal's trailer, the four men had detoured into Durham and, at Pascal's suggestion, found two puny kittens eating from a Dumpster behind a fast-food restaurant. Pascal fed them both chocolate-flavored Ex-Lax, and he and Evers loosed them in Jo Miller's car. They had walked through the woods, crept up to Jo Miller's Lexus and tossed the kittens into the interior. Jo Miller called Evers the next day at his apartment in Norton. He hadn't gotten there until late in the evening, after work. "I can't believe you put those cats in my car, Evers. You did that, didn't you?"

"What cats, Jo Miller? What are you talking about?"

A week afterward, Evers and Pascal drove into Winston-Salem to see Ruth Esther. The brothers were dressed in suits, and Evers had bought a new pair of shoes for Pascal. Ruth Esther had just sold five Ford vans to a school district and was in a good mood, glad to see Pascal and Evers. She hugged them both. They went out for dinner at a nice restaurant, and Ruth Esther paid the bill, even though Evers didn't want her to. After they were finished with their meal, Evers put the bag of green and white stones on the table and told Ruth Esther that he was not going to keep them, that he wanted her to take them back.

"That wasn't the deal, though. You did your part. It's not your fault that my brother stole our money. I want you to have them."

Evers slid the bag closer to her. "I don't have any use for them. I feel bad about the way things turned out. In retrospect, it was a pretty good trip in its own up-and-down way; you were right about that."

"Why don't you at least let me pay you back for your room and the plane tickets?" Ruth Esther asked.

"There's no need," Evers said.

"We had a good time," Pascal added. He and Evers were both sober. They had barely finished a beer each during dinner.

"Where's your brother? Have you heard from him?"

"Oh yes." Ruth Esther sighed. "I've heard from him. He called from Salt Lake a few days after we got back. He was completely broke and at wits' end. Desperate and looking for a way home. He did say that you were right, that Officer Dillon helped him get our money. It looks like he offered the officer the same fifty thousand dollars that the three of us were going to split, and Mr. Dillon accepted my brother's deal. I had no idea—I hope you believe me about that. And, you know, I guess I should've paid a little more attention to what was going on. I thought Artis had told me that the cocaine was in the front seat beside him when the policeman stopped him for runnin' the sign, and that some had spilled while he was trying to hide it. But I got to court late and thought that maybe I'd missed that part of the case or that Artis—who is not always on top of things—had told me somethin' wrong when we first talked about what happened."

"So the police officer, this guy Dillon, threw the case? He screwed it up on purpose, to make sure that Artis would get off?" asked Pascal. "I mean, that's what we figured, but now you're certain, right?"

"It really looks that way," Ruth Esther said.

"Then Artis and the monkey cop split the money, and all's right with the world until the cop double-crosses him." Pascal whistled. "How about that? Evers and I were debating the Dillon scam in Utah, and we finally decided that Dillon had to be in on it from the out-set, so I guess it's no big shock." Pascal whistled again. "Wow."

"If they made this deal, I wonder why the policeman went ahead and arrested Artis and took a chance on going to court?" Ruth Esther asked. "Do you see what I'm talking about? How come they just didn't get on a plane and go? Why risk havin' a court trial?"

"We thought about that, too. I feel sure Artis didn't make Dillon the offer until he had already arrested him and done the paperwork or gotten him to the police station. Even Artis isn't dumb enough to offer the bribe right away. Dillon was too far into the arrest to simply cut him free."

"That makes sense," Ruth Esther said.

"Did Artis know that you'd approached me?" Evers wondered.

"No. There was no reason to tell him and a whole bunch not to. And—to guess what you're going to say next—it probably wouldn't have mattered, would it? It looks like Artis had plans for my share—and yours—that pretty much left out everyone except him and his new partner. He traded my part of the money to keep from goin' to jail." Ruth Esther folded her arms across her chest. "Unfortunately for Artis, Dillon left him in Salt Lake City and took *all* the money. At least I think Dillon took all of the money; it's possible that Artis lost his part or spent it or had it stolen by somebody else. But I'm almost certain that this Mr. Dillon took advantage of Artis, made the deal to let him get away and then took his—our—fifty thousand and Artis' part on top of that. That's what Artis said on the phone, for what it's worth."

"Did Artis mention anything about Dillon, where he is?" Pascal asked. "I can't imagine that he'd come back here. Evers thinks he might come back, but I don't."

"It's not like we have clean hands," Evers pointed out. "What are we going to say or do? Why wouldn't he come back?"

"That's true, I guess," Ruth Esther agreed.

"I'm afraid he'll try to ice the cake and fuck me over," Evers said. "He could very easily say that he was working on the case, followed us to Utah and recovered, say, fifteen thousand dollars of the stolen money, turn that in, turn *us* in and pocket the rest. We'd all look pretty guilty."

"I hope he'll just leave well enough alone," Ruth Esther offered. "Certainly he knows that you're in no position to cause him any real problem."

"Let's hope so." Evers took out a cigarette and lit it.

"May I have one?" Pascal asked. "And a match?"

Evers handed his brother the pack. Pascal offered Ruth Esther a smoke, but she shook her head and refused.

"Well, it's good we've been back for a while and haven't heard anything from Dillon or Lester Jackson," Ruth Esther said.

"Maybe. The one and only thing I discovered is that our friend Dillon is supposed to be on a three-week vacation in Florida. That's what one of the other cops told one of my clerks. I wonder if he's really there. It will be interesting to see what happens when he comes back. *If* he comes back."

"Whatever." Pascal handed the cigarettes back to Evers.

"I hope you left Artis' troll ass in the desert," Evers said.

"I sent him a ticket and some money. I haven't seen or heard from him since, of course." Ruth Esther didn't sound surprised or upset.

"I can't believe you'd do that for him after he fucked us over. Jesus, Ruth Esther."

"He's my brother, Judge Wheeling. What did you expect me to do? I doubt that he's so pathetic and bad by choice; no one would want to be so hopeless and simple. It's his nature. There's not much he can do about it. I'm sure you would do the same for Pascal."

"He always has." Pascal patted Evers on the back, three quick slaps that were both heartfelt and a little comic.

Evers looked at the plate in front of Ruth Esther. She'd ordered a salad without dressing and had eaten only a piece of cucumber and two cherry tomatoes. "Are you sure you won't let me pay for the meal? You didn't order more than three or four dollars' worth."

"It's my treat. I'm glad you both came to see me. I looked forward to it all day."

Pascal put his cigarette on the edge of his plate. "Do you have a husband or boyfriend or anything?"

"No." Ruth Esther smiled.

"I just wondered." Pascal pulled his shirtsleeve out from under the arm of his jacket. "That's good to know."

"I'm flattered that you'd ask about something like that."

"Sure. Whatever."

"So how are things going with your wife and marriage, Judge Wheeling? Any improvement?" Ruth Esther's legs were crossed, and her hands were resting on her knee.

"Hardly. We're going to court soon to see how big a reward she gets for her betrayal and infidelity."

"Well, good luck."

"Thanks." He picked up his napkin and wiped the corners of his mouth. "I appreciate your asking."

"That reminds me. Have you talked to Pauletta since we got back?"

"No, I haven't. Why would I?" Evers wondered.

"She told me you . . . went out while you were in Charleston, and that you had a good time. I just wondered if you'd spoken to her again."

"I haven't."

"Maybe you should get in touch with her," Ruth Esther suggested.

"I might. I might give her a call." Evers hesitated. "Did she get anything out of the trip? What was her cut?"

"She wasn't sharin' any of the money that Artis and Officer Dillon took. That's about all I can tell you."

"I figured as much," Evers said. He glanced at Ruth Esther, then started pushing a piece of noodle around his plate with the tip of a butter knife. "You know—I don't mean to be pushy or rude—but I'm going to stay on this, try to figure it out, find out what the real deal is. You don't blame me for that, do you? It's not going to upset you, is it?"

"It takes right much to upset me, Judge Wheeling," Ruth Esther said.

Pascal turned to his brother. "I don't know why you want to go Ahab on this, Evers. It's pretty much been a full ride already. How much better is it going to get?"

"There's still a lot I want to find out." Evers set the butter knife on top of a napkin. "I feel like I've been looking through a keyhole for the last month or two."

"Whatever."

In the days that preceded the hearing that would determine whether or not Jo Miller would receive spousal support, Evers spent his time talking to his lawyer and eating fast food with his brother, Rudy and Henry. Evers' lawyer was a man named Ike White, a tall, heavy man who wore nice suits and had a deep, theatrical voice. White was polished without being glib or pompous, and he loved going to court.

About a week before the hearing, Pascal began phoning Jo Miller at early hours to wake her and unsettle her before the day in court. There was little need for anyone to phone Evers. He couldn't sleep and suffered from explosive diarrhea. Pascal made him drink Pepto-Bismol and eat cheese biscuits from Hardee's. The biscuit wrappers would not lie flat—the ends were turned up at an angle—and they had all sorts of folds and crinkles and were greasy on the inside, slick to the touch. They were all over Pascal's trailer, empty, wrinkled biscuit papers.

The court date was on a Tuesday, and Evers didn't sleep at all the night before. Pascal sat with him in the trailer, neither of them talking very much. Henry and Rudy had come by, both drunk, and tried to cheer up the brothers. During the night Pascal picked up a few of the food wrappers and cleaned some of his ashtrays. There was talk of thawing out the white shrine, but no one really had the heart for it. "Fuck it all," Pascal finally said. Evers wanted to ask his brother some more about Jo Miller, but things were gloomy and tense enough without opening another wound. Since their conversation at the airport, a lot of their time together had seemed cramped, strange and different; simple conversations spun out webs and traps, words grew double-edged, and talk about women or sex or the Utah trip caused Evers and Pascal to glance at each other without meaning to.

Jo Miller looked especially plain at the hearing. She wore a skirt and a blouse with buttons that were fastened all the way to her neck. Her hair was short, and she wasn't wearing any jewelry. Her attorney, Norman Wolf, was from Raleigh, a tall man with long gray hair. Evers had heard of Wolf, and by all accounts he was a very competent lawyer. Their judge was an older man, Judge Peter Rollins. He was from Charlotte, a special designate who did not know Evers. Ike White knew Rollins and described him as "traditional," whatever that meant.

Jo Miller testified first. She seemed nervous and looked at her hands a lot. After several minutes, it occurred to Evers that much of her nervousness was feigned. She was more poised than that. He wondered if the judge would notice. White asked her several simple questions and then let her testify about her job and her marriage.

"What kind of relationship did you and Mr. Wheeling have?" Wolf finally asked.

Jo Miller looked at Evers. "Evers tried to be a good husband. I think he loves me. But, of course, I didn't get to see him that much because of his decision to leave me and live in Norton."

"Did he help support you, take care of you economically?"

"Sure. Yes. He helped. He's provided a lot for me, a good standard of living." Jo Miller cleared her throat. "I'm not trying to say that

Evers ever did anything intentionally mean. Given his schedule and the job he had and the distance, he did what he could. He did everything he could, I guess."

White looked at Evers and leaned toward him. "Something's up."

"She's just telling the truth," Evers answered.

"Don't be naive, Evers."

"What?"

White frowned. "She's telling the truth now. Too much so."

Wolf picked up a folder from the table and walked toward the witness stand. "Now, Mrs. Wheeling, I understand there is an allegation that you committed adultery with a certain Mr. Falstaf, some months ago. Are you familiar with that suggestion?"

"Yes, sir, I am."

"And is it true?"

"No sir. No. Absolutely not. It's crazy."

Evers looked at the judge. He looked at his wife. At his lawyer. "What the fuck," he said under his breath.

"Mrs. Wheeling, could you go forward and tell the court the circumstances involved in your meeting Mr. Falstaf at the Iron Duke Inn?"

"Yes. Mr. Falstaf is a farmer. He is also a businessman. I met him through my friend Ellen Wyatt. Ellen raises cattle and organizes conventions and expositions, does trade shows, stuff like that."

"Ellen is a fucking, man-hating, feminoid bitch from Duke," Evers said to White. "She doesn't know a cow from a large stone."

"Ellen and Mr. Falstaf and I had thought about buying some property, older motels and so on, and turning them into art deco sorts of places. One of the places we were interested in was the Iron Duke Inn."

"I see."

"So we went there to inspect it. Ellen, myself and Mr. Falstaf." Jo Miller looked at her lawyer, then at the judge.

"Had you mentioned this venture to your husband?" Wolf nodded toward Evers.

"Yes, I had. I'd asked him about investing in it. I didn't really have all the money we'd need."

"Did she mention that to you, Evers?" White asked quietly, his mouth next to Evers' ear.

"What the fuck do you think?" he snapped back.

"And I take it that you were at this motel one night?"

"A lot of nights. Looking at the place. I was there with Ellen, Mr. Falstaf and some other people. We looked at different places, too."

"Did you and Mr. Falstaf ever go there alone?"

"No."

"Did you ever have sex there?"

"No sir. No." Jo Miller set her head and raised her voice.

"Did you ever go there for any purpose other than business?"

"Just business."

"Tell the court about the night you allegedly engaged in what Mr. White has characterized as, let me see, 'gross marital misconduct and adultery with Hobart Falstaf.' "

"We—I mean Mr. Falstaf, Ellen and I—were at the motel looking at some of the rooms. We were talking about redoing them—costs, colors, all sorts of things. And Evers shows up."

"You mean Mr. Wheeling?" White interrupted.

"Yes, and—"

"Was he alone?"

"Yes."

"Go ahead."

"We were in a room—looking at it, you know—with plans and drawings, carpet swatches, paints and chips and so forth. I have all of that with me if the judge wants to see it."

"Had you rented this room, checked in?"

"No. Absolutely not. Ellen had made arrangements for us to see the place, to tour the rooms."

"How did she do that?" Wolf asked.

"I don't know. You'll have to ask her. She dealt with the owners."

Evers looked at White, touched his arm and leaned into him. "This is a total fucking falsehood. I simply cannot believe she would lie like this. It's just brazen."

"She expects to be well paid for her time as your wife," White said.

"What did Mr. Wheeling do when he arrived?" Wolf asked, looking across the courtroom at Evers.

"He was angry. He started acting crazy. He accused me of all sorts of things."

"What did he say, exactly?"

"I'd rather not repeat it." Jo Miller rubbed her eyes. Her voice was soft, and she was looking at the floor.

"Please, Mrs. Wheeling." Wolf looked at Jo Miller. The play-acting was, Evers thought, just awful.

"It's unpleasant, what he said."

"We understand."

"Well . . . he said, 'I know you're fucking the man, I'm just not sure about the woman.' "

Evers hit the desk with his fist and jerked back in his chair. White put his hand on Evers' thigh and shook his head, very slightly, just once. Wolf paused for a moment to highlight the outburst.

"And what did you do or say, Mrs. Wheeling?"

"Well, I just tried to explain things to him and calm him down."

"Were you able to?" Wolf gestured toward Evers when he asked Jo Miller the question.

"No. He just kept yelling and finally left."

"Have you ever talked about this problem?" Wolf asked.

"Not really. Evers left Norton after several days and went to Utah with his brother. He has completely refused to have anything to do with me, just left me. I've tried to call him and see him, but he's cut me off."

"Mrs. Wheeling, have you ever, on any occasion, with anyone, been unfaithful to your husband?"

"No."

"Were you surprised by your husband's behavior?"

"I was. Evers and I always had a decent marriage. This was unexpected. His refusal to see me was unexpected. His behavior now is unexpected." Jo Miller's voice cracked. "This has just been so . . . so bad. Evers had never done anything like this."

"Did you give him any reason to leave you and the marriage union?"

"None that I'm aware of. I loved Evers and tried to do what he wanted. I thought that he was very happy, all in all. I thought so."

"Are you asking for alimony, to help you live until the divorce is final?"

"Yes." Jo Miller started to cry, sucking in air and mucus and dabbing at her cheeks with her fingers. The weeping turned into coughs, and when she covered her mouth with her hands, Evers noticed that she had put on her wedding band before coming to court. Wolf handed her some water and his handkerchief, and waited for her to settle down.

"How much do you make each month, Mrs. Wheeling?" Wolf's voice was low, very understanding.

"About eight hundred dollars."

"Do you have any other source of income, other than your work?"

"No. That's it."

"I believe that we have established through discovery that your husband has vocational income and investment income totaling two hundred thirty thousand dollars per year, correct?"

"I think, yes." Jo Miller looked at Evers for the first time since she began testifying.

"Judge, Mr. White and I agreed that we would submit the parties' tax returns for the last three years." Wolf held up several papers. "They confirm that last year Mr. Wheeling made two hundred thirty thousand, six hundred and eight dollars. We formally would like to introduce these into evidence." Wolf handed the papers to the bailiff, who handed them to the judge.

"Any questions about the documents, Mr. White?" Rollins looked at Evers and his lawyer over the top of the tax returns.

"No sir. That's what my client made."

Wolf stopped asking questions long enough to let the judge look over the tax returns, then continued. "Mrs. Wheeling, I believe, also, that your husband's net worth is somewhere close to three million dollars, exclusive of the farm you're living on in Durham, correct?"

"That's about what it adds up to, yes."

"Has he ever abused you?"

"Physically?" She looked at Wolf.

"In any way?"

"Not really. I understand recently that he has committed adultery, if that—"

"Objection, sir." White stood. "That would be hearsay."

"Sustained. Mrs. Wheeling, just try not to tell us what others have told you, all right?" Rollins was very gentle in addressing Jo Miller.

"I'm sorry."

"That's fine. It took all of us three years of school to learn what to say, what not to." Judge Rollins nodded at Jo Miller. "Let's continue."

"Has he ever abused you, Mrs. Wheeling? That was my question."

"No. Until he left, no." Jo Miller's face was red and damp. "I'm not saying . . . I'm not trying to make him out a bastard or anything. But I didn't want this, and Evers did refuse to live with me and now has completely refused to see me or talk to me. He's just stopped having anything to do with me, deserted me. . . . I'm not sure why."

Evers turned to his lawyer. "She's great, huh? Doesn't seem vindictive, she's wounded just enough, reasonable—shit, what a production."

"Mrs. Wheeling," Wolf continued, "is there anything else you'd like to add?"

"No. I don't guess so." Jo Miller looked at the judge. "No sir." She looked at Evers.

"Your witness, Mr. White." Wolf said this in a very quiet, understated voice, without any hint of triumph.

White rose. "Your honor, could I have about ten minutes to speak with my client?"

"Certainly."

White and Evers left the courtroom and stood outside in the hall, close to each other in a corner. A young lawyer was across from them talking to a boy with wild red hair and pale skin. Evers could smell liquor coming from the boy. The boy's lawyer was using his hands a lot when he spoke.

"She did a good job, Evers."

"No shit she did. We should be able to impeach her, though. She's already admitted being there with Falstaf in your interrogatories, right? Didn't she? Didn't you tell me that?"

"I did."

"Well, nail her."

"That's all she admitted."

"What do you mean?"

White tossed Jo Miller's pretrial answers onto a small table. "Read it for yourself." Evers noticed a year-old *People* magazine and an empty green plastic bottle on the table.

Jo Miller's answers under oath admitted that she was present at the Iron Duke and that Falstaf had also been there. Evers read through the rest of her answers.

"Where is it, Ike?"

"Where is what?"

"The magic question. All you got her to answer is that she was there and he was there. Did you ask her if they committed adultery?"

"It appears that we didn't."

"*We* fucking didn't?" Evers yelled. "Are you kidding me?"

"No."

"You left it out? You sent out twenty pages of questions, and you didn't ask her the most important one?"

"You felt sure that she wouldn't lie, Evers. You told me that. I asked you twice. I thought that tactically it would be wise to let her deal with it the first time here, especially since you said she wouldn't lie. I wanted her to do it cold, without a script. You said she was honest."

"Don't start blaming me for this. Now we can't impeach her. There's nothing inconsistent. It's my word against hers."

"What about your witness, this deputy who was with you?"

"He's not here. You told me there'd be no need."

"Well, I believed you when you said she wouldn't lie. You said to worry about the sign, that she'd hit you with the sign. I didn't want to tip our hand and let her prepare too much."

"I fucking believed you when you said you'd take care of things," Evers shouted. He shook his head. "It's just too obvious to lie about. I can't believe this."

"Try to get the deputy. I'll call and have somebody try to check out the records down there at the motel. I just didn't anticipate this. I can't prepare for something if you tell me it won't happen. Also, we can try to get Falstaf in, maybe get a continuance if you can't find the deputy." White loosened his tie. "Hell, Evers, it looks like they were going to go to the wall anyhow, turn this into a swearing contest. She and her friend are going to say that it never happened, you and your buddy will say that it did."

"Shit. There isn't going to be any contest unless I get my witness."

"Calm down, Evers. Okay? Try to get the deputy."

Evers went to a pay phone, White right behind him. Evers dialed the wrong number. Then he dropped the receiver. Finally he got the dispatcher at the Norton sheriff's office. H. T. Moran was on duty and near a phone. After about five minutes, he called Evers back. He would be there immediately. No worry. No problem. He remembered every-thing. H. T. hung up the phone in Norton, and Evers nodded at his lawyer.

"Let's drag this thing out, okay, Ike? He's going to need some travel time."

"I'm sure she'll have other witnesses, too," White said.

"Let's just stay out here until the judge sends the bailiff to get us. Thank god this is just a temporary hearing. Next time I'll do my own interrogatories."

When the trial resumed, White had his chance to cross-examine Jo Miller. It dawned on Evers that his wife was the smarter of the two, and that she was better prepared. White asked his first questions like a TV lawyer, big looping broadsides without any disguise or subtlety, as if he expected this woman who had just given one account under oath to suddenly change her testimony because a different lawyer asked her the same question and blustered when he did it. "You did commit adultery in that motel room, didn't you, Mrs. Wheeling?" White spread his legs and folded his arms across his chest.

"No."

"And you have in fact committed adultery with Mr. Falstaf, haven't you?"

"No."

"You know, ma'am, that we have pictures of the two of you at the motel? Just the two of you?" He took a step closer to the witness stand, tried to bully Jo Miller.

"You probably do. That wouldn't be all that hard to manipulate since we have been there at the same time."

"And you're telling the court that Mr. Wheeling was there alone?"

"Right." Jo Miller looked directly at White.

"He didn't come with a police officer?"

"Not that I saw." She shrugged.

"And you claim that Miss Wyatt was there, too?"

"Yes. She was. She'll tell you that, too. She's here." Jo Miller was calm.

White hesitated and stuck his hands into his pockets. "You testified that your husband was aware of this potential investment, this project?"

"Sure. At first he encouraged us."

"He did?"

"Yes, Mr. White, he did. In fact, he knew all about us being at the motel that night; that's how he found us. And now he's put together this affair story to suit his own purposes."

"What other businesses does Mr. Falstaf own, Mrs. Wheeling?"

"I'm not sure."

"How many other hotels or motels?"

"I'm not sure," Jo Miller answered again.

"He doesn't own any, isn't that correct?"

"He may. I don't know."

"He's your business partner, but you don't know?"

"All I know is that he had the money and was interested in the project." Jo Miller still seemed very composed.

"The bottom line is that he's a cow farmer with an eleventh-grade education, isn't it, Mrs. Wheeling?"

Jo Miller sat forward in her chair. "Ellen told me that he employs ten or fifteen people and has a substantial payroll. I guess that you could ask her or him about the rest. We needed financial backing, not a rocket scientist."

"Is Mr. Falstaf married?"

Jo Miller twisted a little in the witness stand. "I think so. Yes."

Wolf stood up and objected. "Judge, we've listened to an awful lot about Mr. Falstaf and a lot of other irrelevant information, and I haven't complained. But I think we've gone far enough."

Rollins shook his head. "It's proper. It's proper cross-examination. I'd like to know a little bit about these folks."

"Thank you," White said. He moved closer to Jo Miller, as close as he could get to the witness stand. "How did you discover Mr. Falstaf and his interest in the motel business?"

"Like I said, I met him through Ellen. It's my understanding that they had a booth or program at one of her shows about agricultural things and ways for farmers to diversify. She put us in touch."

"Now, when you claim that Mr. Wheeling left you to live in Norton, the fact is that you left him, didn't you? Refused to go with him?" White stared at her.

"He chose his job over my feelings and my career."

"When he finished law school, you had no career and he had a promising job, and you simply refused to help him, support him or go with him."

"I certainly had no career options in Norton."

"I see," said White. "And in the years since Judge Wheeling moved to Norton, and became a judge, what have you done career-wise? You've done very little in terms of work or further education, isn't that correct?"

"How could I?"

"Well, what's stopping you?"

"I wasn't going to mention it, but since you're trying to make me look so hateful and lazy, one of the main reasons I didn't want to move with Evers is because he uses drugs."

White looked surprised. "Drugs? Judge Wheeling? What drugs? When?"

"Cocaine . . . marijuana. He and his brother smoke hash sometimes."

"That's absurd, ma'am. Do you have any proof?" White tried to sound certain of himself, but he was clearly off balance.

"Well, ask him to take a drug test." Jo Miller looked at the judge, then at Evers.

"Will you, Mrs. Wheeling?" White asked her.

"Sure. Right now. Let's go." She looked at the judge again.

Wolf stood up again. "Judge, Mr. White seems to have opened Pandora's box. I would formally move the court to require both parties to submit to drug screens." He looked across the courtroom at Evers.

"I'm sure my client has nothing to hide and would love the opportunity to clear his name." What else could he say, Evers thought.

Rollins looked at Evers. "Mr. Wheeling?"

"Sure." Evers wanted to kill Jo Miller. She had hooked a small truth to a number of lies. He had never used cocaine or hash in his life, but a positive test for marijuana would make the other untruths seem believable, and undercut his credibility on everything else.

"So be it," said Rollins. "We'll have the tests done before everyone leaves. I'm not sure how relevant it is, but if everyone agrees, so be it. Next question, Mr. White."

"Didn't Mr. Wheeling and an Officer H. T. Moran take you from the motel and drive you to Climax, North Carolina, and abandon you there?" White sat down beside Evers.

"No. That's crazy. What do you mean? When?"

"Judge Wheeling and a policeman found you in bed at the Iron Duke Motel with Mr. Falstaf and soon after, because he was so angry, drove you to Climax and left you on the side of the road."

"That's just not true. Any of it." Jo Miller paused. "My lawyer has an affidavit from Mr. Falstaf, too. Do you want to see it?"

"No ma'am, I don't. Why don't you let me ask the questions?" White forced a smile.

Evers began to have the same foggy, prickly feeling he'd experienced before stumbling into Pauletta's office. His mind began to coast and skip. White was wearing a double-breasted suit and Jo Miller was talking to him and Evers was sweating and for some reason he just had to laugh and he did, heard his own laugh and saw Wolf look at him, and then Jo Miller, and then the judge and his lawyer. Evers closed and opened his eyes and rubbed his forehead; he focused on his wife, on Jo Miller, and her face—very suddenly—changed, came on like an electric fan on a hot day: circles started to catch speed and spin faster and faster, blurring into swirling wisps and whirs inside the edges of her head, leaving a small, framed cyclone where her countenance had been. The storm in Jo Miller's face went on for several seconds, and then, out of the middle of the maelstrom, Evers saw two sharp eyes and pallid skin appear, just spots in the confusion at first and finally growing and pushing full-size into his wife's skull. The spiked eyes looked right at him, and Evers hunched forward and stared back, leaned across the table on his elbows and clenched his fists.

The circling mess balanced on his wife's neck didn't leave until White kicked Evers under the table and pinched his biceps. "Stop staring at her, Evers. You look menacing or crazed or something, like you're trying to frighten her. Sit back." White pulled on Evers' arm.

"She was . . . she wasn't . . ." Evers looked at White, then back at Jo Miller. His wife had reappeared, and she seemed startled, a little scared. Wolf stood and asked the judge to prohibit Evers from "visually threatening Mrs. Wheeling."

"Judge, he was simply upset by some of the testimony that is perjured and inaccurate. It was just a reflex, a reaction, one of shock and disbelief at what he was hearing, not anything malicious," White said in Evers' defense. "Judge Wheeling is stunned by what is going on here today. Quite frankly, so am I."

"I can't help how Mr. Wheeling looks at his wife, Lawyers. Let's try not to squabble and get on with more substantive matters, shall we?" Rollins looked at Wolf, then at White. Evers cleared his throat and slid back in his seat.

When White finished his questioning, Wolf smiled at Jo Miller and leaned back in his chair until the front legs raised off the ground. "Just one more follow-up question, ma'am. Am I to understand that Mr. White is accusing you of having an affair with this man he suggests is a poorly educated, simple farmer? You have a college degree, correct?"

White objected, and Rollins agreed that the question was not a good one. "Although the same thing went through my mind," the judge added. Despite his loathing, Evers had to concede that Jo Miller was bright, clever and poised. He had trouble believing that his wife had settled on Hobart Falstaf as well.

Jo Miller's next witness was Ellen Wyatt. She confirmed Jo Miller's story but did have to admit they were very close friends. She produced all sorts of papers and contracts and receipts to document the women's ongoing interest in the Iron Duke and two other motels. Everything was so complete and genuine that Evers began to believe that perhaps the women had, at one time, considered buying the motel.

Finally, Wolf called Dr. Brockman, who spent ten minutes listing his credentials, then went on to rave and wax passionate about what a fine and admirable person Jo Miller was and how she had "bonded" with her environment and job and something about a "psycho-structure" and this and that and some more about self-esteem and on and on and on and on and Jo Miller's "personality shield" showed a jagged line and a chimney with no smoke and all this meant something.

"Ask him why he doesn't have a job," Evers whispered to White.

"Keep your temper."

"He probably fucked Jo Miller, too," Evers said. "Look at this corduroy charlatan. Elbow patches. Half glasses. Full beard. Those who can, do. Those who can't, teach."

White did a better job questioning Brockman than he had with anyone else so far. His first question surprised Evers, and surprised Brockman, too. "Isn't it true, Mr. Brockman, that you have had sexual relations with Mrs. Wheeling?"

Brockman was so shocked by this stark allegation that he paused and stumbled and fussed before mouthing a feeble, "Why, no." His surprise caused him to look guilty and duplicitous. "No," he said after another awkward silence. Brockman had gone from top-drawer pontificator and intellectual master to a simple longhaired professor with base intentions. The judge wrote something on his yellow pad. Evers could tell that Rollins thought Brockman was a guy who got all summer off and spent most of his time chasing after students and assistants. The judge wasn't certain whether or not Brockman had actually had sex with Jo Miller, but the professor was embarrassed enough by the question to show that he had certainly considered the possibility. Everything he had said before seemed silly. Everything he was going to say would seem hypocritical.

White finished with Brockman, sat down beside Evers and whispered, "Anything else I need to ask?" Evers wrote two questions on a piece of paper and handed it to his lawyer.

"Uh, Mr. Brockman, just a couple more things. Did you and Mrs. Wheeling ever use illegal drugs together?"

"No, we didn't."

"You're sure of that?"

"Yes." Brockman turned and looked at Jo Miller and Wolf. He touched the side of his neck with his hand.

"Did you and Mrs. Wheeling ever invite another woman to engage in sex with the two of you?"

"No. Another woman? Certainly not."

White hesitated. Smiled. "So it was just you two, correct?"

Wolf objected. "That's completely unfair and—"

"Sustained. That's not a good question, Mr. White."

"Are you married or single?"

"Single," answered Brockman.

"Divorced, perhaps, Mr. Brockman?"

"Objection," Wolf said firmly. "Not relevant."

"I agree this time," the judge said. But by now Brockman was damaged goods, spiraling toward the earth with black smoke rolling out from beneath his wings.

"Nothing further, sir." White looked at Evers, bent toward him. "How did you know that stuff? How come you're just now telling me?"

Evers smiled. "I didn't say it was true. I just said ask him."

Before he finished his case, Wolf offered Falstaf's affidavit and then told the judge that the contents would support Mrs. Wheeling's story, denying any adultery.

White objected. "Mr. Wolf knows the affidavit is not admissible, and it borders on unethical practice to offer it and then tell you what it says. It's hearsay, and if they want to get it into evidence, they can bring Mr. Falstaf in here and put him under oath and let him be questioned. Of course, I'm sure they have their reasons for not having him here in person."

"You could have called him as a witness, Mr. White," Wolf answered. "Or taken his deposition."

"They're not trying to get evidence in with an out-of-court statement, Mr. Wolf. Watch yourself. The objection is sustained." Judge Rollins seemed impatient.

Evers' first witness was Pascal. White asked questions about Evers' relationship with his wife, about his efforts to make the marriage successful, about Evers' devotion to his work and Jo Miller's well-being, and about Evers' change of mood and depression over the last several weeks after catching on to the adultery and catting around—as White colorfully put it—taking place at the Iron Duke. Pascal was very convincing and well-spoken, Evers thought. When White finished with his questions, Wolf sat in his chair and stared at Pascal for several moments before speaking. Pascal seemed unshaken, looking straight at the judge, then at Wolf, then at Jo Miller.

Wolf hunched forward in his seat. "Mr. Wheeling, you've not married, is that correct?"

"That's right."

"Have no experience in a marital relationship?"

"I have never been married." Pascal was composed.

"You're unemployed?"

"I don't have a job, that's true."

"And you use drugs and drink to excess?"

White objected. "That's not pertinent, sir, this man's personal habits."

"Sir, this man has testified that Mr. Wheeling is a fit and good spouse, an outstanding husband. I think we need to explore the basis for that, see what 'outstanding husband' means as Mr. Pascal Wheeling defines it."

"Well, then, ask him what he means by that term. Don't ask him about what he does, Mr. Wolf." The judge was sharp with Wolf.

"Yes sir. Mr. Wheeling, do you think a good spouse uses illegal drugs?"

"I don't think it really matters, to tell you the truth."

Wolf leaned back in his chair, raised his eyebrows. "Doesn't matter, you say?" He cut his eyes at Judge Rollins.

"Let me give you an example. I've seen Jo Miller, after she smoked dope, become absolutely affectionate with Evers. When he was in law school and she was stoned, she would just hold him and talk to him and rock him. Wouldn't let him go. Treated him like a prize. She was so . . . so—I don't know—warm and devoted."

Evers looked at White and smiled just a bit. Pascal was bright. He knew what he was doing.

"How about your brother's drug usage?"

"What drugs, when? What do you mean?"

"Well, have you ever seen your brother use illegal drugs?"

"When he and Jo Miller were in Durham, I think they did occasionally. But I've never seen Evers and Jo Miller use drugs since Evers left law school."

Evers breathed very slowly, bit his lip. Pascal's answer was true but misleading. Pascal hadn't seen Jo Miller *and* Evers use drugs since Evers left Durham. Evers hoped the semantics would escape Wolf.

"Never."

"No. Never."

"There could have been times when you weren't around and they did, though."

"Sure."

"Or your brother did?"

"Sure." Pascal paused. "And I'll be candid with you—I've smoked marijuana occasionally. I've done a number of stupid things. I'm not perfect. Evers is the better of the two of us, without question."

"Did you call Mrs. Wheeling several weeks ago and tell her that your brother Evers was in West Virginia, having sex with a woman in a motel?"

"Why would I do that?"

"Did you, Mr. Wheeling?"

"No. That would be crazy. Did Jo Miller say that? Did I understand your question?"

"My question was: Did you call Jo Miller Wheeling and tell her that your brother was in West Virginia having sex with another woman, in a motel?"

"No." Pascal sounded bewildered.

Evers glanced at Pascal. His brother had lied for him. Pascal looked believable. He was handsome and controlled. The question was so strange it made Jo Miller seem less trustworthy for having suggested it to her lawyer.

"You wouldn't mind if we subpoenaed your phone records then?"

"It's fine with me, if it's agreeable with everyone else." Pascal sat up straighter in the chair. "Whatever."

"Do you dislike Mrs. Wheeling?" Wolf's tone was very neutral, hiding something, full of pits and bear traps.

"Jo Miller and I have always treated each other fairly well."

"In fact you dislike her, don't you?"

"No."

"You dislike her because you've made advances toward her in the past, and she rejected them?"

"I've made advances toward her? In a sense, yes." Pascal turned toward Evers. Pascal's face was empty, smooth and impenetrable. "That's true, Mr. Wolf."

"And because she stopped—"

"She didn't stop me. I slept with—"

"That's a damn lie, Pascal." Jo Miller stood and shouted and started crying. "That's a lie." She was gasping, and her shoulders were jerking and falling.

"But my brother didn't know. Until now. I'm sorry; it's a terrible thing to have to say."

Wolf was flustered and confused. Rollins looked at Pascal, then at Evers. He pushed back one of the sleeves of his robe. "Let's all take a few minutes' recess."

Evers, Pascal and White went into a witness room, and White shut the door. All three men stood, even though there were several chairs and a table. The room was dark, despite a window and a light.

"What do you think?" Evers asked his lawyer.

"Pascal helped. Rollins believes him. Wolf's in trouble."

"I don't know," Evers said, then turned to Pascal. "I knew you'd fucked Jo Miller. Thanks, Cain." He was cross and numb and enervated.

"Who said I fucked your wife? I figured I still had a lot of credibility left after being so honest about the dope. I rolled the dice. Maybe he'll believe it. I thought I carried it off well."

"Did you lie, Mr. Wheeling?" White asked. "I can't allow that."

"No, it's all true. Believe it." Pascal winked.

"Don't play games with me, Pascal." White was annoyed.

"Don't fuck up my brother's case, okay? They've defined the rules—whatever we can sell, not what's true or false, that's what can be said. Whatever the judge believes is going to be the truth; and if Jo Miller's lying, then we can, too."

"I don't need a half-assed civics lesson, Pascal. I want to know if—"

"Let's not fight about this," Evers interrupted. "Pascal has testified. Let's get on with it. My brother has told you he's not lying, Ike. That's good enough for right now."

"Thank you, Evers," Pascal said.

"I'm sure we can trust you, Pascal, given that you obviously hold the truth in such high regard." Evers shot him a sour look.

White wanted H. T. Moran to appear before Evers, but H. T. still hadn't arrived when Pascal finished his testimony. White looked at Evers and nodded. Evers stood up from his seat, took several steps across the still room, sat down in the witness chair and looked around the courtroom. He was nervous. He noticed the court reporter; the lady was watching him. She had long, red fingernails, like ten iguana

tongues, Evers thought, and was wearing several necklaces. Her husband probably worked in sales, Evers decided. He remembered one of
the docket clerks in Norton saying that it was not wise to dance with a
man who jerks you on the dance floor. Evers was sweating underneath
his clothes. He thought of bowling balls again.

White began questioning him, and Evers settled down. He told the
judge about his marriage, about his life and about Jo Miller. He told
the judge about discovering her in bed with Falstaf. And, finally, he
told the judge that because he was angry he drove his wife in H. T.'s El
Camino to Climax, North Carolina, and left her naked and tied to a
sign beside the highway. "I was angry," he said again at the end of the
story.

White had been standing near Evers, and he rested his hand on
Evers' shoulder for a moment before he walked back to his chair and
sat down. "Nothing else for this witness."

"Mr. Wheeling, after several years of marriage, is it your position
that you simply want to leave your wife destitute? Pay her nothing?"
This was Wolf's first question. He asked it quickly, as soon as White
had finished.

"I think that's fair, given the circumstances," Evers answered. "She
is able to work, and perhaps her boyfriend could contribute to her
well-being. In addition, when our property is divided, I'm sure that
she will receive a fairly significant share. I just don't think that it is
'fair'—to use your word—that I should have to subsidize her treach-
ery and infidelity on a monthly basis."

"Don't you pay Mrs. Wheeling's power bill, her heat bills, send her
spending money, buy her clothes, provide her insurance, help her
with the upkeep of the farm in Durham and generally take care of
her economically?"

"Is that one question or six, Mr. Wolf?" Evers snapped. He wanted
very much to hit Wolf in the face.

"Mr. Wolf, ask one question at a time." Judge Rollins still sounded
perturbed.

"Mr. Wheeling, you make over two hundred and thirty thousand
dollars a year, correct?"

"Yes."

"And you have very few expenses. You live in an apartment and
have no debts, correct?"

"Right. Exactly. I live in a small apartment and work every day, and
my wife lives in a restored farmhouse on thirty acres and I pay for it."

"That's my point, Mr. Wheeling. Your wife is completely dependent on you financially."

Evers' hands were clasped together, pushing down into his lap. His fingers were wrapped around one another so tightly that the skin underneath his nails was blood red. "Jo Miller has a college degree. She's drifted and dithered and basically refused to work. How can she claim that I've kept her from advancing? There are hundreds of great jobs in the Raleigh-Durham area. Of course, to get one, you'd have to get up before ten and give up the two-hour lunches."

"Mr. Wheeling, now that you've had the chance to criticize your wife, could you just answer my question?"

"What *is* your question?"

"Your wife, and her standard of living during the marriage, are completely dependent on your income?"

"I guess that's true, as long as she elects not to really work, to do no more than she's doing now with her friend Dr. Brockman. Perhaps that job has a lot of noneconomic benefits, though."

"I have nothing else, Judge. I believe the point is made. I would ask the court to strike Mr. Wheeling's last snide remark—it wasn't responsive and is unsupported by the evidence."

"I'll disregard the last comment, Mr. Wolf. It wasn't necessary." Rollins looked at Evers. "You may step down, Judge Wheeling. Thank you." The judge was quiet, almost whispered.

"Oh, one more thing, Mr. Wheeling." Wolf spoke just as Evers had stood up. "Do you now use, or have you in the recent past used, illegal drugs?"

"No."

"You're certain?" Wolf raised his eyebrows.

"I'm certain." Evers had no idea how he was going to avoid the drug test.

H. T. Moran arrived a few minutes after Evers finished his testimony, and White called him as Evers' last witness. H. T. was experienced in the courtroom, knew where to look and how to sit. He wore his uniform. He wore his white boots. He tapped the handcuff tiepin on the front of the witness stand. He supported Evers' testimony, corroborated the details. Evers felt certain that he was doing well. The judge looked at Jo Miller when H. T. testified about finding her in a motel bed; he stopped writing on his yellow pad and folded his arms across his chest.

"Were there any other people in the room, Officer," White asked, "besides you, Judge Wheeling, Mrs. Wheeling and Falstaf?"

"No." H. T.'s answer was quick and firm.

"And Mrs. Wheeling was in bed with Mr. Falstaf."

"Yes."

"Having sex."

"Yes," H. T. said again.

"What did you do?"

"Well, Judge Wheeling up and told Falstaf to get on outside."

"And then?"

"Well, he left. Went outside."

"What was Judge Wheeling's reaction?"

"He was right smart mad."

"How did the confrontation end?" White asked.

"What, now?"

"How did all this end, who did what?" asked White.

"Well, me and Judge Wheeling, we, you know, left and drove back to Norton." H. T. turned and looked at Evers for some clue, a hint. Evers suddenly felt sick and sweaty again. H. T.'s lips were closed, his eyes wide and round. Everything in the courtroom seemed dark and baleful. There was no way he could communicate to H. T. what he needed to say, no way to let him know about the earlier testimony. Evers nodded his head, very slightly, just down and up.

What the fuck does that mean, H. T. Moran must have thought. H. T. decided that it meant to continue the lie. Evers was staring at H. T. White looked at Evers, and Evers leaned toward his lawyer. "Help him, damn it. Lead him."

"And then, Officer Moran, you and Judge Wheeling went to Climax, North Carolina?"

Wolf hit the table with his open hand. "Leading. Mr. White's question is improper. I object."

"Sustained. Rephrase that, Mr. White. I don't appreciate your prodding the witness." Rollins seemed upset. H. T. still appeared uncertain. He looked at Evers. He wanted to help.

"Where did you go after the problem in the motel room?"

"To Norton."

"And before that?"

Evers nodded again. Wolf pointed at him and stood up. "Judge, Mr. Wheeling is coaching this witness. He's nodding."

"I'm nodding because I agree with what he said about my wife," Evers said.

"Where did you go before that, Officer?"

"Nowhere." H. T. was looking straight ahead.

"You didn't go to Climax, North Carolina?"

"No."

"Did you leave Mrs. Wheeling in Climax, tied naked to a sign?" White's voice was plaintive, pleading.

"Why, no sir. No. Did she claim that?"

Wolf leaned back in his chair. Jo Miller smiled.

"Fuck," said Evers, almost out loud. "Great."

After the bloodletting, Evers and Pascal drove to a McDonald's to eat. Pascal drank some hard liquor on the way and smoked part of a joint. "How could that policeman be so fucking stupid, Evers? How? Your lawyer practically told him what to say." They were sitting in the parking lot in Evers' car.

"He tried, Pascal. He's just a dolt, that's all."

"Whatever."

"What a pleasant day, huh? I lose my case, end up paying my wife two thousand dollars a month to fuck a man in the house that I paid for, and I'll lose my pissant, tedious job as soon as the drug screen comes back. Hot damn, Pascal, my life is fuckin' great."

"You'll get things straightened out, Evers. This was just a temporary deal, right? A hearing?"

"Yes."

"We'll be better prepared next time. Certainly we can prove the stuff at the motel. People had to see them together there—and after that, too. Or make Falstaf testify or something. And I didn't sleep with your wife by the way. I just said it to help you."

"You didn't? Really? Don't spend the thirty pieces of silver all at one time. I almost forgot to add that brotherly variable to the my-life-is-great formula." Evers finished the sentence with a disgusted grunt.

"I wish you would quit pounding on me—I'm about all you've got right now."

Evers sighed and turned away from his brother, peered out into the parking lot. Two children carrying backpacks and squirt guns were headed into the restaurant, running and hopping ahead of their parents, shooting each other in the face with jets of water.

"I fucking hated how smug and satisfied Jo Miller was. What a bitch." Evers shook his head, kept watching the kids. "You're right—she's the problem, not you." He looked back at Pascal. "How about your phone records, the call you made to her?"

"Not a problem. I called from Rudy's." Pascal's eyes were already turning glazed and heavy. "At least the policeman got part of the story right. God was he stupid." He laughed.

The brothers went inside, and Evers began looking around as soon as he stepped through the door, did a complete clockwise turn in the Mickey D's. Everything was yellow and bright, surreal. He wouldn't have been surprised to see Salvador Dalí walk in and paint a pterodactyl or two. Evers' face was scorched, burning, his head imploding; he was talking nonsense to himself again, running through blender settings. "Blend, chop, mix, whip, liquefy, dice, grate, puree. Great," he said. Pascal ignored him, but the old people and adolescents and midget-league baseball team, all of them were gawking at him or— even worse—not looking, eating in myopia, their gazes fixed, like men at urinals, no right, no left, just straight ahead. He walked through a sticky Coke spill and went to the counter. He left tracks on the floor.

"Cheeseburgers."

"Sir?"

"Cheeseburgers," Evers repeated. "I want a hundred cheeseburgers."

"One hundred?"

"Correct." Evers put his hands on the counter.

"Now?"

"Right."

"Really?" The boy waiting on Evers looked uncertain.

"Yes. No shit. Now. Really. Is that a problem for you?"

"To go or to eat here?"

"To go."

Pascal tapped Evers on the shoulder. "I'm going to get something in the other line and then go outside."

"A hundred to go, right?"

"Yes." Evers' voice got louder.

"It'll take about twenty or thirty minutes."

"That's okay. I'll wait."

"So that'll be, let's see now, okay, ninety-five dollars and tax." Evers handed the cashier five twenties and a ten and told him to keep the change.

He waited twenty minutes while Pascal sat at the end of a slide in McPlayland, and the cooks made a hundred cheeseburgers. The cheeseburgers were stacked in an empty cardboard box. "Would you like ice tea or fries with your order?" the boy asked when he set the food in front of Evers. "I was supposed to ask that when I took your order." Evers thanked him, turned down the tea and fries and carried the box outside to Pascal.

"Evers, what the fuck are you doing with all those hamburgers?"

"You were watching me while I was up there?"

"No. I was playing with Mayor McCheese." Pascal grinned. "I'm buzzed."

"Oh?"

"Shit, Evers, how much money do you need, anyway? And, at least you've got a fairly easy job."

"Thanks, Pascal. And I'll probably lose that when my dope test comes back."

"You know what I mean."

"Yeah."

"Things will work out. They will."

"Well, at any rate, they're cheeseburgers. I just wanted them."

"What?"

"They're cheeseburgers, not hamburgers." Evers sat down on a swing; he looked huge in the small seat.

"Whatever."

"Isn't it remarkable how you're taught things—if you're a boy, I mean—by your father? The portions of your father that you assimilate. Remember Purvis showing us how to buy shoes? I remember watching him bend a pair of black wing tips into a V and tug on the uppers and check the stitching on the sole. He showed me what to look for. I'd like to be a father and teach that stuff, that ritual of shoe-checking, have it pass through me. The same thing our father did. I'd like for that to happen."

"Are you okay?"

"Yeah. Thanks for trying to help me. I know you hate to lie."

"Let's go on over to my trailer and see if the doctor to the cars and Henry want to get the shrine out and drink beer."

"That's some weird shit, isn't it? I mean, I wonder what it is and all, what's going on."

"I wonder about Ruth Esther, too. Do you think that we'll, you know, get to see her, see her much in the future?"

Evers opened a cheeseburger. "It would probably be easy enough, Pascal. You know where the car lot is."

The next night, Evers was in bed reading, and he had to get up around eleven-thirty to answer the phone.

"When are you going to send me my insurance cards?" Jo Miller asked. "The judge said you were supposed to get them to me immediately."

"What?" Evers croaked. "What cards?"

"Health insurance cards and car insurance information."

"I'll put them in the mail tomorrow. That should be quick enough."

"It's a shame things went so poorly for you, Evers."

"I didn't lie as well as you did." He wondered if his wife was recording their conversation.

"Mr. Wolf says I'll get more when we have the real trial."

"We'll see, you bitch." Evers wanted to scream.

"One more thing, Evers."

"What?"

"You have a small dick and fuck like a fag. And, oh, I almost forgot, your checking balance is going to be a little short; I hope you have overdraft protection. I withdrew about fifteen grand. For a two-week cruise, Mr. Falstaf and I."

"How could you possibly have withdrawn that kind of money? I talked to them after you fucked me over with the horse."

"You gave me a check several months ago, remember? For the utilities. I just held on to it. You signed it in blank. I have two others, although I guess you'll stop payment on them now. Ellen suggested that I keep the checks and pay the bill in cash. It was a good idea, like having an insurance policy."

"You have absolutely no shame, do you? This will come back to haunt you in court."

"I guess we'll see. You were so successful yesterday. And I understand your drug test will be back any day now. That should be a big help."

Evers didn't say anything.

"Evers, listen, maybe I was wrong for some of the things that went on while we were married. But think about how it happened. You left me here by myself and sometimes didn't call for three or four days at a time. Then you tied me to a sign. I deserve to enjoy my life now; that's about all there is to it."

"I truly never realized how unhappy and hard you are, Jo Miller, how bitter, how you hate everything."

"I don't hate everything, Evers. I just don't like you. And, right now, I'm not real high on men in general. I've decided that most of you are thin human coverings stretched over flaws and gaps and pettiness, and that you're completely vainglorious in everything you do from work to pleasure. You're—"

"I don't need to listen to this, Jo Miller. I'll stop by a NOW yard sale if I want to get kicked in the face." Evers slammed the phone down. He was so angry that he couldn't finish reading his book, and he had trouble going to sleep. He drank some bourbon mixed with a soft drink, washed and dried a basket full of towels at the Coin-O-Matic and finally fell asleep at about two in the morning—heard a woman's happy, lilting laugh from the Laundromat right before he drifted off, people washing clothes after midnight, the doors propped open to let out the heat from the dryers.

SEVEN

SOON AFTER ARRIVING IN NORTON, EVERS HAD PURCHASED an aquarium and filled the tank with plastic plants, white gravel, a section of smooth, brown driftwood and, finally, fish, which he brought home in small plastic bags half filled with water and sealed with clear, tight knots: swordtails, angelfish, tiger barbs, catfish and black mollies. Evers put the aquarium in his bedroom, across from his bed. The aquarium had a fluorescent light built into its hood, and the light caused the water to appear practically lavender when the room around it was dark. Evers became transfixed by the silver, black and orange fish moving in the colored water. Almost every night, he turned his reading lamp off, laid his head at the foot of the mattress, and watched the fish . . . suspended here and there in the glass and purple-hued container, colors and flashes, fins and tails, neon streaks darting and pausing and then dipping into a corner. Evers watched the fishes' gills opening and closing. "They breathe water," he'd said more than once.

Evers soon bought more tanks, more plastic plants, more silver, black and orange fish. He had an aquarium built into his living-room wall by an old carpenter who wore a nail apron and drank vodka while he worked. Evers would sit there in his living room, in the dark, listening to Benny Goodman records, smoking a cigar and watching the bright fish in the lavender water. Their fins were never still, their gills *always* moved. . . .

One Saturday morning, not long after the alimony hearing, Evers woke up and looked around his bedroom; the only sound in his five rooms was the bubbling, rolling sound of air being pumped into the lavender aquarium water. The sunlight was coming in the windows—bent and angled through one, without interruption through the other—and made patterns and shapes all over the room: a translucent square on the front of the dresser, a diamond on the floor, a series of S's along the windowsill. A bright, clear, still, mollifying room.

Evers set out to enjoy this day, to enjoy it absolutely. "Singular hedonism," he said while still in his bed. He shaved with a new razor and warmed the lather by holding the can of shaving cream under hot water. He took a bath instead of a shower and shampooed his hair twice.

He put on a white shirt with heavy starch and a new suit, then went out to a restaurant. He ordered eggs Benedict, his favorite breakfast, and made a special effort to chew slowly and pay attention to the consistency of his food—the bread, the meat, the smooth eggs. He smelled the meal while he ate it, and when he was finished eating, he wiped his hands and face on a linen napkin.

Evers stood on the curb outside of the restaurant with the hood on his car raised, and he watched the engine run for five or so minutes before driving away. There were all sorts of belts, pulleys and wires, all interrelated.

He went to the public library and read two short stories by Peter Taylor.

He walked around the park.

He went to the Winston-Salem mall and bought a pair of expensive leather shoes and ten yards of silk fabric.

While he was in Winston-Salem, he went to his health club and swam laps and noticed the water on his limbs and his heart's pace after he had finished his time in the pool. He sat in the sauna and breathed the hot, moist vapor into his nose and throat, and occasionally sucked some of the wet air into his mouth. He combed his hair straight back and left it damp. The comb's teeth touched the top of his head, scraped his scalp.

He ate dinner at Wendy's, and asked a teenage clerk to prepare fresh fries even though he could see from the counter that some were already cooked. The fries were hot and glistened. Evers stuck their square ends into small, white cups of ketchup, tasted the salt and sweet and deep-fry oil.

Evers smoked a cigar.

At home in his den, he drank brandy in small sips that caught fire in his esophagus and burned down across his chest. He watched *Casablanca* on cassette, listened carefully to the dialogue and never stopped following the actors' eyes.

He wrote a short note to his father's brother.

He read a *Washington Post*.

He went to sleep.

He didn't call anyone, and kept the phone off the hook so no one could call him.

The next Monday morning, Evers went to work in Winston-Salem. He left early and stopped at the White Spot Grill and Coffee Shop for breakfast, ate two eggs and toast and smelled like grease and smoke when he left. He was finished with his case by ten-thirty—the lawyers involved had asked for a continuance after a witness showed up drunk—and decided to call Pauletta Lightwren Qwai. She was in her office writing a brief and sounded surprised to hear from Evers, but after they talked for a few minutes, and after he suggested it, Pauletta agreed to have dinner with him in Charleston. "It's a long drive just to eat a meal," she mentioned after they'd decided that Pauletta would cook something at home. "Are you sure you want to do this? Don't you think it might be easier on a weekend?"

"I just had a case wrap up early and don't have to be back until two tomorrow. I'll be on the road soon. You should be flattered . . . think of the sacrifice. It's sort of loopy and romantic, isn't it, driving all that way just to see you?"

Evers left Winston-Salem and drove to his apartment. He took a bath and read *The Sun Also Rises* while he was in the tub. The book was new, just purchased, and it smelled like fresh paper and made a crackling sound when Evers turned back the cover. When he opened the drain, the water leaving the tub caused a tiny funnel to twist and spin around the stopper. Evers stepped out of the water before it had all disappeared.

He dressed in his bedroom—blue blazer, starched shirt, khaki slacks, penny loafers, no socks—and thought about buying a dog, an Old English sheepdog or a basset hound. He'd hung a framed studio photograph of Ernie Kovacs on the wall, and he stepped toward the picture while he was knotting his tie. In the glass between him and the photograph, Evers could see, in miniature, his hands working and pulling at his neck, his collar raised, his top button unfastened. "Would you fuck her, Ernie?" he asked.

Evers drank several cold bottled beers on the way to West Virginia. The drive took most of the afternoon, but it was warm, June, and he rode with his windows down, and the air picked up a lot of different scents and smells and filled up his car. About a mile from Pauletta's, he was alongside an attractive lady at a stoplight, and she smiled at him. He raised his beer bottle, toasted the air with it, and then, when the light changed, he drove away, feeling churlish and idiotic. Evers the adolescent. Still, it was a good feeling not being with Jo Miller any longer.

Pauletta was in the kitchen when Evers arrived at her house. She called for him to come in when he knocked on the door but didn't go to meet him. Evers wandered through two rooms until he found her, walked past an umbrella stand, a stuffed peacock and a table full of ceremonial masks and clay pottery.

"My, you look nice," she said. Pauletta was peering at him around her open refrigerator door. Her hands were full—eggs, bread, butter—and she was wearing a pair of jeans and a sweatshirt. She kicked the door closed with the side of her foot.

"Did you forget I was coming?"

"What do you mean?"

"You just don't seem too, well, too prepared," Evers said.

"I just talked to you this morning, and I just now got home."

"Oh. I guess that makes sense. Sorry. May I help you?"

"You could make us a drink."

Evers opened a cabinet near the sink. "Should I use the everyday jelly jars or the formal ones?"

"Why don't you just drink straight out of the bottle, Judge Wheeling?"

"What are you cooking?"

"Omelets. I make good ones, with seafood in them. I have some crab and shrimp. And a salad."

"Sounds good." Evers was pleased. He took a bottle of scotch from a tray on the counter.

"Did you forget your socks, Mr. J. Crew, or are your white, bare ankles proof to the rest of the world that, despite the necktie, you're not a tight ass?"

"I noticed that the guy in the picture in your den had on some really outstanding footwear—men's hose, I think the salesmen call them. With shorts, too. That's a good look. Those smart gossamer-thin nylon jobs and your sporty Bermudas."

"You're lying." Pauletta broke an egg on the edge of a glass bowl.

"Maybe they were a nylon-silk blend then."

"You're lying to me." She smiled. "I really never noticed. Did he really have on dress socks with shorts?"

"Who is that guy, anyway? He seems to be in a couple of different pictures."

"He's not too central anymore as far as I'm concerned."

"No. Say no. You're putting me on. You two make such a handsome ebony couple."

"Not anymore."

"End of story, huh?—to put it in your terms?"

"Pretty much." Pauletta broke another egg.

"Why?"

"I just got tired of him. Like a good song, I guess. You hear it and love it and buy it and then get sick of it."

"I can't believe how cynical you are about romance," said Evers.

"I can't believe how romantic you are about cynicism." She looked at him and made a face. "Clever reversal, huh?"

"You'll probably have fewer disappointments than I, that's for sure," Evers answered.

"Try not to brood so much."

Evers held up a jelly glass filled with scotch and ice cubes. He was leaning against the refrigerator. "To Adam Clayton Powell," he said, and raised his glass.

"To Oral Roberts," she replied.

"Instead of eating at the table, why don't we just take our plates into the den and eat on the couch when you get everything ready? Less formal, less stiff, easier to transition into music and TV when we run out of small talk."

"If you like. You're the guest."

Evers ate one omelet and enjoyed it so much that Pauletta made him another. They sat on her living-room floor, with their backs against a sofa and their plates between their legs. Evers picked up both plates and took them into the kitchen after he and Pauletta finished their food.

"So what do you think of Charleston? Had you been here before, before you came to meet with me?" Pauletta asked when he came back into the living room. She was still sitting on the floor.

"I like the way the city and streets press right up against the hills. Have you ever noticed how the roads sometimes touch this sort of wall—all around Charleston are these stained, water-colored banks. You can see where the hills have been cut into, all the strata exposed, and from a distance a lot of them look like hill fences or walls. Often, though, you can't see the cuts and blasts in the hills until you're pretty close; you have to be in the right spot."

"That certainly attracts a lot of people to the city. Without a doubt, that's why I came. Most people would probably tell you the same thing."

"You asked."

"Did you put the dishes in the sink or the dishwasher?"

"The dishwasher. I'm a neat person and live by myself." Evers cleared his throat.

"That was nice of you. Thanks."

"Thank you for the dinner," he said.

There was a small gap, a little glitch. Nothing came to mind to talk about, and Evers considered whether he should get back on the floor with Pauletta or take a seat on the sofa.

"Let me ask you something else." Pauletta was relaxed; she had taken off her shoes and set them beside her. Her toenails were cut short and painted with clear polish.

"What?"

"How about sex?"

"With me?" Evers was still standing. "The two of us?"

"Yes."

"Sort of a one-time thing or what? This is sort of sudden."

"I think that anything beyond a one-night stand might compromise us both."

"I suppose you could talk me into it," he said.

"Good."

"Good."

"Say the word."

"Really?"

"Yes, really."

"Let's go into your bedroom." Evers hadn't moved.

"No," Pauletta said. "Come here."

"Why?"

"Come here," she repeated.

He took two steps toward her, and she raised herself onto her knees and put her face against the front of his pants.

"Let's go into the bedroom."

"Right here on the floor." Pauletta stood up and faced Evers. Her hands were around him at his waist.

"The lights?" asked Evers.

"On. So we can see each other." She kissed him.

"This is . . . ," he said, not finishing his sentence or his thought.

Pauletta positioned Evers on the floor and got on top of him. He had never touched her before, and her skin was smooth, brown and soft, without any give. He put his hands inside her shirt, first touched her stomach, then her back and then her breasts, underneath them—felt warm flesh on his palms and the backs of his hands at the same time. He lifted the bottom of her shirt, and Pauletta raised her arms above her head. She was on top of him, uncovered, shirtless, wearing jeans.

Evers turned off a table lamp beside the sofa; almost immediately, he reached up again and relit the room. "I'm not going to do it," he said.

"Tell your crotch that. You two are out of sync." Pauletta leaned forward so her breasts were close to Evers' face. She was very attractive.

"I shouldn't."

"Do you want to?"

"Yes." Evers touched her breast with the ends of his fingers.

"Then you'd better do it now, or that's it. I'm not a waiter, Mr. Wheeling."

"I'm not going to."

"Suit yourself." Pauletta didn't change her position.

Evers was still touching her. "I would've hoped you might appreciate my decency."

"I don't know if that's what it is."

Evers wiggled out from underneath her. He was still wearing his clothes and shoes. "Better to have small restraints than none at all. I already have too many aches and pains, without this. You've been kind to me, and I don't want you to think that I drove up here just to sleep with you."

"It's not possible, is it, that you're intimidated just a little bit?" Pauletta sat up some; she was still on the floor.

"No more than the usual butterflies that come on the heels of long anticipation and first-time sex."

Pauletta made no effort to cover herself. "It's your call."

"I'm actually afraid of catching malaria or some incurable African pox. You know that, don't you? That's the real reason."

"Or something even more loathsome?" asked Pauletta.

"True. Masturbation has pretty much become the ejaculation of choice. I'd rather lose my eyes than my immune system."

Pauletta tried not to laugh, but did. Evers smiled.

"Thanks for the insight," she said.

"So to speak."

"So to speak," she answered. Pauletta reached for her shirt and stood up. She turned her back toward Evers, raised her arms one at a time and pulled the sweatshirt over her head.

"I'm going to leave. I'm grateful for dinner. That was a fine thing to do. I'll touch base again before too long. I've got to find my hotel. I'm not exactly sure where it is." Evers walked to the door and stood there for a minute. "Good night. Thanks for the evening. Sorry I'm a little flustered."

"Good night."

Evers shut the door to Pauletta's home and walked across the gravel driveway to his car. He lifted the handle on the door and discovered that it was locked. He tried the other door. Straight up, no resistance, no click. Evers never locked his car, but the doors were locked. He cupped his hands around his face and pressed against the passenger-side window. The keys were in the ignition. "God spoke to Moses through a burning bush," he said.

He walked back across the rock drive to Pauletta's porch, steps and crunches. The lights were still on inside. He knocked.

"Is that you, Judge Wheeling?"

"Yes."

"What do you want?" she asked through the door.

"I forgot my wok," he said.

"You didn't bring a wok."

"How do you know?"

"What do you really want?"

"To have sex."

"Then this can't be Judge Wheeling; you must be a burglar. I'm calling the police."

"What do I have to do to get inside?" Evers asked.

"The house or my pants?"

"The latter."

"Celebrate Kwanza with me."

"Not possible." Evers had his hands on his hips.

"Send me flowers on Dr. King's birthday."

"Done. Agreed. Promised."

"And apologize."

"I apologize."

"And humble yourself by begging."

"I beg. I apologize *and* beg, and, when the big day comes, I'll woo you with the red-clay-of-Georgia bouquet from an enterprise-zone, minority-owned florist."

There was a pause, then Pauletta opened the door. Her jeans and old shirt were lying beside her on a round, brown throw rug. She was unclothed, standing still, and she and Evers were on the floor almost as soon as he went inside the house. They rolled onto the rug and clothes and then off again, back onto the floor, hardwood and polished.

Somewhere after two in the morning, Evers and Pauletta retrieved his keys with a straightened coat hanger.

"You're a fisher of keys," she said.

"And you're a fisher of men."

"I generally just wait for them to wash up on the shore."

"Thanks for the act of kindness."

"It was something I wanted to do." Pauletta was in a long T-shirt, a robe and tennis shoes. She turned away from Evers and started toward her house. "Once," she said while she was walking.

"Oh?"

"I don't mean that harshly," she said over her shoulder.

"I doubt that you mean it at all."

"Romance is a book, Mr. Wheeling. Only so many pages."

"Maybe we could just be friends when you finally get to the index."

She stopped and faced Evers. "I could, perhaps, but I suspect that you couldn't."

"Who knows?"

"It's fair to say, though, that we're never going to marry and raise adorable mulatto children, huh? Or, for that matter, date anyplace where upright, god-fearing people might see us."

"True."

"And why is that?"

"Because you're black. That's easy."

"And because you're white," she added.

"Oh, I doubt we'd be serious if I were differently skinned."

"Why's that?"

"I'd still want to marry a white woman." Evers grinned.

"Under eighteen, of course. You guys could ride around Dairy Queen and steal pocket change from her parents. That's about your speed." She headed down the drive again.

Evers opened his car door and a light came on; it illuminated the interior of the Datsun but didn't get very far into the night, left him in the dark. "Good-bye. Get inside before you get too cool."

"Right." Pauletta opened and closed her front door without turning around, and the tail of her robe caught a little gust just before she disappeared. A light turned on and off in the house.

Evers found a credit-card receipt in his glove box and wrote on the back of the paper with a pencil:

> *"Romance," said Pauletta, "is a book."*
> *But after the pages expire, there's no second look.*
> *So pen it long, dense and hard, that's the trick—*
> *Which leaves me, I fear, a line short of even a bawdy limerick.*

He stuck the poem under Pauletta's door.

Evers was staying at the Omni, in the center of Charleston. He wasn't tired when he left Pauletta's, so he didn't want to go to bed. That left him with the prospect of sitting in an uncomfortable hotel chair, smoking cigarettes and watching infomercials or piss-poor movies or some of the R-rated tease from the "adult entertainment" selections that would, no doubt, feature too many ankle tattoos and quit right above the actors' pubic hair. In fact, almost every late-night possibility in a West Virginia hotel room would cause Evers—alone in his underwear and dress shirt, without a wife or even plans for a wake-up call—to feel like he was at loose ends.

He stopped at a convenience store and bought two white-powdered doughnuts and a cup of coffee. The man working in the store was talkative and friendly and told Evers where to turn to get to his hotel. Evers stirred sugar into his coffee with a flat wooden stick, put a lid on the cup and walked outside. He could feel the hill air on his face, and the coffee warmed the paper cup in his hand. Evers drove around the city for another hour, beneath the gray buildings and hill walls, wasting time, looking at lights in windows and street signs, eating small pieces of his doughnuts.

When he found his hotel and checked in, it was almost three-thirty. He sat down on the side of his bed and called Pauletta. She was asleep but woke up quickly and sounded alert.

"I called to let you know that I made it to my hotel safely," Evers told her.

"Are you stupid? Did it take you two hours to find your hotel, or did you stop somewhere?"

"I rode around some, looked at the city."

"Oh."

"Thank you again for a nice evening."

"You're welcome." Pauletta didn't seem upset by Evers' call.

"May I ask you something?"

"What?"

"I'm still curious, you know, about a lot of things, including Salt Lake City and you and Ruth Esther. Now that everything is over and done with, I wish that someone would tell me what really went on."

"Maybe somebody will, someday." She yawned. "Oh, by the way, has anyone heard from our friend the cop? Dillon . . . what's his story these days?"

"I hear he's still in Florida," Evers said. "He's not back, that's all I know. I hope he stays there. Basically, it's just another thing for me to worry about."

"I'm going back to sleep."

"All right. I left you a little verse in your door. A poetry gift. Hope you like it."

"I'm sure I will," Pauletta said.

"I'll bet that you get out of bed right now and go look at it, in fact. You won't be able to wait until you wake up for work."

"I'm going back to sleep, Judge Wheeling."

"Maybe I'll come up again, and we could do something. If that's agreeable with you."

"I understand there's a monster-truck show coming soon and that Jerry Lee Lewis is playing here next Thursday. I'll see if tickets are still available."

The week of July Fourth, Evers took several days of vacation, leaving two opinions and several divorce files on his desk undone, and drove to see his brother. Pascal, Rudy and Henry were playing Monopoly in the kitchen when Evers pulled up at the trailer. Rudy had a large lead, a lot of property and green houses, and was paying Henry a hundred dollars each turn to roll the dice and move his piece for him. "A wealthy man doesn't roll the dice," Rudy said. "Plus, I'm trying to keep Henry and Pascal solvent." Everyone appeared to be sober. Pascal was the only one drinking, and he had a beer in front of him.

"Sorry about your case, Jo Miller and all; I meant to mention it before now, but it slipped my mind," Henry said. He'd just moved Rudy's thimble eight spaces and was looking at a deed when he spoke.

"Thanks," said Evers.

"We've been trying to get you for a couple days," Pascal said.

"I've had the phone off the hook a lot. Did you try the office?"

"Lost the number and forgot the name of the court. I knew you were working in Winston-Salem, though. I just didn't have the energy to try all the possibilities in the phone listings. How about writing it down again for me?"

"So what's up?"

"You didn't see?" asked Rudy.

"See what?" Evers looked around the kitchen.

"Outside."

"What's outside?"

Henry laughed. "Check the drive, Evers."

"Rudy got his car," Pascal said.

"He got the . . . the what?" Evers stuttered; he felt a twitch run from his face to his abdomen to his knees.

"Can you believe this? We just got it a couple days ago." Rudy was excited; he spoke quickly. "Like I say, we've been trying to call you for a while, but Pascal felt pretty sure you'd said you were coming down today so we didn't worry a whole lot."

"What kind is it?" Evers asked.

"A Packard," Rudy said. "I wonder if we only get one wish with the smiling talisman?"

"Is that what you wanted?" Evers said. "I can't remember."

"Well, I asked for a Packard limousine, and this is just a standard passenger car, but I'm okay with that."

Evers sat down. "Rudy, you swear this isn't a joke or trick? I don't think you would lie to me, but this is fucking me up. You really got this car?"

"No joke. Just like Henry got the money."

"How?"

Rudy grinned. He stopped playing Monopoly. "Three years ago, this guy's eating at Donald's Pit Cooked over in Concord. It's hot as shit, and he gets food poisoning. Hits him quickly and violently. He thinks he's having the big myocardial infarction—a heart attack. He comes to the ER; I get him stabilized and healthy. Turns out that he owns Red Brick Industries—they make and sell brick all over the place. Guy's name is Hall. James Willard Hall. Check the *Fortune* list, he's about number thirty or so. Megarich. We talked about cars while he was in the hospital. He had to stay overnight, and I hung out with him. He was a collector. Nice guy, knew his automobiles. Each year he sends me a Christmas card and letter."

Evers looked at his brother. "Is this true, Pascal?"

"As far as I know. Rudy mentioned the guy to me before."

"Anyway, I talked to him and got his gastrointestinal problems cleared up, and he liked me. I understand he had a wife but no kids or brothers or sisters. So he dies a couple of weeks ago and leaves me a Packard. They called me and trucked it right down here. The guys who brought it said he had over seventy cars."

"Probably like givin' away a TV or sofa for a guy with that kind of money," Henry said.

"If that," said Pascal.

"By the way, I left you guys as beneficiaries for my lottery checks if I die before they're paid out." Henry seemed a little embarrassed.

"Thanks, Henry," said Pascal.

"Yeah, thanks," said Rudy at about the same time.

"I guess that leaves you and me, Pascal." Evers looked at the game board. Everything was sloppy. The houses were crooked, the money and deeds scattered everywhere.

"Just you, I guess." Pascal smiled. "I'm about as happy and serene as I can get. I love my life and my friends. I don't have any worries, don't have any responsibilities."

Rudy handed Henry some Monopoly money. "Jo Miller probably shouldn't fly anytime soon." They all chuckled a little, but no one glanced at Evers or stopped looking at the board.

"Guess who's coming to visit us tonight, brother."

"Who?" Evers asked.

"Guess."

"I don't know. Charo? David Copperfield? Baby Doc Duvalier and the Ton-Ton Macoutes? Paul Lynde?"

"Paul Lynde is dead," Henry noted.

"I'll take Rose Marie to block," Rudy said, snickering.

"So who's coming?" Evers asked again. "I give up."

"Ruth Esther."

"Really? Ruth Esther? Why?"

"She was supposed to be here by now. She's late, but she said she was coming."

"Why?" Evers wondered. "Why's she coming?"

"I called her," Pascal said, "and invited her to play some double-wide Monopoly with us. I thought it would be nice, since you were coming down—sort of a reunion."

"It's Parker Brothers' real estate trading game," Henry quipped, "the most popular board game in history."

"And she's coming just to hang out?"

"That's what she said."

Evers looked around the corner into the den. "That explains why you guys are sober and everything's so clean."

"I found this service, a cleaning service called Maid for You. Cute name, huh? They came in a van, about five of them, and cleaned the kitchen and bathroom and den and started on my bedroom. They'd only set aside an hour, so they didn't get all the way through."

"I think I'm going to have to break over and have just a small hit," Rudy said. "Just a little bowl. She's late anyway. Watch my empire for a moment, Evers, okay?"

Evers sat down in Rudy's chair. "Welfare as you know it just ended, Henry. I'll be moving my piece all by myself."

"Damn. That's cold. Cut the safety net, why don't you? Pascal and I will get some signs and bullhorns and fat union guys and sisters with litters and an all-caps acronym—SURGE or something like that—and a chant and picket your big-ass, red, Boardwalk hotel. You may want to think again. Or we might burn and loot for a while over on Baltic, just to show our colors a little bit."

"Civil disobedience," Pascal remarked.

"I'm merely the landlord. You'll have to take your issues up with the car doctor."

Ruth Esther knocked on the door while Rudy was still in Pascal's room smoking marijuana, and Henry let her in. Everyone stood up when she walked into the kitchen. Rudy yelled "hello" from the back of the trailer and announced that he'd be out in a few minutes, after he "finished reading the last few lines of an Emily Dickinson poem."

Ruth Esther seemed happy and relaxed and flattered by all the attention and preparation. Pascal started the game over, and the four men and Ruth Esther played Monopoly and talked and told stories until one in the morning. Pascal had bought her a bottle of Riesling from a regional winery, and she drank three glasses of the wine and ate some crackers and a small piece of cheese. The men drank beer, but not that much, and they occasionally went back into Pascal's room to read more Emily Dickinson, but not that often. Rudy and Henry left for about twenty minutes, to get cigarettes and candy bars. "I love my new car," Rudy proclaimed when he walked back into the trailer.

"That was fun," Ruth Esther said after the last game ended. "Thank you for inviting me." She was wearing a pair of modest denim shorts and a white T-shirt underneath a darker, long-sleeve shirt. The long-sleeve shirt was tucked in and buttoned about halfway up. It was the first time Evers had seen Ruth Esther in clothes with color.

"Thank you for coming," Pascal said.

Ruth Esther asked if she could spend the night at the trailer, and Pascal offered to let her stay in one of the bedrooms. Henry and Rudy also volunteered a room for the night. Ruth Esther thanked them and decided to stay at Pascal's. She hugged the car doctor, Henry and Evers, kissed Pascal's cheek and went to bed in the extra bedroom.

"Nice," said Pascal, and the other three men agreed and winked and grinned. Henry finished a beer and tossed the empty into a grocery bag beside the trash can.

"Let's go to Carowinds tomorrow," Rudy said. "It's supposed to be hot and we can ride the water rides and play arcade games, get a little buzz, drink some good beer. You can buy Guinness Stout at Lowes now."

"It's usually crowded this time of year," Evers said. "The lines are too long, especially for the good rides."

"Who cares?"

Henry spoke up. "I'd probably have to take my wife."

"Maybe Ruth Esther would like to go," Pascal said. "I might ask her."

"Well, call me in the morning, when you—" Henry didn't finish what he was saying.

Ruth Esther walked back into the kitchen. "I'm sorry to bother you," she said. "There are a lot of things on the bed in my room—clothes and a rifle and a whole bunch of Nintendo cartridges. What do you want me to do with them?"

"Oh, sorry. Damn. Just put everything on the floor. The maids didn't make it that far."

"Okay." Ruth Esther had her hands in front of her, her second fingers pressed together, the tips almost touching her chin.

"Do you need some help?" Evers asked.

"Oh, no. I'm just sorry to be a problem."

"We're glad you came," Pascal said. "We don't get many guests."

"Where are you going to sleep, Judge Wheeling? You're not leaving tonight, are you? Am I taking your bed?" Ruth Esther asked.

"I always sleep on the sofa," Evers said.

"Do you want me to sleep on the sofa? I'll be glad to," Ruth Esther offered.

"Please, take the bed. Really."

"I don't want to put anyone out."

"You're not. We're glad you're here," Pascal assured her. "In fact, we were thinking about going to Carowinds tomorrow, the theme park near Charlotte. The weather's supposed to be good, if you'd like to go."

"I'll think about it; we'll see. That might be fun."

"Good."

"I hope you'll come." Rudy smiled at Ruth Esther.

"My wife might go," Henry said.

"Thank you all for asking me. Let's talk about it in the morning." Ruth Esther took her hands down. "Good night. If you have trouble sleeping, Evers, let me know, okay? I don't want to kick anyone out of his bed. By the way, what happened to the window in there? It's so dark."

"Oh. Right. A rock flew out from under the mower and busted it. Henry and I nailed particleboard over it. We need to repair it. Sorry."

"That's okay. It just really seems kind of shut up."

After Rudy and Henry left for the night, Evers and Pascal went into the den and turned on the TV. Pascal had purchased a satellite system with some of the money Henry had given him from the lottery winnings. A black-and-white movie was on, and the men kept the volume low so Ruth Esther could sleep.

"It's just too much of a coincidence, Rudy getting that car," Evers said.

"Whatever."

"It's a beautiful car, really sharp."

"It is nice." Pascal nodded.

"I'd like to have a car like that, now that I've seen Rudy's." Evers put his feet on the sofa.

"I've often thought that there are really just two sentiments in the world: envy and pity. The world's divided into people and places below you and above you."

"You're probably right. I'm just too indifferent to notice these days." Evers started taking his shoes off.

"So how's your wish coming?" asked Pascal.

"I can only hope. Think I need to put her picture and a map to her house in the freezer with the decanter?"

Pascal rubbed his eyes. "She's a bitch, Evers." His voice was very matter-of-fact.

"What do you mean?"

"Just what I said."

Evers stared at the TV. The movie was a romantic comedy. A black-and-white man with slicked-back hair was laughing, but Evers had trouble hearing what the actors were saying. "Did you have sex with her?"

Pascal didn't answer for a moment. "Yeah. Yes."

"Why? Jesus."

"There really isn't any excuse, is there, Evers? It's all pretty much the same."

"Depends. Sometimes it's capital murder, sometimes just involuntary manslaughter."

"Ah, Judge Wheeling. It must be nice to be able to grade evil."

"So tell me."

"Well, it was several years ago, a long time ago, when we all went to Wrightsville Beach. Remember? There were about ten or twelve of us and we were . . . it was at the beach. And I was fairly drunk and stoned—no excuse, Evers, I know—and you and Henry had gone out bowling and drinking and I swear it happened just like that. She came into my room when I was in the shower. I did it once. One time. I had no idea beforehand. No flirting or anything. No warnings or brushes under the table. It was really sudden. She tried for two or three years afterward, all the time. I'm sorry. I shouldn't have." Pascal stopped talking for a moment. "I mean, you know, I liked it. I liked the sex because it was so wrong and nasty. I'm not going to lie about that. But it was a one-time mistake, at the beach, with a buzz, years ago."

"I can't believe you'd do it, as close as we are."

"That sort of made it easier, in one sense. I knew you would forgive me. And the way Jo Miller was—is—and the way she acted, it wasn't like I was ruining something that was sacrosanct or pure. I think she really must hate you. I know she hates me."

"Like I said, I guess it doesn't matter now."

"It does matter; I was wrong. I'm sorry. I should've told you when she did it." Pascal had his head bowed when he spoke.

"Sure."

"You know, Evers, I wrote her and called her a couple of times before your trial, to try to, I don't know, make some kind of peace, try to get her to settle things without dragging us through all this. To tell the truth, I sent her a . . . a proposal, I guess you'd call it, not long ago. She wrote me back just as hard as nails, said that what she was doing was best for everybody concerned, whatever the fuck that means. And I tried to get her to say something or write something that you could use against her, but that never happened. She was too smart to admit to anything, even over the phone."

"She wrote you? Wrote you back?"

"Yeah."

"Do you still have the letters? I'd like to see them."

"No. Why would I? I . . . I threw them away. Well, actually, maybe I still have them somewhere . . . around here."

"Did you fuck her again, Pascal? Did you?"

"Lord, no."

"It wouldn't surprise me."

"I didn't."

"What the hell are you doing trying to settle my case, making offers without asking me?"

"I was trying to help, Evers. Just trying to help. Almost anything would beat another trip to court, and at least it kept some dialogue going."

"Dialogue? You think you're Henry-fucking-Kissinger? What the hell does that mean—dialogue?"

"I'm sorry. I really am. I screwed the whole thing up from start to finish. I do hope it makes some difference to you that she initiated the sex." Pascal looked up at the TV.

"That's a good excuse. I'm sure you battled and struggled for what was right." Evers was suddenly very mad.

"I don't know why you're defending Jo Miller, Evers."

"Don't blame her, Pascal. She didn't provide the hard-on. You're just as wrong as she is. All you had to do was say no. Just like you've said no to a million other things."

"Whatever."

Evers was angry. He stared at Pascal. "I get tired of all your Gandhi, passive bullshit and pissy resignation."

"Sometimes you just sort of give up and trade your land for shiny beads and a drink. You know what I mean, Evers?"

EIGHT

THE NEXT MORNING, EVERS AND PASCAL WERE STILL NOT awake at eight-thirty; they had fallen asleep and left the TV on all night. When Evers woke up it was raining, a dopey *Love Boat* episode was just starting, and someone was knocking on the door. Evers assumed it was Henry or Rudy, but upon opening the door, he didn't recognize the two men standing on the steps. Both were wearing suits. One was dressed in a vest and a polyester tie, the other had on cowboy boots and a large belt buckle inlaid with turquoise.

"Are you Judge Wheeling?" The man in the vest was speaking. He was shorter than Evers and almost bald. The man with him was taller and handsome.

"Yes."

"Could we talk with you for a moment?"

"That depends. Who are you and what do you want?" Evers' tone was brusque. Cool.

"We'd like to speak with you for a moment. We're policemen."

"Do you have some sort of identification?"

Both men held up metal badges in small plastic wallets, only inches away from Evers' face. "This is Investigator Loggins, and I'm Investigator Greenfield." Loggins was the good-looking one. He hadn't spoken yet.

"I'm sorry. Sure, come in."

"We have some bad news for you." Greenfield looked straight at Evers. "Your wife is dead."

"Come in," he said again. He tried to recall what the kitchen looked like. As best as he could remember, no dope was in plain view. "Dead. Jo Miller? My wife? Oh . . ." Evers made a quick sweep with his hand, beckoned the officers through the door.

The three men sat down at the kitchen table. The game board and several cans and ashtrays were still on the table. Evers sat next to Greenfield.

"Do you mind if we smoke?" Loggins asked. It was the first time he had spoken.

"I'm trying to cut back, but everyone else around here does, so go ahead."

"If it bothers you, I won't." Loggins reached inside his coat pocket and took out a pack of cigarettes. The package was almost flat, the cellophane torn at one corner. He didn't make an effort to remove any of the cigarettes, just held the pack in his hand. "We're sorry about your wife."

Evers looked at Greenfield, then Loggins. He knew they were evaluating his reaction. "To be honest, we were getting a divorce and pretty much despised each other. I can't say I'm disappointed that she's dead." Evers put his hands on the table in front of him and noticed a note from Ruth Esther underneath the thimble and terrier tokens from the Monopoly game.

"Oh, I see. We'd heard that."

Evers looked at the table and put his chin in his hand. "What a sorry mess." The men were quiet for a moment. "I guess you suspicion that I have some involvement in her death," he finally said.

"Why do you say that?" asked Greenfield.

"I assume that's why you're here."

"Well, not really. No. It looks like she killed herself."

"What?"

"Suicide," said Loggins, pronouncing the word "sewer side."

"Why did you think something was out of the ordinary, that we were here because we suspected you?" Greenfield cocked his head when he spoke.

"I've been a judge for several years. You didn't show up here telling me in somber tones that you wanted to talk just to deliver the grim news. You're watching me to see my reaction. If everything were routine, you would have simply called, or at least given me the sad report with downcast eyes and hit the road."

"How do you know she didn't just have a heart attack or get hit by a bus?"

Evers looked at the policemen. He raised his voice slightly. "Because you said 'your wife is dead.' Not 'your wife has been killed in an accident' or 'your wife had a heart attack.' I know the routine, okay?"

"Sure."

"How did she kill herself?"

"Pistol. One shot, through the temple."

"Did she die right away or at the hospital or something?" Evers asked.

"Right away, evidently."

"If I had . . . " Evers stopped speaking and looked behind him. Pascal walked into the kitchen wearing a gray T-shirt, blue sweatpants and the cheap shoes from Utah. "Good morning, brother."

"Hey," Evers said.

Pascal looked at Greenfield and Loggins. "Selling insurance?"

"They're policemen, Pascal. Detectives from Durham."

Loggins stood up. "I'm Detective Loggins. This is Detective Greenfield."

Pascal looked embarrassed. His neck turned red. "I'm sorry. I didn't mean to insult you. I like the police. Someone broke into my car about a month ago and the folks down here did a real nice job on the case. Sorry." He picked at a yellow crust in the corner of his eye.

"No problem."

"So what's up?" Pascal asked.

"Mrs. Wheeling is dead."

"Damn." Pascal looked at his brother. "That's hard to believe. Dead? Geez."

"What I was saying, gentlemen, is that if I had some involvement I would've been coy enough to keep my deductions to myself." Evers looked at one of the ashtrays close to him and thought he saw the ragged, burned end of a roach. The little bit of dope made him uneasy. He was trying to read the note from Ruth Esther without tilting his head or letting the policemen see his eyes shift.

"What happened to her?" Pascal was standing beside Evers.

"Well, it appears to be suicide."

" 'Appears' is the key word, evidently," Evers said.

"Well, it is a little strange, some things. There were wet clothes in the washer, and she wrote the note on her computer instead of by hand."

"Her name was spelled wrong on the note," Loggins said abruptly. "And she was in her bedroom, not at the computer."

"Misspelled?"

"Miller was wrote out M-i-l-e-r. Just one 'l.' "

"That is peculiar," said Evers.

"Yeah."

"I know how to spell it, Detectives. Two 'l's.' " Evers picked up a Monopoly bill.

"You're awfully defensive, Mr. Wheeling." Loggins smiled.

"Is there anything else?" Evers looked at Pascal, then at the detectives.

"You don't seem too upset." Loggins' tone was unpleasant, challenging.

Evers hesitated. "I'm not, to be honest. I'm glad she's dead. I just told you that. She ruined our marriage. She repaid my kindness and good nature with infidelity. If she killed herself, the world's a better place for it. If someone killed her, he or she probably had a compelling reason. I didn't kill her. I'm sure you're not going to tell me the time of death before you fish around a little while longer, but I was here most of yesterday and all last night. Our friends left a few minutes after one this morning, and Pascal and I were awake until at least one-thirty watching a movie. Black-and-white romantic comedy. Anything else?"

"She died early this morning—sometime after midnight. And it ain't but about an hour down to Durham from here," Loggins said.

"Hour and ten minutes." Evers stared at the detective.

"Well, Mr. Loggins, Evers was here at about two-thirty. I was up, and I know he was right here."

"You a light sleeper, Mr. Wheeling?"

"Whatever," said Pascal.

"I mean, that's right convenient that you get up and see him at two-thirty."

"You guys are phenomenally good at your job," said Pascal. "How long have you been detectives?"

"Long enough." Loggins put the cigarettes back in his pocket and hitched his thumbs under the top of his belt buckle.

Pascal walked across the kitchen and squatted down in front of him. They were almost face to face. "You're sort of hinting that I'm lying to cover for my brother, aren't you? That it's just too extraordinary to believe what I'm saying? It's like the alibi's just too perfect. That's because you're skilled at your job. Tell you what: Check our phone records, Marshal McCloud. Around two-thirty. Nine hundred number, Carolina Date Line. I call women on the phone and talk to them about sticking vibrators in their pussies. I have a lot of free time on my hands. And check the months before, too. You'll see this wasn't the first call in the early morning, just in case you think I staged this one." Pascal had moved his face closer to Loggins as he spoke, so that their noses were almost touching when he finished. Pascal stayed in Loggins' face after he had stopped talking, not batting an eye, breathing the detective's pissed-off air right back on him.

"Gentlemen, this is getting out of control." Greenfield put his hand on Pascal's arm. "Come on. We're not suggesting anything." He turned and looked at Evers. "Judge, you understand, I hope. This is our job. You are certainly a routine suspect. Right now, this looks like a suicide. Crazy people probably don't proofread their suicide notes. There's nothing really that we're trying to do to you." He let go of Pascal.

"Sure." Evers' tone was flat and noncommittal.

"The medical examiner said it looks like she had sex before she died," Loggins said.

"Must have been really shitty, huh?" Pascal was still crouched down in front of the policeman.

"That should help us a bit. A little lab work might tell us who'd been with her just before she died."

"That ought to eliminate me," Evers said.

"Like I told you, we aren't here to point fingers," Greenfield said.

"Of course not."

"We thank you and your brother for your time." Greenfield stood up from the table, took a step across the kitchen and patted Pascal on the shoulder. "No hard feelings, Mr. Wheeling. I hope you understand." Greenfield made eye contact with his partner. "Let's leave these gents alone; we need to get on back."

When Loggins got up, Pascal stood up with him, and the two men kept looking at each other until Greenfield spoke again and said he'd be in touch if anything important happened.

"Damn," Evers said once Loggins and Greenfield had left and pulled the screen door shut behind them.

"No shit," Pascal said, heading back into his bedroom, the flip-flops slapping against his heel and the floor, the pops and snaps picking up speed as he got farther away from the kitchen. Evers heard *Fantasia* start, and soon he smelled dope smoke. He walked to the bedroom door and looked in; Pascal was sitting in the recliner with the bong in his hands.

"That's some pretty unpleasant shit. Jo Miller winding up dead, then the police coming by."

"They seemed dumb, Evers, didn't they? Didn't they seem dumb to you?"

"I guess." Evers sat down on Pascal's bed. "Give me a hit for the road."

"Is Ruth Esther still asleep?" Pascal asked.

"No, she's gone. She wasn't here when the police came. She left us a nice note." Evers handed his brother the note from the table.

Dear Pascal and Evers:
When I woke up it was raining pretty bad. I guess the weather's a surprise, and that it ruins our trip to the amusement park. The week of the fourth is always a busy time at work, so at least I can try to sell a few cars. We'll have to go to Carowinds some other day. I enjoyed seeing you all and will try to call you if something fun comes up in Winston. Please call me again, too. Thank you, Pascal, for the wine and being so nice to me.
Ruth Esther

"You're not, I mean, you're not upset about your wife, are you?" Pascal was holding Ruth Esther's note in one hand and the bong in the other.

"No, not really. It's just strange; that's about all I can say."

"There's no reason to let it get to you. You're better off without her. I know that sounds callous . . . hard, but you know. . . ."

"Don't worry about it."

"So everything's all right?" Pascal looked up at his brother.

"No doubt. Everything is all right."

"Okay." Pascal lit the bong and sucked in as much smoke as he could. The water in the pipe boiled and gurgled.

"Did you really check on me when you called the nine hundred number?"

"Check on you? Right. Yeah, I did. Whatever."

Evers rubbed his fingers back and forth across his chin. He hadn't shaved yet. "Why are you acting so strange? What is it?"

"Nothing. I'm fine." Pascal put his lips inside of the bong and relit the pot in the bowl.

"I was in the room, okay? Not on the couch. Ruth Esther and I changed places. She couldn't sleep where she was. Is that what it is? Did you really get up and call?"

"I really called. I'm fine. I'm with you." Pascal was holding the smoke in his lungs and talking at the same time; his voice came out deep and strained, a cough just under the words.

"Don't worry about it, okay?"

"I'm fine."

"You're sure?"

Pascal blew the smoke out of his mouth. "Yes."

"So nothing's bothering you?" Evers asked.

"No. It's just weird, that's all."

"You're positive."

"I'm positive." Pascal handed the water pipe to Evers.

Evers was still sitting on the bed, and he smoked some of the pot and gave the bong back to his brother, watched a wisp of smoke curl out of the bowl and turn into nothing. "I'd better call her family before I leave. That should be delightful."

Evers left Pascal's trailer in the afternoon and drove, just drove around, without any place to go, until he was tired and his eyes turned red and his legs started to feel heavy and stiff. Even though he was weary, he couldn't sleep; he rested at a wayside near the Virginia–North Carolina border, closed his eyes for a few moments there and listened to an oldies station on the radio. He checked into a motel near Richmond, bought some peanuts and crackers from a vending machine and took a shower. While he was drying off with a thin, scratchy towel, he decided to drive through Chatham and then back to Durham to check on the farm and his wife's funeral.

Evers left Richmond at night. He traveled rapidly and did not dim his lights a single time. The road to Chatham wasn't crowded, and the car lights illuminated the night well up the highway. Empty road, empty lanes. Near Danville, "Lay Lady Lay" came on the radio, from beginning to end, and he turned up the volume.

When he reached Chatham, Evers drove slowly through the town and by Chatham Hall, the school for girls. The campus was asleep and tranquil, nothing stirring, empty except for a few summer students and three or four teachers who had nothing to do until chapel at nine. It was early in the morning, almost light, but not quite. Evers parked his car on the street in front of the school and walked through the fading dark up a brick path to Pruden Hall, a large, classical building with a porch, columns and wrought-iron railings. The entrance was locked, so he went into the building through a back door and climbed a flight of stairs, sliding his hand along the smooth, slick oak banister until the wood wound into a spiral and ended. He saw the school's crest on each and every riser in the steps, and noticed the marks and scuffs and impressions left by hundreds of young feet, late to class or eager to meet a parent or friend waiting in the formal parlor. The ceilings were high, the floors ash with old Oriental rugs, beginning to grow threadbare in their centers.

The smell was there, too, the flush, ripe, sweet scent that Evers recalled from his Woodberry visits, a joyous, invisible vitality commingled with the air, a scarce touch of the past and present so pure that it seemed to strain and buck in an effort to separate itself from the dull breaths spread by the rest of the ordinary world. There was time in the Chatham Hall air, a lot of time.

Evers sat down at the top of the stairs. He and Pascal had been here once, double-dating, the both of them boys. They had rum in silver flasks, and Pascal ended up fucking his date in an earth-science classroom. Evers remembered that it had been warm, springtime, and that Pascal was so at ease, so blithe, reckless and bright, perfect for that time of his life. The next afternoon they played golf and drank beer and tomato juice, and Pascal decided to stay another day before driving back to William and Mary. What happened, Evers wondered, to all that, the girls who came on weekends, the lacrosse sticks and rugby jerseys, the friends standing with him in a cafeteria line, waiting to eat, talking about all kinds of things.

A girl in a housecoat and sweatpants walked by Evers. He had been sitting on the landing for about ten minutes, looking down. "You're not supposed to be here," she said. "Are you waiting for someone?" The girl was pretty. Her hair was flat against her head, and she wasn't wearing shoes.

"I know," Evers answered. "I was just resting a moment. My wife just died. My brother and I used to come here. Once, we came here together. I came a lot, but once we both did. He had sex with a girl—I can't recall her name now—in the earth-science room over in Holt Hall. I sucked face, but that was about it. He was a freshman in college then. Be on guard, you know?" Evers knew he was acting rude and bizarre, but that's how he felt, and certainly he was entitled to a few days of latitude.

After wandering the campus a little longer, he drove to Durham and out to Jo Miller's farm. Evers and Jo Miller had never divided their ownings, nor had there been any court orders—beyond the temporary support award—regarding their money and property. In an effort to be generous, Evers had told his in-laws—a mother, two sisters and two brothers—that they could stay at the farm until the funeral was over and they'd collected Jo Miller's personal belongings. Now, driving up to the farm, he saw that Jo Miller's family had taken most of the furniture, a stereo, two TVs, a freezer, an antique bed and all the china and silverware and loaded it all into a large moving van. Evidently, their work was not finished; the van's loading door was still open.

Jo Miller's family, especially her sister Aimme, was surly and belligerent, and Evers was in no mood to quarrel with them. Aimme was strident and angry and shrieked at Evers, started crying as soon as she saw him. The youngest brother was theatrical and threatened to hit him. Mrs. Covington, the mother, stood behind the children with her head down; she was the only one who didn't sail into Evers the moment he stepped out of his car. In fact, Evers had a hard time deciphering her mood. She wasn't as spittle-throwing rabid as her sons and daughters, and it struck him that, for some reason, there was a measure of understanding and pity in her stooped shoulders and mute hands. She smiled at Evers when she saw him, but the corners of her mouth wrinkled down instead of turning the other way.

"This is all your fault," Aimme blurted.

Evers was standing beside his car. "I suppose you and your brothers have forgotten who cheated on whom, who screwed a cattle farmer and an associate psychology professor, and who refused to live with me?"

"She wouldn't have done anything," Aimme yelled, "if you'd been a decent husband and supported her."

"Right, Aimme. Her adultery and promiscuity are my fault. All I did was buy her a farm and drive to visit her every weekend so she could live in Durham and fuck somebody actually *called* Falstaf and work at her bullshit, half-assed job with Brockman. To hear Jo Miller talk about it, you would've thought the two of them were just a paper or two away from a Nobel Prize."

"You belittled her, and then abandoned her when you couldn't have everything exactly your way." The whole family—except Mrs. Covington—had clustered around Aimme. "You could have been just a little more patient, Evers. You put everything in front of her."

"Speaking of which, you and your vulture family can unpack my freezer and stereo and furniture."

"So now you're going back on your word," Clifford said. He was the oldest. He taught computer classes at a South Carolina community college.

"No, Clifford, I'm not. I said you could have her personal belongings. You may not raid this home—my house—and take my personal property."

"It's her house and her stuff." Aimme was inhaling hard, almost choking, sucking in spastic gulps of air one right after the other.

"The deed is in my name and, anyway, as her husband, I inherit all her property. Besides, I bought it. All of it."

"Oh. Mr. Lawyer now, are we?" Clifford snarled. "We'll just see."

"We will, Clifford. Unload it or get sued. You can take her clothes, pictures and books, and that's about it."

"We'll go to court for our fair share," said Russell, Jo Miller's other brother.

"Your fair share? Are you serious?"

Mrs. Covington raised her head a little. "I can't see that anything good will come out of fighting with Evers."

"I can't believe you didn't even go to the funeral home to see her," said Aimme, ignoring her mother.

"You mean to see if she's really dead?"

"Are you even going to go to the funeral to pay your respects?" Clifford demanded.

"No. That would make me a hypocrite. Look, I'm sorry this happened, but that's about the best I can say."

"You're so vicious, Evers. Such an asshole."

"I can't believe your attitude," Clifford added.

"You are all morons." Evers hit the top of the car with his fist. He'd promised himself that he would not come unglued, and now he had. He hit it again. The noise was deep and hung in the air for a second or two. "Morons," he shouted.

"You'll see," Aimme said. "We told the police we think you are mixed up in Jo Miller's getting killed. Think about that."

"Evers—" Jo Miller's mother started to say something but didn't get to finish.

"Your sister shot herself, Aimme. You think about that." Evers got into the Datsun and started the engine. He rolled up his window and roared down the gravel and dirt driveway. Before he pulled onto the blacktop, Evers looked back and saw Mrs. Covington standing alone outside, staring at him through the dust. She wiped her forehead with the back of her hand, and Evers made a left turn, felt the tires leave the gravel and take hold of the pavement.

While he was riding back to Norton, Evers started thinking about Jo Miller; he looked at the road and sky and highway signs, stopped for a beer at a store and also bought some animal crackers. After an hour in the car, Evers had the memory of his wife cooking at the Durham apartment in her underwear, her back to him and her hair pulled on top of her head in a knot. He couldn't shake the image: his wife when she was happy with him. And then he remembered, although it had nothing to do with what he had just considered, something that Pascal had said after one of his woman-chasing, ganja-ripped trips to the Caribbean: men like sex, women like money and the two very much go hand in hand. Pascal also liked to say that you're only young once, but you can be immature forever. Evers got so wrapped up in his thoughts that he missed a turn and drove twenty miles out of the way.

Evers got home in the middle of the afternoon, and he went into the kitchen and had a drink from a bottle of scotch he had taken out of Pascal's living room and forgotten to return. He had several more swallows out of the bottle and went into his bedroom and climbed underneath the sheets with his clothes on. He feel asleep, and when he woke up it was dark as pitch in the room, and he couldn't see anything, not even outlines and shapes. He heard the steady click and hum of the dryers underneath him in the Coin-O-Matic laundry. The phone rang, and he ignored it. About half an hour later, it rang again, and this time he got out of bed and answered it. It was Pauletta; she was working late and had decided to call him. Evers told her what had happened, about Jo Miller's death and about the police coming to Pascal's trailer.

"I'm sorry. My goodness. I really am sorry—about all of it."

"Thanks."

"Sure." Pauletta paused. "So how are you taking all of this? Is this a bad time to call? I just was taking a break, wasting time, and just wanted to check on you. To tell you the truth, I called to see if you really were coming up here again. So . . . uh . . . what's going on with you?"

"Who knows? My wife's dead, I'm living in an apartment with brown plastic paneling and I'm probably going to lose my job and end up as a blurb in *USA Today*. Could be worse, could be better."

"You wonder sometimes, Judge Wheeling. About all kinds of things." Pauletta sounded sympathetic.

"I guess."

"I hope you feel better."

"So do I. I mean, it goes without saying that my wife and I weren't on good terms when she died. It's just strange to have someone you know so well die."

They were quiet for a moment. "Well, it's nice to talk to you. Anything I can do to help, to lift your spirits?" Pauletta's tone was gentle.

"Thanks. I don't know why I'm sort of melancholy. I love having everything behind me, and I can't tell you how many times I wished Jo Miller a long, gut-wrenching death."

"You probably didn't hate her long enough to be pure and absolute about it." Pauletta's voice picked up. "You know, I read this story in the paper about drug runners who smuggle dope into the country inside of snakes. They force the cocaine into the snake's rectum—boa constrictors, I think—and then send them to the States. A bunch got held up in customs, and some died from the heat, some because the drugs began leaking into their systems. I hate snakes, but it still really seemed cruel and pitiful."

Suddenly, Evers was very sad. He looked around his apartment and out the window. You start out asking for so much, wanting it all, rich illusions, and then you settle for so much less because of simple certitude, the feeling that you can get a certain tiny portion without a bent back and upheaval in your stomach—a comfortable marriage, a home, a kiss, a child, a fire and a thick paper on Sundays. And then you become disillusioned when Fate, preoccupied, blinks at a cinder in her eye, the clouds crowd in and the small lot you've accepted because of its availability becomes distant and otherworldly. People cheat, people deceive, people grow disenchanted. Homeless ladies lift their skirts to piss on the sidewalks on Fifth Avenue, even at the good addresses.

"I have a theory about my wife," Evers said. "About women."

Pauletta almost laughed. "Tell me. I'm sure it's entertaining."

"I believe that sperm is venomous."

"Maybe serpent sperm, yes?"

"I have concluded that women are sterile, squeaky-clean vessels unless and until they become acquainted with number three, at which time, Miss Qwai, like a catalyst of some sort, the semen begins to—very insidiously, mind you—poison their natures. It corrupts their fineness. Have you ever seen a dishonest spinster? An acerbic nun? A less than wholesome girl-child?"

"Or a monstrous mother—even yours, perhaps, Judge Wheeling? Are you overlooking your own viscous origins?"

"A small amount builds up an immunity. Too much from different sources is toxic. Lethal. Women change from charming schoolgirls to disillusioned shrews, and the only qualitative change is the passage of both time and sperm."

"Number three, you called it."

"Yeah. One is—"

"Would my personality improve if I were to cut down my exposure?"

"I think maybe we could save you with cobalt treatments."

"Do all white men your age like the Doobie Brothers and golf, Judge Wheeling, or is that just a stereotype?"

"It's pretty much true, I think."

"So what do you want to do about visiting?" Pauletta asked. "Are you coming up here?"

"I think you should do voice-overs. Your diction is so faultless."

"I called to try to make amends. Certainly you're going to give me a chance."

"Pax Pauletta. Peace in our time. Apologize for what?"

"My attitude after we had sex," she said.

"Oh?"

"I'd like to take you to dinner."

"A few weeks ago I was George Wallace, now we're going to break bread together?"

"You still are George Wallace."

"Implicit in this call is your admission that I'm not an ogre."

"Implicit in this call is my admission," Pauletta replied, "that I shouldn't fuck you and then shun you, when nothing has changed."

"Nicely ambiguous. But I'll sign it." Evers had no desire to hold a grudge. He liked Pauletta. "It'll be nice to see you."

"Good."

"So we're best friends again, with secret codes and our own clubhouse?"

"Why don't you come up here in a couple of days? I'll take you to Fazio's for a good meal."

Detective Greenfield called Evers right before his lunch, around noon, on a Monday when Evers was working in Norton. Evers had just finished talking to H. T. Moran; H. T. was late with the lie-detector report because he had been in Raleigh at a mandatory diversity-and-sensitivity training program.

"Hello, Judge Wheeling."

"Hello, Detective. What can I do for you?"

"Well, we wanted to let you know that your wife's fingerprints was the only ones on the gun."

"And?"

"Lab tests showed her hand had some residue on it. Gunpowder residue. Chemical tests, you know, tells if you fired a gun."

"That's not surprising if she shot herself," Evers said.

"Gun had been fired twice. It was a twenty-two revolver. Two empty casings in the gun. Only one in her, though. Can't figure that out. Just wondered if you'd ever seen her shoot, or if you'd ever shot the gun yourself?"

"I know she bought it when I moved to Norton. She used to shoot it occasionally for practice. I've never shot it."

"We have a suspect, too. I guess that's the right word. Some of this ain't fitting so good."

"Besides me?"

"You read us wrong."

"I hope so." Evers was starting to feel agitated.

"Seems her boyfriend—I don't mean nothin' by that, sir—this Falstaf was over at her place twice in the last few days before she died, once about dark. Neighbor says he left mad and shoutin', spinning tires, all that kind of stuff. They was arguing out in the front yard. Right hard. Seems he wanted to get married, and she already had a new interest. I don't mean, sir, to seem disrespectful with any of this."

"I've already told you that my wife and I weren't getting along. Say whatever you want to."

"She was seeing a college kid. Young guy. Evidently Falstaf didn't take to that too well. He was drinking at a roadhouse later that night, got there around three in the morning. That we know." Greenfield seemed pleasant enough.

"Well, thanks for keeping me up to speed."

"We've checked your brother's phone records." Greenfield paused. "They're pretty much like he said."

"Pascal has strange interests."

"Women ain't really no strange interest. But talking to them on the phone like he does is somewhat unusual."

"Maybe it helps him sleep."

"Right." Greenfield kept talking. "Only problem we got is that two of Falstaf's buddies was with him after he left drinking. They went back to his farm, all of 'em, and stayed there till morning. Least that's what they say. Problem is, that don't tell us much about where he was before. He claims he was with the victim until right late, then left her and went straight to the bar."

"Well, you're the detective. I'm sure you'll figure it out. My bet is that she killed herself."

"I wish you weren't so sore about all this, Judge. I reckon we got off on the wrong foot." Greenfield sounded earnest.

"I understand. Don't worry about it." Evers leaned back in his chair, closed his eyes for a moment.

"One of the guys with Falstaf got a real bad record, couple of felonies. Other one works for him. Never know."

"Not the best alibi witnesses, I guess," Evers said.

"You know, your brother being up is right strange." Greenfield sounded uneasy.

"Maybe he killed her."

"You don't think so, do you?"

"No. Hell no."

"After we check on Falstaf and this boy, if they don't match up, we might ask you for some samples, you know, to see who had been with her before she died."

"Great. I'm glad to see your trust is so deep and sound."

"No offense, Judge Wheeling."

"Anything else?"

"Right strange about her spelling her name wrong, ain't it? That's still hard to figure."

"Nice to hear from you again." Evers hung up the phone without waiting for Greenfield to say anything else.

Fazio's is an Italian restaurant in Charleston, West Virginia, with four large dining rooms and family pictures, mostly unframed, on every wall. Joe Fazio, Joe's dad, Joe's kids, Joe's wife, Joe's uncles and aunts, all of them singly or in smiling combinations, color and black-and-white, fastened in one-dimensional, corner-curled glory to every flat space in the building, except, of course, the floors and ceilings. Evers was supposed to meet Pauletta at seven, and he was about twenty minutes late. Pauletta was waiting for him in the last and largest room in the restaurant. She was drinking wine; there was a bottle on the table.

Evers and Pauletta ate salads and a pizza and drank the bottle of wine Pauletta had ordered. They were unable to agree on toppings, so the pizza was divided into two halves, with different ingredients on each. After they had eaten the pizza, Evers ordered a second bottle of wine. When that had been emptied, the waiter brought a handwritten bill and four red-and-white peppermints, and Pauletta interrupted the story Evers was telling about skiing in Colorado. "What's going on with your wife?" she asked. "You haven't said anything about that."

"Well, if she didn't kill herself, they think that maybe her boyfriend did the deed." Evers studied a small red-edged crust remaining on the pizza platter.

"Really?"

"Yes." Evers looked at her. "That's what the police told me. They called the other day."

"Are they still interviewing you? Now they don't think it's a suicide? Is that what you're telling me?"

"I'm not absolutely sure." He looked around the restaurant. "It's nothing to me, one way or the other."

"It would—" Pauletta stopped talking. Two men and a woman had come up and were standing in front of their table. Evers had noticed them earlier, when he came in. The men had on dark cowboy hats decorated with turquoise and elaborate feathers; the woman was wearing tight jeans and boots with synthetic leopard fur around the top. The men had worn their hats while they were eating pasta and drinking beer from clear plastic pitchers.

"Yes?" Evers said, looking up.

"How you tonight?"

"I'm fine, thank you."

"I didn't know they served niggers in this here restaurant," one of the men said. He was standing behind Evers and sounded drunk.

"I reckon I knowed they served niggers, but I didn't know they'd feed a man what would eat with a nigger." This from the man who had spoken first.

Pauletta stared at the men. She didn't speak, didn't move. Her face showed nothing. Stone. Blank. Empty.

"Are you gentlemen on break from Amherst?" Evers said. "Summer school not back in session yet? My, they give you lads such long holidays now."

"Naw. We're from the zoo. Come to pick up the go'riller."

"How about that, Miss Qwai? Young scholars on an anthropological quest."

"Fuck you, smart mouth. Why don't you and your nigger lady just get up and go on back to your shack."

"Why don't you leave?" Evers turned in his chair.

"Why don't you?"

"Why," said Evers, "don't you make me, hillbilly?"

Thawp. That's what Evers heard. Flesh slamming flesh, a noise, Evers recalled later, like the sound that wet balls of toilet paper made when he chucked them against the ceiling of the boy's bathroom during his one year of public high school. All the pupils did it, threw sopping tissue against the ceiling. The dried masses looked like fuzzy stalactites. *Thawp.*

Evers was knocked backward by the punch, reached for the table, missed it and landed on the floor on his rear and elbows. His chair was partially underneath him; it followed him down. He was looking at a pair of cowboy boots with intricate leatherwork on their sides, angular toes and a border of red-orange mud on each heel. Evers tackled the boots, grabbed on to them at the top near a brown rose outlined in white stitching.

He kept his butt down, his head up, lifted just a bit with his shoulders and drove with his legs. "My legs are magic," he shouted. That's what he was thinking, so he shouted it. He forced the boots and the man in them across the floor into another table—plates, silver, glasses, napkins and bottles falling off the edge—and kept pushing the whole mess across the room, like a bulldozer moving dirt and roots, until the man and the furniture were wedged against a wall.

Evers stood up from his crouch. He looked at the man, moved his face as close as possible to the hillbilly's. The eight or ten other people in the room were all watching. One couple, teenagers, had jumped up from their table when it appeared that Evers might shove the redneck into their meal.

"That was for Bobby Seale, you piece of shit." Evers was breathing hard and trembling.

The pinned man cursed Evers, and so did his friends. The other man and woman were still standing beside Pauletta. "I still ain't afraid of no nigger lover," said the man nearest Pauletta.

"I'm not a nigger lover," said Evers. "Am I, Miss Qwai?"

She shook her head.

The hostess and two men in white T-shirts and aprons rushed up and separated Evers from the man who had hit him. His hat had fallen off during the scuffle, and Evers could see that his adversary was very much bald, with only a long, thin fringe growing around the back of his head. The hostess said the police had been called. The men in aprons told Evers and the others to sit and wait. Another man, Italian, in a suit, came into the room.

"This is certainly unpleasant," Pauletta said as she and Evers sat at their table, waiting for the police.

"Yes, it is."

"And whose fault is that, Evers?"

As far as he could recall, Pauletta had never called him by his first name before. He snorted. "Certainly not mine."

"Shit. It's certainly not theirs."

"What?"

"It's not theirs."

"They started it. They were the aggressors. They punched me. Christ."

"They don't know any better. They're simple, dumb brutes."

"The fucker hit me, Miss Qwai. He hit me and provoked me. And he impugned you."

"What would you have done if a ten-year-old retarded child had slapped your precious head? You would've ignored him, yes? Or called the manager or walked away?"

Evers pointed at Pauletta. There was a scratch on his arm, and his head ached. "This man is not a ten-year-old, pitiful dullard."

"Oh yes he is, more or less."

"That's idiotic."

"It is? Did you hear the two of you? 'Leave.' 'No, you leave.' 'Make me.' 'Hit me first.' 'I dare you.' Jesus. You two sounded like you were in a sandbox. You simply demeaned yourself. Would you argue with a pet? Put yourself on the same level as a dog?"

"Don't you have any pride at all?"

"Pride shouldn't be confused with passion," she answered. "What would you have given up by ignoring that hillbilly? Tell me that?"

"Drop dead. I defend you, and you ally yourself with those assholes. Fine. Great."

"You scuffled because that man struck you, not because of any commitment to me or to principle." She was twisting a ring on her middle finger.

"He wouldn't have hit me if I hadn't been with you. That's de facto commitment, okay?"

"Hardly."

"You'll probably tell the cops it was my fault." Evers was still shaking.

"Legally it wasn't."

"You have no character. None whatsoever." He raised his voice.

The men in hats and the woman with the fur-ringed boots had refused to sit down, and one of the men had pushed the Italian in a suit. They were still cursing and fidgeting when the police arrived. There were two officers, and they talked to the men in aprons. The policemen had their backs turned toward Evers; the men in aprons were gesturing. One policeman took his hat off. After some discussion, the police turned and started to Evers' table. Only then did he notice that one of the officers was black. Evers looked at Pauletta, and he smiled. Then she smiled. "Go figure," she said.

The black policeman introduced himself and took out a pad. "Do you want to file a complaint?" he said to Evers.

"No, he doesn't," answered Pauletta.

"I certainly would," said the policeman, a young man with an immaculate, pressed uniform and polished leather belt and holster. "I would if I was in your shoes."

"That's all right," Evers said. "I'm not too concerned about what happened to me. I would like to see that the owner is compensated for the damage, though."

"You don't have to pay, sir," the policeman said.

"I agree. That's not what I meant. Why don't you arrest them for drunk in public or destruction of private property or something? That way they'll have to pay for the damage they've caused, and I won't have to fool with driving up here for an assault-and-battery trial."

"I don't see why you won't file a complaint. The man hit you, sir, with no right."

"I'd rather not bother."

"If you change your mind, let me know." The policeman handed him a card and joined his partner, who was arguing with the rednecks, trying to persuade the ringleader to walk to the squad car without another fracas.

After Pauletta and Evers left the restaurant, they walked through the parking lot and she asked why he didn't file charges.

"I couldn't," he said.

"Why?"

"I just don't feel like another battle right now. But I didn't elect not to prosecute the assholes because I agree with you."

"No, I guess you didn't, and that's sad."

"No it's not. Not really. Old women who work in fast-food restaurants are sad. Somebody's mother or grandmother in one of those polyester uniforms, serving burgers and chicken. Think about that."

"You're not that compassionate."

"Yes I am." Evers put his hands in his pockets. "I've had all of these fights recently. None of them have turned out too well, even though I've done my best. I'm worn out, Miss Qwai. Fucking worn out."

"Where are we going?"

"I think we should get high and go to an automatic car wash, a drive-through, one of those with the big, whirling blue brushes. Are there any of those around here?"

"Are you serious?"

"Moderately."

They decided instead to go to Pauletta's house. Evers followed along behind her in the Datsun, touching the side of his face every few miles to see if it was swelling. Near the end of a long, two-lane straight, a raccoon darted in front of his car, caused him to swerve and bounce off the highway onto the shoulder, and he heard the tires change rhythm and gravel rattling in the wheel wells.

"You are unbelievably pigheaded," Pauletta said the moment Evers stepped into her living room, where she was sitting on the couch.

"I try to be agreeable. I really do," he replied.

"You're the most unyielding, unbending individual I know. Selfish, too."

"Just think, Miss Qwai. If men were a little more flexible, we'd have no need for women."

"With that attitude, you have no need for women now. Little wonder your wife didn't stay with you."

"It depends, O chocolate sage, on what you want." He was still standing near the doorway.

"I'm never too sure about what you want, but I know what you deserve." Pauletta was looking him in the eye, but he couldn't judge her mood.

"You are my woman, Bess. Don't forget it."

She smiled. "I noticed something in the parking lot—you need to bend your knees when you walk. You look like an old, stiff claymation figure." She got up and poured some scotch into a wineglass, then handed it to Evers. "Maybe this will loosen you up a little, get you out of that really hip robot stroll you've got."

He took the drink and sat down on the sofa, lowered himself in little mechanical jerks and lurches. "Danger! Danger, Will Robinson." He kept his arms stiff and extended, his whole hand wrapped around the glass.

"Actually, I was thinking more along the lines of that sissy gold thing in *Star Wars*."

Evers relaxed and took a sip of scotch. "Don't you have a more suitable glass?"

"I'm sorry. I don't." Pauletta didn't sit down. She pulled her hair back and closed her eyes for a moment.

"You're not drinking," Evers pointed out.

"I suddenly don't feel too good. I don't know if it's the food or your conduct."

"What's wrong?"

"My head . . . I think I may have a fever. And my stomach's upset."

"I'll bet you're pregnant."

"Maybe you're the father."

"Why don't you take something?" Evers asked.

"I think I'll get some water. Some ice water." Pauletta went into the kitchen. Evers heard the refrigerator door open and the tap running, then she came back into the living room.

"Another fine goblet. Did you get that one out of a box of detergent or with a ten-dollar purchase at Burger King?"

"What is it with you and glasses?"

"It just seems so out of character. You have nice clothes, expensive furniture, a beautiful leather briefcase in your car, all grades of first editions on your shelves, a laser disc collection, a frigging stuffed peacock and not a single decent glass."

"This one's a jelly jar."

"Charming."

"Look. Couldn't we do this some other evening? I feel terrible. I really need to lie down."

"Come on. I drove all the way up here. And you just handed me a drink. At least you can talk to me for a few minutes."

"Couldn't you be a little more gracious?"

"Not at the moment, no."

"I'm going to lie down. Come in the bedroom, then." Pauletta went into her bedroom, got in bed and pulled the covers up to her waist. She left her clothes on, and her jewelry. "I feel awful."

"You do look sort of sick."

"Were the situation reversed, were you sick, and had you asked me to leave, I would have. You're like an oil spill, Judge Wheeling—unwanted and persistent."

"Actually, it's been a pretty long night. I'm burned out, too. You're probably right. I think I'll go ride around in the city and eat doughnuts. Next trip up, though, maybe I can stay here instead of the hotel. I think I'm losing ground. I stayed here the first night we went out, had sex soon after, and now I'm meandering through the wall of hills counting the number of lit windows in bank buildings."

"So you're leaving, right?"

"Yes. And no matter how much you plead, I've decided not to have sex with you."

Pauletta laughed a little. "Go away."

"I'll see you," Evers said.

"Okay."

"Can I get you anything before I go?"

"No, thank you."

"All right, then."

"You really think it's the height of niggerdom that I don't have a certain kind of glasses, don't you?" Pauletta said from her bedroom when Evers was walking into the den.

"I wouldn't put it that way." Evers started back to the bedroom door.

"Good."

He stopped before he got to the room. "Do you think you might be inclined sometime to tell me what you guys got out of our trip to Salt Lake? This isn't the first time I've asked. I'm not a bad person, not greedy, not trying to meddle. I'd just like to know."

"Perhaps. Maybe I will sometime."

"So why not now?"

Pauletta sat up in bed. "It's a confusing story, and I feel bad."

"It's not all that epic, is it? Can't you just tell me?"

Pauletta was quiet.

"Why won't you tell me?" Evers inched closer and leaned against the door frame. "Haven't I paid my dues? I constantly look over my shoulder, worrying about Lester Jackson, Warren Dillon, my job, prison and Artis. And, to make things even worse, there's always this undercurrent, you and Ruth Esther never missing a chance to be tight-lipped and inscrutable."

Pauletta looked up at Evers. "I got close to two million dollars; that's what I got."

"You *what*?"

"I got two million dollars."

"For what? *How?* There wasn't that much money. There wasn't, not there in the box, no way." Evers jumped and rambled over his own words. "Did Ruth Esther pay you? She gave you that kind of money?" He kept talking, excited. He took a step into the room. "There was something else, right? You guys went somewhere else. Where? Shit. I mean, that's fine, I'm glad you got the money. I don't want it or anything. Good for you. I don't know why you wouldn't tell me, though."

Pauletta waited for him to quiet down. "I'd like to know something from you now."

"From me?" Evers asked.

"Yes."

"What?"

Pauletta had stopped looking at Evers. She was rubbing the top of her sheet between her thumb and second finger. "What did the letter say? The letter in the box?"

"Why do you want to know?" Evers wondered.

"Why do you want to know what I was paid for the trip?"

"I just glanced at it, at the letter. I skimmed it. As you may recall, everyone—yourself included—was scolding me for being such a ham-fisted knave. Remember? It was pretty ordinary, though, the parts I

read. 'How are you?' 'I'm fine.' Pleasantries, something about a car. It
was hard to read . . . the script was so elaborate and Artis the half-wit
donkey boy was kicking and screaming."

"Who was it written to?" Pauletta asked.

"To Ruth Esther."

"You're certain?"

"Well, it began 'Dear Ruth.' "

"Anything else you remember?"

"Like I said, there was some mention of a car, and a thank-you for
something, 'enjoyed our time together, I have a lot of affection for you,
good luck.' What I saw, it was just, you know, a letter, not a map or
some . . . I don't know . . . valuable document."

"Who sent it?"

"How would I know? I assumed it was her father." Evers spread his
hands out in front of him. "It's more than a little hypocritical for you
to quiz me about the letter, isn't it? After you yelled at me and berated
me for opening it?"

"Did you see the signature, who signed it?" Pauletta had sat all the
way up; her back was straight, and her hands were in her lap, her legs
crossed at the knees.

"That I do recall. William—that was the name. William. It sticks in
my mind because I remember thinking that Artis had such an uncommon name, and 'Ruth Esther' is sort of rare, and I wondered about
their father."

"I don't think Ruth Esther's father is named William."

Evers nodded several times. "I saw the name John—John English—
on the book at the bank, the ledger for the bank box, but I figured that
it could've been a scam or an alias or something."

"Actually, I think her father's name *is* John," Pauletta said. "I wonder who William is. Did you see the surname on the letter, Judge
Wheeling?"

Evers tilted his head back, closed his eyes. "There wasn't one. Just
William." Evers walked all the way into the bedroom and sat down on
the corner of the bed. "So what's the deal with the letter? Lester mentioned it, too, remember?"

"That I don't know." Pauletta's perfect speech was slower than
usual. She paused after each word, and her voice got fainter as she
came to the end of the sentence; when she stopped, it was almost all
whisper and air.

"Was there something I missed? The little bit I saw read like casual
correspondence, just, you know, a cordial letter. Of course the writing
was hard as hell to read, very elaborate. There was nothing else in the

envelope, nothing in the letter. Maybe it was in code or something. Or more clues. Is that what you think?"

"I truly don't know," Pauletta said. "I thought maybe that you could shed some light on things."

"Sorry."

She handed Evers her glass. "Would you get me some more water? With lots of ice, please. And let the spigot run for a moment so the water will be cold."

Evers took the glass out of Pauletta's hand. "So tell me what you got, how you got all this money."

Pauletta smiled. "You probably won't believe me."

"Maybe, maybe not. We'll see."

"I got the envelope," Pauletta said.

"The envelope?"

"Right." She smiled again and kicked Evers from underneath the covers. "Would you go get my water, please?"

"In a minute. So what's the deal with the envelope?"

"Did you notice, Judge Wheeling, that it was old?"

"I did. It was fairly yellow. It did seem old. I noticed that. I figured it had been in the bank for a while, but it seemed older than four or five years. And the calligraphy, the rococo writing was old-fashioned. It flashed through my mind that it was a keepsake or some family missive, an heirloom or something—and that's what Ruth Esther said, too."

"It was written in 1918."

"In 1918?" Evers scratched his head. "Are you sure?"

"Yes. At least that's when the envelope was originally sent. It's possible that the letter you saw didn't go with the envelope. I don't know."

"Did someone noteworthy—"

"The stamps, Judge. I got the envelope and the stamps."

"And they're worth two million dollars?"

"Thereabouts. Do you know anything about stamps and stamp collecting?"

"No. Beyond James Dean and Elvis and a few other postal flim-flams, no. Do you?"

"I collect them," Pauletta said.

"And these stamps are worth two million dollars?" Evers was having difficulty believing what he was hearing.

"The envelope had six twenty-four-cent stamps on it. I'm not sure why there were six, although I'm guessing that there was something besides the letter in the envelope when it was mailed. And some people are overly careful and use extra postage; that could explain it. The six stamps all have an upside-down airplane on them. The plane is a Curtiss 'Jenny' biplane. They're known as 'inverted Jennies.' Are you following this?" She poked Evers with her foot again.

"So far."

"The stamps, obviously, contain a printing error. They were issued in May of 1918. It's generally agreed that four hundred were printed, but until I found these six, only a hundred were known to exist. Most collectors assume that the postal service caught the error and destroyed the remaining stamps. The 'Jenny' stamps are the most valuable stamps in existence."

"I noticed them when we were in Utah, and the address. New York. Addressed to Ruth Esther. To tell the truth, that's what made me curious. I wasn't sure why the letter would have stamps if her father had just left it for her. It—the letter, I mean—was sort of out of place. That's why I got it out of the envelope and looked at it."

"Well, each of these biplane stamps is worth a minimum of a quarter-million. Probably more, since they're all together and in fine condition. And it will be a novelty—their sudden appearance after all these years."

"People pay that much for a *stamp*?"

"People are willing to pay much more for Jackie O's trifles, bad paintings and the carcass of the Elephant Man. People pay for all sorts of things, Judge Wheeling, from oral sex to quarter horses and pieces of meteorites."

"Are the stamps real?"

"Yeah, they are. I've had them insured and called Sotheby's. They're doing some appraisals and word of mouth, and they're having a large stamp sale in about two months. These will be the headliners."

"So that's it?"

"That's it." Pauletta relaxed her back and shoulders.

"Pascal and I got a trip, you got close to two million dollars, Artis and Dillon got a hundred grand . . . well, Dillon did. What did Ruth Esther get? The letter?"

"That's it. She wanted the letter."

"If it was written in 1918, how could it be to her? Her name was on the envelope, I'm fairly . . . certain about that. I think that's right. I know I saw the name 'Ruth.' "

"Well, the name on the envelope is 'Ruth Wright.' Like I said, I have the envelope. There's not much debate about that."

"You're right. Now that I think about it, you're right. I wonder if Ruth Esther is Ruth Wright? Maybe the letter *wasn't* written to Ruth

Esther. Damn." Evers scratched his head again. "Any ideas about how we can figure out what was in the letter? Anything else you know?"

Pauletta smiled. "I'm afraid that my plan was to ask you."

"Incredible."

"Yeah." Pauletta rubbed her eyes with her thumb and index finger.

"I wonder why she included you? Why she gave you the stamps?"

"I'm not sure. Not sure at all. I've always tried to do right by Ruth Esther, and I've done some legal work for her, but I'm still not sure why she gave me the stamps. She knows they're very valuable. But she insists that she wants me to have them. She has from the first time we talked about the clues her father left."

"I'll go get your water."

"Thanks. Thank you."

Evers rolled the glass back and forth between his palms. "I was thinking I might stop by to see you tomorrow on my way out of town. If that's okay. I don't want to bother you."

"That would be fine."

A fter breakfast the next morning, Evers went by Pauletta's office to say good-bye and to take her a gift, a coffee mug with a picture of Gumby holding a West Virginia state flag. Evers had bought the mug in the hotel gift shop. He hurried past the receptionist and slouched down behind a newspaper while he was waiting outside of Pauletta's door—he didn't feel like talking to anyone, especially people with pressing legal problems. Evers had read all the classified ads—puppies, cats, cars, foreclosures, furniture, houses, baby clothes, washers and dryers—before Pauletta's secretary led him into the trees and plants. Pauletta was sitting in front of her desk, in one of the client chairs, talking to a man in the other chair. She ignored Evers for a moment, then stood up. "Hello, Judge Wheeling."

"Good morning."

"I'd like for you to meet someone. You'll recall that I spoke to you earlier about Marvin Ross, one of my clients. He's charged with murder."

Marvin Ross kept sitting in his chair in the small clearing near the middle of the office, didn't stand. He nodded at Evers when he was introduced, bent forward and offered his hand. He was around fifty years old, thin, small and wiry, and he had on glasses with gold metal frames, big glasses that were too large for his head and eyes. Ross was oddly slow and deliberate when he moved, as if he were tired or his hands and neck and face were weighted down. He was wearing a black shirt with a large silver X across the chest.

"How did you get out on bail, Mr. Ross?" Evers asked. "I remember Pauletta telling me some time ago that you were in jail."

"They lowered it. Miss Qwai got it done."

Evers looked at Ross. "Oh." He paused. Without any more transition or warning he turned toward Ross and invited him to breakfast. "I've already eaten once, but I'm still hungry."

"Me or her?" Ross said. He looked confused.

"You, Mr. Ross. The two of us."

"Why would you want to have breakfast with Mr. Ross?" Pauletta asked.

"I just wanted to talk to him. You told me I might be able to give you some help with his case."

"I don't think that it's a good idea," Pauletta said.

"How come?" Ross asked.

"You won't enjoy it, and you won't benefit from it." Pauletta folded her arms in front of her.

"What kind of judge are you?" Ross drawled. "You from here, from Charleston?"

"From North Carolina. I'm a superior court judge."

"You buy?" Ross looked at Evers.

"Sure," Evers said.

"Then let's go. You're serious, right?" Ross pushed his glasses up his nose with his middle finger.

"I'm serious."

"Any man good enough to ask me, I can sit at a table with." Ross looked at Pauletta and winked. "He'll be all right."

"Meaning what?" Pauletta asked.

Evers smiled. "Ponder this, Miss Qwai. First, Lorne Greene used to do commercials for Alpo, right? And Lorne told us that Alpo tastes great. That's what he said, that Alpo tastes great. How did Lorne Greene know how it tastes? Second, consider the fact that 'Jesus Is Coming Soon' is a negro spiritual written around the turn of the century."

"What in the world are you talking about? *What?* And you consider this. If you fuck up Marvin Ross or his case, I'll castrate you. I swear it." Pauletta clenched her jaw. "I don't know what's wrong with you sometimes. I've just about got a manslaughter plea worked out for Mr. Ross. And where are you going? I thought you had to be back at work by early afternoon. Why is it that you want to act like a fool half the time?"

"I'll probably be losing my job soon anyway. And one of the job perks is that I'm my own boss."

Evers and Marvin Ross ate at a Shoney's, ordered steak and eggs, had square cuts of meat that were well done and the same color all the way through. Ross drank coffee and smoked cigarettes while he ate.

"What was the name of the man you shot?" Evers asked Ross.

"Ancie Penn."

"So what did you think after you shot Ancie Penn?"

"That I done fucked up." He looked at Evers. "I knowed you was going to ask me that."

"You were right. I did."

"Yeah. Well, he deserved to be shot."

"Did you feel good about it?"

"Yeah, I sure did. He'd been screwin' my old lady. Screwin' her while I'm at work, then puttin' on my cologne and smokin' my cigarettes. Then, because he's that kinda shitass, he's got to tell me to my face, you know."

"It was fairly cold-blooded, wasn't it? Pauletta told me you just walked up to him and shot him, then went home and washed your car."

"It wasn't a wrong thing to do, okay? I know I'm gonna pull some time, but Miss Qwai figures it won't be much. Says a jury might be sympathetic, so she thinks she can make a deal. She got some letters and cards between my old lady and Penn from the D.A. They had to give 'em up because of some motion she filed. They're some shameful shit. She's right smart, ain't she?"

"She is."

"Yep."

"Still, killing a man over a little trim is kind of excessive, don't you think?" Evers smiled at Ross.

"Figure it's sin for sin. Adultery and killin'. Pretty much even."

"What about your wife?"

Ross smiled back at Evers. "She ain't worth the trouble. No need to punish a whore, she's already common."

"Where'd you get that shirt?" Evers asked.

"Nephew give it to me," said Ross.

"You're a fan of Malcolm X?"

"Naw. I figured it was somethin' to do with football at first. The Raiders, maybe. I got too many problems of my own without worryin' about whether enough brothers gettin' to be astronauts or manage baseball teams. Things for me is a little more day to day, right?"

Evers laughed.

"How come you want to eat with me?" Ross stubbed his cigarette out.

"Why not?" Evers wiped his hand on a paper napkin.

"What you wanna do after we eat?" Ross leaned forward in his chair.

"How about we get some beer and go bet on the dogs?" Evers offered.

"For real? You want to?"

"Sure."

"Fuckin' A, yeah. If you wanna, yeah."

"We'd probably do well to take a cab if we're going to drink."

"Pretty long ride out to the track," said Ross.

"My treat."

"So you really a judge, huh?"

"Yep."

"How 'bout that." Ross picked up his glass. "Grab a handful of them Captain's Wafers from the salad bar 'for we leave, okay? They'll go good with the beer."

Two hours later, Evers called Pauletta from the track to report that Marvin Ross and he had won four hundred and fifty dollars betting on a dog named Frankenstein. Pauletta was annoyed and hung up the phone. "You're drunk," she said before leaving the line. It wasn't even one in the afternoon.

"You call her, Ross," Evers suggested.

"No way."

"Come on."

"You been dippin' into that, ain't you?" Ross bit a cracker.

"Pardon?"

"You and her been gettin' it done, ain't you?"

"No way."

"Tell the truth now," said Ross.

"I've tried, okay? I'll admit that much."

"Right. I knowed it. I sure did."

Marvin Ross and Evers laughed, a drunken, conspiratorial laugh that men can laugh because they know they're able to assume certain things about each other, just as well as they know that those certain things are inescapable—god's imprimatur, Il Duce's code, serial numbers that may change in the end but share the first five or so digits. After all of the races were over, they sat down and pressed their backs against a wall near an exit and ate Captain's Wafers until a security guard made them leave. Evers dropped Ross off at his home, then took the cab to Shoney's and picked up his car. He rode around the city for an hour after that, looking at the hill walls and dull, drab buildings, wondering if he should go by to visit Pauletta again and spend another night in West Virginia or begin driving back to Norton. He had called his office from the dog track and canceled court for the day, explaining to his secretary that he had the flu and a bad headache. There were people talking in the background when he called, and the public address announcer began recapping a race right as Evers was about to hang up, but what was she going to say to him?

Evers had given Marvin Ross almost all the money they had won at the track, and had kept two twenties for the ride home. He bought some gas and coffee and a microwave sausage biscuit and started back to Norton; he decided not to call Pauletta or see her again before leaving Charleston.

The next morning, Detective Loggins called Evers at his office in Norton. Evers felt fairly good and settled. He had sobered up during the drive back to Norton and slept for nine hours.

"Good morning, Judge Wheeling."

"It is. What can I do for you?"

"We're treating your wife's death as a homicide now. Not a suicide."

"What does that mean? Do you give the file a different color tab or something?"

"Different number, actually." Loggins' voice was so plain that Evers couldn't tell if he was serious.

"Anything else?"

"Would you be willing to take a polygraph?" the detective asked.

"Fuck no."

"Why?"

"You know why. They don't work, you can't use them in court and even if I pass it, you'll keep bothering me. I have nothing to gain."

"Do you care if some of us come up there and do a little longer interview?"

"Leave me alone. Don't call anymore. Don't come up. Go away."

"Well, let me tell you one more thing. I talked to the doctor yesterday, the medical examiner, and he told me your wife was just about eaten up with throat cancer. Had a year or so to live at the most. She was real bad off."

Evers was startled, surprised. He leaned back in his chair. "Say that again."

"She had cancer and was going to die."

"Help me if I'm wrong here, but wouldn't that be a reason to shoot yourself? I haven't done this as long as you, don't have that hard-to-get, two-year criminal justice degree from the community college, but wouldn't this tend to suggest that she killed herself?"

"I don't think she knew. We checked her primary physician—she had one of those health plans where everything goes through one doctor. She hadn't been in for over a year. And no referrals. The doctor was just as surprised as you."

"Maybe she used another name or went somewhere else," Evers said.

Loggins chuckled a little. "Well, I don't have no law degree, but why would she do that? Plus, she ain't mentioned it to a single, solitary person."

"Sometimes maybe you just sense things. I don't know."

"I think I'd find out if it was a sore throat or cancer before I shot myself," Loggins said.

"What else did you want to ask me?"

"Where were you sleeping that night at your brother's?"

"I went to sleep on the sofa," Evers answered. "Why?"

"And the phone's in the kitchen, next to the den?"

"Yeah, good memory. So?"

"So how come you don't wake up? That's a small trailer, and he'd walk past you and then be right there in the kitchen, talking and all."

"I never said he didn't wake me up." Evers shifted in his chair.

"You sure acted surprised when he told us. He was standing right there on the phone and you don't wake up or nothing?"

"Well, you know he made the call. That much you can't deny. And I imagine he listened, not talked, right? It's phone sex, Detective. He pays them, not the other way around."

"Just odd, you not knowing about it. You didn't know, did you?"

Evers was angry. "You're the sleuth. You figure it out."

"By the way, I have a four-year degree from East Tennessee State in physical education. I can run fast and jump high, that kind of shit."

"You can jump up my ass for all I care. Did you call just to vex me and waste my time, or is this some new police technique?"

"Other than the fact that you hated your wife, did you have any reason to shoot her? Girlfriend, anything like that?" Loggins was suddenly hostile.

"Just the insurance policy, I guess." Evers coughed.

"Insurance?"

"Yeah. A cool million. I bought it about three weeks before she died. So what?"

"Really?"

"No, of course not, Columbo. Jesus," Evers said, then slammed the phone down.

He sat in his office, gazing out of his window and thinking about the thick stands of hardwood trees all around Norton, old North Carolina oaks and poplars whose branches and leaves and limbs could block out an acre of sky. The high, green canopy made him feel as if he were sitting at the bottom of a bowl, looking up. Norton, the Tupperware town. He thought about the place mats at Howard Johnson's and how much fun it would be to design them. Can you find ten things wrong with this picture? Can you unscramble these letters to spell five common words? Then he thought about cycling. And Pauletta. And Jo Miller and Pascal, the two poles in his life. "Zounds," he said to his office.

NINE

NOTHING MUCH HAPPENED FOR A COUPLE OF WEEKS; IT began to get hot—heavy, stupefying heat—and sluggish, everyone stayed sticky, baseball was on all the cable channels at night, and swallows started chasing gnats and flying bugs when the dusk-to-dawn light switched on in front of Evers' apartment at the Coin-O-Matic. Pascal called one evening and told Evers that the trailer dwellers had run an extension cord from the mobile home out to the sofa so they could hook up a fan. Pascal was wearing old Bass loafers and short pants all the time, no shirt, and smoking dope inside until the sun went down. No one had heard anything from Ruth Esther. Evers went to work and stayed busy. He'd phoned Pauletta the day after he got back from Charleston, and her secretary said she wouldn't be available for several days. Summer had flattened out, turned muggy and prosaic.

Finally, one night when Evers was sitting in his apartment eating a pizza and reading *Cosmopolitan*, Pauletta called. "I thought that perhaps you were angry with me," he said. "About the track, when Mr. Ross and I called you. I'm sorry about that. I called . . . it's been close to two weeks ago, I guess . . . called to apologize."

"I've been away. I just got back. I assume my secretary told you that."

"She told me you wouldn't be available for a while. That can mean many things."

"I wasn't snubbing you or being rude, if that's what you're thinking," Pauletta said.

Evers turned the volume down on his TV. "The Atlanta fucking Braves are on every channel. Have you noticed that? Cinemax, HBO, Discovery, the Weather Channel. Nothing but baseball, always the Braves. And Ted Turner's always sitting there in the stands, looking washed out and a little off center."

"I don't watch much TV."

"So, where have you been, if I may ask?"

"I went to a seminar." Pauletta paused. "I went to D.C. for a seminar, the Black Trial Lawyers Association. It was a good trip."

"I've always wondered about that. Could I join?"

"No. You have to be black."

"Oh." Evers laughed. "That doesn't seem fair. Or at least it seems ironic. Sort of separatist and discriminatory."

"Most things are discriminatory in some sense, Judge Wheeling. Dumb kids don't get into good colleges. Try as they might, work like Trojans, they're just not smart enough. That's discrimination—they're being excluded because of the way they were born. Unattractive men and women cannot be fashion models. Congenitally hobbled people cannot compete in most Olympic events or drive a city bus. Accidents of birth. The world's full of doors and pits and barriers. You know that."

"I really wasn't trying to start a battle. Or provoke a scolding. I just wanted to know. I wasn't planning on actually signing up and then boycotting hotels or restaurants or the NBA if I didn't get my way."

"I wasn't trying to be contentious either. Sorry. But you *did* ask."

Evers grunted. "I did, didn't I? I should've known better."

"Listen," Pauletta changed the subject. "Here's why I'm calling. Are you still curious about the letter, about what was in the envelope?"

"Sure. Yeah. I'm just disappointed you don't know the whole story."

"I've tried to find out a little about Ruth Esther and haven't gotten too far. And I don't want to make her uncomfortable or do anything unethical."

"I agree," Evers said. "I've really grown to like her myself. She's been pretty decent and straight up with all of us. You especially."

"She's a good person. And a good friend. I've never met a better person. But what about Artis? Maybe we could find out a little about their backgrounds that way." Pauletta's tone turned sour and lost its warmth when she mentioned Artis. "When he was convicted before, when he went to prison, there had to be a presentence report, correct? You do that in North Carolina, don't you? Parents, schools, work history, place of birth, the whole nine yards. Maybe that would help us some. I'm assuming you could get that with no problem."

"True. I guess I could."

"So what do you think?" Pauletta asked.

"Sounds good."

"When would you be able to look?"

"I'll go first thing tomorrow," Evers said. He took a bite of pizza and balanced the slice on his knee. "This may seem a little simplistic, but I guess you have asked her about the letter. It's possible she might tell you what's in it or why she wanted it so badly."

"I've asked. She was like she often is—very polite, very nice, but completely quiet about her business."

"I'll look tomorrow. It will give me something to look forward to. I'll let you know."

"Thanks. Call and tell me what you find out."

The next day, Evers drove to the courthouse in Winston-Salem, but he didn't get to look at Artis English's report until after lunch. Before he began his first case, he had his secretary retrieve eleven different files and not sign any of them out; he had no interest in the other ten, but didn't want any more connection with Artis and Ruth Esther than was absolutely necessary. Evers figured he would get to the file before noon, but the morning turned hectic and roiling. The lawyers were cranky and unprepared, Evers started court late, a defendant tried to run out of the courtroom after Evers sent him to jail, a crazy woman in a red wig representing herself in a traffic case kept demanding that Evers read her copy of the Magna Carta, and things got balled and knotted and jammed into a clump of poor timing and well-burnished idiocy that wouldn't move, wouldn't go anywhere. Evers finally got through with his morning work at one-thirty, and he went into his chambers, shut the door and lit a cigarette. He sorted through the files on his desk until he found Artis', and he had just opened the folder when he heard a knock on the door. He looked up, and his secretary had stuck her head into his office.

"I'm sorry, Judge, to bother you. What a morning, huh?" Geneva Pullins had worked in Winston-Salem Superior Court for thirty-three years, since she was twenty-three years old, and was a nice contrast to Evers' inexperienced, middling secretary in Norton. Geneva had gray hair, rouge-pink cheeks, and took quick, choppy steps when she walked. Evers liked her; she was kind and helpful, and she knew where everything was. "I just heard—this is really hard to believe, really bad. John Waddell, the deputy, just told me, and I thought you'd want to know and you wouldn't mind being bothered since it's important and all, but Deputy Waddell told me that Warren Dillon got shot last night. Shot and killed, down in Florida, on his vacation. He'd taken some extra time, had some more vacation and was even thinking about retiring, I hear. And how about that, he got shot." Geneva shook her head. Her glasses fell down almost to the end of her nose, but she kept talking and didn't bother to slide them back up. "Just like that, that's what I hear, he got shot."

Evers put his hands on the edge of his desk and shoved his chair back; the chair rolled over the floor on four metal balls. "Warren Dillon got shot? Really? Do they know what happened?"

"It seems, well, I should say Deputy Waddell told me, like I say, told me just this minute, and I knew you'd want to know and that's why I bothered you, he told me it was just an accident, that he got shot by a man in a gang or something like that, got caught in the middle of these two gangs fighting. They caught the man right away, the man who shot him, that's what I understand. At least that's good, that they caught him. It's just terrible. He was getting out of his car at a restaurant, and all that time as a policeman, and to get shot on vacation—what a shame, huh? Get shot for no reason while you're on vacation."

"What do they know about the suspect?"

"He was in a fight with another man, they were shooting at each other, one of them was in a car, and poor old Warren was in exactly the wrong place at the wrong time. Just bad luck, that's all, bad, bad luck."

"So it was just—"

John Waddell stepped around Geneva, into Evers' office. He was wearing a blue police uniform, and he rested his hand on her shoulder for a moment. The policeman was almost a foot taller than Evers' secretary. "Did Geneva tell you about Officer Dillon?" Waddell asked.

"Yes, she just was."

"Terrible."

Evers scooted his chair forward, closer to his desk. "Yeah. Yes, it is." He put his forearms and elbows on top of Artis' file so the name and number were hidden. "I understand they have the man who shot him?"

"Yeah. Complete accident. Guns and drugs. The world's just gone crazy, Judge."

"I used to never even lock my car door or my house," Geneva pointed out. "When I started here working for Judge Cummins, I just parked out on the street and never worried about it, didn't even think about it, about something happening to me or my car."

"I'm sorry to hear about Officer Dillon," Evers said. "Let me know about the arrangements."

"Evidently, he was going to retire down there. I understand he'd put his house up for sale. He was eligible for that early retirement program, too, because he had in twenty years of service."

Geneva spoke up. "That's another thing. We just keep on lettin' all these foreigners into our country, one right after the other, thousands of them, without checking or looking into their backgrounds, just let them pour in and this is what we get. Where was this man who shot Mr. Dillon from?" Geneva looked at Officer Waddell. "You told me. Tahiti—what did you say? Where was it?"

"Haiti. An illegal immigrant, evidently. Fighting over drugs, I'll bet you anything. Or a car, or a street corner, or a woman. People are somethin', Judge." Waddell raised his hand. "Good to see you, Judge Wheeling. I'll get out of your hair and let you get back to work. Just thought you should know."

"Well, well, well . . . ," Evers said under his breath after Waddell left and Geneva had gone to get him a soft drink and a vending machine sandwich. Evers lit another cigarette and opened Artis' file again. He found the presentence report and turned through several pages until he got to the section on family history.

FAMILY AND SOCIAL HISTORY:

The author of this report is unable to verify English's exact age. English's biological mother is deceased, his father unknown. He has one sister, Ruth Esther English, who is a car saleswoman. She works regularly and maintains a close and supportive relationship with the defendant. English's biological mother died in New York in 1989. In 1985, she brought English and his sister to the Anchor House program in Columbia, South Carolina. She placed the children in Anchor House for adoption. English's mother had a lengthy history of psychological problems and repeated hospitalizations. According to records from South Carolina, she told the workers at the Anchor House, depending on her mood and mental state, that her children were born when "Jesus touched her, like on the roof of the Sistine Chapel," that she "found them," and that "Apollo had sent a swarm of lightning bugs" and that she conceived when she walked through the insects at night while they "all flashed at the same time." Records also indicate that English's mother struggled with alcohol and drug abuse.

Finally, it is noteworthy that English's mother claimed that the children, who were teenagers when they came into Anchor's custody in 1985, were born before the turn of the century. English's age was guesstimated to be sixteen at the time. He was allowed to pick a birthday for himself and chose February 2. English and his sister were legally adopted by John and Nadine English in 1986. Mr. and Mrs. English are both dead. Mrs. English was a homemaker, Mr. English was a retired missionary. English and his sister refer to John and Nadine English as their parents, even though they were adopted by this family late in their teens and spent most of their lives with their biological mother. The children both took the last name English. Artis English was signed in to the Anchor House by his mother as "Artis Matthew Wright." There were no birth records or other documents available from the mother when she appeared at Anchor.

Evers turned back to the beginning of the report to read about the theft from Lester Jackson.

OFFENDER'S VERSION OF EVENTS:

English claims that his sister and adoptive father actually planned the crime and broke into the antique business of Mr. Lester Jackson. English claimed that he had nothing to do with this offense. The victim reported $10,056 in cash missing as well as some other small items. Nothing has been recovered. English's version seems extremely suspect since he was found trapped in the building by the police. English has offered to "turn state's evidence" and testify against his father and sister. Both have alibis, and the author of this report feels certain that Mr. English's accomplice was someone else.

Evers looked through the rest of the report and put it back into the file. He called Pauletta and told her what he'd found.

"So John English isn't her real father?" Pauletta asked.

"Correct. He adopted them. Ruth Esther's birth name is Wright. Just like the letter."

"And their mother was crazy?"

"It's not good, not acceptable, to use the word 'crazy.' You should know that. Her mother was 'profoundly disturbed.' " Evers was smiling a little. Geneva scuttled into his office on the balls of her feet and put a Coke and a sandwich on his desk. The sandwich was cold and in a sealed, clear plastic triangle.

"Nothing more than that?"

Evers mouthed thank you to Geneva, and she hurried out of his office. "Well, Artis claimed that he wasn't even there, and sly Lester only reported ten thousand and change missing and a few other things. The 'other things' would be our letter and envelope, I'm sure. It goes without saying that he didn't really feel like explaining why he had a hundred grand in drug cash lying around."

Pauletta was quiet for a while. "Well . . . so, anyway, thanks for looking. We know more now than we did."

"That's not the news of the day, however."

"Oh?"

"Oh no. I hate to sound sinister, but the good news is that Warren Dillon will no longer be plaguing us."

"Why? How do you know? Did you talk to him? Is he back in North Carolina?" Pauletta rushed through her questions.

"Because he got killed in a drive-by shooting in Miami, at some restaurant. The monkey man was getting out of his car at feeding time and some crackhead Haitian shot him. An accident, so I hear. I can't say I'm all broken up about it."

"Shit."

"Yeah."

"How about that?" Pauletta's voice was faint, as if her mouth was not very close to the receiver.

"I'll let you know if I hear anything else, but so far it's just a random thing," Evers said.

"How about that? How about that?" Pauletta kept repeating. When she hung up, she still seemed a little ruffled.

Evers worked until after five-thirty. He left his office and drove to his health club in Winston-Salem; he wanted to take a swim before driving back to Norton, to jump in the pool and go all the way under and then pop back through the surface and shake the clear beads of water out of his face and eyes. He would put his suit and shirt and tie back on after he got out of the pool and leave his hair wet, comb it straight back and let it dry on the ride home. Evers drank a mini bottle of scotch and smoked most of a joint during the ride—a little celebration of Warren Dillon's demise. "Feting fate for a change," Evers said out loud so that he could hear the words.

After parking and surveying the splashing mob in the outside pool, Evers decided to swim inside because that pool was almost empty. The indoor pool was covered by a clear dome, and you could see the sun and sky when you looked up. Before he went into the locker room to change, Evers saw a small girl, six or seven, sitting on a towel beside the water, her legs crossed Indian style. The child was bent over a coloring book. She had thick black hair and a ring of chocolate around the circumference of her mouth. As Evers walked past, she looked up and said hello.

"How are you?" Evers asked.

"Okay." The girl had on a yellow sundress and tennis shoes with purple Quasimodo faces. "I'm coloring."

"I see that," Evers said.

"I have to stay here," the girl volunteered. "At home I can get into the little part of the pool, but I can't here. That's my dad." The girl pointed to a man swimming laps.

"I'll bet you're a good swimmer," Evers said.

"Nope. Not really. I can swim a little and open my eyes under water and jump off the side. I can do that."

"I'm impressed. That's good for someone your age."

"Do you want to see what I'm coloring?"

"Sure."

The child held up her coloring book. She was using an orange crayon to color a horse.

"Nice. Good-looking horse." Evers grinned. His mouth was dry from smoking the marijuana.

"Do you want to color something? My dad is still swimming."

"Me?" Evers asked.

"Yep."

He looked at the book and the crayons. "Okay. Pick your page and I'll pick mine."

"You don't want to really." The girl started twisting and giggling.

"Yes I do. Let me see your crayons."

"Really?"

"I'd enjoy a little coloring."

Evers leaned over the book and turned a seal burnt umber, a color he picked because he liked the name and the shade. He pushed down hard with the crayon and made a dark outline around the seal when he finished coloring the inside. The girl was still working on a lion.

When he put his crayon down and looked at the burnt umber seal, it appeared to come off the page, to move through the air in front of him, sailing around, its flippers and tail moving up and down in gawky, two-count flaps. Evers shook his head and rubbed his eyes. He looked at the pool and the girl and then the pool again, and all the cuts and sparkles in the pool ran together into quiet, white waves, like a flooded shroud, the water covered over by light, the seal working in the air under the clear dome. He could taste the dope and liquor in his mouth, a lot of bitter alcohol and a few patches of sweet, burned pot, pits and nicks on his tongue and cheeks and the roof of his mouth that were different from everything around them. Not a bad sensation, he decided.

Evers crawled to the edge of the pool, stuck his head under the water, opened his eyes and breathed out. Bubbles came out of his nose and mouth under the water in different shapes and sizes, heading to the surface. Evers stayed underwater as long as he could, and when he took his head out of the pool the seal was gone, his summer jacket and starched shirt were wet to his chest with water and the little girl was laughing, looking at him, clapping and pointing. Evers started laughing, too. He thanked the girl for letting him use her book and crayons and shuffled back through the club toward the parking lot, forgot about swimming. The dope and scotch pumped up everything along the way, brightened all the colors and moved the plants and pictures and furniture an extra space or so from where they really were.

He decided to drive back to his office, even though it was late and everyone would be gone for the day. He wanted to call Pascal and talk to him. He drove slowly, stayed in the right lane and kept his window down. A car with three yellow and black Wake Forest parking stickers and a bad muffler passed him, and the kids in the car— five of them, all college students, no doubt—glanced over and kept on going, straight and too fast for the speed limit, driving someone's parents' hand-me-down car, traveling too quickly for no reason. Evers watched the trunk of the car and wished he were back in college, and that he and Pascal could drink beer and eat deli sandwiches for lunch and speed around town and fall asleep watching sports on TV.

When Evers called, a message from Henry was on his brother's answering machine. "Gone to the creek to pay our respects to the shrine. Leave a message." Evers was still damp from the pool, but his head had started to clear; all the fuzz and jitters had gone away. He had no idea what the message meant.

The next day, Evers checked his answering machine when he got home from work. There were two messages, the first one a call from Detective Loggins. He was coming to Norton in the morning to talk to Evers about an "important development in your wife's death." This despite Evers telling him not to, and that he didn't want to see either him or Greenfield anymore. Jo Miller's mother had also phoned and asked Evers to call her back. "Right. I need to get screamed at some more," Evers said after he heard the message from Mrs. Covington.

Loggins arrived at ten-thirty sharp in Evers' office. Evers ignored him and made him sit in the waiting area for almost an hour. Evers stood in his office and peered out at the streets and buildings in Norton, saw old slate roofs, vehicles with red mud speckled on their quarter panels and a farmer selling tomatoes off the back of a flatbed truck; two men with newspapers under their arms were talking in front of the post office. He knew that Loggins wasn't about to leave after driving so far.

When his secretary let Loggins in, Evers did not get up from behind his desk. Loggins walked across the office to the edge of the desk and reached his hand across. Evers shook it and released it very quickly.

"More good news, Detective?" Evers asked sarcastically.

"Bad news, I'm afraid." Loggins sat down, wearing his customary cowboy boots and bolo tie.

"What?" Evers pretended to be interested in some work, caught the bottom corner of a paper and lifted it up so he could see the sheet underneath. "What bad news?"

"I have a good hunch about what happened to your wife."

"Oh?"

"I think she was killed."

"I know that's what you think. That's why you're here, even though I told you—several days ago—not to come."

"You know who my feelings tell me done it?" Loggins asked.

"Has the law changed overnight? I thought we were still under the old system—you know, facts, evidence, reasonable doubt. I probably should've watched the news last night."

"I think I can prove who done it. Know I can. I think it was your brother."

"Shit. Good luck." Evers snorted. "You have a new villain every day. Tomorrow it'll be Professor Plum."

"I know he was up in the morning. I think that the call's too obvious. And guess what else? I got a charge slip on the day she was killed from a gas station right outside Durham; it's got your brother's name on it and his license plate number. He was down there when she was killed."

"Wow. That's really overwhelming." Evers laughed at Loggins. "You'll need a little more than that."

"White Caucasian hair at the farm, not Falstaf's, and not William Reilly's—he's the college boy. Bet it'll match your brother."

"I'll bet it doesn't. And what if it does?"

"Carpet fiber from a very expensive Persian rug in Pascal's car. Exactly like the rug at the farm."

"Could have been there a week or a month or a year. Could've come off my shoes or pants. Could've come off *any* of a hundred rugs. You and I both know that fiber analysis is one step above voodoo."

"One more thing." Loggins' voice had a bite in it. He was pleased with himself, almost excited. Evers stared at him. He was not going to ask the detective; that would dilute Loggins' delight some. They sat there like stones, quiet and hard, until Loggins finally gave in. "Well, besides all that, he told me he done it. Signed a confession."

Evers stood up out of his chair and turned his back on the detective. The sky was blue and beautiful, and Evers could see that Joe Pendleton had propped open the door to the barber shop with a painted white brick. "Fuck you," he said without turning around.

"I reckon he done it."

"Fuck you, Detective. Get out of my office."

"I was just trying to be decent by lettin' you know before we arrested him formally."

"You came here to gloat. Or to find something out." Evers turned around. "Now leave."

"I'm sorry."

"It's still a shitty case. What about the man who'd just fucked her? What about—"

"It was Falstaf. He admitted it; tests confirmed it. But he's got a real fine alibi. His story checks out."

"His alibi is that he was screwing the victim, then got drunk with his convict buddies later on. That's 'real fine?' " Evers stepped toward Loggins.

"I didn't come here for you to try my case, Mr. Wheeling. You ain't judgin' this one." Loggins' voice was strained. "I'm sorry about this," he said, and walked to the door. "I don't guess it's much use askin' you to tell me all you really know, is it?" he said without turning around, then walked out.

Evers ran past his secretary and out into the hall. He reached for Loggins' throat, but the policeman grabbed his wrist and twisted it. Their chests touched. "If you come back here," Evers said, "I will charge you with trespassing."

"I might just charge you with assault, Judge. This time. Today."

"Right, Roy Rogers. I'm sure you'll have a lot of luck with that."

After Loggins left, Evers called Pauletta at Sparkman, Roberts. While the phone was ringing, he thought about her sitting in her office surrounded by trees and high plants. The last time he was there, when he met Marvin Ross, pictures of Martin Luther King, Maya Angelou and Miles Davis were on all the walls, half-hidden behind rows of green leaves. The photographs were black-and-white, the frames silver.

"Say that again," Pauletta said after she came on the line and recognized Evers' voice. He had started rattling away without telling her who it was. "You need to slow down some."

"My brother. Has a problem." Evers made two sentences from one.

"What's that?"

"It seems that he confessed to killing my wife, and that the police have a little bit of corroborating evidence. Fibers, a credit card receipt."

"Why would he kill your wife?" Pauletta asked.

"Public service, maybe."

"Very funny. But did he say why?"

"No. I haven't talked to him yet. If he's not in jail, I'll get him to come up here to tell me about it. I was hoping you'd talk with him, too."

"I'd be glad to. Is he out on bond or what?"

"He hasn't been arrested, as far as I know. In fact, I haven't been able to locate him for several days."

"Why would he do it? For you? I hope you didn't encourage him."

"Encourage?" Evers snapped. "I think she killed herself or her boyfriend killed her. If you're diplomatically asking about my involvement, I don't have any. Is that what you're getting at?"

"So why did he do it?"

"He didn't. Not that I know."

"Confess, I mean. Why did he confess?" Pauletta was calm, and her words crisp and certain.

"Well, maybe he didn't. Maybe the cop just told me that to work on me a little. If he did confess, I have no idea why."

"Do you want me to drive down there?" Pauletta asked.

"Yeah. Even if I can't find him, I could use the company. He might not show up. I don't know . . . but if, well, it would just be nice to see you. It's kind of you to offer."

When Evers hung up, his secretary came in to tell him that Geneva Pullins had called earlier from Winston-Salem to let him know that Warren Dillon was being buried the next afternoon in High Point. "Call her back and tell her I can't make it, okay?"

"A couple of people in the sheriff's office said that the state police were looking into some things. They found a bunch of money in Mr. Dillon's motel in Florida, and it may be that he was mixed up in something illegal. Supposedly it was over two hundred thousand dollars. I heard that they think some of the money came from payoffs, him charging to let people go or let them get off in court. I don't know if it's true, but that's what's going around."

"I'm shocked," Evers deadpanned.

That night, at about six-thirty, Pauletta called Evers from a pay phone at the Hardee's in Norton and asked for better directions to his apartment. He'd forgotten to tell her about a turn, and she couldn't find where he lived. Evers told her to stay where she was and drove in the Datsun to meet her. He had found Henry, but Rudy and Pascal were still missing. Henry said that Pascal had bought two half gallons of El Toro tequila—"the cheapest kind they sell, the one with the bull on the front"—about a week ago and started planning a trip with Rudy. Henry had decided to ride with Evers to meet Pauletta; Prince Hal was worried and fidgety, and he kept changing the radio station and tapping his knuckles on the window. They met Pauletta at the Hardee's parking lot, and the three of them went to the Norton Kountry Kafe for dinner.

Evers had very little appetite. He picked up some Jell-O with fruit cocktail suspended inside it and a piece of chocolate pie from the buffet line. He glumly picked a grape out of the Jell-O and brushed the red gelatin from around it with his spoon. Pauletta and Henry started a conversation about basketball, and Evers left the table and went into the bathroom. A blind man was in there, standing at a commode and tapping it with his cane; he shuffled forward until his shins hit the bowl and then urinated, holding his cane under his arm while he was pissing.

When Evers got back to the table, Pauletta and Henry were talking about Bill Russell. "White people liked Bill because he could defend

Wilt Chamberlin, and Wilt was so ferocious and black and good," Pauletta said, and looked at Evers.

Henry laughed.

"This is just terrible," Evers said. "No one should have to go through this." He was looking at the slick, greenish-brown grape he'd extracted from the Jell-O.

"Don't mope, Mr. Wheeling," Pauletta responded. "Quit being a pussy."

Henry quickly looked away upon hearing the word "pussy."

"Imagine," Evers suggested to Pauletta, "imagine time that has been assembled—rogue seconds bound into minute bundles—by a union of crabbed and sweating Gorgons, warlocks and doomsayers, this guild of hellish artisans, clucking and snorting and grunting over the hours of mischief being twisted into form by their furious labors and tiny, yellow-nailed hands. Or, better still, imagine . . . Ted Bundy hosting the Ted Mack Amateur Hour. Bad, bizarre times. That's what this is like."

"Don't mope," Pauletta said a second time. "You say some crazy, off-the-wall, weird things."

Evers sighed. "Things were just starting to get better."

"So you don't know where they are, not at all?" Pauletta asked Henry.

"Nope. They have a lot of tequila and some dope. Pascal was talking about getting on a train, taking a train trip, so they could drink and still travel and sleep. They took the Monopoly board, too. It sounded like a good trip. I would've gone, but if it lasted four or five days my wife would've killed me." Henry stopped talking for a moment. He cut a piece of country-style steak and daubed it with mashed potatoes. "This isn't much help, is it? What I'm telling you? I'm sorry. They didn't say where they were going. I guess we could check the train station." Henry put the piece of meat in his mouth.

"Did Pascal ever mention the police, Henry?" Pauletta asked. "Did he tell you what was going on?"

"No. I didn't hear about it until Evers called me. Maybe he told Rudy, but I didn't know about it. Evers said he's in a fair amount of trouble."

"He is, from what I can tell." Pauletta looked down at her plate for a few moments. "But you never know."

Henry agreed to drive to Pascal's trailer and look around there. They all decided that he would go in—the door was never locked—and scout around for brochures and schedules, press the redial button on the phone, see what was missing and listen to the messages on Pascal's machine. He promised to call Evers if Rudy and Pascal checked in or returned to the trailer. "It's no big deal, the two of them leaving for a couple of days, Pauletta," Henry pointed out. "They wander around and meander and drive and travel like this all the time. We all do. I hope you don't read anything irregular into it."

"I understand," Pauletta said. "I didn't think that they were fleeing or hiding. Don't worry."

Henry left for Pascal's in the Datsun, and Evers and Pauletta drove in her car to Evers' apartment. Evers put on a Count Basie CD, and they sat in his den and talked and watched the fish swim back and forth in the aquarium. Evers drank part of a beer, and he gave Pauletta a bottle of Coke which turned out to be flat and tasteless. They decided to call Ruth Esther. She was at home, and was happy to hear from them, but she hadn't spoken to Pascal or seen him since leaving the trailer the morning after they'd all played Monopoly. Evers told her what had happened, and she sounded concerned. "I'll call you if I hear from him," she promised. "I hope he's okay. Call me when you find out more, will you? Let me know what happens."

Evers assured her that he would phone her when he knew something.

"Thanks," Ruth Esther said. "I'm glad that you told me all this."

"Sure." Evers hesitated. "May I ask you something?"

"Certainly. Uh . . . hang on a second. Hang on. I think I hear a car out in my drive." Ruth Esther put the phone down, and Evers heard two or three footsteps and a door opening. "No luck," she said when she came back. "It was someone turning around in my yard. I live at the end of my street—it happens all the time."

"What kind of car?" Evers asked.

"A white Suzuki. Looked like a bunch of teenagers in it."

"Oh."

"What did you want to ask me?" Ruth Esther wondered.

"Did you see anything . . . I don't know . . . out of the ordinary the night that you were at Pascal's with us? Evidently, that's when Jo Miller got killed. Do you recall anything strange?"

"Well, I was with you guys until I went to bed. Then I talked to you a little when I came out to get on the sofa."

"Did you hear Pascal on the phone?"

"No. Not that I can remember. You mean at night, while I was in the den?"

"Yeah."

"No. Of course, I guess I could've slept through it. But I don't think so."

"Around two-thirty, he was on the phone, right in the next room, in the kitchen."

"I didn't hear anything. I left for a little while around then."

"You left to go home?"

"No, I just went out for a minute," Ruth Esther said. "I had to run an errand."

"You left and came back?" Evers asked. "In the middle of the night?"

"Well, yes. I went to the Lowes. I saw it when I was coming in. It's hard to believe that a small town like that would have enough business for an all-night grocery store."

"Huh." Evers looked at Pauletta. "I didn't know that."

"I wonder how come you wouldn't? The store's right there on the way to Pascal's, and it has a banner, with big red letters, saying that it's open twenty-four hours."

"I mean I didn't know that you'd left that night," Evers explained.

"Oh." Ruth Esther was quiet.

"Why did you go to Lowes?"

"I needed some saline solution for my contacts. They were hurtin' my eyes. They're extended-wear, but I think all the smoke bothered me and messed them up. And I'm not used to drinking and staying up as long as we did."

"Most people carry that sort of thing with them," Evers said. He looked at Pauletta again and pointed at the receiver.

"I didn't plan on staying with you guys that night, and I usually don't have a problem."

Evers motioned to Pauletta, and she changed seats, sat down beside him and put her ear on the phone so her head touched Evers'. "How long were you gone?"

"Thirty minutes or so, I guess. Are you askin' me all this because you think it might help Pascal? Is that why? Or are you trying to get at somethin' else?"

"Certainly, I . . . I . . . there's no way you know much that would help, I don't guess. You don't know anything about this, do you? About what happened?" He turned the receiver so Pauletta could hear better.

"Well, I'd be glad to tell the police or whoever that he was there with us until, what was it, like one in the morning? And he was there when I left that morning at about seven-thirty. I looked in on him. And you, too. And after you and I switched that night and I got on the couch, I never heard him come out or come by. And I don't sleep very deep. And—listen—I just thought about this. Think about this, okay? When I left, I drove Pascal's car to Lowes. One of your buddies—Rudy, right?—had left his fancy Packard behind my car when he got back from the store. They went out to go get candy and beer between games, remember? The Packard was still there when I left *and* when I got back. Henry and Rudy must've ridden in Henry's car when they went home. The Packard was there when I left and still there when I got back. So was my vehicle and so was yours. I took Pascal's big old Lincoln, since it was the easiest to get out. So no cars were ever gone. That ought to help. I could tell that." She sounded pleased.

"That still leaves a few hours, I guess. After you got back." Evers was facing his aquarium, and he noticed that the fish were unusually still in the water, not moving or swimming very much at all.

"Ask her about the store," Pauletta whispered, "who she saw, how she paid."

"So you were gone for, what, say half an hour?" Evers asked Ruth Esther.

"More or less. Probably closer to an hour."

"Oh."

"There was no one in the store, and I stayed a few extra minutes and talked to the little girl runnin' the cash register. It seemed like a lonely job, so we talked for a while. Lilly. Her name was Lilly. She said she knew Pascal, that her dad had done some work on his trailer and that she'd seen you in the store with him."

"I don't think I know her," Evers interrupted. "Pascal probably does. He knows most of the folks in the grocery stores and convenience stores around there—anywhere alcohol is sold."

"Well, she knew him. The store was getting ready to throw away some bunches of flowers, and this girl, Lilly, gave me a couple. Some were pretty bad off and brown, but I got a good arrangement out of the two bunches she gave me. Took the best ones from both and put them together."

"So I guess you didn't drive to Durham and shoot Jo Miller in the head with a twenty-two caliber pistol?"

Pauletta frowned at Evers and pushed him in the side with her elbow.

Ruth Esther made a strange noise, a short, second-long "hummm," a single burst out of her throat, close to a groan. "Lord, no. Lord. I can't imagine doing something like that. If I were going to kill your wife, Judge Wheeling, I certainly wouldn't want to shoot her with a gun."

"Right. I was just—"

"You were just trying to help your brother and figure things out. There's nothin' wrong with that."

Evers said good night to Ruth Esther, thanked her for her help and hung up the phone.

Evers finally got Pascal on the phone the next day.

"Are you on heroin or something?" It was about five in the afternoon, and Evers thought that his brother sounded groggy and slow.

"No. Uh-uh. Just nappin'." Pascal sniffed.

"I'm not talking about that. Did you talk to that simpleton policeman?"

"Yes."

"Did you tell him you killed my wife?"

"Yes. I told him that."

"Signed a confession?" Evers nearly shouted.

"Sort of."

"Sort of? Pascal, this isn't a game or a joke. Do you want to go to jail? Wear a jumpsuit and get butt-fucked? Play cards for cigarettes all day?"

"Evel Knievel and Elvis did all right in jumpsuits. And the Godfather of Soul looked pretty smart in that TV commercial we saw."

Evers didn't speak.

"Evers?"

"Yeah."

"Don't worry about me, okay?"

"Why in the world would you confess to killing my wife? Is this another lark or stunt or prank? This guy, dolt and clown that he is, is still a policeman, and he's going to arrest you if he already hasn't."

"They haven't yet. I've been gone." Pascal's voice was grainy and nasal, laced with indolence, backed up in his head.

"God."

"Don't worry, Evers. Don't worry about taking care of me."

"Do you have money for a lawyer?"

"Maybe I'll get a court-appointed lawyer. I figure my case will be pretty easy to handle."

"Meaning what?"

"Let's talk about it, Evers. I'll come up and see you. I'll get Dr. Rudy to come, too. Be there soon."

Evers was impatient. "Pauletta came down yesterday. She came to talk with you and to get this straightened out. She stayed until lunch, but she had to go back. You need to call her."

"I will," Pascal said. "It was nice of her to do that."

"Where have you been? And what's all this about taking the shrine to some creek?"

"I'll tell you when I see you. It's nothing important."

"By the way, did you take a check out of my book? I'm missing a check."

"No. What brought that up?"

"I got to the last check in my book, the last one in sequence, number two ninety-nine, and it's not there. I thought you might have taken it."

"No."

"So you didn't get it?" Evers demanded.

"No."

"You're sure?"

"I'm sure, Evers. Though I'm certainly getting blamed for a lot recently. You want to grill me about Amelia Earhart? Hoffa? Chronic Fatigue Syndrome? Original sin?"

"I'll just call the bank and have it stopped."

"Whatever. I'll see you soon."

Evers went into his bedroom, sat down in a chair, and began watching his fish and trying to think. The water in the aquarium was purple and glowing. Evers got up and sprinkled food across the top of the tank, and the fish popped and darted at the flakes. The phone rang and Evers debated whether or not he should answer it. He didn't feel like talking, but thought it might be Pascal calling him back or perhaps Pauletta. When he picked up the receiver, Aimme was on the line, and he could hear the rest of Jo Miller's family in the background.

"Mr. Wolf contacted us today, Evers." Her voice was taunting, almost singsong.

"What, Jo Miller still owes him money?"

"It seems like that test you took a while ago didn't go so well. Mr. Wolf is mailing us a copy. Looks like it was positive for marijuana."

"Those tests aren't reliable. They're wrong. Anyway, what's it to you?"

"We plan on letting your employer know, the bar know, the media know and the district attorney know." Aimme sounded like she was reading from a script.

"Okay, good. The tests are wrong. I've had them done here, and they're clean." Immediately after his hearing, Evers had avoided dope for several days and had drunk herbal tea, goldenseal and lots of water to clean out the THC residue in his system. When the next test was done, he ended up with urine as clear as Perrier and a negative drug screen from Dr. Rudy and the hospital lab. Rudy had initially suggested simply swapping samples, but that plan stalled when Evers couldn't think of anyone whom he trusted *and* who could also piss clean.

"If you let us have her house and farm and belongings, we'd drop everything."

"No thanks."

"Wolf said we'd have a good chance of winning a civil suit against your brother, even if we can't get anything from you or hold you responsible for what happened."

"Wolf just wants a fee."

"Do you really want all we know to come out?"

Evers laughed. "Pay your money, get your lawyer, go to court, do your best."

"You know, the policeman told us about Pascal. He thinks you're involved, too. So do we. I know it. He's got a good case against Pascal. It's just a matter of time before he gets you."

"You're full of shit, Aimme." Evers hung up the phone. Almost as soon as he turned away from the table, it rang again.

Evers grabbed the receiver before the first ring ended. "What the fuck do you want?"

"Evers?"

"What? What? Pascal?"

"Yeah."

"Sorry, I thought it was somebody else."

"Good. I'm glad you're not quite that pissed at me."

"What's up?" Evers watched a piece of fish food begin to sink through the lavender water. "I thought you were coming down here. What are you doing? We've got a lot to do. You need to quit fucking around and get down here." An angelfish dived after the falling food.

"That plan isn't going to work. The police are here now, and they just arrested me. They tell me I'm going to need a bond to get out of jail."

"Shit."

L ater that night, Evers picked up Pauletta at the Raleigh-Durham airport; it was her second visit to North Carolina in two days. It had been raining hard since noon, and Evers saw several jagged flashes of lightning right before he got out of his car at the terminal, like orange, bony fingers stretched out in the downpour. The sky and roads and cars in the parking lot all seemed gray, as if every other color had been washed away by the storm. Pauletta's was one of the last flights to arrive at the airport, and her plane was an hour late.

"Thanks for coming down again," Evers said after he put Pauletta's bags and CD case in the backseat.

"You're welcome. I've never been to Durham. I understand it's a nice area. And I'd like to go through Chapel Hill if we have time—maybe on the way back here."

"It's not too far out of the way."

"Sorry about the delay. The storms really set us back. I hope you didn't have to wait too long."

Evers shrugged, switched on the ignition and started out of the airport. "It's not a problem. I'm just glad you got here safely."

"It was a pretty nasty flight."

"In the face of all the shit in my life, I have some more good news," Evers announced.

"What?"

"My in-laws are threatening to tell the world about a drug test I failed."

"Why did you have a drug test? What exactly are you talking about?"

Evers told Pauletta about his support hearing with Jo Miller. "If word gets out, you'll lose your job, won't you? You guys are elected, right?" she said.

"Probably. I do have a second test, and that one's clean."

"How do you explain the first one? The one you failed?"

"It was one of the really quick piss tests the court service units do. It's my feeling that I got a false positive." He winked at her. "The one administered at the hospital by the infallible Dr. Rudy just a few days later is correct, of course. The bottom line is that I had another one done as soon as I found out from my attorney that I allegedly failed the first one. At least that's what I'm going to say."

"Any problems with the bar or the state and your license?"

"I don't think so. I might have to go to a seminar or write an essay or something. It's not a 'moral turpitude' crime, so I'm okay, I think. Maybe they'll make me pee in a jar occasionally."

"If they find out."

"I'm sure my in-laws will see to that."

"You'll lose your job," Pauletta said again. "How do they do that in North Carolina? Impeach you? A recall election or something?"

"To tell you the truth, I'm not sure. It's not something that happens a lot."

"Maybe it won't get out."

"Well, at any rate, I figure I need to just stare the beast in the face. That's what I think; I'm going to be sloppy and stubborn about it, like the guys who show up falling-down drunk in court to enter a guilty plea for DWI. I've got a small bag of dope that Pascal gave me, and you said one time that you might sample some with me. What do you think? It should make the trip more pleasant. And it should help your counterculture bona fides at the next march."

"How long will it take us to get where we're going?"

"It's twenty or thirty miles. It'll take a while in this weather." The windshield wipers were slapping, and there was a swoosh of water whenever a truck passed them. "Anyway, thanks again for coming. I guess you have better things to do with your free time."

"I canceled a trip with a very fine man, as a matter of fact." Pauletta opened her CD case. It was dark, so she switched on the interior light.

"The slick, Billy Dee Williams type? Sharkskin suit and a Cadillac filled with Asti Spumanti?"

"Put this in." Pauletta handed Evers a disc, Handel's *Water Music Suites*. "Do you like classical music, Judge Wheeling?"

"*Fantasia*'s about it."

"Figures." Pauletta put her CD case behind the seat. "Where's the dope?"

"In the glove box."

"We won't be able to see your brother tonight, right? It's already after eleven."

"Right. We'll get a room and see him in the morning. We won't get to Durham until after midnight. Can you roll a joint?"

"I haven't since college," Pauletta said.

"Well, try. I'm not very good at it either, and I'm driving. Let's get out of this traffic and all the lights just a little bit more, too."

Pauletta opened the glove box. "Do you think that your chances of having sex with me are improved since I'm smoking dope with you?"

"Are they?"

"Nope."

"Are you angry about missing your date with your slick black prince?" Evers looked at her, then back at the highway. He grinned. "I'll bet you really didn't have another trip."

"Of course I did. Why would I lie to you?"

"Before I get stoned, I want to ask you something, okay?"

Pauletta didn't answer.

"Did you like having sex with me?"

"It was adequate. It wasn't like fucking the Tin Man or something."

"Adequate?" Evers laughed.

"In the top twenty percent of all white men. Top fifty of all men generally." She smiled. "Maybe someday you'll get a chance to improve," she said in her deliberate way, then smiled again.

"What is a tin man, anyway? I mean, a lion is a lion, a scarecrow I know, Toto's a dog, but what the hell is a tin man?"

Pauletta looked across the car at him. "How smart is it of you to be using drugs right now? Sort of self-destructive, isn't it?"

"Who knows."

Pauletta rolled a joint, and she and Evers passed it back and forth between them. The end was orange, and the marijuana burned unevenly and too quickly. Evers and Pauletta cracked their windows. The smoke hung in the air for an instant and then skipped outside, into the rain and dark. After about fifteen minutes, she said, "I can't believe we're doing this."

"We are."

"Let's check out a McDonald's or something. I'm starving."

"I am, too, but that's a lot of effort and interaction."

"No it isn't. We need to eat."

The marijuana shortened Evers' sentences to rudimentary phrases. "Drive-through, then."

"Okay."

"Who pays?"

"I'll pay," said Pauletta.

"My sentences are short."

"Mine, too."

They both laughed.

"Drive-through," he said.

"I'll pay."

"That was a tiny sentence."

"Yes."

"Will you order?" Evers asked.

"I'm too high."

"I can't."

"Tell them we'll have whatever they select for us," Pauletta offered.

"Too complex."

"Just do it."

"What if it's a McFun pack or some other kid's thing?"

She tossed her hands up. "I can't taste anyway."

"Don't you feel stupid talking to the fucking sign?"

"What sign?"

"The menu with speech you order from."

"It's probably—"

"Yeah. It's not the menu that talks. Someone inside."

"An employee."

"Yeah."

"Yeah."

They ate in the restaurant's parking lot, and it seemed to Evers that they took a long while to finish.

By the time they got to Durham, Pauletta had turned quiet and walleyed, and Evers had started to even out his buzz. The world in front of him began to appear less and less like an eight-millimeter movie projected onto a white bedsheet. People moved without jerks and twitches, colors were not overbaked, and background and foreground finally seemed to separate. Pauletta was travel-and-dope drained and fell asleep in her pants and silk blouse on one bed. Evers took a shower and brushed his teeth and slept in the other bed, the one closer to the air conditioner.

At the Durham jail, Pascal was practically giddy when he came out to meet his brother and Pauletta. He was clean shaven, his hair was combed, and he walked quickly and relaxed when he sat down.

Pauletta and Pascal were glad to see each other again. They talked for a few minutes about music and movies while Evers held his sunglasses by the earpiece and flipped them around in lazy circles. Pascal was going on about a CD—*Cabaret Mañana*—that reminded him of cocktails and narrow ties, and he suddenly stopped and started talking to Evers.

"Oh, Christ, I meant to tell you. I had a great idea this morning, something that could really pay off. We should market reproductions of ticks with gummed backs. Kids would buy them, stick them in their heads or on their arms and frighten the shit out of their parents. A gold mine."

"We have other problems right now, Pascal."

"Evers can be very focused sometimes," Pascal said to Pauletta.

"Myopic, I'd say." Pauletta answered without much thought. "Why do you have your sunglasses out in here?"

Evers was suddenly angry. "What's wrong with you? Both of you? Pauletta flies two fucking hours down here, Pascal, and you stroll out here like some monarch, all carefree and smiles and record reviews. What the fuck is your problem? Perhaps I'll just leave you in here and not bond you out. You can do Rex Reed for the crooks and pinheads in your cell."

"Damn, don't do that." Pascal seemed concerned. He was wearing cheap blue jeans and a denim prison shirt with a black number stenciled onto it. "I'm sorry. I'm glad you came. I am. I just don't want you to be so worried, Evers, so weighed down by everything. A little levity helps sometimes."

"Amen," said Pauletta.

"So what's the story, Pascal?" Evers said, still cross. He jammed his glasses into his shirt pocket.

"Is it safe to talk here?"

"What do you mean?" Evers asked.

"Bugs, microphones. Whatever."

"It's safe," Evers said.

Pascal lowered his voice. "The confession won't do them a lot of good."

Pauletta leaned forward. "Why?"

"Well, first of all, when McCloud and that other dickhead came to visit me, I'd been drinking. Was drinking. I told them I shot Jo Miller. Nothing more than that. No detail, no elaboration. They asked me to sign a confession. Loggins writes it down on this form with my rights across the top. I waived my rights and signed the confession. As a matter of fact, I signed Purvis' name."

"Our father," Evers explained to Pauletta. He was still irritated and ignored Pascal's strange statement.

"Why did—?" Pauletta started to speak, but Pascal held up his hand.

"I signed it sloppily, but if you look, it will be pretty clear that it's 'Purvis,' not 'Pascal.' When I handed it to Loggins, I knocked a beer over onto the paper. Spilled all over it."

Pauletta started writing on a legal pad.

"Right after they left, I took Rudy's old Toyota out and drove it into a ditch. Before I wrecked, I'd drunk a pint of bourbon and at least six beers. I had most of the pint and two of the beers after the cops left. Gulped the shit down. I called Rudy when I left, and he phoned the police anonymously a minute or so later. Guess what? Fifteen to twenty minutes after I confessed I'm arrested for DWI with a point-one-six blood-alcohol level."

"No confession then," Pauletta mumbled. "If you were drunk, the *Miranda* waiver wasn't knowing and voluntary. If you're convicted of DWI, that's proof you were drunk. The state kills its own confession."

"They'll dismiss the DWI," Evers said. "Greenfield will pick it up and dismiss it."

"We can still use the blood test," said Pauletta.

"I doubt he'll find it. I drove across the line into Randolph County to wreck. It won't be in court where I live, and these guys are down here in Durham."

"What about the fibers and the credit card?" Pauletta was still writing. "Have you heard that news?"

"The cops mentioned that stuff when they were walking me out to their car, right before they did that classic move where they push your head under the door frame. Can't help you with the fibers. Certainly, though, that's not enough to convict me."

"They have a credit card record that indicates you were in the area on the day she died." Pauletta didn't look up from her pad when she spoke.

"Yeah. For a while that really threw me, because I was . . . I couldn't figure out how that happened. And then it dawned on me that after Evers left that morning, Rudy and I drove to Raleigh to buy some dope from a guy called Oscar. He's an accountant, works on Saint Mary's Street. He's been selling us pot for a couple years. On the way down, we stopped to buy gas and bought some beer and doughnuts at a Shell station. But it was like ten or eleven in the morning. The police had come and gone, and Jo Miller was already dead." He kicked the floor with the toe of his shoe. "It hardly seems fair that the police would use that. Is this the kind of thing they do—take things out of context?"

"I wonder if there is any way to establish the time as well as the day?" Pauletta said. "Did you pay at the pump? Did you talk to anyone? Buying beer and doughnuts before lunch isn't all that common, so maybe someone will recall seeing you and when you made the charge. Is the store open twenty-four hours? We need to check."

"I hope so," Evers said. "The drug dealer doesn't sound like a good witness."

"He's a CPA, Evers. He doesn't have to tell everyone exactly *why* we were there. And Dr. Rudy was with me the whole time."

Evers rolled his eyes. "I'd probably prefer to count on the drug-dealing CPA."

Pascal waited for Pauletta to look at him. "We paid inside. And they used one of those metal things they put your card on and then a slip and then run over the top of everything. I don't remember much about the clerk. I think it was fairly busy, though."

"We'll look into it."

"Whatever."

She put down her pencil and squinted at Pascal. "So what's going on? Why in the world did you do all this?"

"All things given, it was the best I could do."

"What the fuck does that mean, Pascal?" Evers felt his neck get hot.

Pauletta was perplexed. "Did you shoot her, Pascal?"

"Does it matter?"

"It would be helpful to know, yes." Her speech was paced and controlled. "I would like to know."

"But does it matter?"

"Pascal—"

"If I told you I did it, it would really limit your options, wouldn't it? Ethically, I mean. If I confessed to you, you couldn't let me testify to something different. I'm right about that, aren't I? Aren't I, Evers? You told me—"

"How did you figure out the confession stuff?" Evers interrupted.

"Read about it. Went to the Supreme Court Library in Raleigh and read *Strong's North Carolina Index* and a couple books on criminal procedure. It's pretty basic stuff, Evers, and I did graduate from college. Then I got Rudy to call legal aid from a pay phone and run it by them. He told them his name was Hector and used this great Spanish accent, sounded like Ricardo Montalban."

"What about Rudy?" Pauletta asked Pascal.

"Completely trustworthy."

"So are you going to tell us what's going on?"

"Whatever."

"We need you to help us, Pascal. Obviously, there's something you're not telling us." Pauletta slid her seat toward Pascal while she was speaking.

"I've told you everything you need to know."

"I'll have you bonded soon, and we'll drive you to your house before we go back. We need to get you a local lawyer, too. And before we leave, I'll have Pauletta get the lab reports, a copy of your confession and the credit card information."

"What do the reports say, exactly?" Pascal's voice lifted; he seemed uncertain for the first time.

"Evidently, a hair was found at the scene that isn't consistent with Falstaf's or the college kid she was running around with, and they claim the carpet fibers in your car match some rug at Jo Miller's."

"What does that mean? Do they completely match? I mean, can they tell if they're the same ones?"

Evers shook his head. "They can't say they're the same ones, that they came from her rug, but they can say that they are just like the ones in her rug. Same origin, same weave, same material."

"What kind of rug?" Pauletta asked.

"Fairly rare Kermanshah," Evers answered.

"Certainly there's more than one, though. And who knows when they got in there? They could've come off me when I was there months before. Or off Evers after he'd been at Jo Miller's. That doesn't seem like much." Pascal shrugged. "That's not much at all. What about the hair?"

"They can be pretty definite on that, I'm afraid. Have they asked you for a sample yet?"

"Yeah. I gave them one a while ago. They came about two weeks ago and searched the car and took a bag full of hair clippings."

"Did they have a warrant?" Pauletta was writing again.

"No, I gave them permission. They wanted to search the house, but I wouldn't let them. Rudy told me that after I was arrested, the police were at my trailer and went through everything anyway." Pascal looked at Evers. "I meant to tell you that. I know it's important, and I meant to tell you when it happened."

"Any problem with the search?" Pauletta asked.

"Probably find some pot and a few bongs."

She laughed.

Evers stood up. "I'll post the bond, Pascal. We'll be back in an hour or so, I guess."

"Thanks. And thank you, Pauletta."

"You're welcome. It was nice to see you."

She and Evers walked out of the jail without speaking. When they got outside, it had started to rain again, a steady, mean, messy wetness that had already made small pools in the parking lot and on the sidewalk.

"What do you think's going on, Judge Wheeling?" Pauletta wondered.

Evers shook his head.

"Is Pascal normal? Is he all here?"

"Yes."

"Did any of that make sense to you?" she asked.

"No." Evers was looking at the ground. "Don't try to make sense of it. That would be like playing a Beatles album backwards or something."

"It's very possible that he did it, and when the police came to search the car, he got the message and decided to sabotage their case with the clever confession. He keeps the DWI quiet until the confession is introduced at trial, then gets it punted, and he's home free. Can't be tried again, and without the confession the case against him is shit. Even if they turn up the DWI before trial, or if his lawyer raises the issue before trial, he's still in good shape. They'd either dismiss the case or plea bargain. He might be very guilty."

"It's possible that she killed herself or that Falstaf shot the bitch. We need to hire an investigator to check into that. Falstaf was there. He was pissed off, and he threatened her. He had a reason to kill her. Her name was misspelled. Pascal wouldn't do that. Plus, Falstaf's alibi doesn't seem too great to me. Oh—there's something else. She was virtually dead anyway. The autopsy showed horrible cancer, and maybe she knew. That's got to be to our advantage. We need to get her medical records."

"How do you know, and why are you just now telling me?"

"The cops told me."

"Do you think the police have been accurate, that they've been telling you the truth? Why would they tell you all this about their case and what they know?"

"Why not? I don't think they really thought Pascal was involved to begin with."

"Why didn't they arrest him right away?"

"Because they're stupid? Or knew they had a weak case? And he said he'd been gone; I guess they couldn't find him. Who knows?" He put his hands in his pockets and started through the rain to his car. "Let's go find the magistrate and see about getting him out."

Evers and Pauletta picked Pascal up from the jail and drove to a convenience store. They bought a carton of Corona, and each of them opened one in the car.

"How long is it to your house, Pascal?" Pauletta was in the front seat.

Pascal was folded and cramped into the car's small rear, the hatchback pressing down against him. "Hour and a half or so. We'll need to stop again for beer." He raised up and put his hand on Evers' shoulder. "Thanks for taking care of me, Evers."

"I'm glad to do it," Evers said, glancing back at his brother.

"Maybe we should let Pauletta visit the smiling white shrine before she leaves," Pascal said.

"What's that?" asked Pauletta.

Evers shook his head. "It's too foolish, Pascal. Too foolish and not a good idea."

"Tell me about it, Pascal."

Evers turned and looked at his brother. "Pascal, why? Why bring that up? I thought you didn't want anyone to know about it anyway." Evers was irate and frustrated again.

Pascal raised his voice. "Pauletta's a good person; she—"

"You've known her for a few weeks, Pascal, and been with her for three days or so in Salt Lake City. How would you know?"

"I can tell. I want her to check it out. Besides, she's my lawyer."

"Suit yourself."

"Tell me what you are talking about," Pauletta said again.

Pascal wedged his beer bottle between his legs. "The shrine is this white talisman. An albino charm that seems to grant wishes."

Pauletta pivoted all the way around in her seat. "Let me ask you what I asked your brother. Are you okay? Sane, that sort of thing?"

Pascal laughed. "Ask Evers. He's seen it, too."

"He's not reliable. The first time I encountered him he was babbling and crawling around my office. Seriously, do you think you're okay?"

"Sure. I'm fine."

"The confession plan is great. You're not trying to convince me you're crazy, are you? It won't do any good to persuade me—you'll need to convince a psychiatrist and a judge."

"Ask Evers. He's seen the thing work."

Pauletta turned back in her seat, toward Evers. "Have you?"

Evers kept driving, didn't speak.

"Are you pouting, Judge Wheeling? There's no need to be sullen. What do you know about the shrine?"

"You and Pascal figure it out," Evers said.

"It's lucky, right?"

"Right," Pascal answered.

"It's difficult for me to make much sense out of a lot you say, Pascal. You want me to visit this charm?" Pauletta asked.

"Right."

"What is it, a statue or relic or some kind of icon? A photograph? What? And what sort of wishes do you get?"

Pascal tapped Pauletta on the shoulder and handed her an empty bottle. She opened another beer and handed it back to him. "Well, my friend Henry won the lottery. Rudy got a classic car."

"Come on, now. A real good-luck charm? You're pulling my leg. Really? It's hard to get a grip on you two. Is this a prelude to something else? A parable? Nonsense for my entertainment . . . travel talk? What?"

"It's true," said Pascal. "Hard to believe, but true."

"What did you and Evers request?"

"I wanted to be beatific," Pascal said. "And Evers wanted his wife dead."

"Four for four, right?" Pauletta took a sip of beer.

"Whatever."

"Is this religious or spiritual or something?"

"I think so," Pascal said.

"I think so, too," said Evers.

"Are you religious, Pauletta?" Pascal asked.

"Not really."

"An infidel, are you?"

"An independent. We backed John Anderson for god." Pauletta looked up, and she and Pascal met each other in the rearview mirror.

"You know," Pascal said, "when I was in high school, I had this scheme to test the patience of the divinity. You're probably aware the book of Revelation holds that if you alter the word of god, then you'll suffer all sorts of horrific plagues. I figured that if you wanted to test the limits and validity of your religion, you could rewrite a few pages, spread them around and see what happens."

"I don't think that I want to take the chance, Pascal." Pauletta was amused.

An old, long car passed by Evers, Pauletta and Pascal. Evers saw a CB antenna stuck to the trunk, bending in the wind like an animal's tail as the car traveled down the highway.

"I wish we had some smoke," Pascal said. "Especially since we're going to thaw the shrine. I'm sure the jackbooted fuzz took the last bit I had at my house."

"Your brother has some, Pascal."

"Where'd you get dope, Evers?"

"You gave it to me about a month ago."

"And you still have it?"

Pauletta laughed.

Evers grinned, then laughed. "Hard to believe, huh, Pascal?"

"Yeah."

Evers slowed down the car. "What's all this about the creek, going to the river or something like that, whatever it was on your machine that replaced the *Star Trek* message?"

"Huh?" Pascal stuck his head between the seats. "What are you talking about?"

"On your answering machine. The spiel about going to the creek or stream with the shrine."

"Oh, right. We've been taking the albino shrine down to the little stream behind my trailer. We started going down there because it has been so hot, and it's cooler by the water. And it's in the woods, too, so you have lots of shade. Best of all, the water seems to enhance the smiling white charm, seems to cause it to work better, to do different things, to look different."

"I'm sure that it's a real special-effects wonderland," said Evers. He pushed the gas, and the car began to pick up speed.

The rain was coming down hard when the brothers and Pauletta got out and started walking through the woods to the stream. They had changed cars at Pascal's trailer, gotten into Pascal's banged-up Lincoln and driven through a field behind the mobile home and then down a hill. Big, heavy drops tapped and bounced off everything outside, so clear that they seemed bright and lit when they were falling.

"What a storm, what a storm!" Pascal was high and held his hands, palms up, toward the sky, and let the rain fall on his face. "This is great."

"It is a hellacious rain," agreed Pauletta, cutting her eyes at Evers. All three had on raincoats and hats, and Evers was carrying a couple of blankets.

Pascal had brought three cheap lawn chairs to a clearing at the stream. Evers and Pauletta sat in two of the chairs, and Pascal sat down on the ground beside his brother, left the last chair folded up and propped against a stump. The rain made a rattling sound in the trees above their heads. The stream was rising, picking up pace and swallowing stones, and rivulets the color of old copper were pouring in from the banks.

"What now?" Pauletta asked.

"We just wish and think. Talk. That's about it," Pascal said. "Isn't this great?" He put the liquor decanter holding the albino tears on the ground in front of them.

"What's in there? And why is it frozen?" Pauletta held her hand above her eyes to block the rain.

"I don't know if we can tell you. It might undercut the magic or somehow gum up the shrine or, I don't know, cause a crimp or change or problem." Pascal bit his lip. "I'm not sure."

"Then why did you bring me out here?" Pauletta asked.

"So . . . I guess so you could see it. And make a wish. Maybe . . . make a wish if you wanted to."

Pauletta reached down and picked up the glass decanter. "It looks like a frozen thimble. Or the top off something." She rotated the container in her hands and looked in from a different side. "Is it a cocoon, some sort of chrysalis? Are you hatching something?"

Evers looked straight ahead at the creek and didn't say anything. Rain was dripping off the bill of his hat, his nose and his chin.

"Whatever." Pascal shrugged.

"Why won't you tell me what it is?"

"Why are we out here in the rain?" Evers complained. "Why?"

"It adds atmosphere, Evers," Pascal answered.

"I'm fucking drenched." Evers hunkered down in his chair.

"If I tell you, Pauletta, you have to promise you won't mention it to anyone else, okay?" Pascal pointed his finger at her.

"Sure. I promise. You have my word."

"It's full of white tears. And they really do seem to affect things. In a good way."

"White tears?" Pauletta repeated.

"Yes."

"You're serious?"

"I'm totally serious," Pascal answered.

"Where did you get them?"

"Guess."

She laughed. "How would I know? How could I possibly know?"

"Guess," Pascal said again.

"I have no idea. It's a bunch of tears, right?"

"Yes," Pascal said.

"So tell me." Pauletta reached down and pushed on Pascal's shoulder.

"Ruth Esther," Pascal said excitedly. "Ruth Esther is the mother of the albino tears shrine. How about that?"

"How did that happen? How do you happen to end up with . . . you know . . . how did you get them?"

"Evers got them. He knows the story. Tell her, Evers."

"This isn't a gag, right?" Pauletta quizzed Pascal.

"Absolutely not. Give her the yarn, Evers."

Evers watched the hard rain, listened to it hitting the ground.

"Come on, Judge, tell me. I'm really curious."

"Why do you care?" Evers asked.

"It sounds like a good story. And because it's important to Pascal."

"All right." Evers pulled the edge of a blanket over his head and told Pauletta the entire tale, starting with the scrambled, spinning, hungover first meeting he had with Ruth Esther. "So now you know," he said when he finished talking. "That's how we got the shrine."

"Wow." Pauletta had listened the whole time Evers spoke without interrupting him. "You'd almost like to believe there's something to it."

The three of them sat in the woods for another fifteen minutes, thinking and fighting the weather and watching the white shrine shed its frozen sparkles. The rain started to fall faster, and Pauletta suddenly began to feel uncomfortable. They'd all smoked some of the joint while they were in the Datsun, and her mouth was dry and she started shivering. The brothers were making her uneasy; they were crazy, odd and elusive without meaning to be, tangled up in each other, blurred together, sitting around her rapt and intense, waiting for something impossible and haunting to happen. Pauletta wondered what was about to start, what in the world the two of them were expecting. She looked at them and worried about herself, thought about Jo Miller. The dope, the rain and the woods were making her paranoid.

"I'm too damp to stay much longer," she said suddenly. Her voice was trembling.

Evers looked at her. "You're scared, aren't you?"

"Yes. No need to lie. This is too weird. It just happened all of a sudden. I was fine and now I'm really uncomfortable, almost ill. Some of it's the pot—I'm not used to it."

Evers got out of his chair and stood in front of Pauletta. He unfolded one of the blankets and laid it on the ground.

"Come here."

"Why?" Pauletta didn't move. She was wearing an expensive, long raincoat, and part of her hair, in the front, was soaked and flat, stuck against her forehead.

Evers reached down and took her hand. He sat down on the blanket and guided Pauletta toward him so she sat down between his legs, her back to his chest. Evers wrapped the other blanket around them both. He put his chin on her shoulder, his arms around her. "Don't worry. It fucked me up the first time, too. And it's strange out here right now."

Pascal looked at Evers and Pauletta. He got off the ground and into the seat Evers had been sitting in. "I approve, brother."

"You don't know everything, Pascal," Evers said.

"We'll see," he answered.

"The two of you are so bizarre. Crazy. Evers especially."

Evers shifted behind her, moved his legs and tugged the blanket down farther over their faces so it blocked more of the rain. It was dark underneath the blanket, like sitting in a soaked cloth cave. "I'm getting cold, too," he said.

Pauletta's mind jumped from thought to thought, omitting a few bridges and niceties. "I perhaps am sitting in dark isolated woods with two madmen, one of whom is a murderer."

"Whatever," Pascal said.

"Don't worry," Evers said, and kissed Pauletta on the neck. Her skin felt warm on his lips. She leaned back against him and closed her eyes.

"We need to make our wishes." Pascal seemed relaxed and stoned. Every so often he would stick out his tongue, tilt back his head and swallow a mouthful of rain.

"Who goes first? I think we should . . ." Evers quit talking. He thought he'd heard something, a voice or a step or a noise, and he squeezed Pauletta's shoulder. Pascal had turned in the same direction and straightened up in his chair.

"You hear something?" asked Pascal.

"Where?" Pauletta sat up and looked through the rain.

"Across the stream, on the other side." Evers pointed. He pushed the front of the blanket up with the palm of his hand.

"Beside the big tree, the one closest to the water." Pascal pointed, too.

Pauletta kept looking. She was cold. The rain was hitting her in the face and turning into explosions on her cheeks. The drops were large, poured thick and dense out of the sky. "I don't see anything."

"Right there straight in front of us," Pascal said, "looking at us— what is that? It's sort of bright, like it's electrical." He talked in a normal voice.

Pauletta blinked. The rain was beating down on her at an angle, blowing into her eyes, coming in waves of transparent, pounding confusion that thumped and pecked her skin. "I can't see anything. There's nothing out there. I can't see shit."

"Hello." Pascal stood up. "Rudy? Hello?"

"Pauletta, look. It's no more than thirty yards away. Like a white blur. Right there."

"You and your brother have a different kind of vision than I do, Judge Wheeling. I see rain and trees."

"It's as bright as day, Pauletta," Pascal said.

"There's nothing out there. You two are either crazy or liars. I've seen enough of this. I don't know how I let you talk me into this shit. It's a glorified parlor game with two fools. Let's go." Pauletta's head was clearing.

"You really don't see anything?"

"I see you and Pascal. I see rain and woods. Nothing else. I guess in your bizarre, labyrinthine, stupid and incomprehensible world order, this is another trip that has some meaning for you two. It's way too strange for me. And I resent being jerked around."

Pascal looked down at Pauletta, then crouched beside her. His hair was soaking wet. She could see his eyes, wide and earnest. "Evers didn't want to come. I brought you just because I like you and I know Evers does, and I wanted you to enjoy the shrine. I swear we didn't mean any harm. We're not trying to be crazy or prove anything or fuck with you. We'll take you back, and I'll cook us something to eat and get you some dry clothes. I'll even get the space heater out of the closet and warm you up. Okay?" He touched her arm. "Okay?"

"Thanks. Thank you, Pascal. I'm sorry I didn't see anything. Maybe on a better day." She unfolded Evers' arms and got up.

"I told you it was a poor idea," said Evers. He looked at the shape across the water, then reached down near his feet and picked up a cold stone with pointed, irregular edges. He threw the rock toward the creek, and it left his hand and raced into the heavens and heavy sky, disappeared.

"What're you doing?" wondered Pascal.

Evers heard a noise, very quick and sharp, above his head, and he looked up. Pascal also looked up. They heard the noise again, and this time, right after the sound, a tree limb snapped and fell toward the ground. The limb was large, about the size of a man's thigh where it broke off from the trunk, and a smaller branch brushed Pauletta's shoulder before the whole tangle landed in the wet leaves and moss.

"Are you okay?" asked Evers.

"I guess." The chair she'd been sitting in was nearly invisible beneath the tree branch.

"Let's go," said Pascal.

"No argument from me."

The two men and Pauletta walked out of the woods and did not look back. Evers put his arm around her. "I'm sorry about all of this. I really am. Everything recently has just been a fairly bad quagmire. Thanks for sticking with me."

"Sure."

"I'll try to make it up to you," Evers promised, and Pauletta flickered a weak smile that faded almost as soon as it started. They were in sight of the car.

"You can be very decent at times," she said, "when you're not acting in character."

"Why do women like men so much when they're not themselves?"

Evers asked. "I've never understood that. Women love aberrations, don't they?"

"What brought that up? You just ramble and chatter sometimes."

"I thought you might be able to help me with that. I've always wondered about it."

"You appreciate small things when you have to go through a lot of shit to get them. A sprinkle of water in the desert makes you very grateful."

Pascal opened the door to his car. "See there, Evers. Now you know."

"I hope we aren't stuck," Evers said. "There's a lot of mud."

"We won't be."

The car started and moved across the ground without any problem.

"So what did it look like to you?" Evers asked.

"You're not going to believe this," Pascal said. He had both hands on the steering wheel and was traveling slowly through the field. The windshield wipers were on high, slapping down clear spreads of water over and over again. "You tell me. What did you think? Tell me first."

"Well, nothing really. Nothing . . . identifiable. Sort of like Abe Lincoln's head, going up and down, like it was on a Slinky. Up and down."

Pauletta started laughing. "I'm sure that's exactly what it was, Judge Wheeling. Why would you think that's out of the ordinary?"

He ignored her. "So what did you think it was, Pascal?"

"Well, to tell you the truth, it looked like—to me, anyway—like Ruth Esther, very bright and lovely."

Pauletta laughed some more. "That's great—postmodern visions. Everyone gets to see what he wants to see. I like that. A little dope, some rain, a thimble of frozen pus in the woods and you get Jackson Pollock and Robert Motherwell to paint your path for you."

Pascal put a cigarette in his mouth and pushed in the lighter. "And you didn't see anything, right?" He looked up in the rearview mirror.

"Sorry," Pauletta answered back.

"You've really changed your tune quickly, haven't you?" Evers said. "You were all revved up about the shrine a few minutes ago."

"What?"

"Nothing. Forget it."

"What do you mean?" Pauletta pressed Evers.

"Just forget it, okay? Maybe now we can spend a little time figuring out the more practical aspects of Pascal's defense."

TEN

PASCAL INSISTED ON HAVING HIS CASE HANDLED BY A PUB-
lic defender. Evers offered him the money to hire a private
lawyer, but he refused. "How much did you pay Ike White to forget to
ask the right question?" Pascal finally said. "Besides, I've got good
facts, and you and Pauletta will be holding my hand every step of the
way."

Evers and Pauletta both agreed that Pascal's lawyer seemed competent. He was a fifty-year-old, jolly, rumpled southerner who went to
college at Amherst and law school at Boston University. His name
was Adam Wampler, and as far as Evers could tell, he did everything
he could for Pascal, although he was as bewildered as everyone else
about the confession. Pauletta would help him at the trial; she'd also
done the research for the confession issue, and had written a memo-
randum and copied all the relevant cases.

Wampler and Pauletta had buried the motion to suppress the confession among a number of other requests and motions, many of them
routine. The lawyers had deliberately been low-key and had camou-
flaged their intentions as much as possible. Wampler had told the district attorney that there "wasn't much to" any of the fifteen motions
that took up almost an inch of Pascal's court file. To confuse the genuine issues as much as possible, Pauletta had included motions and

briefs that challenged the legality of the search of Pascal's car and one that suggested the case should be dismissed because the police officers had been "rude, unpleasant and overbearing." Adam Wampler loved the last one and chuckled when he read it. Like Pauletta, he did not, in general, care for the police.

The lawyers and judge had agreed to arrive at court an hour before the jury was due to report, to deal with all the motions Wampler and Pauletta had filed. When Pascal and the lawyers got to the top floor of the Durham Judicial Center, Evers didn't stay with his brother. There was no one in the jury room, it wouldn't be used until time for deliberations, and Evers went in and sat in a wooden chair with a three-slatted back and thought about the trial. There was nothing else to think about. The sun was shining in Durham, and Evers could see out of the window.

He felt sorry for Pascal and his waiting. Waiting for uncertainty and little else, for his chance to be considered by people who didn't know him but would judge him anyway, and who probably would judge him on things they were never meant to consider—his posture or his looks, or their impressions of Wampler and Pauletta, or someone's half-baked recollection of courtroom myths and bromides overheard ten years ago in an uncle's toolshed. You might, it occurred to Evers, more easily win the favor of a juror, or two jurors, or even three, by entertaining them with the first seven pages of a 1981 Eldorado owner's manual and ignoring the facts and facets of Pascal Wheeling's life. You very well might. " 'Do your best' sort of sums it up, doesn't it?" Evers said aloud.

After she and Wampler had met with the district attorney, Pauletta came into the jury room and found Evers sitting in the wooden chair with his feet resting on the seat of another chair. His hands were laced behind his head, elbows out, like a prisoner on a forced march.

"Adam in here?"

"No." Evers didn't move.

"Who were you talking to?"

"To whom was I talking, you mean? I was talking to myself. I said that we'd do our best for Pascal, but that something else, something we never touched on, might decide the case."

"Like what?" Pauletta asked.

"A lot of things."

"Such as?"

"That's just it. Anything—his race, your race, mine, the wind, a TV show, bad hearing, a hair out of place, nothing at all, shirt selection, breakfast cereal—"

"I can see that you're prepared to add a lot of substance to our effort."

"I'm nervous, to be honest," Evers said.

"Well, don't be. It's on our heads. It's our case, our client, our responsibility."

"I know that. He's my brother, though."

"Try not to talk to yourself when you testify."

"Thinking is talking to yourself, isn't it?"

"Don't think out loud." Pauletta was tense.

"Stalin and Churchill, allies at Yalta, return home to wrap up the war." Evers rocked back in his chair.

She looked at him and didn't say anything else.

Granger Hands was the district attorney in Durham. He was a well-dressed man, handsome, average height, with no hint of a North Carolina accent. He was civilized, frank and aggressive, in Evers' estimation. He was also quite skilled in court, but overworked.

Pascal's judge was a man named Moses Pendleton. Pendleton was fat, pallid and bald, with small square teeth that could fairly be characterized as stained, though they were not quite yellow. He bit his lip from time to time, and the exposed, discolored teeth caused him to look like a field mouse or a hamster. Evers imagined him reared on his haunches, paws clutching a flat seed, white-bellied and bubble-eyed. Still, Pendleton struck Evers as fair and evenhanded, just not very bright.

As a professional courtesy, Pendleton had agreed to allow Evers to sit in on the motions hearing, although he wouldn't be allowed to speak or argue. Evers was still sitting in the jury room when Adam, Pauletta and Pascal came in, about ten minutes after Pauletta had left him sitting there brooding.

"We ready to go?" Evers took his feet out of the chair and started to get up.

"Not yet," said Pauletta.

"We have a decision to make," Adam said. He took several steps into the room and was standing behind Pauletta and beside Pascal.

"What decision?" Evers asked.

"Adam suggests that we go ahead and show our cards now, see what the D.A. will offer. He thinks Hands will be objective." Pauletta's tone was professional and open-ended. "Show him our evidence, see what he comes back with."

Adam looked at Evers. "He doesn't want to lose a murder case with an election just around the corner. Plus, these aren't local people, and the case hasn't received *that* much attention for a murder, given it's a judge's wife and his brother. Granger doesn't want to look like a fool; he'd rather get something than nothing, so I think we should tell him what we have. He doesn't have time to react anyway. What can he do between now and nine-thirty? We don't have anything to lose."

"Get a continuance?" asked Evers.

"Not with Pendleton. Especially since we filed our motions more than a month ago."

"What do you think?" Evers asked his brother.

"Whatever."

"Let's try it then," Evers suggested. "What do you think, Pauletta?"

"I think it's a bad idea. I think we have a sure winner, and we go to trial and drop it on them. Why give Hands time to prepare his witnesses and do some research? Maybe he'll get a continuance and more time to prepare."

"But what can he change by preparing?" Adam countered. "The wrong name is on the confession, and Pascal was legally drunk moments afterward. None of that will change. And without the confession there's no case. Nothing. He'll know that and make a decent offer, maybe even dismiss this. Pendleton could make the wrong call on us. He's not all that courageous." Adam made his points quietly.

"Loggins and Greenfield will get a quick tutorial, and all sorts of things could happen," Pauletta said. "The original confession might disappear. I don't trust the state. Let's have a hearing and argue the motion. Or reserve our right to challenge the confession and do it in trial with the jury excused. It doesn't make sense to call the enemy camp and tell them you are going to attack an hour in advance, even if you have a flamethrower and they have slingshots."

"What do you think, Pascal?" Evers asked again.

"Whatever you decide." Pascal seemed nervous and uneasy. He was wearing a dark suit and looked very pale.

"Go get Mr. Hands," said Evers, and Pauletta shook her head.

Adam went outside and came back with Granger Hands, who greeted everyone and was cordial and polite. He sat down at the table beside Evers.

"What can I do for you folks?" he asked.

"We had hoped to discuss a compromise," Adam said. He was still standing, along with Pauletta.

"Always glad to listen." Hands sounded sincere.

"I think that you have some problems with your case, Granger. We wanted to let you know in advance, try to save you a little embarrassment and, of course, help Mr. Wheeling. Maybe work out a plea agreement."

Hands scratched his head theatrically and then put his hands in his pockets. "I've got a dead woman, a confession, a credit card receipt that puts Mr. Wheeling's car in the area, carpet fibers—good slides and lab stuff that juries love—and a reason for Mr. Wheeling to kill his beloved brother's evil wife. Am I missing something, Adam? Miss Qwai? I'm not a great lawyer, but I think I can do okay with this one." He looked at everyone except Pascal.

"Suppose you didn't have a confession?" Adam asked. "Then what?"

"Suppose I didn't, but I do."

"Suppose you didn't," Adam said again. "Then you wouldn't have a case, would you, Granger?"

"It would make things difficult," he agreed.

"You couldn't get past a motion to dismiss, could you?"

"It would be a challenge." Hands smiled. "But he confessed. I've checked the forms. He signed off on *Miranda* and signed the confession. And he confessed at his own home. No coercion or anything."

"Do you have the confession, Granger?" Adam asked.

Hands looked through his file and handed a typewritten statement across the table to Adam.

"The original one?" said Adam.

"The policeman has it. We sent you copies several weeks ago. You're not going to stand there and tell me some chickenshit story about discovery, that you didn't get the confession copy?"

"We got it, Granger." Adam smiled. "Don't get upset."

"I've always been aboveboard with you, Adam."

"I know. I'm not questioning your ethics. Would you get it from the cop?"

"Sure." Hands walked to the door and summoned Greenfield. Evers noticed that the jurors were beginning to come in. Two older men were talking to each other, and a young woman wearing a sweat suit was reading a paperback book. Most of them looked uncomfortable.

Hands handed Adam the original confession. "Short and sweet," he said.

"Look at the signature," Adam said. "Read it." Adam laid the paper on the table.

Hands put his finger underneath the signature and leaned forward. "It looks like 'Purvis Wheeling' or something. The writing isn't too great."

"Exactly."

"Well, the defendant signed it in front of two officers."

"You'll agree that his name is 'Pascal,' not 'Purvis.' "

"Maybe it says 'Pascal.' " Hands picked up the confession and looked at it again, held it closer to his face. "Even if there's some debate about it, he still signed it and admitted his guilt to the officers. It may be an interesting abstract problem, but we can get around it, I think. Is he going to deny signing it and deny talking to the police? He'll lose that swearing contest. And the jury will probably be pissed if they figure he signed the wrong name to be cute. This will hurt him, Adam. You know that."

"That's not the end of the story."

Hands put the confession down and drummed on the tabletop with his fingers. "What's the rest?"

Adam set his briefcase on the table. Evers heard the hard plastic hit the wood and the case's fasteners pop open; for some reason, it reminded him of customs in the Caribbean. Adam dropped a copy of a traffic warrant onto the table; the paper fluttered then cut a rapid zigzag before it landed. "Check it out."

Hands looked at the warrant. "Mr. Wheeling has been convicted of DWI. Great. Impressive. You want concurrent time or something?"

"Check the date and time. It's within a half an hour of the confession. I've got the two officers here to testify that he was so drunk he could barely stand. He was found guilty, his blood-alcohol content was way over the limit, and therein lies the problem. He was drunk when he confessed, and so drunk that he signed his father's name to the confession. In fact, he was drinking when he signed it and spilled beer on the paper. There's a stain on the lower left-hand side. If he's drunk, he can't effectively waive his *Miranda* rights, plus there's the question of the accuracy and voluntariness of the statement. Last but not least, the confession has no detail. None."

"Huh." Hands folded the DWI conviction in half and slid it toward Adam's briefcase. "You say these guys are here?"

"They're subpoenaed. Officers Brown and Hancock."

"I saw them listed but figured they were just character witnesses since you used their home addresses and didn't let on that they were policemen. Especially since they were from up around where the defendant lives."

"I can't tell you everything, Granger."

"You care if I talk to them?"

"No. There's a guy from Duke Hospital, too. A Dr. Lane. He wasn't subpoenaed. He'll tell you that you can't get a point-one-six in twenty minutes. Mr. Wheeling was drinking when he talked to Loggins and Greenfield."

"They didn't mention it," Hands said. "Let me talk to these folks, and I'll get back with you."

"What do you think?" Evers asked after Hands had shut the door.

"Granger is usually reasonable," Adam said. "We'll have to see, I guess."

"Excuse me," Pascal said. "I'm going to wait outside. Maybe take a look at some of the jurors, see if any of them have long hair, tattoos . . . scars, needle tracks, tremors—just check things out. Let me know what happens."

Evers got up and looked out the window. He saw a pickup stop at a light several blocks away. A man wearing a plaid shirt and carrying a paper sack got into the truck. Evers thought about Winston-Salem and his summer job at the factory, all the shift workers and their hardscrabble, simple happiness. Homer, Butch, Snake, Lula, Pumpkin, Myra and Maddog. There were Pucketts, O'Dells, Lawlesses, Branches and Gwynns. And they were all interchangeable in a certain way, mix and match, a Butch Lawless, a "Snake" Morris—they all had identical backgrounds, the same common clump of experiences and the same knockabout mentality that at its most creative aspired to memorizing the ingredients on the back of a soft drink can during a break from work. These were people who were unable to accomplish anything greater than an extra pack of Camels in their glove compartment, but they were happy, most of them. Numb and happy, bound up in routines and certainty so sure and lifeless that two hours to hunt alone in the woods on a Friday morning seemed like a blessing, and a trip to the fish house for fried seafood and hushpuppies once a month was a good part of life. Evers couldn't recall the last time he'd been happy or could rely on anything at all. He and Pascal used to joke about the Plant People, and now he envied their bland days and easy moods.

Evers heard the door open behind him, but he didn't turn around, just kept looking out the window and watched the truck drive away.

"So what do you think, Granger?" Adam sounded anxious, a hint of beggar in his tone.

"Not much I can do, Adam. Greenfield and Loggins say he was coherent and not drinking. Plus I've got Mrs. Wheeling's family on me like a cheap suit. I give you something, they'll write letters to the editor for months. As you well know, mine is an elected office." Hands paused. "Best I could offer is twenty years on second degree."

"Losing a murder trial isn't going to help your standing in the election either," said Adam. He sounded angry, but constrained. Evers still had not turned around.

"Twenty on second degree. That's better than the worst that could happen."

"Fuck this," Pauletta said suddenly. "Let's let the judge decide it. This is a waste of time." She picked up her suit jacket and file and walked out of the room.

Evers walked out behind her and went to use a pay phone. He passed Pascal, seated by himself in the courtroom, and gave him a thumbs-down sign. Pascal shrugged and smiled.

Judge Moses Pendleton was not happy to have to make a difficult technical decision. He held the suppression hearing in his chambers and kept rubbing his forehead and looking at his watch. He released the jury until one that afternoon.

Adam called the two state policemen who had arrested Pascal to testify. Hands had taken some of the edge off their testimony, but they were generally effective. He introduced their field notes, which showed the arrest at 3:26 p.m., twenty-three minutes after the time on the confession. They conceded that Pascal was unaware of where he was, had trouble communicating and was very unsteady on his feet. Pendleton seemed most intrigued by the alcohol-stained confession with the wrong signature. "This isn't even his name," he said twice to Granger Hands.

Dr. Lane told the judge and lawyers that the body could "evacuate" or process approximately one twelve-ounce beer or one mixed drink with two ounces of alcohol every hour. Each beer or mixed drink produced a blood alcohol content of .015 to .020, so that it would take, theoretically, sixteen to eighteen beers in half an hour to reach Pascal's BAC reading. However, it was virtually impossible for the body to absorb that much alcohol so quickly. It was Dr. Lane's expert medical opinion that Mr. Wheeling would have to have been drinking for at least an hour to ninety minutes prior to the test to produce such a high blood-alcohol content.

Loggins and Greenfield testified that Pascal was not drinking, was sober, coherent, and that he'd turned over an old, warm beer can sitting on the kitchen table along with a lot of other trash and debris. "He was absolutely normal, Judge," Loggins insisted.

When the two detectives finished testifying, Pendleton stood up from behind his desk. "This is close, Lawyers. Of course, the test is what was his condition when he signed the waiver and gave the statement, not what his condition was half an hour later. The detectives who were there say he was fine, but the doctor from Duke says that with his BAC he would have been impaired. Signed the wrong name, too." Pendleton repeated what everyone knew.

"But he signed it," interrupted Hands.

"The defendant going to testify in rebuttal?" asked the judge.

"No sir," answered Adam.

"Have you all talked about a plea?" Pendleton wondered.

"Yeah."

"What did you offer, Granger?"

"Twenty years on second degree."

Pendleton raised his voice. "Off the record, please." He looked at the court reporter, and she stopped typing. "You can do better than that, Granger. This is right on the edge."

"I have an unhappy family and the reputations of two very good policemen at stake. That's the best I can do."

"You've got an election coming up, and you're going to make me call it. Don't bullshit me, Granger." Pendleton sounded mad. "I'll be your whipping boy if you lose this one. We answer to the voters, too, you know."

"Not for another two years, though." Hands was calm. "Jesus, Judge, he admitted killing a woman. What do you want me to do?"

Pauletta stood up. "Judge Pendleton, if I could speak. We haven't rested in rebuttal. Mr. Wampler is correct that we will not call the defendant, but we do have a witness in rebuttal, Dr. Rudy Williams. Perhaps this debate will be more appropriate after all the evidence is in. And perhaps the rebuttal evidence will give the court some additional factual assistance." Adam turned and looked at Pauletta and Pascal. Evers was seated in a corner behind them all, staring at the floor.

"I'm sorry, Miss Qwai, I guess I was hasty. I didn't mean to cut your case off." Pendleton bit his lip. Evers thought of an exercise wheel and pine shavings.

Evers had rehearsed Rudy as well as he could over the phone, providing him with some simple facts and an easy story to recite. When the car doctor arrived, he had on his white physician's jacket, a tie and a beeper. He looked perfect. They had to wait about twenty minutes after the other witnesses finished for him to make the trip from Norton, but Pendleton seemed glad to have the break.

Pauletta questioned Rudy from notes that Evers had given her.

"Your name?"

"Rudolph Astin Williams."

"Your occupation, please?" Pauletta was wearing a dark business suit. She was poised and appeared confident, although she had only a general idea of what Rudy was going to say.

"I'm a physician." Rudy gave his credentials and experience.

"Did you have occasion to see Pascal Wheeling on July twenty-sixth at two-thirty p.m.?"

Hands objected. "Leading. Miss Qwai is leading."

"Sustained."

"Did you see Pascal Wheeling on July twenty-sixth?" Pauletta repeated the first portion of her question.

"Yes."

"About what time?"

"Between two and four in the afternoon."

"Where did you see him?" she asked.

"At his trailer."

"Why were you there?"

"Mr. Wheeling had been sick. He'd been drinking too much, plus he had a fairly bad viral infection. I wanted to check on him."

"You make house calls, Doctor?" Pauletta preempted Hands' attack on Rudy's answer.

"Actually, I do. My work at the ER is not totally demanding, and we live in a small town. Also, I know Pascal and like him."

"How do you remember the date?"

"I checked my notes. Also, I recall it was the same day he got a DWI. He asked me to testify at his DWI trial, and I refused. He wanted me to testify about the effects of his medication on his driving skills." Rudy adjusted the beeper on his belt.

"Did you testify at that trial?"

"No. No, ma'am."

"Why is that, Doctor?" Pauletta asked.

"I felt uncomfortable doing so. I work in the ER. I see every day what drinking on our highways can cause. And besides, his medication would not have contributed significantly to his physiological state at the time he was driving."

"But he called you and asked you to testify for him?"

"Called me the very same night," Rudy answered.

"And you told him what?" Pauletta asked.

"Well, to be blunt, I told him that when I had seen him he was drunk, and that the medicine I'd given him did not contribute in any way to his impairment."

"What time did you see him?"

The room seemed especially quiet. The judge looked at Rudy.

"Like I said, in the afternoon. I can't be positive."

"You said earlier around two to four." Pauletta was standing when she questioned Rudy. She took a step toward him after she spoke.

"Yeah. That's a rough estimate, though. Could have been earlier, could have been later." Rudy smiled. "You're asking me to recall a fairly routine visit with one of many patients that occurred over two months ago."

"I understand." Pauletta hesitated. "And what was his condition when you saw Mr. Wheeling, the defendant?"

"Drunk and disoriented. He was seriously impaired. His eyes were red and glassy. He exhibited a strong odor of alcohol. His balance was poor, his coordination affected. His speech was slow and slurred on some words. He was febrile, congested and dehydrated."

"Did he recognize you?"

"Yes. Certainly."

"What did you do for him?" Pauletta gestured with one of her hands, raised it just a little and pressed four of her fingers together.

"Checked his blood pressure, took his temperature, reminded him to stay inside and rest, and told him that if he didn't stop drinking, he would kill himself. Also, I got him some water and ice. I was concerned about the effects of both a fever and drinking in terms of his remaining hydrated."

"Was there anyone else at the home?"

"No. Not that I'm aware of."

"Did you see anyone when you left?"

"Two men were there, coming to the door. Two policemen."

"How do you know who they were?"

"I asked. We talked for a moment or so." Rudy smiled again.

"Do you recall their names?"

"Lord, no."

"Did they say why they were there?" Pauletta asked.

"Just to see Pascal. I told them he was sick and drinking."

"Did you tell them not to bother Mr. Wheeling?"

"Oh, no. No, ma'am. I didn't know what they wanted, and I assumed it was none of my business. I did tell them that Pascal had been drinking."

"Did you tell them he was drunk?"

"No, ma'am, I didn't. Maybe I should have. I'm sure they found out as soon as they got inside." Rudy's watch beeped, and he pushed a button on its side to make it stop. "Sorry."

"Did the officers go inside?"

"I guess. I mean, I don't know. I'm not sure exactly what this is about. There was no medical reason for them not to approach Mr. Wheeling, okay? He had a virus and was drunk. I told them that, basically, and left. There were no medical reasons for them not to talk to him. I left them alone, ma'am." Rudy raised his voice and sat absolutely erect in his chair. "I know what these policemen have to deal with. I see it in the ER all the time. And I wasn't going to tell them to leave Mr. Wheeling alone. It wasn't my business. In fact, if anything, I thought seeing two officers might straighten him up a little." Rudy shifted his weight and seemed agitated. He never looked at Evers, and Evers was glad of it.

Pauletta held up both hands. "Doctor, I'm sorry. I didn't mean to suggest that you did anything wrong."

"Well, it sounded like we were heading that way."

"Just a few more items, sir." Pauletta's tone never changed.

"Okay." Rudy relaxed.

"How would you characterize Mr. Wheeling's mental capacity, clarity of thought and, most important, his competency when you saw him on this date?"

"He was intoxicated. Clinically speaking, his mental processes were significantly curtailed, and his competency, temporarily of course, was extremely questionable."

"One final question, Doctor. Have you seen either of the policemen you saw on that day again?"

"No. Not until today."

"Today?"

"Yes, ma'am. I saw one of them today sitting outside in court when I came through."

"Could you describe him?"

"Nice-looking man, rugged, western-type clothes. He's right outside."

"How about the other officer outside, sitting with the man you described? Do you recognize him?"

"It could be the man who was with him at Mr. Wheeling's, but I'm not certain. The one man stands out, but I'm not certain about whether or not I could identify the second man."

"Thank you, Doctor." Pauletta asked the judge to have Loggins step in, and Dr. Rudy confirmed that he was the policeman at Pascal's. When the judge called the other policeman in, Rudy couldn't say for sure whether he'd met Greenfield that day.

Hands was not taking Rudy's testimony at face value. He was very thorough when he questioned the car doctor. He had a yellow legal pad full of scribbles he'd made during Pauletta's examination, but he didn't look at it very often.

"What kind and color car were the policemen driving?" Hands asked.

"I'm not sure. I don't think it was one with lights and so forth, or I'd recall. But it could've been. I'm not sure."

"You can remember, from a brief conversation months ago, a man's face, but you missed something as big as a car?" Hands seemed skeptical but was still polite.

"I can remember one man who was very distinctive. I can't identify the other one. I'm not sure about the car. I'm sorry." Rudy sounded contrite.

"What kind of driveway is it? Didn't you have to get past the police car?"

"It's a little semicircle in front of the trailer. I came in on one side, from Route 813, turned in the first entrance since I was coming from the hospital."

"I see."

"They must have been on the other side, used the other entrance. Or I could have backed around them."

"Now, you and Mr. Wheeling are good friends, correct?"

"Yes." Rudy nodded.

"Did he know you were coming that day?"

"I told him a day or two before that I'd come by that morning. Then I got tied up in the ER until the afternoon, so I was late."

"What time was it again?" Hands asked.

"Afternoon, two, three, maybe four."

"Could it have been later?"

"Than four?" Rudy seemed confused.

"Yes."

"Maybe, I guess. But I doubt it."

"Who asked you to testify here today?"

"Pascal Wheeling."

"When?" Hands looked at his pad.

"About a week ago or so."

"Were you subpoenaed?"

"No." Rudy paused. "I mean, not that I know of. I haven't gotten a subpoena."

"How did you know when to be here?"

"Pascal told me that his lawyer would call if they needed me. That way I wouldn't miss work. They called me this morning."

"Who did?"

"Evers did. Evers Wheeling." Rudy looked at Evers for the first time.

"Did he discuss your testimony?"

"He asked me if I remembered what time I saw the policemen."

"What did you tell him?" Hands cleared his throat.

"What I told you and the lady. The same thing I've said several times today."

"Did Mr. Evers Wheeling make any suggestions to you about your testimony?"

"No. He told me to come and which floor and room I needed to find. I had trouble with the directions and had to get a pen. He asked me about the time, about when I saw Pascal. That was it. Then I drove down here." He crossed his legs and looked at Pauletta.

"Would it surprise you to know that both officers have no recollection of seeing you or talking to you?"

"I'm not sure. I don't remember one of them, either." Rudy turned his wrist and looked at his watch.

"No sir. They don't have a problem with recollection. They are certain, both of them, that you were not there and that you never talked to them. Are they lying?" Hands was very firm.

Evers saw Pauletta start to stand and then sit back down. She glanced across the room at him.

"Sir, I would never say a policeman is a liar. I know what they have to do, and I respect them. I would never say that. I know when I saw them and where. I've told you everything I know. If they say something different, and it's important to what's going on, then I don't know what to suggest."

"They're not being honest?" Hands said.

Rudy leaned forward and glared at him. "Listen. I'm not a lawyer, and I don't know what's going on here. I do know this, however. First, this lady has suggested that I'm guilty of malpractice, and that she knows more than I do about the practice of medicine. Now you're calling me a liar. I've had just about enough of both of you."

Hands raised his voice. "What did the defendant ask you when he contacted you a week ago? Did he go over your story?"

"He asked me what I recalled, and I told him."

"You weren't subpoenaed here today, were you?"

"No," Rudy snapped. "Haven't you already asked me that?"

"Just came to help your friend."

Pauletta objected. Pendleton told Rudy to answer the question.

"I came because I was asked to."

"Do you have an office practice?"

"No. I don't."

Pauletta objected again. "How is this possibly relevant?"

"I think we need to know just what kind of doctor we have here."

"I think it's a proper question," Pendleton said. "And I understand his answer to be that he doesn't. Go on, Mr. Hands."

"How long have you known the defendant?"

"About five or six years."

"Been in his home, done things with him socially?" Hands asked his questions more quickly now.

"Yes. Occasionally."

"And you're sure you saw these two officers at his trailer on this day?"

"It was the day he got a DWI, because he called me."

"What did you prescribe for his illness?"

"Amoxicillin and Tavist D."

"Did you give him a prescription?"

"Yes." Rudy didn't seem shaken by Hands.

"When?"

"Three or four days before. Maybe five."

"Was it filled?"

"It was. I called it in. Called it in to Revco at the shopping center. You can check, if you wish. The lady there, Jane, the new pharmacist, I can't remember her last name, filled it. It was sitting beside the sink in Mr. Wheeling's kitchen when I went by."

"You didn't bring any notes or files or records?"

"No, I didn't know I'd need them." Rudy turned angry again. He pointed at the phone on the judge's desk. "Pick up the phone and call if you want. Nine-one-nine four-eight-six two-three-two-one. Call and ask."

"Thank you, Doctor," Hands said.

Hands had Dr. Rudy remain in the room while Greenfield testified again. Greenfield denied ever having seen Dr. Williams when Hands asked the car doctor to stand up and face the detective. Loggins, when he was called to testify a second time, also was emphatic about not seeing the doctor that afternoon at Mr. Wheeling's mobile home.

Adam didn't ask Greenfield any questions. When Hands finished with Loggins, Adam at first said he had nothing to ask, then had Loggins come back and sit down.

Adam stood up. "Let me make sure I understand your position, okay? You say the defendant was not drinking, but we all agree he knocked a beer over on the confession, right? There's that stain."

"He wasn't drinking; he was fine. The can was warm when I picked it up. It had cigarette ashes on the top."

Adam nodded. "I see. And the defendant wasn't impaired, even though he signed the wrong name?"

"Right. He was fine."

Adam nodded again. "And the defendant wasn't drunk, even though he had a point-one-six blood-alcohol level half an hour later?"

"He wasn't drunk." Loggins shifted his weight. His hands were folded across his lap.

"He was not drunk even though within a half an hour of your leaving, two other officers say he was very drunk?"

"Maybe he got that way when we left."

Adam paused. "And along those same lines, you never saw or talked to Dr. Williams, the man seated there to your left?"

"Right."

"And even though you *truly* believe this defendant confessed to a murder, you just drive off, don't arrest him?"

"We . . . had to go get a warrant and have our chief approve everything. Didn't want to take no chances."

"But you *could have* arrested him right then and there, and didn't."

"We didn't arrest him."

"There are a lot of inconsistencies, huh?"

"Some, I guess."

When Loggins left, Rudy got up as well, and Evers followed them both outside and caught up with Rudy in the hallway. "Thanks," he said.

"Sure. It was almost fun. I liked the attention and all of the trappings and dignity."

"I didn't know you had a beeper. That's a nice touch."

Rudy smiled. "It's a garage-door opener. It was a good prop, though. A nice addition." He looked up at Evers. "I hope I did okay. You didn't tell me about the car. I was nervous about that. I figured they would've had a plain car, being detectives and all, but I didn't want to take a chance. You told me not to guess, to just stick to the simple version."

"You did great." Evers saw Loggins standing farther down the hall, smoking a cigarette and watching them. "Did you really phone in a prescription?"

"Yeah. Pascal had a nasty bug and fever. Of course, he was pretty much over it by the time all this happened, but I had called in something for him."

"Great."

"So I did well?" Rudy asked again.

"Yeah. Now leave before they call you back to testify. And don't talk to the policemen. Just leave and drive home."

"Don't worry. What's going to happen to Pascal?"

"I'm not sure," Evers said. They shook hands, and Rudy started walking down the hall. Loggins tried to talk to him when he passed, but Rudy waved his arm at him and kept going. The detective took a few steps after him, then stopped.

By now, it was almost noon. When Evers stepped back inside, Judge Pendleton was reading the cases that Pauletta had submitted. Hands wanted more time for research, but Pendleton didn't seem inclined to go along with the request. As soon as the judge laid the file and Pauletta's cases on his desk, Hands started speaking. "Judge, you've got two officers' reputations at stake in this thing," he said.

"Which two, Judge?" Pauletta shot back. "Maybe we need to have another trial on the DWI."

"Judge, this is—"

Adam cut Hands short. "Judge, I don't know how this plays into things, but she was terminally ill anyway. Her autopsy showed that she had a significant, irreversible cancer problem."

Hands slapped the arm of his chair. "That's not even remotely relevant to what we're doing here. Sick people aren't fair game for killers just because they're sick. Murder is murder, for heaven's sake. I guess you get a free assault if the victim has a cold, right, Adam? We're talking about a technical point here, not the facts. I can't believe you'd bring that up, Adam."

"Is it true, Granger?" Pendleton ignored what Hands had just said.

"She did have cancer in her throat, but as far as we know, she was unaware of it. For that matter, I may have it myself, right now, but certainly that doesn't entitle you to shoot me. In fact, Judge, it makes the crime worse, like taking a dollar from a poor man. It's depriving someone who has very little left."

"I just thought the judge should know," Adam said.

"Well, that's not—"

Pendelton interrupted. "I gave you a chance to get out on this one, Granger. There's just too much against you, and it's your burden of proof. The statement's out. I'm excluding it. I'm going to lunch, the jury will be back at one o'clock. We can start then if you want."

"Judge, without this confession, we have no case against a man who admitted to a killing." Hands was red-faced. "Aren't we overlooking a lot of substance and facts in the name of some legal niceties?"

Pendleton picked up a pen and pointed it at Hands. "This ain't no goddamn technicality. You can't take a good statement from a man who's out of his mind. And there's plenty of lying going on, and from everything I can see it's just as good a chance it's coming from your boys as anywhere else." Pendleton raised up in his chair and stretched toward Hands. "For a murder case, a lot of this seemed awful surprising to you. Maybe if you were a little bit more prepared, this would go better. I don't want to hear another word about it. You made me call it and I did."

Hands stared at the judge for a moment and then started jamming his legal pad and books and files back into a leather satchel. He walked out of the room quickly, leaving the door open behind him. The rest of them sat in Pendleton's office for a few minutes longer, until the judge got up from behind his desk, picked up his bag lunch and blue blazer and stomped out without saying anything else. Adam and Pascal went off to find a soft drink and a snack. When Evers and Pauletta left Pendleton's chambers and walked out through the court-room, Aimme and Clifford were sitting in the front row of the gallery. Aimme stood up and pointed her middle finger at Evers, pumping her hand up and down. "Fuck you, Evers," she shouted. Mrs. Covington was sitting away from them, near the end of the bench.

"You guys get the judge paid off?" Clifford said. "Even if you and your piece-of-shit brother get out of this, we're going to sue you civilly. We already talked to Mr. Wolf. You and Pascal will never, ever rest. Do you understand me?"

Evers slowed for a second but kept moving. He was about even with Jo Miller's family. "Well, Cliff, this one's pretty much over for you," he said.

"Fuck you, Evers. Mr. Hands said that Pascal's looking at twenty years in jail."

"How about twenty minutes?" Evers stopped walking. He had gone past the Covingtons and was looking back at Aimme and Clifford.

Aimme put her hand down and turned toward Pauletta. "And you're scum, too, lady. Just common shit. Helping killers and dope fiends. I hope you're real proud."

Pauletta set her briefcase on the floor. "Ma'am, Judge Wheeling may be willing to sit here and listen to you curse him and attack him, but I am not." Pauletta worked on every word, didn't get in a rush. She pointed at Aimme. "If you wish, if you want to, if you feel strongly about it, if you want to continue this encounter in that kind of nasty vein, then I will come over the back of that seat and flat beat your ass. I will. I'm not as passive and thick-skinned as most of my brethren. You call me shit, and I'll punish you for it." Pauletta's face looked like a dark sketch, tight and compact, all the bones apparent, her muscles spring-loaded, all the turns, curves and lines sticking out.

Pauletta started through the benches toward Aimee, and Clifford stopped her, put his hands on her shoulders. A police officer, standing with a group of people near the back of the courtroom, shouted at them, and Pauletta said, "I'll kick your pathetic white ass, too, Clifford. Take your skinny hands off me." Pauletta slapped Clifford's hands; the skin-on-skin sound—a pop, like a child's cap gun firing—was sudden and loud in the courtroom. The officer trotted past Evers and wedged himself between Clifford and Pauletta; Aimme's mouth was open and she was close behind Clifford, looking at Pauletta over his shoulder.

The policeman seemed more amused than alarmed, and he patted Pauletta several times in the middle of her back after he walked her out of the benches and into the aisle.

"Thanks," Evers told him. "Sorry to cause trouble for you."

"No problem. It's hard to keep getting called every son of a bitch in the book and just take it all the time. Believe me, I know."

Pauletta looked back at Aimme before she walked on, and Pauletta's face caused Evers to think of a goddess, a boiling, irate, spectacular deity, standing up from a simple throne, provoked into impatience, bolts and thunderclaps on the tips of her fingers. The policeman escorted them out of the courtroom into the hall, wished them well and left. Evers took his suit coat off and folded it over his arm. He and Pauletta began walking down the hall, toward the elevator. Right behind them, Mrs. Covington opened the door of the courtroom and called Evers' name.

"Just keep walking," he said to Pauletta. "She's too old for you to thrash. Don't turn back, don't say anything. By the way, I think you could've taken Cliff."

"I'm still angry. We should not have to listen to personal attacks for doing our jobs. I wonder how many accountants and physicians get mauled and called 'motherfucker' and 'piece of shit.' I'm not going to put up with it."

"For what it's worth, it's a side of you that I appreciate. You look like equal parts Joe Frazier and Nelson Mandela. Very noble anger. In a feminine way, of course. You weren't looking like a brute or anything." He put his arm over her shoulder.

"Evers! Miss Qwai!" Mrs. Covington had walked into the hall and was pacing Evers and Pauletta.

Evers and Pauletta continued on toward the elevator. "And I am going to resist being treated poorly by fools and imbeciles for honorably practicing my trade." Pauletta was breathing hard, Evers noticed. A few strides away from the elevator, he looked around for the steps leading to the ground floor. He didn't want to be trapped in front of the elevator staring wistfully at the illuminated down arrow while Mrs. Covington chewed on his ears and wagged her finger in his face.

"It's like banging the lion's cage with a stick," Pauletta continued. "We get attacked because people know we won't respond." She was exhaling small, abrupt snorts out of her nose.

"I thought that we were above certain kinds of conduct," Evers chided her. "I seem to recall your scolding me in West Virginia for defending myself."

"We are—"

"Evers, I want to talk to you. I'm trying to help," Mrs. Covington shouted. She wasn't running, wasn't really chasing Evers and Pauletta, but was just walking along behind them, getting farther and farther away at the other end of the hall. A young girl and a man with a long beard looked at Mrs. Covington when she yelled at Evers. Evers and Pauletta both glanced back, and Mrs. Covington kept coming, her purse swinging in time with her steps. She walked up to Evers and stopped in front of him. Evers pushed the button to call the elevator.

"You want to help us?" Evers was apprehensive. He was leaning back, and his legs were stiff and his fingers were touching his palms, folded into loose fists. "Help us to do what?" He was watching Mrs. Covington's hands and her purse, worried about a gun or knife or something sharp in one of her pockets. Or she might throw something on him, throw acid into his eyes. He'd read about a case in South Carolina where a victim had thrown acid on the defendant's face right before court started.

"I've called you twice Evers, two times. Didn't you get my calls?"

"Yes."

"You didn't call back."

"An in-law ass-chewing about once a month is generally all I need."

The elevator arrived—a small electronic bell rang—and the doors withdrew into the walls on each side, made an air and lubricated sound, full of grease and wheels and metal. Several people stepped around them and got in.

"In a way, I guess, I'm glad you didn't call me back. In a way." Mrs. Covington was a small and tired lady, in her sixties, looking up at Evers, wearing a circle of pinkish lipstick, although some of the color was well off her mouth. Her hair was fixed, perfectly in place, and she smelled like perfume and old clothes, a damp, soggy smell, like the back of a bedroom closet. The perfume was porous and weak, and the musty, closet scent ran through it, overwhelmed it. She licked her lips. "All of this has been hard for me and my family."

"I'm sure," Pauletta said.

"I'm a decent woman," Mrs. Covington said. "And I'm healthy and fit and expect to live a lot longer." She smiled and turned her head, looked at Pauletta and Evers from a different angle. "I don't want the wrong thing to come out of this."

"Neither do we." Pauletta had regained a lot of her breath.

"Did Pascal tell the police that he shot my daughter, Evers? Did he? Everybody tells me that."

"They say he did. That's what we've been told, that he confessed. He's never told us that, though, Mrs. Covington. He's never told Pauletta or me he's guilty. Never." The doors to the elevator slid shut.

"It's hard for me to understand."

"What do you want to tell us, ma'am?" Pauletta asked.

Evers noticed that the hall was getting crowded, filling up with criminals, lawyers, police officers, clerks and people with yellow traffic summonses in their hands. A group of four men came out of another courtroom. The men were smiling and laughing and shaking hands with a short, weedy man wearing a blue baseball cap that had the letters NRA written across the front.

"I . . . I don't know what happened. I think Pascal's a good boy. I don't know how to explain everything. But . . . what I wanted to tell you, and I've tried to tell Evers, tried to call twice, and I sort of go back and forth on it, change my mind, is that Jo Miller left, well she sent it, mailed me, a copy of her note. The note they say was on the computer. She sent it to me."

"Sent it? The same note? When?"

"It came in the mail two days after she died."

"How do you know *she* sent it?" Evers relaxed his hands and bowed his head closer to Mrs. Covington.

"It was her writing on the envelope, and she signed it. And wrote some more to me across the top. A little message on the top. Not much, just a little bit more for me. She just said she thought what she was doing was best for everyone."

"The same letter that was on the computer screen?"

Mrs. Covington wet her lips again. "From what I can tell, yes."

"You're sure it was from her?"

"Yes, of course."

"What did it say?" Pauletta asked. "What was added?"

"Nothing that would make any difference to you, just some personal things."

"So she sent you a signed suicide note, with an addition in her own writing." Pauletta looked at Evers and raised her eyebrows.

"Do you still have the letter?" Evers asked.

"I don't . . . know." Mrs. Covington shook her head. "This is very hard for me. My other children blame you for this, Evers. Some of what they say makes sense."

"Like what?" Evers frowned. "Why am I getting vilified for all of Jo Miller's choices and failings? Why?" He folded his arms across his chest.

Mrs. Covington turned her head again, licked her lips. "It's like watching a movie, Evers." She stopped and licked her lips some more, made a sucking sound. "Like a movie, it depends on where you come in on it. You start in the middle and you may see someone do something that confuses you or seems mean, uncalled for, but it wouldn't seem that way if you'd seen what came in front, if you'd started watching during another scene that came earlier. Very few things happen between two folks without a little push or word one to the other. Jo Miller didn't just up and shoot herself without some help from you, Evers. Things don't happen that way. Nope, they sure don't."

"What exactly are you saying?" Evers glared down at Mrs. Covington, his arms still flat against his chest. "That I shot her? Or that I somehow caused her to shoot herself? Made her do it by treating her badly? What?"

"Some of that's what I'm telling you, yes. Yes."

Evers rolled his eyes and exhaled loudly. "How in the world could—"

"Judge Wheeling, you need to listen and think about her point. Just be quiet. This isn't a debate that needs to be happening out here in the hall in front of hoodlums and strangers."

Evers unfolded his arms and held his hands out in front of him, like he was pushing something away, blocking himself off. "Fine. That's fine. You're right. I'm sure it's an argument I'm not going to win anyway." He put his hands down. "Did you tell the others about the letter, that Jo Miller sent you a signed note?"

"No." Mrs. Covington sighed. "I didn't. I don't think it would make any sense to."

"Did you mention the letter to the police?" Pauletta inquired.

"No, I didn't. But I did try to call Evers twice. He didn't call me back. And now I'm telling you. And I'm not sure how important it is or, I don't know, if it's important at all since Pascal said he did it."

"So would you tell the truth if we called you as a witness, ma'am?"

"I will tell the truth." Mrs. Covington closed her eyes for an instant and dropped her head. "I will tell the truth, yes."

"Thank you, ma'am," Pauletta said.

"Yeah. Thanks, Mrs. Covington. Thank you," Evers added. "We didn't know about this."

Mrs. Covington stood a little straighter and adjusted a pin on her jacket. "Like I said, I haven't told anyone else. I'd really just like to stay out of all the court goings-on, now that I've cleared my conscience. I would."

"I understand," Pauletta said. "It's a problem without an answer."

"Was there anything more specific, more detailed, in what she wrote to you, Mrs. Covington?" Evers asked, very suddenly. "Any explanation as to why she might decide to . . . to shoot herself?"

Mrs. Covington tightened her face, made her eyes and features smaller and flat. "Because, Evers, she didn't want to be a cipher. To be almost forty and have nothing. Have to start all over. It's easy to take hold when you're twenty, but that's when you begin, not when you're halfway through your life. She told me about a month before she died that it was like eating a slice of white bread, and you've eaten all of the white part, eaten the center, and there's nothing left on your plate but the brown crust."

"I'm sorry," Evers said. "Most of the time, I tried my best."

"Can you imagine what it was like after she walked out her drive and put that letter in the mailbox, what it would be like walking back, by yourself, opening the door, shutting it, going in your house to take your own life?" Mrs. Covington's voice quavered. "That's what I see. Her walking down that road, by herself. No children and no husband with her."

"Did she know about the problem with her throat? Maybe that had something to do with it."

"I don't think so. She'd been sick some, but that's all. She never mentioned it to me. I knew that she was upset, but I had no idea this was coming. We talked the day before and she was chipper, in a real good mood."

"Well, I appreciate your telling us. I'm sorry I didn't call you back. I didn't know what you wanted."

Mrs. Covington smiled a little and shrugged, then turned around and walked back down the hall, away from Evers and Pauletta.

Evers shook his head. "That's a nice spin and some colorful window dressing to put on her daughter's shiftlessness and promiscuity, huh? It's a little more fundamental than all that, and way less pure, isn't it? Fucking a college kid, a cow farmer, and not really working because you prefer to sleep in and sip cappuccino with your friends. I think I just heard her make it sound like Jo Miller had this Albert Schweitzer melancholy, this metaphysical vapor lock and broken soul because she'd dropped the only vial of medicine that would've saved all the kids in the village from rheumatic fever. Shit." Evers was watching Jo Miller's mother walk down the hall; her pace and gait were steady, and she didn't look back. She made a right-angle turn, very crisp, pivoted almost, to reenter the courtroom; a nicely dressed man held the door for her.

"I'm glad to see you're so sympathetic and chastised." Pauletta was watching Mrs. Covington as well.

"Oh, fucking wonderful. What am I missing, huh? Tell me." Evers threw up his hands. "Thanks for all your backing."

"I'm on your side, Judge Wheeling. Your wife did some unpardonable things. You have the moral high ground. But nothing happens in a vacuum. All sorts of different outcomes are possible, depending on who does what. And even if you're totally blameless, you should still try to find a little bit of forgiveness in your hard heart. That's all I'm going to say about it. This isn't the time to discuss it, okay? We need to find Adam and Pascal and let them know about Mrs. Covington. Her testimony is gold. Absolute gold."

"She shot herself, Pauletta. Jo Miller killed herself."

"She did, didn't she?"

"She shot herself," Evers said again. "I knew it."

Evers found Pascal eating peanuts and drinking a soft drink in a jury room. Pauletta was trying to locate Adam, so the brothers were by themselves, seated on opposite sides of a cheap table. Pascal's tie was loosened, and his jacket on the chair next to him.

"So the confession is gone, correct?"

"Yes," Evers answered.

"Why do I still have to go to trial?"

"Because the D.A. is demanding it. Don't worry. The case will go out on a motion to dismiss. We won't even have to put on evidence. We're home free."

"I still could lose, though. Anything is possible in court, right? Isn't that what you told me?" Pascal put a foot on the table. His shoes were brand-new, the bottoms still tan and slick.

"I don't see how."

"Whatever."

"And our case just got even better," Evers told his brother.

"Oh? How's that?"

"Jo Miller killed herself. That's what I came back here to tell you. She sent the letter on the screen to her mom. Signed the fucking thing. Let me say that again. Signed the fucking thing. And added a little message at the top. She shot herself, Pascal. And her misspelled name and two dim-witted policemen have turned this thing into a tar pit as black as coal and as big as the doublewide."

Pascal tugged at the button on his shirt collar. "So . . . wait a minute. When did you find out about the letter to Mrs. Covington? Is that something they had to divulge at trial? Something that Adam got from the D.A.? Why are you just now telling me? How could there be a signed letter?"

"Believe it or not, Mrs. Covington told us. Just a few minutes ago. She'd called me a couple of times, but I didn't call her back. I assumed that she was just calling to scream at me. That's my fault, isn't it? But I'm not a mind reader. Sorry. Who would've thought?"

"Is the letter . . . real?" Pascal looked bewildered.

"Sure. It has to be. Why would Jo Miller's mom make up something to help us?" Evers closed his eyes and tilted his head back. Both of the brothers were silent for a moment. Evers kept his eyes shut, rested the nape of his neck on the top of his chair. "Tell me why you confessed, Pascal," he said, still not looking at anything. "What in the world was going on? This has to be the time for you to tell me." Evers sat up and gazed at Pascal.

Pascal took his foot off the table and pulled his chair closer to the edge. The chair made a sudden, sharp metallic squeaking. The noise seemed loud and filled up the room's quiet. "You know why, I guess."

Evers felt hot and light, like he had felt in Pauletta's office. The chair noise was still vibrating in his ears, still in the room. "No, I don't," he said. "Why?"

"It was something I owed you." Pascal's voice was low, almost a whisper, but it came through the noise in Evers' head like a burrow into his brain, violent and direct. Evers' face and neck turned crimson; the color switched on all at once, and a blood-red current jolted its way across his skin, buzzed around in his cheeks and chin and circled his throat. His lips came apart and made a smacking sound. Pascal moved closer. "I had to do something, to get all of the shit and failure and letting you down out of me, Evers. To even us up, make us brothers again."

Evers closed his mouth, began running his bottom lip between his teeth. "I . . . I," he stuttered and gave up, tried to talk but couldn't.

"And I'm mixed up in it, too. I let you down. Caused a mess. This pays back some of my part."

Evers put his head on the table, dropped his forehead onto the wooden edge so the table was pressing into his skin; his eyes and mouth were left suspended in the air over the floor. He wasn't able to speak for a few minutes. "What in the world have you done?" he finally said. "Have you lost your fucking mind? Have you?" He didn't raise up when he spoke to his brother, kept his face down and talked to the floor.

"Isn't it wild and strange that she was going to die anyway?" Pascal said. "That's the scary part—the wishes and the shrine and everything. That's got to make you think."

Evers didn't move or speak or lift his head. Pascal got up from his seat, walked around the table and knelt down beside him. Pascal kissed the side of his brother's face. Evers kept his brow on the hard edge, kept his eyes closed so the room was blacked out; his neck was red and scalded, and the noise from the chair had gotten into his skull and was spinning around like a pinwheel in a rush of wind. Evers and Pascal stayed silent for a few moments. Evers was finally able to sit up, and when he did he put his hand on his brother's shoulder. "None of this plays out so well, Pascal. Are you trying to take the blame for me because you think I did it? Is that it? The other possibility is even less palatable—I damn sure didn't want *you* to kill her."

"Well . . . it did look pretty bad, I mean, you know, you wishing her dead and everything else. And you were all fucked-up after the police left."

Evers let go of Pascal's shoulder. "This doesn't make any sense at all. I fucking *told* you the next morning where—"

"Where you were and the couch story—I know. Like you're going to tell me you drove down there and killed her. I thought I was making the right call." Pascal almost lost his balance, put his hand down to keep from tipping over. "Shit. Wow. So you really didn't do it, huh?" He made a clicking sound with his tongue and teeth. "Shit. So much for my grand plan to pull you out of the fire."

Evers looked at a brown plastic pitcher in the center of the table, and he knew—without even checking—no water was in it, that if he took hold of the handle the pitcher would come right off the table with no resistance at all, light and empty and full of nothing. He started reaching for the container anyway, stopped almost as soon as he started and peered down at his brother. "Get up off the floor and let's talk about this before we go back outside."

. . .

Hands was in a little better mood when he returned from lunch, but still angry. He met with Adam, Pauletta and Evers in Pendleton's office before the judge returned.

"You sandbagged me, Adam. You screwed me on this. I think you told me twice that the motions were routine. That's why we heard them today."

"I filed them well in advance, and I file similar motions in every confession case. The motions were routine. The facts were compelling."

"Pretty fine line, isn't it?"

"That's what we do, Granger. We're lawyers. Semantics and elliptical commitments."

"It will affect the way you and I do business, I can tell you that." Hands was petulant.

"So be it. I have a clear conscience. My job is to represent my client diligently and to deal with you honestly. I did both."

"You fucking misled me, Adam. Intentionally. I didn't expect that of you, and I'll remember it in the future."

"Maybe if you'd worked a little more thoroughly," Pauletta said calmly, "you wouldn't have to rely on the kindness of strangers, Mr. Hands. We're not an information co-op, you know."

"I didn't say anything when you were rude to me earlier. But you are ignorant and unprofessional, ma'am. And I guess it's easy to look good when witnesses like your doctor choose to lie under oath, and you choose to encourage it."

"You weren't looking too good with your two redneck, lying cops." Pauletta raised her voice.

Adam stood up. "Folks, let's not squabble. Maybe we can still do some business. Certainly you have a better offer now?"

"Let's just try it," said Hands.

"Granger, you don't have a case. Zero. Right now you have an adulterous, terminally ill woman with a suicide note and a boyfriend who threatened her. The best you have is some carpet fibers that could have come from my client's brother or some other carpet or been there for who knows how long. And some inconclusive hair fragments. That's what the lab report said. Some common points, but inconclusive. And I think we can show that my guy was in Durham after the police had already visited him at his trailer. I gave you his accountant's number, remember? One more thing. The powder residue on her hand—that's going to be hard to explain."

"Mr. Hands, for what it's worth, my brother didn't kill Jo Miller. He didn't do it, and he's not a bad person." This was the first time Evers had spoken to Hands. "Putting him in jail isn't going to solve anything." Everyone in the room looked at Evers. "Can't we come up with something that will save face for everyone?"

"We have a strong case, Granger," Adam said.

"If it's such a great case, Adam, then let's try it," Hands snarled. "You shouldn't be worried."

"I agree," Pauletta said. "Let's go."

"Same offer?" Adam asked. "That's all you can do?"

Hands thought for a moment. "Three years to serve on involuntary manslaughter, ten suspended. Plus you release the information on the boyfriend and his threats, put it in the record when we do the plea."

Adam was quiet. "That's not what I had in mind. Of course I'll have to ask our client."

"Okay."

Pauletta looked at Evers, then at Hands. "There's no way he'll take it. This case will never get to a jury. And when it's discussed, I'll tell the press exactly what went on and how cowardly and scheming you were throughout. That's a shitty offer." Pauletta stared at Hands. "And, in fact, we have another little surprise for you. We have a suicide note, one that Jo Miller Wheeling signed and mailed."

"Is that so, Miss Qwai?" Hands smiled. "I don't really care what you have or what you do. In fact, because you're so belligerent, I may just withdraw my offer."

Adam touched Pauletta on her shoulder. "Let's go talk to Mr. Wheeling." He looked at Hands. "You know it's not a good offer, Granger. And you know we'll all tell him not to take it."

"I don't care. I don't," answered Hands. He stood up and walked out of the room.

"You don't actually have the note, do you?" Adam asked. "The actual note? We'll just have to use her mother's testimony, right? I'm correct about that, aren't I?"

"Correct," Evers said. "But I think that Mrs. Covington will tell the truth if we have to rely on her."

"I'm not sure how much it matters," Pauletta remarked. "Why is your neck so splotched, Evers? You look like you're about to faint; I noticed it when we got back from lunch. Are you okay?"

"I'm fine. This is just stressful."

"Why?" Adam wondered. "Why are we not concerned about Mrs. Covington?"

Pauletta reached inside her suit jacket and took out a single sheet of paper. "This was left for me in the courtroom when we came back after the break. It would seem to be a copy of the note."

"Damn," said Adam. "Good news falling out of the sky. Hard to beat that."

"You have the letter? You have it? I didn't know that."

"I just found it a few minutes ago, Judge Wheeling. You were with your brother."

"May I see it? I'd like to know what it says." Evers held out his hand.

"I will read it to you. You may not have it—I think giving it to you would be a breach of trust. I feel I have some obligation to Mrs. Covington."

"For heaven's sake, Pauletta. That's fine—read it to me then. As if that makes a big difference. You can be so fucking sanctimonious sometimes. Maybe you should just whisper it to Adam and let him tell me after you leave."

"Maybe I shouldn't tell you anything, because you have no sense of decency, fair play and courtesy. The world spins around on small, kind gestures. You have no respect for that, do you?"

Adam ducked his head, opened one of his files and started shuffling and arranging everything inside the folder. He was wedded to the task, was not about to look up or join the argument.

"I'm sorry. I apologize. Please, read me the letter. I'm sorry."

"I doubt you are."

"Tell me what it says, Pauletta. Please," Evers pleaded. His shirt was wrinkled, and he had taken off his suit coat.

"You owe Mrs. Covington quite a debt."

"You're right. I'm sorry. I was just really anxious to find out what my wife had written."

Pauletta peered at Evers over the top of the letter; the paper blocked all of her face below her eyes, made her look like a robber or a highwayman. "The handwritten part reads: 'I'm sorry it has come to this. Sorry for us all. I wish things could have turned out differently, but I truly believe that I have been a good person and a good wife and that this is the right thing for me, for you, for Evers, for everyone. I deserve my freedom. Jo Miller.' "

"Christ," Evers snorted. "What is she, in high school or something? 'I deserve my freedom'? What is that? How absolutely trite."

"It strikes me as really bland, Judge Wheeling, sort of passionless and generic." Pauletta pursed her lips. "Really . . . aloof," she added after thinking for a moment.

Adam raised up. "That's what I thought, too, Pauletta. Pretty damn cold for the last thing you write your momma."

"What did you guys expect?" Evers asked. "Flannery O'Connor?"

"It's just so empty," Pauletta mused.

"So was she," Evers said.

The three of them went into the courtroom and took Pascal out into the hall. Adam explained again that his confession had been suppressed, and that it was almost a certainty that he would be found not guilty. On top of that, there was Mrs. Covington's information about the note and the copy Pauletta had discovered. There wasn't even enough evidence for the case to go to the jury. After the state rested, the charge would be dismissed. There was very little risk, in Adam's opinion. Or Pascal could take three years in jail.

Pascal turned to Pauletta. "What do you think?"

"Not a very tough call," she said in her perfect speech. "There is simply no case against you. There is no risk."

"There's always a risk," Pascal said. "Strange things happen. Weird things, inexplicable things. What do you think, Evers?"

"You have a very strong case." Evers put his hands in his pockets. "Pauletta is correct."

"How long would I be in jail on three years?"

"A matter of months," Adam answered. "Six or seven, maximum."

"You're certain?" Pascal asked.

"Probably less," said Evers.

Pascal stepped back, rocked against the wall and folded his arms in front of him. Evers could tell that he'd gone outside and smoked a joint. Pascal was tight and careful when he moved. "I think the plea agreement is fair. That's what I want. The three years. That's my choice."

Pauletta knotted her face. She stepped toward Pascal. "What is wrong with you? You're a bright man. You're getting ready to give up several months of your life to the state. Plus you'll be a convicted felon. For no reason. In a few hours you can walk out of here free."

"She's right, Pascal. I have to tell you I disagree with your decision." Adam was dumbfounded, all his features filled with shock.

"Tell him, Evers," Pauletta raised her voice. "Don't let him make a bad choice."

Evers looked at his brother against the wall. "Pascal can choose what's right for him. Everyone has to make their own peace, deal with things the way they see them."

"You're both fools," said Pauletta. "Crazy. Why the hell did you confess to begin with?"

"Pauletta, listen. I understand what I'm doing. I hope you understand, too. You and Adam have been kind to me and great lawyers.

But I want the time. I deserve it, in a sense. Balance the scales. Cell life for a month or two—very ascetic." Pascal practically mumbled the last part. He straightened up. "Come here," he said to Pauletta. Pascal put his arm out and around her. "It's a good deal for me."

Pauletta and Evers left the courthouse, and Evers walked with her to the passenger side of his car. He opened the door for her, but she didn't get in and sit down; she stood outside the car holding her briefcase and looking straight ahead. She was silent and stubborn, standing beside the door with her chin tilted up, staring off down the street, catching the tops of buildings and a billboard and the lowest part of the sky . . . barely paying attention to what was in front of her. "So," she said.

"So what? What's wrong with you?"

"So are you going to tell me what's going on? About all the switchbacks and detours we took to get here? Or is the story too sinister and pathetic?"

"Oh, no. No. It's a good story. A great story."

"Really?" Pauletta dropped her chin and looked Evers in the eye.

"Yes, it is."

"Then suppose you tell me what just happened," Pauletta demanded.

"It's a wonderful story, especially when you're expecting black smoke and sulphur and the sort of run-down, inevitable trailer-trash coda that should come from all of us—fatalistic dope smokers who've made giving up an art form. It's a great thing, what Pascal did. There's nothing bad or depraved about it."

"Really." Pauletta kept her eyes locked on Evers, kept standing beside the Datsun. "Are you going to tell me?"

"Sure. You should know. Pascal thought I'd killed Jo Miller, so he confessed and took the blame to protect me. He thought I was involved and was trying to help me."

"Help you?" Pauletta grunted.

"Exactly. Pascal got up to make the nine hundred call, the couch was empty and his car was gone—Ruth Esther took it to Lowes, remember? He'd been smoking a little dope, and he figured that I'd killed Jo Miller. I was in the bedroom; right after the police left the next day, I told him that Ruth Esther and I had switched places. I told him, told him that she had gotten on the sofa because the bedroom was too dark and cramped, but he thought I'd just made everything up, that I wasn't telling the truth about changing places."

"Didn't he check the bedroom, look in to see who was in there?"

"He said that he saw Ruth Esther's car, so he didn't bother. I wasn't on the sofa, he knew the Lincoln was gone, and Jo Miller turns up dead. Plus we'd just been talking about, well, about how poorly she'd treated me."

"She did kill herself, right?"

"She killed herself," Evers said very deliberately. "But Pascal didn't know that, and he became convinced that I'd done something to her."

"That's pretty remarkable. Huh . . . Pascal was trying to help you. So that's why he confessed." Two pigeons flapped onto a ledge above the street, and Pauletta looked up for a moment. She pointed at Evers with her free hand. "When did you figure all this out? Damn—you didn't know the whole time, did you?" She laid her briefcase on the roof of the Datsun, laid it down flat and kept her fingers on the handle.

"I just found out, just now. Think about it, Pauletta. What more could someone do for you? Think about what he did for me. Or, well, what he tried to do."

Pauletta let go of her briefcase. "He just falls on his sword for you, without asking you about anything? Just guesses that you killed your wife and decides to confess? How smart is that? This still sounds a little crooked to me. Are you sure about this?"

"I was a little angry and pissed and baffled at first, too. I almost puked, felt like I was going to pass out or collapse or something. Then I thought about it, thought about Pascal."

"So why is he going to jail for no reason?" Pauletta asked.

Two state patrolmen in sunglasses walked by the car, and Evers waited for them to pass out of earshot before he answered. "I guess there's always a little risk in every trial, even the ones you're sure you can't lose. You know that. But, I think, I think . . . after talking to him, that the main reason he took the deal is because he's . . . well, he was . . . sort of broke."

"What?"

"He was just broke. He'd gone through so much, and gone through everything he had, and this was his way to settle things with me. I mean, obviously, I didn't want him to go to jail. He didn't have to do that, but I think he wanted to."

" 'Broken,' you mean. Is that what you're saying?"

"That too. That's what I'm saying. But now he's pretty much restored, and even with me." Evers looked at the ground and smiled. "I can always count on Pascal in the long run. That's for sure. For certain. The other day, there was this uprooted tree at the edge of my yard, a big maple laid on its side, and its roots were everywhere like tangled-up red-and-white hair. And I was thinking—there's just so much to battle. You close your eyes at night and you see dots and lights that just spin and bounce wherever they want to. A fan belt breaks. A gene mutates. Things jump and start, and you feel like a dwarf reaching up trying to grab a banana off a shelf or something. It snows in May. But in the long run, there's one little stick of certainty in all the shit and unfairness and chaos."

Pauletta sat down in the car seat. "You have a good brother. Maybe this will straighten him out a little."

"Maybe."

"So that's it?" Pauletta asked. "Now we know?"

"That's it," Evers answered.

"The whole story?"

"Yes."

"You're telling me the complete, absolute truth?" Pauletta was starting to relax.

"I swear." Evers raised his right hand.

"It's pretty remarkable. Even for you guys."

"Did you really think he was involved? Or that I was?"

"I certainly considered the possibility, but all of you are so lazy and shiftless and obstinately detached that I decided it would be far too effort-intensive for you or Pascal or Henry or Rudy to drive a couple of hours to kill someone."

"I knew you believed in us," Evers said, and he shut the door to the car. Pauletta looked up at him through the glass, and Evers saw a little spread of cheer in her face and eyes. He started around the car and noticed that she'd left her briefcase on the roof, and he smiled and pointed at the top of the Datsun.

He and Pauletta had dinner in Durham, and they ate a long, full meal and drank two bottles of expensive champagne. Evers got a little buzzed, a little high, but it wasn't the spastic, wallowing kind of doubled-over obliteration that he worked up to sitting in the bug-zapper light drinking scotch and red wine until every bottle at Pascal's trailer was empty. He and Pauletta were giggling and laughing when their bill came, and they asked their waiter to help them remember some of the words to the theme song from *Gilligan's Island*.

When they got in Evers' car to leave the restaurant and were sitting in the dark, before Evers cranked the motor, he kissed her for a long time, and when she stopped kissing him she put her head on his shoulder and her hand on top of his thigh. They sat there in the car, in the parking lot, for over an hour, closing their eyes and almost falling asleep, not saying anything, and occasionally Pauletta would move her head or her hand, little rubs and shifts, and for a while Evers could feel her breathing on his neck.

They slept in different beds in the same hotel room, and he woke up before she did, still in his dress shirt and suit pants. He left her a note and walked several blocks to a convenience store, bought some orange juice and doughnuts. He stopped at a pay phone on a wall outside of the store and put his juice on top of the metal box around the phone. It was early in the morning, and the sun was out, a warm, plain, blue day. The phone cord was twisted and coiled, a trail of stiff metal segments, and someone had left a beer bottle on the ground next to Evers' feet. He called Jo Miller's mother, and the phone rang a long time before she answered.

"You ever notice how the pay phone cords look like a metal snake?" Evers said when his mother-in-law finally picked up.

"What?"

"This is Evers. I'm calling from a pay phone."

"Why are you calling? Did you say something about a snake?"

"You can keep the farm. All of it. Whatever's there. I want to give it to you."

"Why? What's the catch?"

"No catch. I'd rather for you to have it than your wicked brood, but that's up to you. I appreciate what you did for Pascal. And I don't have the resolve for another year of jungle warfare with Aimme and Cliff. It would be nice if you could get them off my back; you could do that for me."

"You're sure about this? Are you drinking?"

"It's eight in the morning, a little early even for me. I'm certain."

"All right."

"Good luck to you, Mrs. Covington. Good luck."

"I'll have Mr. Wolf draw up the papers."

"You do that."

When Evers got back to the hotel, it was quiet in his and Pauletta's room, and he could hear the air conditioner running, pushing cool air out of the vent next to the window. The curtains were closed, and the room was dim. Evers went to Pauletta's bed and woke her. He had to shake her, and when she opened her eyes she was startled for a moment, jumped a little with her arms and legs.

"What? What do you want?" Pauletta was cross. "Why did you wake me like that?"

"I thought of something last night, right before I fell asleep. I know how we can find out about the letter."

ELEVEN

LESTER JACKSON RAN A NICE SHOP. HIS BUSINESS WAS IN A good neighborhood of Winston-Salem, operated out of a portion of an old tobacco warehouse that had been refurbished, painted, reclaimed, track-lit and gentrified. The front of the building was brownish brick with thick mortar joints, the floors inside tongue-and-groove oak, and all the beams and trusses were shellacked and exposed. Lester's store was full of mahogany and inlays and claw feet, sturdy secretaries, sideboards, tables, chairs, armoires and low-boys. When Evers first spied him, Lester was Nazi-starched and walking around—hands held behind his back—with a thin, coffee-tan, chemical-peeled, middle-aged woman. The woman had on expensive shoes and a business suit, though it was doubtful she worked anywhere, especially since it was three o'clock on a weekday afternoon, and she barely, slowly, moved, like a brown, languid snake on a warm rock, coiling through headboards and a pair of end tables, no hurry, nowhere to go except perhaps to another store or out to Reynolda Road to meet a friend at the contemporary art gallery. Lester was at her heel, straight and sinister, nodding and chatting, a breath or two away from her ear, master of all the furniture and knickknacks and whatnots he surveyed.

He glanced at Evers, apparently didn't recognize him at first and returned to the coffee snake and a dark headboard she was rubbing with her hand. Lester leaned in to tell her something, and then he twisted back abruptly, jerked his head around, and looked up and down at Evers and scowled at Pauletta. "Excuse me," he said to his client, who hardly looked up from the wood she was examining. Evers and Pauletta stopped walking, and Lester squeezed through a desk and the back of a dresser to meet them.

"Judge Wheeling. Miss Qwai. My, what a surprise seeing you here." Lester was tight and erect. "Well, now."

"Hello, Mr. Jackson," Pauletta said.

"Hello."

"Quite a fine store," Pauletta remarked.

"I doubt that the two of you fancy antiques, and I'm sure you didn't stop by for tea and scones and patter. And since you've already successfully stolen my property, I'm at a loss to explain why the fuck the two of you are here. Standing in my store. With your hands on your hips and wearing frowns. I should be the unhappy one, yes?" He flashed a crisp, snide smile. "So what can I do for you?"

"We want to talk to you. Perhaps take a little of the sting out of your loss." Pauletta took her hands off her hips.

"What is it that you want? You've stolen my money, and Ruth Esther and her troll brother have my letter." Lester turned and looked back at the coffee snake. The woman had moved to a fainting couch and was pushing down on the cushion with the heel of her hand. "I understand that . . . I heard that your wife had passed away, Judge Wheeling. Is your visit somehow connected with that sad problem?"

"No, it isn't," Evers snapped. "How could it be?"

"You tell me."

"My wife shot herself."

"I believe that I read something about your brother being involved, yes?"

"We're here about the letter." Evers raised his voice.

"I see." Lester rubbed his chin with the back of his wrist. "I'm confused, of course." He took a step forward. "Would you like to sit down or come back into my office?"

"We're fine here," Pauletta answered.

"Tell me what it is that I can do."

"You're out roughly a hundred thousand dollars, correct?"

"Among other things." Lester sat down in the middle of a sofa. He bent forward and tugged up both of his socks.

"Mr. Jackson, the money was ill-gotten. We all know that. That's why you didn't report all of it missing. That's why, I'm sure, you claimed only a ten-thousand-dollar loss with the police and your insurance company. Pretty fucking hard to explain how you made a hundred grand in cash selling tables and bric-a-brac to dentists' wives." Pauletta took a step closer to Lester. "You—"

The serpent lady had finally belly slid to Lester, and she touched him on the shoulder from behind the sofa. "I may come back for the bed. I just need to think about it, you know, try to visualize it in the space, and try to colorize it with everything around it. So I'll call or come by later."

"I appreciate it. It's a beautiful piece." He stood up and walked the woman to the door of his shop. "Where were we?" he said when he got back to Evers and Pauletta. He sat down on the sofa again, in the same place, and crossed his legs.

Pauletta sat down beside him. "You're out a hundred thousand in drug money. You're out a shitload with the letter. But there's nothing you can do about that, either. It's a safe bet that you got the letter from Artis. He stole it from Ruth Esther, and you either had him steal it or knew it was stolen when you took it from him. And the kicker, Mr. Jackson, is that you probably gave him drugs in exchange for the letter and envelope. So you have a stolen letter that you got from a drug-addled, cutthroat runt in exchange for cocaine, and now you've got nothing except a pitiful little insurance check. No letter, no stamps, no cash, nothing. Zip, nada."

"You're full of theories and supposition, Miss Qwai. Wonderful stories. And what if they're true? I'm not saying they are. But if you're correct, so what?"

"Am I right?" She stared at Lester.

"You are correct that I obtained the letter from Artis."

"What did you pay him, Lester?" Evers asked.

"That, Judge Wheeling, would be proprietary information. Why does it matter?"

"You know the letter didn't belong to Artis." Pauletta leaned back some so her shoulders rested on the back of the sofa.

"I do now. Of course when I acquired it, I thought he was the rightful owner. I bought it in good faith."

"I'm sure," Pauletta said sarcastically.

"I've since come to discover that some of the pieces he traded me were perhaps—and I emphasize the word 'perhaps'—not altogether his."

"He stole the letter from his sister, Mr. Jackson. You know that." Evers was still standing, still looking down at him.

Lester uncrossed his legs. "Why are we going through all this hide and seek, all this hunt and peck and asinine circling?" He reached down and pulled on his socks again and smoothed the cuff in his pants leg. "Artis came to me from time to time trying to peddle a few odds and ends. The first time we did business, he brought me a lamp, some old books and an exceptional inkwell, a really nice piece. One day he came in with a good side chair in the trunk of his car—the fabric needed to be redone, but it was a very impressive piece. Probably 1870s. I sold it to a chiropractor's wife from Kernersville. I encouraged him, of course, to bring me other items when he had the opportunity. He brought me the letter and envelope along with an old frame and a steamer trunk."

The phone rang, and Lester glanced toward the back of his business, toward his office. "I have an answering machine," he said. Two women walked into the store, and Lester greeted them without getting up, told them to look around and that he'd be glad to help if they needed anything. "Anyway, when I received the letter, I knew that it was valuable—at the time, I guessed around three or four thousand. I had no idea. . . ." Lester stopped and fingered his socks and pants again. "I have to confess I had no idea that the stamps were so worthwhile. No idea at all. I'm not a stamp man. It's such a prissy business; tweezers and magnifying glasses, fussy, ill-kept collectors. I don't keep up with the trade at all."

"I can see how you'd find selling lamps and inkwells a lot more ballsy," Pauletta remarked, and Evers let out a blunt, barbed cackle directed at Lester Jackson.

"You'd be surprised," Lester said to Pauletta. "You'd be surprised." He was as rigid and pressed as ever, not a curve or wrinkle anywhere on him.

"I doubt it," she answered.

"That was my mistake, the stamps. And, to be honest, I doubt I would've ever paid much attention to them, although sooner or later I most likely would've discovered their significance. Ironically, it was the claims adjuster for my insurer who suggested I check the envelope; he figured maybe there might be a hundred dollars or so worth of old stamps. Needless to say, I didn't attempt to claim the several million they're worth. The letter I could've sold in a couple of weeks. Then it was stolen, along with a great deal of money. Overall, I'm out close to ninety thousand dollars—I was only able to claim the loss of the letter and around ten thousand when I dealt with my insurance company. I didn't have an adequate paper trail to prove the existence of the other money, and there were also some tax concerns. I'm sure that you understand what I mean."

"It's not hard to figure out," Pauletta said.

"And, naturally, that figure doesn't include my loss of the stamps."

"A pretty big hit there," Evers noted.

"So there you have it." Lester was watching the two women walk through his store. "Women come and go, talking of Michelangelo," he remarked when he looked back at Pauletta and Evers.

"I wouldn't have thought the letter was worth more than a thousand dollars, if that." Pauletta's expression didn't change.

"There's a huge market for historical documents. Letters, canceled checks, autographs, signed contracts. The few items I get I sell to a company called Write On Incorporated. I don't fool with the stuff myself. They have about twenty stores. They frame the document, matte it, spruce it up and sell it. They've got a great store in the mall in Las Vegas, the one on the Strip next to the Frontier. Everyone from Robert E. Lee to Albert Einstein."

"But four thousand for this letter? Even given the author, that seems steep."

"Two hundred and fifty thousand dollars seems a lot to pay for a canceled postage stamp, wouldn't you agree?" He pivoted on the sofa so he could see his two customers. "Let me know if you're finding everything all right," he called to them.

"But four or five thousand dollars?" Evers shook his head. "Wow."

"The insurance company paid me four thousand seven hundred and fifty dollars, actually."

"That's based on what—the time when it was written, or the writer, or the age?"

"It's . . ." Lester stiffened his lips. "You tell me."

"Tell you what?" Evers demanded.

"Who wrote the letter."

"Why does it matter?" Evers asked.

"It must matter to you and Miss Qwai."

"We know who wrote the letter. We've read it." Pauletta looked Lester Jackson in the eye.

"Then tell me who wrote it," Jackson insisted.

"You're forgetting the script, Lester. We have it. We've read it. Remember? Remember out in Utah? You were overdressed and hiring thugs to steal our bags. You had that cutting-edge Banana Republic safari look, and your hirelings on mopeds fucked up a fairly simple street crime. I'm not even sure that you ever *had* the letter. So you tell *me* what was in it."

Lester Jackson sighed and popped his thighs with his open hands.

"This is getting us nowhere. Get to the point, please. What do you want?"

"I'm sure that you copied the letter, correct? For your records. For insurance."

"I photograph every piece of furniture and copy every document which finds its way into my store."

"And you have a copy of Ruth Esther's letter."

"Yes. In fact, I made a copy when I got it, right away, and another that I attached to my duplicate of the letter I sent to my contact at Write On. I should have two copies, as best as I can recall."

"We would like the copies," Pauletta said.

"Really? That's what you're after?"

"Correct." Pauletta didn't flinch, didn't show Lester anything at all in her face.

"Why?" Lester looked puzzled. "What am I missing?"

"You don't need to know."

"Are you trying to somehow cover up something for Artis? That doesn't make any sense." Lester started tapping a fingernail on his watch crystal. "Or to protect yourselves, to get rid of any connection between you and Artis and Ruth Esther? What? I'm bamboozled. And I don't want to get screwed twice."

"How much for the copies?" Evers asked Lester.

"Maybe I have several copies. What then?"

"We would need all of them, obviously," Pauletta answered quickly.

Evers started to speak. "Actually, we only need—"

Pauletta glared at him and cut him off. "Actually, we know we can trust you—right, Judge Wheeling? We only need your assurance that you will give us all your copies. That's correct, isn't it, Judge Wheeling?"

"Right, yeah." Evers felt his neck get hot. "That's correct."

Lester left his watch alone. "What would you offer for my copies?"

"What are you asking?"

Lester split his lips and gave a short whistle through his teeth. "What am I asking? Let's see. How about the ninety thousand I've been fucked out of?"

"Shit," Evers exclaimed. "Guess again."

"How about five thousand dollars?" Pauletta offered. "That's five thousand more than you have right now or will ever get from this deal."

"Twenty."

"Ten," Evers said.

"Twenty."

"No chance." Pauletta chuckled.

"You must really want these copies. It has to have something to do with Artis—it has to. And, oh yes, now the policeman is dead. I'll bet you're both a little uncomfortable. The answer's right around there, isn't it? I'm getting warm, aren't I?" Lester sat up even straighter on the sofa, so erect that it looked like he was trying to unloose a kink in his spine. "I'm very close, aren't I?"

Pauletta reached into her purse. "Here's ten thousand dollars, Lester. This is it. This is your only chance. Bring us the copies." The money was in an envelope, and Pauletta held it in front of her, shook it up and down some, like bait for an animal or a flapping paper lure.

"You are a brutal negotiator, Miss Qwai. Wait here." Lester stood up from the sofa and walked to the back of his store, through a door. When he came out again, his two shoppers had settled on a small marble-top end table, and Lester took their check and helped them carry the table outside to their car.

"Not really a quality piece," he said when he walked back in. "I was glad to move it." The phone rang, and Lester looked back toward the sound. "The machine will get it," he said for the second time.

"Here's your money." Pauletta handed Lester the envelope. He took the bills out, counted them and put them back into the envelope.

"Here's your letter. Both copies." Lester handed one set of papers to Pauletta, the other to Evers. "And you can trust my discretion should the police or any other authorities happen by."

"I'm sure we can, Mr. Jackson," Evers said. "We all have something to lose in the long run, don't we? I think I mentioned to you once before that no one wins a nuclear war."

Lester smiled and held out his hand. Evers halfway expected him to snap his heels together and salute the Reich. "I enjoyed our time together," Lester said.

Evers and Pauletta shook his hand and walked off.

"It's a pretty colorful bit of history, isn't it?" Lester said as they were leaving. "Mischief seems to run in the bloodline. I'd thought about contacting some historian or biographer or archive, but decided to let the dead rest in peace."

"That's generous of you, Mr. Jackson," Pauletta said.

It was hot when she and Evers stepped out onto the sidewalk, hot and quiet, only a few cars driving by and two or three people window shopping. "Did you hear the copier come on?" Pauletta started laughing.

"Yes. Oh, yes. Our friend Lester, always scheming. It sounded like someone had started a cement mixer in his office. What a dishonest, slippery piece of shit. He'll probably call next week and tell us he has just 'found' another copy. Unbelievable."

"Lester is a creepy man."

"I'm sorry I almost fucked up your pitch, Pauletta. I didn't catch on right away."

"Don't worry about it. We got what we came for. I knew that if we gave Lester a chance to cheat us, he'd jump right on it."

Pauletta and Evers got into the Datsun. He started the engine, rolled the windows down and turned on the air conditioner. He was sweating; spans of slight beads had formed across the top of his lip and popped out above his brow. "I hope this is worth five thousand dollars apiece," he said while unfolding his copy. "It's going to have to be pretty entertaining for ten grand."

"I have to admit that I like the way having lots of money makes everything seem less expensive," Pauletta remarked.

The letter was written on four small sheets of paper, and Lester had copied the smaller sheets onto eight-and-a-half-by-eleven paper, so the writing was in the middle of the page, framed by black borders on each side:

Dear Ruth,

I have received and thank you for your correspondence of April 24, 1918. It found me in good health and average spirits, somewhat tired from various travels. I am writing this from Washington, having just arrived here after leaving on business some ten days ago. The return trip was arduous but uneventful, and the city is now taking on its spring colors; the rebirth has taken over the city, and all about the town it seems as if everyone is a little more gay and a little more inclined to linger in discourse with a friend or to study nature's blooms and craft, even with the bitter war on everyone's mind. You know how I urged all who would listen—even President Wilson—to have us stand neutral in Europe's conflict. But that debate is well passed and long ago decided, and we must now take the world as we find it and hope for a speedy and merciful resolution to this battle that has consumed so many.

I am constrained to say that I also enjoyed our most recent visit and your company. Your New York is a bustling town, although I must confess that I am finding that the relatively gentle pace of my old Lincoln and the simple countryside are more suited to my disposition. I am also considering a move to Florida, as the climate is so constantly pleasant I am told.

Like you, I have become quite a convert where the "horseless carriage" is concerned, and I am beginning to share your enthusiasm for this form of transportation. As I mentioned, I had owned only two automobiles until the acquisition of the new Model T which you recommended to me. It is much superior to the Stanley Steamer and the Oldsmobile I purchased in 1902. The price of $420.00 for the Ford was quite reasonable, and I occasionally, I must admit, simply drive it for pleasure without having any real destination in mind.

I am not at all certain how to respond to the more personal and intimate concerns you raised in your letter. Like you, I am now and have been for some time rent and tortured, in my passions and my intellect, about our involvement. I am mortified and ashamed that we allowed it to become carnal, and have prayed that this sin and all that might come in its aftermath will be forgiven. Given my substantial years and your bare youth and inexperience, I must accept all of the blame. I also sadly must agree that it is not wise for us to meet again, despite my affection, love and fondness for you.

The Lord forgives us our sins, and he understands temptation and doubt. His own Son cried out on the cross, just for a moment, feeling the burden of uncertainty and the pull of evil. I have asked that He might forgive me, and I entreat you to remember me kindly in the coming months despite my transgressions. This letter is at once your absolution and your dismissal, my declaration of my love for you and my harsh departure from your wonderful countenance. I hope you will have it with you always, to make you complete, to present as your pardon, to use as your shield and to lay upon your bosom so that I can touch your heart.

If you would care to write me, please address me at my new lodging: William Jennings Bryan, the Stanley House, 112 E Street, Washington, D.C. This address should find me for about another month. Again, I ask that you forgive me our misdeeds and continue to hold me in your thoughts. You are wise, preternaturally so, past your young years, heavenly and beautiful, a godsend. I hope that I have not disturbed any of that.

Yours,
William

P.S. I am enclosing a small locket and have added several postage stamps to insure a speedy and safe delivery into your hands. I purchased the stamps this morning and observed that they were printed incorrectly—quite a novelty, I think, and perhaps somehow appropriate for this correspondence. All my best.

"Shit," said Evers. "William Jennings Bryan?" The air conditioner was blowing on him, the fan was on high and the car engine was running. He wiped the sweat off his lip. "What in the world?" He turned back to the first page and rolled the window up. He read the letter again and got hotter, then turned the vent so it was blowing air hard into his face. He began to fight with his breath; he couldn't slow his breathing down, started gagging in air that never made it into his windpipe. Pauletta saw his expression—captured and panicked, his eyes wide, spellbound sights—and she put her hand on his arm. "Are you all right?"

"Yeah."

"Are you sure?" Pauletta's speech was perfect and clean. "You look like you're having a heart attack."

"I'm just hot and I'm—think about this, Pauletta, what this is. Think about it." Evers' lungs seemed scorched and constricted, squeezed together. "This is like being at the foot of an avalanche."

"I don't follow you."

"The letter. It's from William Jennings Bryan. Put this all together."

"Put what together?" She took her hand off Evers' arm. "I'm a little disappointed, to tell you the truth. I'd hoped for Rasputin or Scott Fitzgerald, or at least a presidential candidate who'd won the election."

"It all fits," Evers said.

"I'm not sure I know what you mean. Are you shocked to learn that a hypocritical old populist and itinerant pitchman for the Lord serviced a young girl and then blew her off with a lot of blandishments and silly flatland piety? You look absolutely sick. Are you sure nothing's wrong?"

"You don't get it?"

"Get what? That it's a good thing he wasn't elected president? That he fucked a young woman while thumping the Bible—the world's full of that. Should we contact his biographer? The National Archives, what? *A Current Affair?* It's sad, it's interesting, it's good minor history, but so what? It's hardly breathtaking."

Evers wiped his forehead with the cuff of his sleeve. "It's Ruth Esther. That's why she wanted the letter."

"What?"

"The letter is written to Ruth Esther, okay? It's written to her."

Pauletta pulled back until she was pressed up against the window on her side of the car. She arched her eyebrows and pushed her chin into the top of her chest. "Have you lost your mind? What are you talking about?" She laughed. "You're stoned, aren't you? You went into the restroom when we stopped for gas and smoked dope, didn't you? You sad motherfucker."

"That's why she wanted the letter—she had the affair. It's her letter."

Pauletta put her hands over her face for a moment. "The letter was written in 1918. That would make Ruth Esther something like ninety-five or a hundred years old. She's not that old. She looks like she's in her mid-twenties."

"Why else would she want it? It's worth maybe five thousand dollars, and she gives up millions to get it. It's addressed to her. She—"

"It's addressed to 'Ruth,' not 'Ruth Esther.' "

"She—the woman in the letter—loves cars." Evers waved his hands to make his point.

"So does John DeLorean. And Dale Earnhardt. And Mario Andretti. So what?"

"She never eats. Never."

"She does eat, just not very much. Maybe she surfeits herself on Swiss Cake Rolls and chocolate milk when you're not around."

"The alabaster tears? Explain that," Evers demanded. He waved his hands again. Sweat started running from his temple to the bottom of his jaw, and he didn't bother to wipe his face, just let the water go where it wanted to.

"Your friend Doctor Rudy explained that to you. Don't you remember telling me that when we were sitting in the woods with Pascal and your piece-of-shit shrine? You have a plastic top full of frozen pus."

"The wishes. I'm serious about this. Rudy gets a car. Henry wins the lottery. Jo Miller kills herself, *and* she had cancer—a double winner."

"And Pascal asked to go to jail. That was his wish, right?" Pauletta was still leaning against the door of the Datsun.

"I think he wanted some piece of mind and equilibrium and a chance to square off his life. To do something for me. And that's what he got. I already told you that. In a way, that was the start of all this, the first little glimmer, my brother being so good to me."

Pauletta studied him and didn't say anything. He was still gasping and panting and perspiring. "So what, Evers, what? She's a vampire, a goddess, some divinity? She's a hundred years old? Oh. And this. Think about this. If she's a child in 1918, or at least a young woman, how is she still the same age in 1980 when her mother took her to the shelter? She was a teenager when she turned up at Anchor House. And her mother is like a hundred and fifty years old? That's your take on all of this, right?"

Evers looked out through the windshield. Two men walked into Lester's business. A man with a dog on a leash passed the Datsun and waved at Evers and Pauletta; the dog stopped and peed on the base of a parking meter. "Listen. You're the one who constantly tells me not to mope and to believe in something, right? That the world isn't just bingo balls popping around on compressed air?"

Pauletta looked confused. Her voice came out in a high pitch, and she slurred her words. "You're serious, aren't you?"

"Yes."

"Really?"

"Yes. Really."

"When did you figure this all out?"

"Just now, when I read the letter. It's not conventional, but it makes sense," he added.

"I guess that's good, then. Good for you." She watched him for several seconds. "So what do you think Ruth Esther is . . . what?"

"A godsend. Just like the letter said. Think about this, and bear with me. All the pieces that go into this, the trail from beginning to end, how it worked out. This much coincidence and fortuity can't just be coincidence, the way this all lies down together. I get Artis' case, meet Ruth Esther, Rudy gets a car, my wife is wiped off the planet, my brother ends up with a chance to redeem himself and I get word that the world has a sense of order and get out of all kinds of muck and quagmire. And I meet you. You believe in the rightness of things— hard work, reward, subjugating chaos, that sort of thing. Plus we're a good match for each other, whether you want to admit it or not."

"I think . . . that there's a lot going on, and that the world's hooked up to run in a fair fashion. I think everything carries its own weight. But you put happenstance, fate, luck, fortune, divine ordination and jackass schemes in a bag and shake them out and turn them over in your hand, and you can't eyeball the difference, tell which is which. You can't see behind the curtain, whether it's full of cogs and wenches or dead solid empty."

"I thought that you were a little more spiritual than that." Evers wasn't panting as much; he turned the fan down.

"You are a manic man, foolish. Zipping from one state to another.

You go from thinking that the world's a claptrap, ramshackle shit-storm to divining supernatural guideposts from irrational, impossible assumptions and half-assed references in an overwrought love letter. Sitting here in your car with four pages of copy paper. Sweating like a morphine addict, perspiration about to turn your collar a different color. All this sudden enlightenment, after years of bad decisions, bad living, flippant, cavalier attitudes and endless bellyaching. Just like that?"

Evers dropped his head back and stared at the roof of his car. His breathing had almost returned to normal. "You're right. But some good things can come out of tragedy of your own making, I guess. I can try to make amends. To do better. The cranks we turn, all the levers we pull. Oedipus ended up blind but sage . . . and Paul, Paul on the road to Damascus . . . and Nixon. Look at Nixon or . . . " Evers quit speaking, just stopped. "I don't care. If you don't think it makes any sense, I don't care. That's your business."

"Well, I'm happy that you're uplifted, at least. A zealot's nutty enthusiasm will certainly be more pleasant than all of your glum mumbling." The disbelief had gone out of Pauletta's face. "It's your life. What will it be next week—crystals and pyramids, or Amway?"

"I thought you'd be a little more encouraging."

"I'll tell you what. Let's ask Ruth Esther. See what she says, get her reaction." Pauletta flattened her feet against the floorboard and pushed herself up in the seat.

Evers thought for a moment. "I'll bet you she's gone. I'll bet she's not at the car dealership, and that she's moved. Disappeared. Vanished. We will never see her again."

"But you'll always know she's there, right? That's the way the fable works. When you look into the sky on a cold, cold winter's night and a star dims and brightens, winks at you, or tumbles and somersaults across the horizon, when you look up or feel down, she'll be watching over you, moving you around with gentle nudges and heavenly reminders."

"I don't know. Why not?"

"And your shrine, your holy relic, is literally a few abnormal tears. Tears with some strange discharge in a liquor decanter. And these drops in a ketchup top are the key to the church, dilithium crystals for the engine, correct? It's like E equals mc squared to physics, penicillin for bad throats and venereal disease. Am I on the train? Yes?" Pauletta was trying not to grin, her lips bunched up and straining at the corners.

"Let's go show her the letter; I think that's a great idea. And you've seen the tears—they look like liquid marble. Don't try to downplay that. And why in the world do we end up in Salt Lake City? Huh? With this big stone temple looking down on all this—how did Ruth Esther put it, that her money was 'watched over'? I'll ask about that, too."

"Okay. You do that. I hope we can find her though, get to her before she turns into mist."

"So you tell me why Ruth Esther gives up millions and pays thousands to get a letter worth a few grand and works like a Trojan to make sure she recovers it. You still haven't answered that."

"That's a valid point. But there are several explanations. And it assumes, of course, that Lester gave us the correct letter."

"I saw the letter in Utah. This is the same letter."

Evers drove the Datsun from Lester Jackson's to the car dealership where Ruth Esther worked. He and Pauletta walked into the showroom and asked a receptionist at a switchboard where they could find Ruth Esther.

"She's gone," the receptionist said. She had on a headset, and a small mouthpiece was in front of her chin. The mouthpiece was covered by a black ball of sponge. "Vaughn Ford-Lincoln-Mercury-Jeep-Eagle-Isuzu," she said into the air. " Please hold." She punched a button and repeated the greeting to another caller.

"I knew it." Evers made a fist and hit the flat of his hand. "I told you."

"When did she leave?" Pauletta asked the receptionist.

"Vaughn Ford-Lincoln-Mercury-Jeep-Eagle-Isuzu. I'll connect you." The receptionist looked up. "I'm not sure."

"I told you, Pauletta. Miss Naysayer, Miss Hypercritical Castigator of the Weak."

"Did she say where she was going?" Pauletta wondered. "Or leave any kind of information that we could use to locate her?"

"Is it an emergency or something?" The receptionist pulled her microphone away from her mouth.

"Sort of, yes."

"Well, she and Chuck Lofton, one of the other sales representatives, went to a dealership down in Hickory to pick up a vehicle. We swapped a blue Grand Cherokee for a champagne-colored one. Ruth Esther had a customer who wanted that color with a couple of options, and we put it up on the locater and found it right off. They should be back pretty soon. They left this morning. Do you want me to call the dealership down there and see if they've left?"

"Hickory, huh?" Pauletta said.

"Yes. If it's important, I can try to get her there or try her cell phone."

"If she's due back soon, we can just wait." Pauletta looked sideways at Evers.

"She's not here yet," he stuttered. "She hasn't walked through the door. We'll see."

"Your prediction is looking very, very feeble, Judge Wheeling."

The dealership was full of people and banners and refreshments, and the showroom was noisy and busy. "What's going on today?" Pauletta asked.

"It's all week," the receptionist answered. "From Friday to Friday. It's our Door-to-Door promotion. A really big deal. Help yourself to the food or drinks. And if you're in a hurry or need something right away, I can get another sales rep for you."

"Thanks. We'll just relax and wait for Ruth Esther."

The receptionist took them into Ruth Esther's office and shut the door when she left. She came back a few minutes later with soft drinks and two green apples. Evers set his drink and fruit on the corner of Ruth Esther's desk and didn't touch them again. Pauletta left for a while and looked at cars and flipped through brochures. When she came back, she mentioned to Evers that there was a circus truck in the parking lot, getting ready to unload some kind of animal. Right after that, Evers saw Ruth Esther walk into the building. The receptionist said something to her and pointed toward Evers and Pauletta. Ruth Esther came into her office smiling and surprised. She grabbed Pauletta's hands, kissed her cheek, then held on to her hands and took a step backward. When she let go of Pauletta, she hugged Evers and asked him how he was.

"Okay," he said. "I'm fine."

"It's so great to see both of you."

"It's nice to see you, too," Evers replied.

"I'm afraid that our visit isn't completely social, Ruth Esther," Pauletta said.

"Oh. What is it? I hope nothing's wrong."

"No. However, Judge Wheeling wants to ask you something. He has some questions left over from Utah."

Ruth Esther sat down behind her desk and started fanning herself with a magazine. "It's still hot, isn't it? I don't think it will ever cool down." She kept waving the magazine. "What else is there about our trip, Evers?"

He bit his lip before saying anything. "Why did you want the letter so badly? I'm not asking to be, uh, prying or pushy or anything, but you gave up tons of money and took considerable risks to get it."

"Why do you think I did it?" Ruth Esther laid her magazine down and put her fingertips under her chin. "I'm not sure what you're getting at. I wanted it because it was important to me."

"Why is it so important? That's what I'm trying to find out. How much could a letter from William Jennings Bryan mean to you? And how do you get a letter from someone in 1918?"

"What is it that you think, Evers? Tell me." She glanced at Pauletta. "How did you find out who wrote the letter? Did you see that when we were at the bank?" Ruth Esther lowered her hands but kept her fingers together "It's funny that you'd know and not say anything about it till now."

Evers looked at the floor. "Well, I . . . to tell you the truth, I bought a copy from Lester. I hope that doesn't offend you, and I don't think it will since I needed to find out about the letter anyway. See, I think it's all connected. Strange, but connected. To answer your other question, I think you wanted the letter because it was written to you." He picked up speed, blurted the sentence out. "I think that it was critical that you get it for a number of reasons. First, because it's personal, you know, romantic, a love letter. And over and above that, it shows that William Jennings Bryan was a cad, a hypocrite and a masher. You need to have the letter to safeguard his reputation. And most importantly, it shows very bad failings on the part of two divine instruments, you and William Jennings Bryan, which would compromise and erode faith and order and decency even more than they've already been diminished. People don't like to see their standard-bearers with their zippers down. Except me. I mean—I don't care about the zipper part—I mean that for me, I'm probably the one person you could recruit who would find something good in all this. And that's why I'm in the loop and dealing with this." Evers put his hands, palms down, on the front of Ruth Esther's desk and swayed forward. "That would sound silly to some folks, but you tell me where I'm wrong."

"Well, to begin with, I'm not a hundred years old or however old I'd need to be. Are you serious? I get the feeling you're pullin' my leg." Ruth Esther's lips were open just a little, and she blinked several times, as if something uncomfortable was under her eyelids. "The letter isn't to me. It's to my grandmother, Ruth. I'm Ruth Esther. That's why I use two names. She's the only tie I have, the only family I know about. My mother's mother. My mother was . . . she was a little touched, sort of crazy. And she was a bad drinker. The letter and a few other things are all I have about my family. My real family. That's all there is to it. Understand? I don't have any family—except Artis—and don't know anything about my blood and background except for this letter and a few pieces of furniture and some pictures. See, the Englishes adopted us—they weren't our real parents. Everybody prizes different kinds of stuff, usually stuff that you don't have or that's hard to get. The letter's like my family Bible or family farm or grandfather's watch, you see. It means more to me than money. Some things you can't put a price on. I don't think that's really your business, or else I would've told you to begin with. But now you know."

"I don't believe you. I don't. I don't mean that harshly. I think this whole thing is connected in a fantastic way, and that you've delivered me from a lot of hand-wringing and funk and indifference." Evers raised up. "How many judges would've been so restless and unhappy that they would have gotten involved in a scheme like this? And there's so much more. Our buddy Warren Dillon gets shot, the shrine comes alive at the creek one day. And you try to tell me that this is all just spilled out, coincidence piggybacking on good fortune. Shit. And you're saying, you're telling me, that you went through all this and gave up thousands of dollars for a letter with sentimental value. That's a crazy, patchwork, unbelievable tale—"

"As opposed to your more compelling explanation, Judge Wheeling, that Ruth Esther is over a hundred years old and has supernatural powers." Pauletta grinned at Ruth Esther, and Ruth Esther giggled. "And I didn't see a thing when we were all sitting out there in the woods in the pouring rain. Nothing came alive for me."

"Well, *I* sure don't know anything about a creek," Ruth Esther said. A little of the giggle made its way into her words.

"I'm convinced. You two can laugh all you want, but I'm convinced."

"Judge Wheeling has a convert's zeal, I'm afraid, Ruth Esther. The same world looks brand-new to him today."

Evers wasn't through. "You gave up these stamps, all of this money, gave millions to Pauletta, just to get a letter you want for your scrapbook? Why give her anything more than her hourly rate? Tell me that. And what about the lottery and the car and Jo Miller and the white, smiling tears?"

Ruth Esther was wearing a white blouse and pants one or two

shades darker. "I don't know about the lottery; it's just luck, isn't it? And the car, didn't someone's will leave it to Rudy? I'm not sure what that—or your wife—has to do with anything. And Pauletta is my lawyer and friend. She risked a lot, her job and everything, talkin' to you and making offers to you and going with us. Her job was at stake. And it's possible that we might never have found the stamps, and then she would have been in pretty bad shape—a lot of time for nothing. It could have been good for her, could've been bad. Turns out it was good."

"Whatever. Tell me about the white shrine. You didn't mention that. Explain that," Evers demanded. "You just happened to dive into a bathroom stall when I'm there and leave this incredible, white curiosity. That had to be planned. The albino smile was the come-on, a little taste of opium to whet my appetite."

"Well, it's an eye disorder, just the way I am. And I was pretty crazy I guess, when I first met you, chasin' you into a bathroom. I'm embarrassed about all that now. I almost wish I hadn't done it. You as much as made me give them to you, remember? You came down to the dealership and said you didn't trust me."

"I simply don't believe that you would give up millions for no reason. That's why I'm convinced I'm right. Every explanation you two have is just terrible. I know what I know; I know what makes sense."

"I'm sorry I'm no more help," Ruth Esther said. "But I'm flattered that you are sayin' such nice things about me." She walked out from behind her desk and stood beside Evers. "If you're feeling better, I'm glad that I helped. And you're right about Mr. Bryan; I think it's pretty neat and all that he's in my background, that he wrote the letter. I guess you pretty much know that he ran for president and was in the monkey trial and was an important religious figure. He was a big deal in his day. That much of what you're saying is right."

"I don't imagine there's any reason to sit here and debate this all day." Evers shrugged. "I'm not going to say anything else about it. Well, one more thing. I thought of this on the ride over here. Why, after you went into Lester's, would you not get your letter back immediately? That's why the three of you broke in to begin with, to get your letter. The money was probably an afterthought or just punishment for Lester. You and your father didn't break in that store to get cash. No way. But then John English doesn't give you your letter, doesn't give you what you really came for, but hides it with the money. Even though he has it right there, and it has nothing to do with him or Artis. That was odd, and it sets up this whole thing, sends you on this headlong dash to get your letter back. Like a rock in a lake, all these ripples come out of that, something that happened years ago and made no sense at the time."

"I've never even thought about that. I sorta see your point. But the reason my father put the letter with the money is to make sure I didn't just forget about the money and Artis. He wanted to make sure I looked after Artis when he was in jail and then would take him to where the clues said. I don't think I would've looked for the money unless my letter was with it, and if I hadn't looked for it, Artis would never have found it. Of course, I don't guess our father figured that Artis would screw himself out of the money. And, it made us stay, you know, in touch."

"Well, like I said, I'm not going to argue with you two anymore. But I knew from the beginning—hell, I told Pascal and Henry and Rudy—that this whole thing didn't make sense if you just look at it in ordinary terms."

"It makes sense to me, Judge Wheeling, but what do I know." Pauletta picked up Evers' apple from the desk and took a bite.

The three of them talked a little while longer, mostly about Pascal, then Ruth Esther hugged Pauletta and Evers, told them to come back anytime, and that she wanted to ride with them one afternoon to visit Pascal. Maybe in a week or two. She stood in the doorway to her office, and Evers and Pauletta started out across the showroom floor, past a long silver car, and Pauletta touched Evers' shoulder and slowed down. Men and women and children were everywhere, looking at price stickers and opening hoods and moving around, and two girls were making hot dogs and pouring soft drinks. A man with a large TV camera was filming the crowd and the cars, walking along with another man. The second man had on shorts and tennis shoes and was carrying a bright light on a skinny metal pole.

"So, listen. Tell me this: If Ruth Esther's magical or an angel or the deputy prime minister for the heavens, then why wouldn't she tell you? Why wouldn't she just get on with it, since you've been converted and figured all this out? That doesn't make any sense, her disclaiming all of her work and good deeds. Have you thought about that?"

Evers stopped walking. Three children with helium balloons ran past him, the last child bumping Evers' leg when he passed. "That's the most critical part, Pauletta. The linchpin. I have faith, you see. You have to take a little step, a little jump, trust a little. Faith. And that's what I was missing, why everything was a broken-down, soupy, nasty morass for me. A little bit of belief, that's what I needed. You can't imagine how good I feel. Just like that. When I figured this out, I just . . . just . . . can't explain it. Just like that—I feel so much better." He looked past Pauletta. There was a live elephant out in the parking lot. Two kids were on the beast's back, sitting on a colorful blanket. There was a line of people waiting to take a ride, children and adults, most of them with cameras. The elephant was led around in a circle by two handlers, and the kids on its back held on with both hands. "Check that out," Evers said, pointing out the window. "That's what was in the truck."

"Couldn't you believe in gravity or the Red Cross or air-traffic controllers, something a little less bizarre? Or, if you need something religious, how about the pope? He's better documented, more popular, and the faith requirement would seem to me to be a little less demanding. Or Billy Graham. He seems like a kind, devout gentlemen. You're sort of at the Jim-Jones-levitation-and-chants end of the spectrum."

"It's not like I just made all this up, Pauletta, or that I'm a fool. Think about it."

"I have."

"Do you want to get in line, ride the elephant? El Elephanto." Evers started walking again. "Imagine getting on that thing if you were stoned."

"No. Stoned or otherwise."

"How come?"

"Why would I want to ride an elephant?"

At the door leading outside, Evers reached in front of Pauletta and took hold of the handle. She hesitated and caused Evers to jam into her shoulder and side.

"Does that offend you," he asked, "civility and old-school courtesy? Is there something in the black feminist code that condemns door opening? Too contrived, too condescending, too full of alpha-male symbolism?"

"Not at all. I'm just unaccustomed to it. Respect and courtesy and kindness—even if just for an instant—all play well with me."

She walked through the door, and Evers saw the elephant turn a corner in its ring, saw its eye the size of a fist and its trunk dangling off its face, limp and wrinkled, pink at the very end. Evers followed Pauletta out the door and suddenly heard thunder—BOOM! BOOM! BOOM!—and light poured into his eyes, white glare that popped open his pupils and sent them reeling. Ruth Esther's name came out of the sky, deep and electric, out of the ceiling and sky, more behind him than in front, and through a lot of white, dilated blindness, he saw some colors, sparks and streaks, red flares in the sky, and he heard the elephant bellow, saw its trunk hooked and rolled in the air. BOOM! Again, BOOM BOOM BOOM! Evers felt the pavement vibrate under his feet. He saw more color in the sky and began to get used to the brightness in his face.

He looked back over his shoulder into the showroom, located Ruth Esther, and she started to fade in and out, a fifties jungle-radio transmission, flickering paler and whiter, mixed and flecked with shimmers, coming and going, in and out, steam from a stove pot, and then she was returned, solid and apparent, one more person among all the cars and food and tacky decorations. She began walking toward him.

Evers recognized the camera in his face and the brightness retracted into a square, into the light on the tall pole, and a man in a suit was shaking Evers' hand. BOOM! Sparkles and bright showers were in the air—fireworks—and the elephant had stopped in the lot. Evers rubbed his eyes with the heels of his hands; the light was causing them to water and sting. Then Ruth Esther was standing beside him, and Pauletta in front, beside the cameraman. He heard Ruth Esther's name called out on the paging system again.

"Congratulations! Congratulations," said the man shaking Evers' hand. People began to close in and started clapping.

"What?" Evers said. BOOM! More fireworks exploded above his head. The man dropped Evers' hand and stood shoulder to shoulder with him. He looked at the camera and put his arm around Evers' neck.

"I'm Cannady Vaughn, owner of Vaughn Ford-Lincoln-Mercury-Jeep-Eagle-Isuzu, and you are the one millionth person to step through our dealership doors. We started with my daddy in 1946, and we've been the longest continuously open Ford dealership in the tristate region. We're proud of that."

At least a hundred people had surrounded the door and were listening to Cannady Vaughn. The crowd was chewing gum, eating hot dogs, holding babies, and clutching giveaway hats and plastic ice scrapers.

"Good. Great," said Evers. He reached behind Cannady Vaughn's back and touched Ruth Esther, pushed on her arm with his open hand. He wanted to make sure that she was solid, cloth and flesh and bone.

"Have you followed our promotion on K98, our Door-to-Door Sweepstakes?"

"Not really. No."

"What's your name, sir?" Cannady Vaughn asked.

"Evers Wheeling."

"Where are you from, Evers, around here or out of town?"

"Norton. I live in Norton." Evers' eyes had adjusted to the camera light. People in the crowd were beginning to move around, and the elephant and its handlers were getting ready to start circling the lot again; two teenagers, a boy and a girl, were at the front of the line, ready to ride.

"What brings you to Vaughn Ford-Lincoln-Mercury-Jeep-Eagle-Isuzu?" Cannady Vaughn was smiling and his head was slanted; he looked right into the camera after he spoke to Evers. Evers guessed that he did his own commercials, local TV spots that had too much backlight and showed him standing in the middle of his car lot, ending with a finger snap or goofy gesture and a tired tag line.

"Why am I here?" Evers repeated.

"Exactly."

Pauletta started laughing.

"I . . . uh . . . well, I came to look at a truck. Black full-size." Evers hesitated. "I drove it a few months ago, took a test drive." He began to pick up steam, turned toward the camera. "Looked all over Virginia and the Carolinas, and I couldn't find a better truck at a better price. So I came back here today. Came back to Vaughn Motors. And I had a great saleswoman. I really appreciated the way I was treated. Ruth Esther English. She's a real professional."

"Well there you have it. People are gonna think we set this up, Evers." Vaughn winked at him, then smiled at the camera. "Of course if we weren't on the level, we would've waited till dark to let off those fireworks. They were still somethin' though, right? They showed up real good I thought."

"I didn't have any trouble finding them." Evers gave everyone a stagy smile. "Is this live? Are we on TV or something?"

"No. We'll use this for our fall commercials."

"Oh."

"So let me tell you about our Door-to-Door giveaway, Mr. Evers."

Pauletta snickered and made a face at Evers.

"One million people have walked through the doors of Vaughn Ford-Lincoln-Mercury-Jeep-Eagle-Isuzu," Cannady Vaughn began, "and we see each one as a special client, an old friend and a buyer with individual needs. We want everyone to leave here feeling well treated by courteous, experienced salespeople and a great service department with state-of-the-art equipment and technology."

Cannady Vaughn rattled on and Evers leaned back toward Ruth Esther, talked over his shoulder through the corner of his mouth. "I don't see how you sell anything. This blowhard fool would scare away any rational buyers."

"People like Cannady," Ruth Esther whispered. "He's actually real honest. Sometimes he's just a little too hyper."

Evers leaned further back. "Hyper? That's a little understated, isn't it?"

Finally, Vaughn was getting to the payoff. "So, Mr. Evers Wheeling, of Norton, North Carolina, we plan to take you from this door to the door of any vehicle on our lot, and that car will be yours. Door to door. You pick the vehicle, we give you the title."

"I won a car?"

"Correct. Any car on our lot. Plus a trip to Cancun and five hundred cash dollars to spend while you're there, courtesy of Vaughn Ford-Lincoln-Mercury-Jeep-Eagle-Isuzu."

"Wow." Evers grinned. "Thank you. That's hard to beat."

"Are you still interested in that truck?" Cannady Vaughn asked.

Evers ducked his head and smiled at him, a slick, over-the-top smile. "I think I'll take a look at one of the Lincolns now that my budget has changed." The crowd laughed, and Cannady Vaughn slapped Evers on the back. BOOM! More fireworks, and the cameraman swung around to take in the people and elephant and explosions in the sky. Evers stepped back and put his mouth beside Ruth Esther's ear, felt a few soft strands of her hair when he turned his cheek to talk. "Thanks," he said.

"You're welcome."

"Thanks for everything."

"You're welcome."

"I don't guess you're going to confirm my suspicions, are you? Suddenly confess? Tell me the truth?"

Ruth Esther turned away from Evers, changed positions so that she was close to his face, her hand on the round part of his shoulder. "I've told you all I can tell you," she said, and when she stepped back, Evers was sure that he saw a sly cut in her eyes and a winking, ephemeral smile.

BOOM! BOOM! The crowd began to scatter, and Evers tried to locate Cannady Vaughn and Pauletta. People were milling around and winding through the cars and trucks like ants in red-powder dirt. "What a treat," he said. "What a treat."

Prisons, all of them, have the same smell, especially right before or right after a meal—grease, cabbage, disinfectant, perspiration and cigarette smoke, a dank caldron of odors that don't belong together and catch in your nose and throat as soon as you walk through the gate. Pauletta had discovered, about a year after starting her job in Charleston, that all corrections officers, even those with lopsided mustaches and heavy bellies, try to avoid the smell of boiled food and prison fog by wearing a lot of cheap cologne—Old Spice, Brut or the pungent products from Avon that somebody's wife peddles from the back of a dusty, stickered-up minivan. The prison where Pascal was being held, in Statesville, North Carolina, was no different. The guard who walked with Pauletta through a metal detector and two sets of cellblock doors smelled like aftershave, hair oil and mouthwash, all the scents of a middle-aged alcoholic without the undercurrent of whiskey; the matron who patted Pauletta on her arms, legs and trunk was wearing some sort of drugstore perfume, an unrepentant mix of flowers and hammers. The two guards in their ill-fitting uniforms were tiny, filtered breaks in five acres of low-grade stench.

Pauletta hadn't been terribly surprised when she called her office from Norton and got word through her secretary that Pascal had phoned from jail and wanted her to call him back. She had called Charleston from her car, in the morning, just before driving out of the parking lot at the Coin-O-Matic. Evers was still in bed. They had slept together, but didn't have sex, just kissed two or three times and stayed next to each other for most of the night. A new white Lincoln was parked beside the Datsun; Evers had brought the new car home the night before, driven eighty miles per hour most of the way from Winston-Salem to Norton. Three Mexicans with heads of thick black hair were standing around the door to the Laundromat, chewing on toothpicks, watching Pauletta, staring at her while she talked on the phone. She stopped about a mile outside of Norton, and a man in bibbed overalls at a roadside stand with a few apples and a slew of watermelons told her how to get to Statesville.

When he was brought into the interview room, Pascal was wearing prison clothes and handcuffs, but he looked the same to Pauletta, still had good color in his face and plenty of energy when he walked and moved; he picked up his feet, held his shoulders back and took good, long strides to get where he was going. So many convicts barely move, seem to wind down like mechanical toys or cold car batteries, get slower and slower each day, each week, each month—a result of, Pauletta guessed, having nowhere to go, nothing to do and ten years to live in a black hole with bars. Pauletta felt sorry for Pascal, felt a touch of pity seeing him in manacles. Pascal held out both of his hands, splayed them as best he could with the shackles on his wrists, folded up Pauletta's hand in his and squeezed her tight enough that she could feel her fingers jam together. The chain on his handcuffs rattled and clicked when he held on to her. "Thank you for coming. Thank you."

"You're welcome. How are you? How's life in the big house?"

Pascal used his foot to push a chair away from the table. "Not as entertaining and romantic as I'd imagined, but tolerable. I got my parole documents last week. My mandatory date is about two months away." He sat down.

"Is that why you called? Is there a problem with that?"

"Oh, no. No. That's fine. That's all fine."

"Good." She sat down next to him. "Oh, by the way. While I'm thinking about it—I left a carton of cigarettes and twenty dollars for you at the prison canteen."

"That's thoughtful. Truly kind. Thanks."

"You're welcome."

"Evers told me you guys made some progress on the letter. Found out what it was."

Pauletta took her jacket off and laid it on the table. "We did. It cost us ten thousand dollars, but we found a copy."

"Wow." Pascal was wide-eyed for a few seconds. "That's pretty pricey."

"Did Evers tell you any of the details?" Pauletta asked.

"No. My calls are limited to three minutes. He called last night—I guess you'd just driven back to his apartment. Anyway, said you'd gotten to the bottom of everything. And that he'd just won a car. He's coming down on Sunday to visit. I'm anxious to know the whole deal; it should be a really interesting story. And I'm assuming that everything is good, that everything turned out okay, since Evers sounded upbeat on the phone and you're here and no one's in jail besides me."

"It's quite an ending. I'll let your brother give you the whole story. I won't spoil the surprise. Plus, we might have different versions of the facts—you know how Evers is. I'll leave it to him." Pauletta winked at Pascal.

"That's the best idea, no doubt. It'll be nice to have something to look forward to besides a shower and kitchen duty."

"Well, I don't want to steal his thunder. He'll enjoy telling you the tale and embellishing it all the way through."

Pascal took a deep breath. Pauletta saw his chest move, his mouth open. "Do you know why I wanted you to come? Thanks again, by the way. At least you were already in the state."

"You're welcome."

"I needed to talk with you."

"Okay."

"We still have a privilege, right?" Pascal asked. "Everything is confidential?"

"Yes."

Pascal looked her straight in the eye. "Even from my brother? Even from Evers?"

"Absolutely."

"Are you two seeing each other? How is it that the tattooed, menacing, African American felon in the cell across from me put it? 'Talking'? Are you and Evers still talking?"

Pauletta grinned. "Maybe a few words here and there. We don't quite have a steady, traditional romance yet. It's pretty halting. I don't know."

"You know, I thought about getting a tattoo while I'm here. I thought MOM and a heart would be plenty safe and might even pass as high hip in some circles."

"Why not, Pascal? A tattoo might be a nice touch."

"At any rate, I need to tell you something. Just you, no one else."

"Okay."

"Do you have an idea, any clue?" Pascal wondered.

"No."

"Do you think Jo Miller killed herself?"

"You mean, I guess, do I think you killed her?" Pauletta's enunciation was perfect, every word immaculate. Her voice barely told anything; she could have been asking someone to pass the salt or open a window.

"That's one way to put it."

Pauletta leaned back in her chair and gazed up at the ceiling, saw two fluorescent lights covered by a wire cage and a spider's web in the closest corner of the room. A tan, dry, translucent wing from a mosquito was caught up in the web, hanging straight down, dangling ten feet above the floor, as lifeless as could be. "Now that you've asked me the question, I certainly have—what should I say?—an open mind on the issue. Two things have always stuck with me, Pascal. There were a pair of discharged casings in the gun, but only one wound. That's strange. And the letter, the one she mailed to her mother. When I went back into court, after we saw her—saw Mrs. Covington, I mean—she had left the copy for me. Remember? Bless her heart, she was truly paralyzed by the whole thing. I'm sure that she left it for me. Who else would have? I thought that was very strong, very courageous on her part."

"Yeah, it was. I agree."

"But the letter, when I saw it . . . I don't know. The writing was so deliberate and impersonal, and it was across the top of the page. I'm sure it was Jo Miller's writing; her mother would know that. And it came to Mrs. Covington in an envelope with a handwritten address, so, well, that was important. But you know how it was signed, Pascal? Just 'Jo Miller.' Not 'love' or 'Jo' or 'see you in heaven,' just her name. A pretty restrained good-bye, huh? The other thing, clothes in the washer? That's a third thing, I suppose. I said there were two things, but I guess that there are three problems for me. If I were going to kill myself, I'd at least take the day off. Why is she doing clothes in the middle of the night if she's getting ready to shoot herself?" Pauletta crossed her legs and studied Pascal. "In the end, Pascal, the way I look at it is that the state didn't have enough to prove you guilty beyond a reasonable doubt. And that's really all I do, all I'm concerned with, you know?"

"But that's not all there is to it."

"That depends. That's all there is to it for me."

"Well, I need to tell you. I shot her. I did it." Pascal bobbed his head up and down. "I shot Jo Miller."

"You did?" Pauletta was very collected. She didn't move, didn't change her position, didn't blink or gasp or recoil.

"I did. I shot her. It's a lot to carry around with you, even if you feel you had a good reason for doing it."

"I want to make sure we're on the same page. Let's take this in steps. You murdered Jo Miller, your brother's wife. Is that what you're saying?"

"That's what I'm saying." Pascal rested his hands on the edge of the table, and the metal chain on his cuffs scraped the wood, made a harsh, deep sound.

"Shot her?" Pauletta had started inching forward, moving closer to Pascal.

"I shot Jo Miller." Pascal's voice was determined; he seemed to be pushing the words out of his mouth.

"You shot her with the twenty-two pistol?"

"Yeah."

"Her twenty-two, the one the police recovered?" Pauletta asked.

"That's correct."

"How is it that she had discharge residue on her hand?"

"Simple. That was the second shot. I shot her, put the gun in her hand, squeezed the trigger and fired the second bullet into a backstop. A piece of firewood laid over a copy of *War and Peace*. It was the thickest book on the shelf, and I thought it would score pretty high irony points, sort of playful and appropriate."

Pauletta nodded, thought for a moment. "So . . . so how did you get the gun? Find it in her house or—wait a minute. Let's backtrack. How did you get into her house in the middle of the night?"

"I wrote Jo Miller when Evers told me what was happening, about catching her in the rack with Falstaf. I knew they were going to get a divorce. I tried, you know, to talk Jo Miller into not being so punitive and greedy. I was sincere at first, really tried to work things out. I called her on the phone, too. She wrote me back and told me, basically, to drop dead. I tried a couple more times to get her to settle things with Evers, sort of tried to broker things, threw out some possible offers, even tried, tried one time, to get her to call Evers and see if they could get back together. I did *not* want them to go back to court after the first hearing was such a nightmare. Pauletta, Jo Miller was rattlesnake mean, all fangs and venom. I finally told her I had some pages that Evers might be okay with, an outline of a separation agreement, and that I needed to sneak it to her and talk with her about it. If she'd go along with the proposal, I promised her that I'd twist his arm a little. I told her that the whole thing was making life tough for Evers and me, that it had really caused problems, my testifying about sleeping with her, and that we needed to get something done. That was, all in all, pretty much true."

Pauletta waved her hand to cut him off. "Did you sleep with her? I'm assuming that you did, right?"

"Yes, once. Years ago."

"Was she married to your brother then?"

"Yes."

"And Evers knew this for sure?" Pauletta asked.

"Yes. But you're getting too far ahead. Hang on." Pascal took his hands off the table and put them back in his lap. He seemed rushed and hurried, but eager to tell Pauletta every piece of the story.

"Okay."

"Will it bother you if I smoke?" Pascal asked.

"No, of course not. Go ahead."

Pascal took out a cigarette, tapped the open end on the table several times, bent his head toward his hands and stuck the cigarette between his lips. "Okay. Here's the truly sad, amazing-as-hell thing. I get up and Ruth Esther is gone in my car. At first, I figure it's Evers, but I look in the bedroom, and he's in there. So I talk on the vibrator-and-leather-boots line for a while, wait for Ruth Esther to get back, sneak out through my bedroom window, roll my car out of the drive and take off to Jo Miller's. I called her from a pay phone to tell her I'm on the way. Now—and this may strike you as small, insignificant, all things given—now she has to shoo Falstaf out of her house, and they'd just had sex, remember? That was the final report from Loggins and Greenfield. The lab analysis. I didn't know that at the time, of course. So here I am, and she opens the door at four o'clock in the morning in a short T-shirt and a thong. No shit, Pauletta. She's wide awake, got makeup on, hair combed, the whole nine yards, just unbelievably arrogant and vain and corrupt, and just got through with another guy. And you know she was doing all of this just to rub my nose in it, to tempt me and to hurt Evers." Pascal had been talking with the cigarette in the corner of his mouth. "Would you help me with this, help me light this thing? It's sort of hard to strike a match with my hands like this."

"I don't have my lighter. They made me leave my purse at the front desk," Pauletta said. "I'm sorry."

"My matches are in my shirt pocket. Just reach in and get them."

Pauletta found the matches and lit Pascal's cigarette. He inhaled as much as he could, held the smoke in and then breathed it out through his nose and mouth at the same time. "I left a boom box at the corner of Jo Miller's porch with a Halloween tape in it. It's a great tape. Ghosts and goblins and screams. We've had it for years at the trailer. Scares the shit out of the kids when they come to the doublewide trick-or-treating."

A guard opened the door and stuck his head into the room. "Everything okay in here?" he asked.

Pauletta swiveled in her seat and faced the guard. "Sure. Why are you asking?"

"Just policy. We have to check by every so often."

"Everything's fine."

"Good." The guard shut the door, and Pauletta smelled a little wave of cologne waft across the room.

Pascal was taking drags off the cigarette, sucking in smoke and exhaling it while he spoke. "I showed Jo Miller this outline, this agreement I'd done about two weeks before, and while she's gone to get a beer for me and to get a pair of sweatpants—she's cold, right?—I tell her I hear something, go out, punch the play button on the box, come back in, and then, of course, she hears something. I ask her for the gun, tell her to go to her room and lock the door. I go back out, stay a few minutes, walk back in and tell her that it was a couple of raccoons in the garbage."

"You're still in her bedroom?"

"Exactly. She sat down on the edge of the bed, and I ran over and put the barrel right up to her head. Oh—I guess it goes without saying that I put on gloves when I went outside. The whole thing took about twenty minutes."

"The suicide note?" Pauletta asked.

"I took the last page of one of the letters she'd written me. I just thought of it that night, thought up the whole plan right after I went into my room. It absolutely broke Evers' heart when I told him what I'd done—you know, sleeping with Jo Miller. I mean, we'd talked about it before, and he probably had some suspicions, especially after the trial, but when I told him for sure, it really hurt him. I've never seen him cry, but he got really upset, and I stuck my head out of my bedroom after I left to go to sleep and, well, he was just sobbing, had his head in his hands. More because of me, what I'd done and what it would do to us, more because I'd let him down than anything Jo Miller had done." Pascal had smoked his cigarette almost to the filter, and he dropped it onto the floor and stubbed it out with his foot.

"I'm not sure I understand. I can see why Evers was upset, but I'm not sure how you managed to produce a suicide note."

"I just took the last page of one of her letters to me, typed the suicide message on the computer, and printed it out on that same page under her signature. I had the letter at the trailer, and I just took off the last page. I'll never forget it: 'I'm sorry that it has come to this. Sorry for all of us. I wish things could have turned out differently, but I truly believe that I have been a good person and a good wife and that this is the right thing for me, for you, for Evers, for everyone. I deserve my freedom.' Pretty dramatic, huh? She wrote it on rose-colored stationery with an embossed monogram, too. How perfect. Like I said, I just thought of it that night—right after I'd decided what I was going to do."

"That's clever, Pascal. And lucky—if that's the word you want to use—lucky that you had a page with no more than that on it."

"I'd really tried to work something out, right up to the end," Pascal said. "I didn't start out trying to get her to compose a suicide note, not at all. The only tiny fly in the ointment—if anyone had ever really looked at the letter, there were no fingerprints on the paper. I'd handled it, so I had to completely clean it up, wipe it off. And I fucked up her name; that wasn't good."

"How'd you get her to mail it for you?"

"That was a little trickier. I took a check with me, one of Evers', forged his name and wrote it for fifty thousand dollars, told Jo Miller it was good-faith money. She didn't trust me to hold it and I didn't trust her, so we agreed we would send it to her mother while we worked out the deal. If she didn't sign anything, we got the check back, so on and so on, and you get the picture. I just used the envelope she'd written out, and the check never got sent. I was even going to use her saliva, but her mouth was full of blood after everything happened, so I used tap water. I couldn't be sure that her mother would let someone know about it, but it was a pretty good bet. Made it easier to take the dive on the confession, too, knowing I probably had a little backup. And there you have it."

"So you really killed her? This isn't a joke or feint or trail to nowhere?" Pascal had put another cigarette in his mouth, and Pauletta lit it for him.

"Yeah."

"I guess I'm . . . a little shocked, but this isn't a total surprise. I always thought there were a few gremlins in this one, some stray pieces and rough edges. To tell you the truth, though, I figured that most of it had to do with Evers. That he was involved or knew more than he was letting on."

"Nope. He has no clue. None."

Pauletta glanced up at the spider's web in the corner above her head. "And I guess I know why you shot her, because—"

"Because she was absolutely vicious and had just about ruined Evers. Steady betrayal, lying to him, taking his money, taunting him. Then when I told him what I'd done, about sleeping with her, told him the truth, it almost, like I say, killed *him*."

"Perhaps, if we're handing out punishment for betrayal and causing Evers suffering, you should have shot yourself as well. You were as guilty as she was."

Pascal reached up with both of his hands and took the cigarette out of his mouth. "I was guilty once and regretted it. I asked Evers to forgive me. She was guilty again and again and reveled in it."

"And simply getting rid of her wasn't enough. You needed to do something for your brother, but you couldn't just tell him that you'd killed his wife. He'd stew and worry and fret and live on eggshells the rest of his life, wouldn't he? And he'd probably condemn you for it. Even as much as he hated her, he wouldn't want to cross that line."

"Exactly." Pascal nodded. "At first I wasn't going to tell him anything. I was just going to do it for him and let it be."

"But then you get the chance to wipe the slate clean with the fucked-up confession. The problem's gone, and you repay your brother in currency that he can accept and appreciate."

"Right."

"Damn smart plan." Pauletta's tone was noncommittal, all lawyer.

"It sort of fell into place over time. The confession and DWI, that helped me out in two ways. It let me appear to do something for Evers; that was very important. But at the same time, it settled things with the police and let me get on with my life. Over and above making things right with Evers, giving me the chance to do that, taking the blame for this got a lot off of me. This thing was a hell of a lot more than I expected. I never should have done it. Never. I was mad and guilty and ashamed and pretty desperate to do something with my life other than burden Evers. That was a terrible, pernicious combination. Jo Miller deserved it, but I shouldn't have been the one to pull the trigger." Pascal's lips trembled, his voice caught. "She deserved it, but I shouldn't have shot her." He stopped for a moment, and neither he nor Pauletta said anything. "At any rate, I had to get it settled, ended, over. I couldn't stand the guilt and all the worry, worrying about the police finally finding out what really happened. I couldn't leave it open, so I brought it to a head and built in some escape routes and booby traps. Confessing helped me twice over, really." Pascal squirmed some; Pauletta could tell that he was becoming agitated, uneasy.

"And it worked. You'll serve a few months, and that's it. You're off the hook, can't be retried, you're even with your brother, a martyr in his eyes, his evil wife's dead as a doornail and all the people you care about think you're a hero of sorts."

"One problem, you see." Pascal started coming apart; his hands began shaking, rattling the chain on the handcuffs, and he wrapped his fingers together in a tight, bloodless fist. "Shit. You don't know how bad this is when I look back on it." His voice was uneven and his eyes were wet to the rim, a wall of tears balanced on the brink, about to break and scatter. "This really didn't make me any less of a fuck-up. It probably made things worse."

"I don't get it. Why the change of heart? You're remorseful? I'm not following you."

Pascal dabbed at the corner of his eye with the back of his arm. "Two things. The big thing, the most important thing, is the shrine and Ruth Esther. Jo Miller had fucking throat cancer. She was going to die. Henry wins the lottery. Warren Dillon gets shot. Rudy asks for a car . . . gets it. I ask to be beatific and suddenly my life is good, fun. I meet a nice woman—Ruth Esther, who seems to like me. There's something going on there. Oh, and don't forget, Ruth Esther takes us on this crazy trip, all that's part of it, too. I was . . . well, meddling, sticking my nose in. Some kind of interloper. So then I'm sitting in here—this is the second thing—and it dawns on me that Ruth Esther who is . . . holy—believe what you will, you've got to believe in something—Ruth Esther tries to stop me that night by taking the car so I can't go. Everything was already taken care of, out of my hands. That, Pauletta, was a sign. 'Don't do it. Your fucking car is gone.' "

"I agree that you were wrong, Pascal, and that you should be punished. Everything else is just chance and things happening. It's good you're remorseful. You should be. Don't fuck it up by feeling that way because you're cowardly or afraid, or because you suddenly believe in voodoo and fairies. You should feel bad—feel terrible—because you killed a woman."

"You can't know how shitty this is, how scared I am."

Pauletta held up her hand, shook her finger at him. "Actually . . . when you think about it, Ruth Esther's taking the car and leaving was sort of a good thing as far as your fabrication goes. It made your story that much more believable to Evers. Right? Do you see what I'm saying? Your discovering the car gone—and Evers knowing that it was gone—made your reason for confessing seem to have some decent sense to it. I'm not buying into Evers' and your . . . " Pauletta stopped. "Into your theory that all this is running on some sort of schedule and according to plan, but you could just as easily read something good into Ruth Esther using the car."

"It was a very clear warning, and I ignored it. It's that simple."

"Well, I think most of what you're saying is silly, a lot of rot. But regardless of all that, I can see why you feel so awful."

"I do. I do. You can't imagine." Pascal choked. He had started to cry, was sobbing. "Believe me I do. I'm not cut out to live with this, either. I'll never get over it, be the same. That's why I needed to tell you. Confession's good for the soul. That's what they say, right?"

Pauletta rocked forward in her seat. "So I've heard. But I don't know that telling me's going to do you any good, Pascal. What difference does it make that I know?"

"Someone needs to know that I'm sorry." Pascal was still crying. "Someone needs to know that I realize I was wrong. And that I've figured it out, figured out that I crossed up Ruth Esther and the relic."

Pauletta laughed and shook her head at the same time. "My, my. You and Evers are going to have a lot to talk about. It looks like I'm the only unwashed heathen left in the group." She hesitated. "Well, there's Artis, I guess."

"Talk to Evers? About what? I'm not sure I understand."

"I suspect you will, soon enough."

"You're not going to tell him, are you? He'd just agonize over it, and

I'd be right back in the same old pit looking up at him, waiting for him to throw me a rope. It would undo the little good to come out of this."

"I'll never mention it to anyone, Pascal. But I can't settle this for you. It's a huge thing, killing another person."

Pascal was drained; he hung his head and slouched down in his chair. He was sobbing, but there didn't seem to be as many tears. "You believe that I know I was wrong, and that I'm contrite, don't you?"

"I do, Pascal. I believe you." Pauletta's voice was gentle, generous.

"Maybe you can fit me in your wishes and petitions and prayers."

"Sorry, that's not something I do."

"Whatever. It's a little like Martin Luther; sometimes you need lightning to strike a tree right in front of you and scare you shitless."

Pauletta stood up and wrapped her arms around Pascal, held on to him and rubbed and patted his back. He was still sitting down, and he started to weep a little harder. "She was a terrible woman, Pascal. People have done worse. And it's good you love your brother so much. That's about all I can give you." She picked up her jacket and walked to the door, left Pascal slumped and bent, bound up in chains, sitting with his legs stretched out in front of him, about to fall out of his seat. She walked out of the room and didn't look back, heard the door clang and shut behind her.

TWELVE

THREE WEEKS LATER, ON A CLEAR FRIDAY EVENING, EVERS WAS
sitting with his legs spread in a V at the edge of the yard in
which he'd grown up. He was wearing shorts and could feel the grass
underneath his legs tickling and scraping his skin. At his apartment
above the Coin-O-Matic, the walls were bare and his plates and
glasses were wrapped in newspaper, but he'd decided to leave a lot
behind. He'd already spent a day filling up plastic garbage bags, haul-
ing them down the stairs and tossing them over the metal lip of the
Dumpster beside the Laundromat; the sacks of trash would clatter and
collapse when they landed, then settle in with the rest of the glass and
cans and junk people had finished with and thrown away.

Evers was cutting small, straight lines with a pair of lawn clippers,
new ones with black foam handles. He was working on the high grass
in front of a flower garden full of vines and weeds and burgundy, yellow, and purple blooms on thin green stems. After lunch, he'd discovered the family's old croquet set in the basement, and now he looked
out and traced the whole game in his mind: the wire wickets, the
stakes with colored bands and grooves lathed into the wood, the turn
near the birdbath where the course curved in front of the flower bed
and headed back to the house. He recalled that Pascal used to carry a

gin and tonic around the layout and swing his mallet with only one hand, barely stooping to hit his ball.

Evers' parents' neighbor, Lizzy Blankenship, came out on her porch and walked across her lawn to the flowers along the yard's border. "It's so nice to see you back," she said. "What a fine surprise."

"It's good to be back." He looked up at her. Mrs. Blankenship was smiling, and her hands were clasped together in front of her.

"How are you doing?"

"I'm doing okay, I think. Just trying to get things in shape around here."

Mrs. Blankenship nodded. "We all need to do that every now and then, I guess."

"I agree," Evers said.

"I heard you were moving back full-time pretty soon."

"Yes ma'am. I think this will be a good place for me. I've already gotten the power connected and phones and some new carpets. I think I'll be happy here."

"I hope so." Mrs. Blankenship paused. The old woman shifted her head and looked past Evers. "Have you gotten some help?"

"Help?" He turned and glanced over his shoulder. Pauletta was lifting a brown bag of groceries out of Evers' car, the new white Lincoln. He dropped the clippers and leaned back on his palms and laughed. When he stopped laughing, he told Mrs. Blankenship simply that Pauletta was his friend. "She's been really good to me," Evers said. "I like her."

"Oh, I see. Yes . . . "

"She's a lawyer, too."

"When will you be coming back for good?" asked Mrs. Blankenship.

"Probably in the late fall, when the leaves begin to change."

"Will your lawyer friend be coming?"

"Perhaps, but you never know with her."

"Of course." Mrs. Blankenship smiled. "So do you have a girlfriend now? I mean, well, you know, I guess 'girlfriend' sounds so old-fashioned."

"Not really."

"I was so sorry to hear about your wife and everything and your brother."

"Thanks."

"How's Pascal doing?"

"He's okay. The last time we were together we talked about the way bread smells in elementary-school cafeterias and how many convicts listen to NPR."

"And you're not going to stand for your office again, is that right? I read in the *Journal* that you're quitting your judge position."

"That's right. I'm not sure I want to judge people anymore, and I'm not sure that I want everyone dragging out my personal problems."

"I see. Good for you. Good. Let me know if I can help you with anything. It's nice to have one of my boys back."

After Mrs. Blankenship left, Evers cut a fistful of flowers and took them with him into the kitchen. He left them on a table lying on their sides, some of the petals folded and bent underneath themselves.

"For me, Sweet Prince?" asked Pauletta. She was standing at the sink with the water running, her back to Evers.

"For the house."

"House flowers, then. Same family as wallflowers?"

"I cut them from the garden on the edge of the lawn."

Pauletta turned toward him, drying her hands on a small cloth towel. "I'm really glad you asked me to spend the weekend with you. I hope this sojourn doesn't hurt your standing with the ancient neighbor."

"I doubt it will. I told her that you were the housekeeper."

Pauletta smiled. "But she still wanted to know if we're sleeping together."

"You know, since you mentioned the subject, it occurs to me that resuming sex might not be a bad idea." He put his hands in his pockets. "Only if you want to, of course. I'd hoped it was sort of implicit when you agreed to spend the weekend with me."

"You need a goal when you fuck. But perhaps I could make an exception. Who knows."

"I need a pleasant, eighteenth-century, white-gloved, gazebo-by-the-water type of romance, all the right parts of instinct and interest. I want to sit on my porch in June and watch cars pass on the highway. I want to hold hands and watch television together on Sunday mornings and eat cereal and pecan twirls in old robes. I want to be sublimely satisfied."

"Then I don't guess we'll be fucking after dinner."

"I didn't mean to suggest that I needed it now, or for that matter that I can't have it with you. Like I said, I think that's part of all this, our ending up together."

Pauletta laughed. "Lord Byron, Keats, Shelley, Evers Wheeling. All the Romantics. You always say the right thing."

"I appreciate your being kind to me. I do." Evers spoke quietly.

"You're welcome."

"I mean it. You were good to help us and all. Very few people would've been so generous."

Pauletta folded the towel in half and laid it down. "Have you heard much from Pascal?"

"All the time. He doesn't like many of the people, of course, but he likes the time alone. He seems a little down, but he'll be out soon. Maybe we can go see him on Sunday. I thought I'd ask you."

"That would be fine." She was facing Evers. "Have you told him about Ruth Esther and your theory and newfound faith?"

"Sure. I wrote him and talked to him. I saw him the Sunday after I won the Lincoln."

"What did he say?"

"His exact words were 'whatever.' " Evers smiled and then started laughing.

"He . . . well, I suspect that maybe he has given it more thought than you might expect," Pauletta said. She leaned against the sink.

"What do you mean?"

"Nothing. Nothing. He's just thoughtful, and you two are brothers. So that's all he said to you?"

"Yeah. You know Pascal."

"Not as well as you do."

"And you still think I'm mad as a hatter, right? Is that going to hurt my chances of sleeping with you? I hope not. And long term, I hope it doesn't derail our time together. Consider it a charming idiosyncrasy, like a goatee or a bad hat."

Pauletta folded her arms across her chest. "I'm not sure what to make of it." She dropped her eyes. "I wasn't sure that I was going to mention this to you and embolden—"

"I'm already pretty firm in my take on all this," Evers interrupted. "Nothing you say's going to matter to me one way or the other. I know the truth. The bottom line is that you can never know anything for sure. Nothing. There are no positives, just shades and degrees of faith. It's like that with everything. Fluke water stain or image of Christ, weather balloon debris or alien ship, Thomas Jefferson slept with Sally Hemmings or he didn't. You bet that the sun will come up tomorrow in the east, your brakes will work, your lunch isn't contaminated with carcinogens or piss from a disgruntled busboy, a dog won't bite and that the gym teacher isn't seducing your teenage daughter. It's just a question of how long and how sturdy the span is between the two sides, like James West—remember *The Wild, Wild West*? Remember how he'd take this terrifically small derringer out of the secret space in his boot heel and load the gun with an arrow tip and rope and shoot the rope across a river or pool of acid or some other threatening gulf? James West would bridge the gap with a single thread and then transport himself over the problem. That's the way things really are."

"Sometimes you just don't know everything, Evers. Little stress fractures that you can't see in an iron support, a plank that looks sturdy but is full of termites." Pauletta thought about telling Evers the truth about Pascal, licked her lips and let the inclination fade away, decided then and there that she never would, that she shouldn't, that it was none of her business.

"I know all I need to know."

"Well, at any rate, on a more immediate and worldly note, I found out Tuesday that the Poverty Law Center in Charleston is closing. Hard to believe, but the white, potbellied solons in our legislature have cut the program's funding to just about nothing. Also, the center's lease is up, and the owner wants to sell the building. Obviously, they need some money. I'm on the board of directors. I could buy the whole building and have it repaired and redone for around a million bucks. And I'm going to do it."

"Good. I'm not going to say anything about it, how nicely that fits."

Pauletta cleared her throat. "You wouldn't have any interest in working there, would you?"

Evers shook his head. "Sorry. My new world order doesn't involve my abandoning common sense and all reason and principle. I still detest affirmative action, welfare, deadbeat renters, scofflaws, criminals, thugs, shoplifters and people who don't pay child support. I'd vote to end the Poverty Law Center, too."

"I'm sure you'd prefer a police state and some sort of Middle Eastern system of justice—hands and feet and arms chopped off in public spectacle."

Evers grinned. "You like me, don't you? I can count on you." He picked up a flower.

"I guess so. You have some good points. Even though there's a lot I don't like about you. I mean, you have very little balance, a strange view of women and you really don't like black people, do you?" She shifted her weight.

"I'm pretty evenhanded with my dislikes and likes. I try to spread them out based on petty self-interest more than anything else. And I like you—you're black."

"Why? How come?"

"Because you're dependable and determined, and I like the way you look," Evers said.

"Perhaps you could be a reference book of sorts."

"Ah, the book theory," Evers smiled. "That's a solid start. At least that'll keep me around for a good long time—dusty and dull, but still in the library."

"Fair enough."

He looked at Pauletta, then looked around the room. "I'm going to sit on the porch while you finish cooking, okay? Before we get into a quarrel."

"Fine with me. I really didn't expect you to help."

"Would you put the flowers in a jar?"

Evers left the kitchen and walked onto the screened-in porch and sat down in a metal chair. He began listening to the first night noises: insects and cars and radios. He could smell food from the kitchen, something Pauletta was cooking, meat and spices. Earlier, after he'd dug out the croquet set, he had bundled up stacks of old *National Geographic*s in the garage, tied them together with a perfect knot that wouldn't let go. He rubbed his fingers across the metalwork underneath the arms of the chair, felt the swirls and ornaments, the hard, smooth designs on each side of him, and for the first time in years he felt braced and sound; the world wasn't shaking underneath him, and he wasn't tumbling around in a slipstream, waiting to hit bottom. He recounted things in his mind, how he'd gotten back to his house, and he thought about his brother, sitting in jail, and decided he would clean up the trailer before Pascal got home, replace the window that had been sealed up with particleboard and fix the screen door. And he was going to get rid of the shrine, the jar of tape and plastic and tears, because none of them needed a frozen ketchup top filled with white crying, not really.

Somewhere in Chatham, Evers imagined, young girls were filing into the dining hall, without a care in the world. Soon, on Sunday, he would see Pascal. He felt a twinge in his stomach, something deep and visceral. He slid down in his chair and watched the world change, shedding its last hues, keeping time, everything working just right.

Miles away at Vaughn Ford-Lincoln-Mercury-Jeep-Eagle-Isuzu, Ruth Esther was talking to a physician, a sad man with irritated eyes, convincing him that he should travel to Mexico to treat her brother for a knife wound that hadn't been reported to the authorities, promising the doctor some money but, most importantly, a trip—a winding, rollicking journey that would right his life and clear his head.

A NOTE ON THE TYPE

THE TEXT OF THIS BOOK WAS COMPOSED IN MELIOR, A TYPEFACE
DESIGNED BY HERMANN ZAPF AND ISSUED IN 1952. BORN IN NUREM-
BERG, GERMANY, IN 1918, ZAPF HAS BEEN A STRONG INFLUENCE IN
PRINTING SINCE 1939. MELIOR, LIKE TIMES ROMAN (ANOTHER POPU-
LAR TWENTIETH-CENTURY TYPEFACE), WAS CREATED SPECIFICALLY
FOR USE IN NEWSPAPER COMPOSITION. WITH THIS FUNCTIONAL END
IN MIND, ZAPF NONETHELESS CHOSE TO BASE THE PROPORTIONS OF
HIS LETTER FORMS ON THOSE OF THE GOLDEN SECTION. THE RESULT
IS A TYPEFACE OF UNUSUAL STRENGTH AND SURPASSING SUBTLETY.

COMPOSED BY CREATIVE GRAPHICS, ALLENTOWN, PENNSYLVANIA

PRINTED AND BOUND BY R. R. DONNELLEY & SONS,
HARRISONBURG, VIRGINIA

DESIGNED BY IRIS WEINSTEIN